Curse Breaker

Book One in Red-Line: The Fletcher Family Saga
J. T. Bishop

Eudoran Press LLC

J. T. Bishop

P.O. Box 117021

Carrollton, TX 75011-7021

www.jtbishopauthor.com

Publisher's Note: This is a work of fiction. Names, characters, places, and incidents are a product of the author's imagination. Locales and public names are sometimes used for atmospheric purposes. Any resemblance to actual people, living or dead, or to businesses, companies, events, institutions, or locales is completely coincidental.

Updated book cover by J.T. Bishop

Book Cover photo images by Nejron Photo and Maksim Shirkov

Author Photo by Mayza Clark Photography

Book Editing and Cover Design by Amie McCracken

Curse Breaker/ J. T. Bishop. -- 1st ed.

Paperback ISBN 978-0692778401

Hardback ISBN 978-1-955370-01-1

To Gwen and Christine,

I am blessed with many friends, but you two have hung around the longest. From the silly stories we used to write in high school, Gwen, to the time I told you I'd written my first book, Christine, you two have always been there.
I suspect that without you, my writing career would have stalled long ago, or perhaps never begun.
I thank you for believing in me and I am honored and blessed to call you friends.

Other Books by J. T. Bishop

Detectives Daniels and Remalla standalones/novellas
The Girl and the Gunshot (subscribers only)
A Hamburger Christmas
The Magic of Murder (subscribers only)
Murder Unveiled—a prequel to Haunted River

Detectives Daniels and Remalla
Haunted River
Of Breath and Blood
Of Body and Bone
Of Mind and Madness
Of Power and Pain
Of Love and Loss
Dominion
Illusions
Vendetta

The Redstone Chronicles
Lost Souls
Lost Dreams
Lost Chances
Lost Hope
Lost Lives
Lost Time
Lost Love

CHAPTER ONE

THE KNOCK ON THE door pounded, along with his head, but Grayson Steele ignored both. He grabbed a pillow from the couch and pulled it over his ears to muffle the sound. The banging came again, and he groaned and pulled the pillow closer. The needles behind his eyes sharpened their aim and sank into his skull. The noise sounded again and the needles became drill bits, burrowing deeper. He still didn't move, expecting the noisy offender to eventually give up and leave.

After a moment, the knocking ended. Relaxing his hold on the pillow, he could make out the soft sounds of the ocean surf. Grayson Steele had no interest in visitors. His only concerns were his dog—a mutt named Max who also ignored the front door because he'd learned early that barking at it mattered little—and his bottle of bourbon, which now sat half-empty on the coffee table. If those two items were not at the door, then he was not answering.

Although the pounding on the door had ended, the pain in his head did not. After a few minutes, he shifted from his prone state on the couch and groaned when his body protested. Despite his relative youth, he felt as old as his house and just as creaky. Seeing Grayson move, Max sat up from his perch beside the sofa and watched him. His doggy eyes peered and his tail wagged, indicating his hope that his owner might pick up the Frisbee and head for the back door.

"Sorry, Max," he said. "No catch today."

He tossed the pillow on the couch and attempted to sit up. Max's eager puppy-eyed look made him sigh.

"You okay, Mr. Steele?"

He jumped at the sound and turned. The pain behind his eyes flared, and he winced. Looking over, he saw a slender but tall man in a light blue suit and yellow tie in his kitchen. He was well-groomed and clean-shaven.

Grayson held his head. "Who the hell are you?"

The man flipped on the faucet in the kitchen sink and began to wash the piled dishes. "My name is Franklin. Franklin Gallagher, sir."

"What the hell are you doing in my house?"

Franklin scrubbed at a bowl and glanced up at him. "Cooper Stone sent me, sir."

"What?" He rubbed at his blurry eyes. "Coop?"

"Yes, sir."

"What the hell for?"

Franklin set a bowl in the drainer and reached for another dish. "He told me to come over here." He held a plate under the water. "He said...and I'm quoting him now, 'Get that asshole up and moving. Whatever it takes. I want him ready for the weekend.'"

Grayson shook his head and immediately regretted the action. "Weekend?"

"Yes. Mr. Stone is throwing a birthday party this weekend at his beach house. I believe it's three doors down from here, sir."

"I know where it is, Franklin. How did you get in here?"

"Mr. Stone gave me a key."

"He what?"

"He said you wouldn't answer the door. He's been trying to reach you for two weeks."

"He gave you a key?"

"Yes, sir."

"That bastard." He moaned and grabbed his temples. "Why didn't he come? Why'd he send you?"

"Mr. Stone recently hired me. I'm his assistant and jack-of-all-trades, you might say. I help him with various tasks as required. He offered me a thousand dollars to come here and..." He looked around the house, eyeing the empty liquor bottles, closed shutters, and the dirty clothes on the floor. "...assist you."

Grayson couldn't believe this was happening. "Assist me? I don't need assistance. I have a housekeeper, Frank."

"Pardon me, sir, but perhaps their skills could use some improvement. When was the last time your help was here? A year?"

Grayson pinched his nose when his head flared again. "Nobody likes a smart-ass, Franklin."

"I apologize, sir."

"And stop calling me sir."

"What would you prefer me to call you?"

"Grayson is fine."

"I'd feel more comfortable with Mr. Steele."

Gray attempted to stand but sat back down when his legs shook. Max continued to sit beside him. "Some guard dog."

Max had no response.

Franklin shut off the sink and dried his hands. He'd placed the remaining dirty dishes in the dishwasher and flipped it on. He looked around the kitchen and viewed the pantry.

"Can I make you some lunch, sir?"

"Lunch?" asked Gray, shutting his eyes. "God, no." Hearing rustling, he opened his eyes and peered into the kitchen. Franklin was poking his head into his pantry. "What are you doing?"

Franklin popped his head out. "I'm afraid I'll have to go to the grocery for you, Mr. Steele. The only thing you have in here is dog food." He pulled out a large bag and dug out a scoop of dried bits. Max immediately reacted and jogged into the kitchen. Frank found a bowl, dumped the food into it, and set it down. "Here you are, Max." He patted the dog on the head.

Gray grunted. "You know my dog?"

"Mr. Stone told me about him, yes."

Franklin began to walk through and gather up empty bottles and trash.

"You can go home. I don't need a babysitter."

"Mr. Stone said you would say that. He told me to ignore you." He picked a shirt up off the floor and threw it on the back of a chair.

Gray shook his head. "He's giving you a thousand dollars to do this?"

"He has."

"I'll give you two thousand to leave."

Frank stopped where he stood, holding a dirty plate and an empty liquor bottle. "He told me to tell you that he'd offer a thousand more than any offer you make. Guess that means I'm up to three thousand dollars." He walked into the kitchen and dropped the bottle into the trash and put the dirty plate in the dishwasher.

"Shit."

"I suppose you could say that."

"Just what exactly does he want you to do?"

Franklin walked back into the room. Seeing something on the floor, he leaned over and picked it up. It was a lacy black bra. "Perhaps you haven't been as lonely as Mr. Stone suspects."

Gray stood despite his shakiness and pulled the item out of Franklin's hands. "Mind your own business, Frank."

"Yes, sir."

"And stop calling me sir."

Gray dropped the bra onto the kitchen table and sat down in a chair. His throat felt as dry as the sand off his back porch, and he knew he needed a shower and a shave. His stomach growled despite his hangover, and he realized he hadn't eaten in twenty-four hours.

"To answer your question, sir…I mean Mr. Steele…Mr. Stone wanted me to check in on you. Make sure you were all right. Then he said to make sure you got cleaned up and ate something. Said you'd probably be hung over and would need a shower and a solid meal. It seems he knows you pretty well."

Gray held his foggy head in his hands. "He should. I've known him since the third grade."

"I know, sir."

Gray lifted his head. "You do?"

"Well, yes, sir." Frank walked back to the pantry and pulled out a broom. "I'm surprised you have one of these." He began to sweep at the crumbs on the floor. "You and Mr. Stone are well known. Most know of your background."

Gray watched Franklin sweep. "They do, huh?"

"Of course. Everyone knows of Stone and Steele Enterprises. You two were self-made millionaires by the age of twenty-five. Mr. Stone was on the cover of *Tech* magazine."

"That was me, Frank."

"It was?"

"Yeah. Coop was on the cover of *GQ*."

"Well, whatever. You both made a name for yourselves at an early age."

Gray rubbed at his eyes. "I suppose so."

Franklin stopped his cleaning. "Do you mind if I ask you something, sir?"

Gray sighed. "What?"

"What happened?"

"What happened?"

"Yes. I did my research when I began this job. The two of you were a popular team. Out in the media. Enjoying the night life. Traveling. Beautiful women. Then, all of a sudden, you dropped out of sight. From what I've gathered, Mr. Stone has been running the business the last few years."

Gray said nothing. After a moment, he stood and spoke. "I'm going to take a shower, Franklin."

Franklin resumed his sweeping. "Yes, sir."

Gray stepped away from the breakfast table but turned before he left the room. "Franklin?"

"Yes, Mr. Steele?"

Gray studied the man cleaning his floor. "You a reporter?"

"Excuse me, sir?"

"Are you a reporter?"

Franklin made a face. "Heavens, no, sir. I wouldn't know the first thing about reporting."

Gray thought for a moment. "I don't like reporters, Frank. So I hope you're telling the truth. A word of this impromptu visit gets out in the press and you'll be sweeping floors for a living."

Franklin gripped at the broom. "I would never speak of this, sir. I highly respect my employer's privacy, and those of his circle."

Gray eyed him as if measuring his honesty. "Let's keep it that way." He turned to walk back to his bedroom. "Oh, and Frank?"

"Yes, sir?"

His stomach grumbled again. "If I'm stuck with you, you might as well order me a pizza."

"Certainly, sir. What kind?"

"Surprise me. Oh, and get something for yourself too. This is on Coop's dime, right?"

"Yes, sir."

"Then order for the neighbors, and get whatever you want."

"Thank you, sir."

"And Frank?"

"Yes?"

He turned and headed for the shower. "Stop calling me sir."

CHAPTER TWO

THIRTY MINUTES LATER, HE re-emerged from the bathroom feeling better but still moving slowly. He walked back into his living room and squinted from the bright light that greeted him. Franklin had opened the shutters and sunshine flooded the room. He raised his hand to block his eyes. The room had been cleared of trash, and his dirty clothes were now gone, presumably in the laundry. Glancing into the kitchen, he saw the clean countertops and empty sink. He had to admit, it looked better. He considered grabbing a beer from the fridge, but he knew he'd regret it, and he walked to the back door and opened it. The sea breeze hit him, and he breathed deeply. Max ran up the porch and jumped up for a pet. He ruffled the dog's head and stepped outside. Franklin was nowhere in sight. He stood for several minutes with his eyes closed and listened to the soft waves and cawing seagulls. Only the beach could calm him when he needed to relax. It was why he lived here now. After all he'd experienced, it was the only place he'd found peace, until the demons reared their heads, and then he'd learned that only bourbon could quiet those voices. And they seemed to speak to him more and more often lately.

The sound of talking reached his ears, and he opened his eyes to see people below on the shore, staring and pointing. He looked down the beach as Franklin joined him on the porch.

"There you are, sir...Mr. Steele. Your pizza is here."

"What's going on down there?'

"What do you mean?"

"Down there." He pointed where the beach walkers looked. Red lights flashed in the distance and Gray could see emergency vehicles. It was hard to make out what was happening.

"I don't know, sir. Perhaps an accident?"

A police cruiser joined the scene.

"I hope it wasn't a drowning," said Franklin.

Gray moved toward the stairs. "I'm going to find out."

"Wait, sir."

Gray turned toward Franklin. "What?"

Franklin turned and went inside. He came back out with a paper towel and a piece of pizza in his hand. "At least eat something while you walk."

Gray almost turned him down, but then his stomach growled and he reached for the food. "Thanks." He turned and headed down the stairs as Max joined him.

"Sir?"

"What, Franklin?" He glanced back.

"You mind if I clean your bedroom?"

Gray considered it. "Have at it, Frank. Just watch out for the spiders." He grinned when Franklin gave him a worried look. "Come on, Max. Let's go find out what all the excitement is about." Max ran toward the water's edge, and Gray took a bite of his pizza. Franklin disappeared into the house.

Five minutes later, Gray came onto the scene. An ambulance pulled away as he neared and a policeman began to roll out yellow tape to keep bystanders away. A fire truck with flashing lights waited nearby and a second police cruiser joined the fray. Gray assumed the ambulance carried the victim until he moved and got a better view and saw what looked like a blue tarp on the sand. He froze when he realized it was a body. Police officers milled around, and he could hear the muffled voices of radio communication coming from their vehicles. Other people had stopped, and they all stared from behind the tape as the police worked the area.

He'd finished his pizza on the walk over, and he curled the paper towel into his fist. Another vehicle drove up, and he saw the words, "Coroner's Office," printed on the side. The car stopped and two men stepped out and walked toward the covered form. Two other men with badges met them. They spoke, but Gray could not hear what they said over the sound of the waves. Max barked at a seagull, but remained at Gray's side.

"Any idea what's going on?"

Gray turned at the voice and saw a woman. Dressed casually with sunglasses perched on her head, she stood next to him, but she watched the police as he did. Her long, dark hair blew in the wind.

"No. No idea."

"Doesn't look good."

"No, it doesn't."

They watched the men from the coroner's office pull equipment from their vehicle. The officers began to question the crowd.

"Do you know who it is?"

A seagull flew over Gray's head. "What?"

"The victim?" she asked. "Do you know her?"

"It's a her?"

"Yes. I saw her before they covered her."

"You did? What'd she look like?"

"Blonde. Pretty. About all I could tell. You're a local, though, aren't you?"

"Excuse me?" he asked.

"You live here? Grew up nearby? Right?"

"How do you know that?"

"You're Grayson Steele, aren't you?"

He groaned, but didn't answer her.

"My name's Gillian. Gillian Fletcher."

He continued to watch the men with their equipment. It was not the first time he'd been approached by a woman on the beach, but at a crime scene?

Still watching the activity, he answered her. "Listen, Miss Fletcher. I'm not interested, okay?"

He could feel her looking at him. "You're not interested in what?" she asked.

"There's a dead body over there. Now is not the time for a hook-up."

"A hook...what, you think I'm hitting on you?"

He turned toward her. She was attractive, and under different circumstances, he might have made the effort, but he was not that man anymore. "Aren't you?"

She smiled. "No, I'm not."

"Then what do you want?"

"Excuse me?"

"You know my name? Know I live nearby? Know I grew up not far from here?" He crossed his arms. "What do you want?"

She didn't answer for a second. "I'm a reporter."

He chuckled. The men on the beach lifted the tarp, but they blocked his view. "Looks like you've got quite the story on your hands. First on the scene."

"I'm not that kind of reporter."

"You're not?"

"No. I work for *Lifestyle* magazine."

"*Lifestyle*, huh? What lifestyle are you interested in?"

"Yours."

He smirked. "Let me guess. You want to interview me?"

"I do."

"Why?"

"Why not? Everyone wants to get an interview with you. You're a millionaire playboy who's become a recluse. The Howard Hughes of our time. You're a huge scoop."

"No, thanks."

"Why not? Don't you want the world to know the truth?"

"What truth?"

"That you're not as messed up as they say you are. That you're not a drug user or psychotic. That you're not building sandcastles in your bedroom in your free time. Or tying up seagulls and eating them for lunch."

He grimaced. "Is that what they're saying about me?"

"Depends on the magazine."

He shook his head. "I'm obviously not keeping up on current trends."

"So tell them that you don't do any of those things."

He tilted his head. "And how do you know I don't?"

She didn't say anything, but her eyes moved back to the beach. The men were moving the body into a zippered bag. They tried to keep the bystanders from watching by holding up a blanket, but a strong gust of wind blew and the blanket moved and he got a quick but clear view of the woman. A chill shot through him when he realized he recognized her. He knew the victim.

"Oh my God."

"What?" she asked.

He felt the blood leave his face, and he stared at the sand.

"You okay?"

He looked for his dog. "Max?" He saw Max chasing a seagull.

"Mr. Steele?"

Max ran up to him and shook out the water on his coat. "Let's go, Max."

"Please, Mr. Steele. Would you consider it?"

He didn't answer her. His wooden legs didn't want to move, but he forced them over the sand, the face of the victim echoing in his mind. He blinked and tried to think back. When had he seen her last? Calculating the time in his head, he grimaced when he remembered. Three days. It had been three days since he'd slept with her. He felt the urge to lose his pizza, but he held it back. Picking up his pace, he walked fast through the sand and ignored the reporter behind him.

"Mr. Steele? Are you okay? Can I follow up with you later?"

Leaving the scene, he said nothing.

· · · ● · ● · ● · · ·

Twenty-four hours later, he sat quietly on his back porch. He'd barely moved since he'd returned from the incident on the beach the previous day. When he'd made it back, he'd kicked Franklin out and grabbed another bottle of liquor. He'd opened it, but something had stopped him from drinking. Going outside to sit, he'd tried to let the sea calm him. He'd sat for hours, thinking about what he had done. He'd been so careful to avoid any possibility of this happening again, but then she'd showed up at his door. When he hadn't answered, she'd come around back. He'd seen her peeking in through the patio door and he'd recognized her immediately. Marilyn. She'd been a childhood friend of his and Coop's. They'd grown up together, attending the same schools, hanging out together and generally making their parents' lives hell. After graduating high school, she'd stayed on the east coast to attend college while he and Coop headed out to UCLA. They'd kept in touch. The summer after their graduation, just before he and Coop hit it big with their business and after Gray had experienced one of the most traumatic events of his life, they'd had a brief fling. It hadn't lasted, and they hadn't expected it to. They weren't in love, but they'd both needed the affection. Soon after, she'd moved to California and he and Coop had returned to the east coast. He'd heard she'd married, but it didn't last and she'd divorced. He hadn't seen her since their tryst until she'd showed up three days earlier on his back porch.

While mulling over her visit and their time together, he'd dozed outside in the patio lounge chair. Marilyn's body zippered into a plastic bag played repeatedly in his head and he couldn't summon the energy to move or even care if he ever did again. He berated himself. How could he have been so stupid, so careless? The phone inside the house rang; he ignored it. It had rung several times since Franklin had left, but he hadn't answered. His cell phone had died during the night. It had messages he'd never bothered listening to. His mind kept returning to Marilyn. He'd let her in when he'd seen her. They'd talked. He'd offered her a drink, and they'd caught up on old times. She'd asked how he was and wondered why he'd chosen to hide from the world, and uncharacteristically, he'd answered her. After hearing his answer, she hadn't lectured or judged him, nor offered any advice. A few hours later, they were both drunk, and she'd leaned over and kissed him, and he hadn't stopped her. Damn, he thought to himself. *Why didn't I stop her? Why didn't I stop myself?*

The sun rising, he'd opened his eyes and roused himself long enough to go inside to use the bathroom. Returning to the porch, he saw the opened, untouched liquor bottle still sitting on the patio table. He grabbed it and a glass and sat, ready to drink the memories away, but he still couldn't bring himself to do it. It was as if he knew he deserved to feel the guilt and despair. Marilyn's face flickered again in his mind's eye. He'd as good as killed her and not drinking would have to be his punishment. He thought of the other women from his past, and he scanned the dark blue, choppy water. If he couldn't bring himself to drink, then maybe there was one other way out of the hell he was in. He wondered how long it would take to succumb.

"Hello? Mr. Steele?'

The voice startled him, and he shifted in his seat, listening for the source of the sound. He cleared his throat but didn't speak.

"Mr. Steele? May I come up?"

Looking through the balcony slats, he could see a woman below his patio. He didn't know her at first, but then his mind cleared and he recognized her. "No," he said. "You can't."

"Just for a few seconds? Please?"

"I told you I'm not giving you an interview."

"How about a Band-Aid?"

"A what?"

"A Band-Aid. I stepped on a shell or something. I'm bleeding."

He sat farther up but couldn't see her clearly, so he forced himself to stand. She stood at the base of the stairs, holding her foot, and blood dripped from her heel. Her sunglasses were still perched on her head, and the wind still blew her hair. Despite his reluctance, he sighed and gave in to her request.

"Fine. Come on up. Rinse it first in the shower below the stairs. I'll get a bandage."

She looked beneath the porch and hopped to the shower, where she turned on the spray and rinsed her foot. He left the balcony and returned with supplies as she reached the top of the stairs. She held a pair of sandals in her hand and dropped them on the deck.

"Here," he said. "Sit." He grabbed a chair and pulled it up. She sat down, and he grabbed another chair and sat across from her. She raised her foot, and he took it and laid it over his knee. She winced at the movement.

"What'd you do to it?" he asked, applying pressure to the cut with a paper towel.

She sucked in a breath. "I took my shoes off. Must have stepped on something."

"Right off my back porch, huh?"

"Talk about a coincidence."

"I'm sure."

He continued to hold pressure on the wound.

"How bad is it?" she asked.

"You'll live. It's bleeding, though."

"I don't need stitches, do I?"

He took the bandage away and checked her foot. The bleeding had slowed. "No." He dabbed at it and found some antiseptic ointment and unscrewed the cap. "If it swells up, though, turns blue, and starts to smell, you might consider seeing a doctor."

"Thanks," she answered. He smeared the medicine on her foot, and she winced again. "I'll keep that in mind."

He found a large Band-Aid and patched it over her foot. "I'd keep the sand out of it, if you can."

She took her foot off his knee as Max stepped out of his dog door and joined them on the porch. He ran up to her, and she petted his head. "Thanks for the first aid," she said.

"You're welcome." He put his supplies on the outdoor table. "So," he said, "you want to tell me why you were snooping outside my house?"

Her eyes widened. "I wasn't snooping. It's a public beach."

He snorted. "Come on."

"What?"

"I know what you want."

"Yes. I told you. I want an interview."

"And you think sitting outside my house is going to get you one?"

"I'm talking to you, aren't I?"

"Not on the record, you aren't."

"Not yet."

He stood from his chair. "It was nice meeting you, uh...what was it?"

She smiled. "Gillian Fletcher. And what's the harm in a short interview?"

"Goodbye, Mrs. Fletcher."

"It's Miss."

"Whatever." He moved to the back door. "Come on, Max."

Max continued to sit next to her, though, and Gillian rubbed his ears. "At least one of you likes me," she said.

"He's a lousy judge of character."

She didn't give up. "Not an interview, then. A conversation."

His lips turned up. "Now you are hitting on me?"

"I want to talk to you, not date you. And I'm persistent when I want something."

"What, you always get your story, is that it?"

"Something like that."

"I hate to tell you this, but you're not getting this one." He opened the back door. "Come on, Max." Max must have realized Gray meant business because he stood and walked into the house. "Have a nice life, *Miss* Fletcher."

He started to close the door when he heard another voice. "Miss Fletcher? Who's Miss Fletcher?"

Footsteps sounded on the stairs and Gray's best friend and business partner, Cooper Stone, walked up onto the back porch. His lanky, yet muscular frame fit his tailored, but casual clothes perfectly. He had the classic polished look, yet he still maintained the appeal of an easy-going, spontaneous college kid. He stopped when he saw Gillian. "Is this Miss Fletcher?" He smiled down at her and his blonde hair shone in the sun, giving him an almost angelic appeal. "Well," he said, reaching for her hand, but instead of shaking it, he raised it and kissed the back of it. "Pleased to make your acquaintance."

Gray swung the door back open. "What the hell are you doing here?"

Cooper grunted, but his smile remained. "Good to see you too, buddy. How about you answer your phone and maybe I wouldn't have to come over here to make sure you're still alive?"

"I'm alive, all right?"

"I can see that." He still held Gillian's hand. "And keeping good company, I see."

"She was just leaving."

Cooper groaned softly. "What a shame. I hope my friend here treated you well."

Gillian took her hand back. "On the contrary, he's been rather difficult to deal with."

"Then allow me to introduce myself," said Cooper, displaying a charming grin. "My name is—"

"—Cooper Stone," she answered for him.

"My reputation precedes me."

"It does."

He grinned. "I hope that doesn't mean we can't get to know each other better."

"Cooper," said Gray.

"What?" he answered without looking away from Gillian.

"Leave her alone."

That made Cooper look up. "What? Don't tell me you like her? I thought you'd sworn off women?"

"I mean, she's not your type. She doesn't want a two-week fling, which ends in a doctor's visit."

"Ouch," said Cooper, straightening. "You need a drink. What's got you all riled up?"

Gray tried to answer that question himself. "She's a reporter. She wants a story."

"I see." He shook his head at Gillian. "And he said 'no.'"

"He did," she answered.

"Of course he did." He sat down in the chair across from her. "Well, since he's being difficult, would you like to interview me?"

"Damn it, Cooper," said Gray.

"What? The lady wants a story. I can give her one."

Gillian sat forward. "It's not your story I want. No offense."

"None taken," said Cooper. "But, keep in mind, I have good stories to tell."

"I'm sure you do, but it's his story I'm interested in."

Cooper sighed. "Good luck with that, Miss Fletcher." He leaned in close to her. "Gray can be a bit solitary when he wants to be." He smiled charmingly at her. "I, on the other hand, can be much more pleasant company."

"For God's sake," said Gray.

"Hey," said Cooper, throwing out his hands. "There's a beautiful woman on your porch and you're ready to ship her off." He looked at Gillian. "I apologize for his rudeness. Would you like to stay for lunch?"

"What?" asked Gray.

"Actually, I do need to get back," said Gillian. She pushed up and stood without putting weight on her heel.

Cooper noticed. "What happened?" He took her hand as she balanced. "Are you injured?"

"It's nothing serious. Just cut my foot."

"Cut your foot?" said Cooper. "Are you walking back?"

"Yes."

"Where?"

"I'm at the Sea Island Hotel."

"You can't walk back there like this." His brow furrowed. "You were going to make her walk back like this?"

Gray didn't know what to say.

Cooper's face dropped. "I'm sorry, my dear. My friend's an idiot." He pulled a cell phone from his pocket and dialed a number. "Dylan? Yes. Can you bring the car around front? Thanks." He hung up the phone and returned it to his pocket. "You sure you don't want to stay? I'm sure we can find something to eat in this sorry man's house."

"I've got cereal," said Gray.

Cooper made an annoying grunt. "Never mind then," he said. "Let's get you out front. My driver will take you home."

"That's really unnecessary," said Gillian.

"Don't argue. Let's go inside to the front door."

"Cooper," said Gray.

"What?" asked Cooper, looking surprised. "You afraid she's going to tell her readers how ugly your house is? About time somebody did."

"It's better than that contemporary crap you like. At least I don't live in a monochromatic crystal palace."

"It's called style, Cochise."

"It's called ugly."

"This way, my dear," said Cooper, leading Gillian into the house. They walked through the living room and up to the front door as Gray followed. Cooper's driver waited outside in the driveway.

Cooper walked Gillian down to the car. "Dylan, take Miss Fletcher back to her hotel, please, at Sea Island."

"Yes, sir."

"Thank you." He held Gillian's hand. "It's been a pleasure meeting you. I'm sorry if my friend was unpleasant. He can be challenging. If possible, I hope perhaps we might see each other again."

"Perhaps," said Gillian. She pulled her hand away and spoke to Gray, who watched from the front steps. "If you change your mind—"

"I won't."

She stared for a moment and then turned, and Dylan helped her into the waiting car. The car drove away as Gray turned and walked back into the house.

"Hey," said Cooper, running up the stairs. Gray almost closed the door on him.

"What the hell is the matter with you?"

"What's the matter with me?" asked Coop, following Gray and closing the door.

"Yes," said Gray. He turned and headed into the kitchen.

"What's the matter with you? She's beautiful."

"She's a reporter."

"So what?"

"She just wants a story."

"Maybe she might want more, if you gave her a chance."

"I can't do that."

Cooper made an exasperated sigh. "Oh, that's right. Because you're cursed."

Gray stopped and turned. "You know what happens, Coop."

Cooper's voice rose in frustration. "Come on, Gray. How long are you gonna believe that crap? Nobody is dying because of you."

Gray walked into the kitchen and grabbed the Cheerios and poured himself a bowl. "I wish that were true."

Cooper watched him add milk. "You should have let Franklin go to the grocery store for you."

The mention of Franklin irritated Gray. "And why did you send your assistant to my house?"

"Because I couldn't get a hold of you."

"So you gave a stranger a key to my home?"

"He's not a stranger. I did a complete background check on him. He can be trusted."

Gray shoved the milk back in the fridge and slammed it shut. "You gave him my key."

Cooper's own irritation grew. "Then if you don't want someone to check in on you, answer the damn phone."

Gray shoved the bowl of Cheerios across the counter, uneaten. "I don't want to be bothered."

"Jesus, Gray. This is me you're talking to. I know you better than your mother. I know you're carrying a load of baggage, but you can't disappear, man. Your whole life is ahead of you."

"Spare me the psychiatric talk."

"Spare me the 'woe is me' crap. What the hell?"

Anxious, Gray walked out of the kitchen, but Cooper followed. Gray paced for a moment before he slumped into a seat at his breakfast table. "You don't understand." He thought of Marilyn. "It happened again."

"What happened again?"

Gray ran a shaky hand through his hair. "She died."

Cooper sat beside him. "Who died?"

"Marilyn."

"Marilyn? You saw Marilyn?"

Gray sighed. "Yes. Three, no four days ago."

"How? When? I thought she was out in LA."

"She was, but she came into town and showed up here. We talked for a while. We were drinking." He stopped when the magnitude of what had happened hit him again.

"And?"

"And she stayed the night."

"You and Marilyn?"

"Come on, Coop. It wasn't the first time. You know that."

"And what's the problem?"

Gray dropped his head into his hands. "She's dead."

"She's what? How the hell do you know that?"

"Because I saw her body on the beach yesterday."

Cooper's jaw dropped. "You saw her body?" He paused. "Is that what had you all upset when you threw Franklin out? He said you were acting strangely."

Gray sat back and stared at the table. "Strangely? Yeah, you could say that. I saw a commotion on the beach. When I went down there to see what was going on, there was a body. The police were investigating. I got a look...and it was Marilyn." He closed his eyes at the memory.

"Are you sure, Gray? Maybe it was someone who looked like her?"

"It was her, dammit." He stood from his seat and paced the room. "And she was with me." He groaned before he said it. "Three days earlier."

Cooper sat forward. "Don't go there. This isn't your fault."

"It's the same damn thing, Coop. I didn't physically hurt her, but anyone I care about and sleep with dies three days later."

"I thought it was only women you were in love with? Or isn't that what you thought?"

"I thought so. I've had flings and nothing's ever happened. I wasn't in love with Marilyn, but I cared about her." He stopped pacing and banged his fist into the wall. "God, maybe this thing is getting worse. Maybe it's anyone now."

"Wait a minute. Get a hold of yourself. This is not a curse."

Gray turned on him. "What the hell would you call it then? You can't deny the facts. First Angela. Then Erin. Then what happened in Mexico? And now this. It's happened every time." He grabbed at a chair and hung his head. "I sleep with a woman I love, and they're dead three days later."

"But you said so yourself. You didn't love Marilyn."

Gray looked back with harried eyes. "Apparently, that doesn't matter anymore."

Cooper shook his head. "Would you please consider the fact that this could all be a coincidence?"

Gray sat down heavily. "When are you ever going to take this seriously?"

"And when are you going to stop believing this nonsense? Yes. These women died. Yes. They were tragic circumstances. Yes. They were with you three days earlier. That doesn't mean that you are responsible. You are not cursed."

"You honestly think that with that track record that something isn't going on here? That there isn't something about my involvement that affected these women?" Gray felt weary.

"They died, but not because of you. What do I have to do to get you to believe that?"

"If I could get one woman I loved to day four, then that would help."

"Then that would require you actually leaving the house," said Cooper.

"I can't take that chance."

Cooper sighed. "Listen. Let me call Kenny. I'll find out what the scoop is on this body on the beach. Maybe you're wrong. Maybe it's not her."

"It was her."

"Then why haven't we heard anything? She was from around here. She'd be easy to identify." He pulled his phone out of his pocket.

"She hasn't lived here in almost ten years. And it's been less than twenty-four hours since they found her."

"Just let me call."

Gray groaned. "Kenny? You have to call him?"

"He's a policeman. He's our best source."

"Fine."

"Don't worry. I'll keep your name out of it."

"You know he still doesn't speak to me."

Cooper held the phone to his ear. "How could he? You never leave home." He listened and left a voicemail. "I'll talk to him, okay?" He put his phone away. "We'll find out what's going on. Until then, don't freak out on me. Let's get the facts first."

"I know the facts. She's dead."

Cooper shook his head. "Can we talk about something else? There's nothing we can do now until we get some more information. So just try to relax."

"Relax, huh?" Gray exhaled a deep breath. "All right. What else do you want to talk about?"

"Not to sound unsympathetic, but my birthday party is this weekend. And I expect you to be there."

"Ah, hell, Coop. I'm not exactly in party mode."

"Grayson. You cannot sit in this house this weekend when three doors down, the party of the century will be taking place." Gray picked at a mark on the table. "You're my best friend. I want you to be there."

"Cooper..."

"I know you've got a lot on your mind." Gray peered up at him. "I'm not making light of it. I know you've been kicked in the ass, but you need to get out of the house. So do yourself a favor and come to the party. Even if it's just for an hour."

Gray bounced his knee. "I'll think about it, okay?"

"You'll do more than think about it. You'll be there or I'll send Franklin over to get you."

Gray crooked an eyebrow. "Did you really offer to pay him one thousand dollars to check in on me?"

"Sure did."

"You realize I offered him two thousand to leave?"

"Which is why he's getting three thousand dollars from me."

"You're kidding."

"Nope."

"I should have offered him ten thousand."

"I'd have paid him eleven."

Gray's eyes widened. "What for?"

"Because, contrary to the asshole persona I may at times project out into the world, I'm actually a decent guy." He dropped his hand onto Gray's wrist. "And I'm worried about you."

Gray looked away.

"You're my friend. And if it means I have to send someone to come check in on you when I haven't heard from or seen you and you don't answer your phone, then I will. I don't care if it costs a hundred grand."

Gray moaned. "I'm sorry, Coop. I know I haven't been easy to deal with."

"Don't apologize. Just answer your phone once in a while."

Gray nodded. "I will."

"And come to my party. I swear, you won't want to miss it."

"That's what worries me."

"Besides, we may have a storm coming soon. Got to get the fun in while we can."

"Storm?"

"Yeah. Heard about it on the radio on the way in. It's a long shot, but it could affect us."

"I hadn't heard."

"That's not surprising. A hurricane could be on top of us, and you wouldn't know it till your roof blew off."

Gray didn't answer, but continued to stare off.

Cooper stood from the table. "Come on. Let's go."

"Go where?"

"To get some breakfast. You could use a decent meal." He scanned the room and headed into the entryway, where he picked up Gray's car keys.

"I'm driving."

"Why?"

"Because by the looks of you, you could fall asleep during a home invasion."

Gray rubbed his eyes. "You're probably right."

"We'll go to Mama Jakes. Have some of her famous pancakes. You're buying, by the way."

Gray stood. "That's fine."

Cooper jangled the keys. "And on the way over, you and I will talk about the lovely Miss Fletcher. You need to let her interview you."

"No, I don't."

"Yes, you do."

Gray and Cooper walked outside. Gray locked his door. "Why?"

"Because people need to know that you don't sleep in animal skins or trade in illegal ivory on the black market."

He stopped on the front steps. "What? Is that what people are saying?"

"That's not even the half of it. Just wait till you hear about how you smear beetle dung on your face to stay young and eat crushed seashells to ward off evil spirits."

Gray's mouth dropped. "You're lying."

Cooper grinned. "Yes. I am. But if you don't talk to her, I will, and she'll hear all about your penchant for insect poop."

"Thanks a lot."

Cooper slapped his friend on the back. "What are friends for?"

CHAPTER THREE

COOPER'S BIRTHDAY PARTY WAS in full swing when Grayson arrived. He'd heard the music the moment he'd opened his back door to leave. Arriving at the house, he dusted the sand from his feet and put his sandals back on as he climbed the stairs to Cooper's large, paved patio. Cooper had bought the house three years earlier when Gray had moved into his family's beach home. Gray's house had been in his family for thirty years, and when his mother announced she was selling it, he'd bought it from her. He'd moved in two months later. Cooper couldn't understand why Gray wanted to live at the beach, but he did understand the appeal of being near the water. So when a neighboring house had gone on the market, Coop had bought it sight unseen. He'd renovated, and now as Gray walked up the tiled stairs, he was greeted by two massive cement lions, each alongside the entrance to the deck. Beside him was the infinity pool which sported a waterfall that faced the beach. The lawn furniture was all white or glass, the only color being the green potted plants scattered around the elaborate porch, or as Coop called it—the outside living room.

A band played off to the side of the pool and waiters served drinks and appetizers. One stopped beside him and Gray took the offered glass of champagne. He had not touched a drop of liquor since seeing Marilyn's body. It was as if that moment had kick started him into reality, and he realized he had some serious issues to face. But now wasn't the time for that. He'd told his friend he'd try to come to the party; he was here. So he stuck a smile on his face and moved into the crowd. He was greeted by many people who knew his name, but he didn't know theirs. He recognized a few and avoided some others. He passed a magician who pulled a dove out of a hat and rolled his eyes at the juggler who entertained a group inside the house. He saw everyone except the birthday boy. He drained his glass of champagne and grabbed another one, along with an appetizer that looked like bacon and shrimp, and eyeing the crowd, began to make his way back onto the pool deck.

"Hello," he heard from behind him.

He turned and stopped chewing. He recognized the woman immediately, only now her hair was up and soft tendrils framed her face. She wore a lovely black dress that framed her slim, but curvy figure. He kept his eyes on her face. "Miss Fletcher."

She held a glass of champagne. "Gillian."

He finished chewing and took a swig of his drink. "Yes, I know. Fancy seeing you here."

"Surprised?"

He thought about his answer. "Actually, I shouldn't be. What, did you invite yourself just to get to talk to me?"

She laughed. "You have a healthy ego." She took a sip of her own drink. "No, I was invited."

"You were?" Then it clicked. Cooper.

"Yes. Mr. Stone sent me an invitation. He insisted I come. Said the whole island would be here."

"I'm sure he did." Gray scanned the room sure he would see Coop staring down at him, laughing his ass off. He didn't see him though.

"You don't mind, do you?"

"Mind? Why should I mind?"

"You look unhappy."

Not seeing Cooper, he looked back at her. "That's not unusual."

"I can see that."

He took a sip of his drink. "So, having fun?"

She laughed softly. "I know no one here. And the one person I do know doesn't like me. So, no actually. But I figure after a couple more glasses of champagne, it won't matter much."

"I never said I didn't like you."

"You don't act like you do."

"I don't like reporters."

She studied him. "Why not?"

"It's been my experience they're more interested in the story, not the truth."

"I'm not like that."

"That's what they all say."

"You are cynical, aren't you?"

A waiter approached and Gray grabbed at another bacon wrapped appetizer. "I have my reasons."

They stood for a few quiet moments and observed the people in the crowd.

"I'll give you approval on the article," she said.

"What?" He swallowed his food. "Approval?"

"Yes. I'll let you read it before it goes to print. You don't like it, I won't print it."

"Your editor will agree to that?"

"He may not have a choice."

"Hmm."

"Think about it."

He drank his champagne.

"What about you?" she asked. She picked up a fresh glass and handed her empty one to a nearby waiter.

"What about me?"

"You having fun?" She nodded at the partygoers. "You should know most of the people here."

As if on cue, a brawny man in a gray suit with a loosened tie and a tall, scantily clad woman with short auburn hair walked out of the crowd. She leaned on the man and laughed while he told a bawdy joke, and it was evident they'd enjoyed several drinks. As he reached for another drink from a passing waitress, he swayed and bumped into Grayson. He would have fallen if Grayson hadn't caught him.

The man looked up to apologize, but stopped when he saw who'd grabbed him. "Grayson Steele," he said.

Gray recognized him. "Hi, Stuart." He nodded at the woman. "Fran."

"Gray?" she asked. She detached herself from Stuart. "What are you doing here?"

"Jesus," said Stuart. "How long's it been?"

"A while." He raised his drink. "It's Coop's birthday."

"He has one every year," said Fran.

Gray remained passive. "I know. But he usually has them in the city or takes some elaborate trip. But since this one was three doors down, it was hard for me to say no."

"It's good to see you," said Stuart. "God. What's it been? Three, four years?"

"At least," said Fran.

"I don't think it's been that long," said Gray.

"What the hell you been doing all this time?" asked Stuart. He looked over at Gillian. "Spending time with the ladies?" He smiled and leaned on Gray's shoulder. Fran did not smile.

Gray pushed Stuart back up to a standing position. "Not much. Just hanging out."

"What, you letting Coop do all the work? You think that's smart? Aren't you supposed to be the wonder boy?"

Gray felt an itch crawl up his spine. "I'm not the wonder boy."

"Sure you are. Everyone knows it's your brains that got the business up and running. Coop's just good at schmoozing the customer. He could sell fertilizer to a cattle ranch. You're the one who made the business what it is."

He shook his head. "That's not true, Stuart."

"Come on," said Fran. "We know you. Don't be so modest. What happened to the arrogant, spoiled kid who used to give Coop a run for his money?" She cocked an eyebrow at Gillian. "You used to be the life of the party."

"Things change, Fran."

She cocked her head. "Who's your quiet friend?"

"Sorry, this is Gillian Fletcher. She's a guest of Cooper's. Gillian, this is Stuart Preston and Francine Thibodaux. We all went to high school together."

"Pleased to meet you," said Stuart, and he swayed again.

"I think you've had enough to drink, Stuart," said Gray.

"Nonsense. This party's just getting started. Right, Fran?" He wrapped an arm around her and pulled her close. "Besides, we're staying in one of Coop's guestrooms tonight."

Fran's desire to pull away was clear, but she let herself be hugged. "Right, Stuart." She finally stopped staring at Gillian. "How long can we expect you to be around?"

Gray wished he could find Cooper. "Not long. I'm hoping to find the birthday boy and then get the hell out of here."

"Oh, come on," said Stuart. "Hang out. Have a few drinks. Let's catch up on old times. Since when do you get to come to a party with an open bar?"

"I can drink any time I want, Stuart. I don't need a party to do it."

"Have you bumped into Kenny, yet?" asked Fran. Gray stopped mid-movement as he brought his glass up to his mouth. Then he continued the motion and drained the glass. "He's here?"

"Yes," said Fran. "He's here."

"No. I haven't seen him."

"You going to talk to him?" asked Fran.

Gray and Fran stared in silent communication when Cooper arrived and stood between Gillian and Gray. "Well, if it isn't all my favorite people all in one place." He put his arm around Gillian. "Miss Fletcher." He looked her over. "How nice that you came to my little party."

Gillian raised her champagne. "I wouldn't have missed it."

"Had any luck yet?"

"Excuse me?"

He squeezed Gray's shoulder. "At wearing him down? Has he conceded defeat?"

She shook her head. "Not yet."

"Give him time. He's not as tough as he looks."

"Cooper," said Gray.

"Glad you came," he said to Gray. "I was hoping I wouldn't have to send Franklin."

"Franklin?" asked Stuart. "Who is Franklin?"

"That would be me, sir," said a man who approached. "Your drink, Mr. Stone." He handed a glass to Cooper.

"Thanks, Frank." He took a sip as Frank began to walk away. "Hey, wait a minute. You need to meet everyone." Franklin stopped and turned, and Cooper introduced him to the group.

Once the introductions were made, Cooper pointed toward Gillian. "Miss Fletcher here wants to interview Gray."

"She does?" asked Franklin.

"Shit, Cooper," said Gray.

"Interview?" asked Fran.

Gillian nodded. "Yes, I do."

Fran eyed Gillian. "Whatever for?"

"My sparkling personality," said Gray, and Stuart burst into laughter.

Gillian answered her. "He's a self-made millionaire who dropped out of sight at the prime of his success. People are curious."

"They are?" asked Stuart, still chuckling.

Fran sipped her drink. "I read in one of those gossip mags that you'd been kidnapped by aliens." Gray rolled his eyes. "Is that the type of magazine you work for?"

Gillian paused, but smiled. "No, actually. I work for *Lifestyle*."

"Really?" asked Cooper. "That would be the perfect magazine for you to be featured in. Women would eat it up."

"Can we talk about something else?" asked Gray. "It's your birthday, for God's sake. Why are we talking about me?"

"Why, indeed," said Fran. She pulled on Stuart's arm. "We need another drink."

"You're so right. Garcon?" He stepped away to grab at two more champagnes.

"It was a pleasure to meet you all, but I have to get back," said Franklin.

"Get back to what?" asked Cooper. "It's my birthday, Franklin. Time to let your hair down. Relax and have a drink."

Franklin looked uncertain. "You're sure, sir?"

"Of course I'm sure. Nobody's working tonight. And Franklin," he said, grabbing at a champagne glass and handing it to him.

"Yes?" said Franklin, taking the glass from Cooper.

"Stop calling me sir."

"Yes, sir...I mean, Mr. Stone." Taking a sip, he walked into the crowd.

Stuart returned with his drinks and handed one to Fran. "Interesting fellow," said Fran.

Cooper agreed. "The guy's irreplaceable. He does whatever I need."

"He should," said Gray. "You pay him enough."

"That's true. I do."

Just then, Stuart shouted over the music. "Kenny!" He turned and grabbed at a man's arm. "Is that you?"

"Stuart," said Fran.

Cooper and Gray made eye contact.

The man turned and his eyes lit up when he saw who spoke to him. Kenny wore black pants and a navy shirt and cowboy boots brought his height level with Stuart's. He ran a hand through his thinning brown hair. "Stuart? How the hell are ya?" He smiled and shook Stuart's hand and Stuart's drink sloshed and spilled, but he didn't notice.

"Come on over," said Stuart. "Look who's here."

Kenny made his way over and saw Cooper. "Hey, Cooper. Where the hell have you been? Happy birth..." He stopped when he saw Gray.

Gray stared back. "Hi, Kenny," he said.

Kenny said nothing at first, but then seemed to collect himself. "Grayson."

Cooper interrupted the silence. "Can you believe I actually got him here? It was like pulling teeth."

Kenny looked around. "How's the birthday so far? Having fun? I can see you invited everyone."

"Of course I did. It's not a party without my friends."

"You've always had a lot of those."

"But my favorite ones are all here." He pulled Gillian close. "Even you Miss Fletcher."

Grayson glanced at Gillian and Cooper and took another swig of his drink. Fran sipped from her own glass.

"I don't believe we've met," said Kenny.

Cooper straightened. "Pardon me. Gillian Fletcher, meet Kenneth Mc-Dougal. Sea Island police constable and all-around good guy."

"Pleased to meet you," he said, shaking her hand.

"You, too," said Gillian.

"She wants to interview Gray," said Stuart.

"Ah, hell," said Gray.

"Good for her," said Kenny.

Stuart had no response. Kenny spoke to Cooper. "You picked a good time for your party. Next weekend might have been a wash."

"What do you mean?" asked Cooper.

"Storm watch is probably going up tomorrow."

"Seriously? It's coming this way?"

"Looks like it might be," said Kenny. "We'll have to keep an eye on it."

Cooper observed the room and laughed. "At least my friends are all here to enjoy my party before the big, bad storm arrives."

Kenny turned serious. "Not all of them."

"What do you mean?" asked Cooper. "Who else could I possibly invite?"

Kenny stood quiet, as if unsure whether to say more. "That body on the beach you called me about? It was Marilyn Horn."

The group went silent, and Grayson froze and felt the color drain from his face.

"What?" asked Fran. "What about Marilyn?"

"It was her?" asked Coop. He glanced at Gray.

"It was. Preliminary results show she drowned."

"Drowned? Who drowned?" asked Stuart.

"Marilyn drowned?" Fran asked. "What are you talking about? When?"

"Sorry," Kenny said. "This wasn't the time to bring it up. But you asked me about it. Thought you should know."

"Yes. Right," said Cooper.

"Marilyn? You mean Marilyn from school?" Stuart asked.

"Yes, you idiot," said Fran. "What happened?"

"Not sure," Kenny answered. "We found the body on shore a few days ago. Just made a positive ID yesterday." He looked at Coop. "How did you know it might be her?"

Gray raised his head and answered the question. "I saw the emergency vehicles on the beach. I walked down and saw the scene. I thought I recognized her."

"Well, you were right. It was her." Gray finished his drink and looked for another one.

"Shit," said Stuart. "Marilyn's dead?"

"I'm sorry," said Kenny. "I should have brought it up later, after the party."

"Nonsense," said Cooper. He put a hand on Grayson's shoulder and lifted his drink. "A toast to Marilyn. A world class friend and confidant. Let's hope she's found peace."

"Here, here," said Stuart as he raised his glass.

"To Marilyn," said Gray.

"She will be missed," said Fran.

"Let me get another drink," said Kenny. He turned and found a waiter and grabbed a glass. "To Marilyn," he said.

They all took a swig of their drinks, and Gillian did the same.

"Well," said Kenny, looking around at the partygoers. "I'm sorry I can't stay long. I've got an early call tomorrow."

"How's police work treating you, Kenny?" Stuart asked. "Bet you've got some stories to share."

"Oh, you know how it is on the island, Stu. Feast or famine. Most of the time, I'm just chasing teenagers smoking weed, or the occasional break-in. Nothing too serious."

"You ever wish you'd moved to the city? Made it big like our two millionaires over here?"

"Come on, Stu," said Gray.

"No, I like my life just fine, thanks." He took another drink of his champagne and placed the rest of it on a passing waiter's tray. "I think that's my cue."

"Oh, come on, Ken. Don't leave yet," said Cooper. "Stay a while."

"Nah, I think I've had enough. Thanks for inviting me, though." He leaned closer. "Try to keep it calm, though. I don't want your neighbors calling me at 3 am."

"The neighbors are all here," said Coop.

"Good," said Kenny. "That should make it easy. It was good seeing you all." He didn't acknowledge Gray. "We should all get together. Talk about old times."

"Kenny," said Fran.

Kenny looked back. "Yeah, Fran?"

"Before you go, can I ask you something?"

"Sure thing. What is it?"

"Can someone explain to me why a woman who swam for exercise, drowned?"

"Excuse me?"

"Marilyn," she said. "She and I kept in touch. She was an expert swimmer. How in the hell could she have possibly drowned?"

CHAPTER FOUR

GRAY WALKED OUT ONTO Cooper's outside living room. Trash littered the ground and glass crunched beneath his shoes. The party over, the pool deck was now silent. The band was gathering their instruments to leave, and Gray looked at his watch. It was 3:30 in the morning. He heard a snore and turned to see a random party goer asleep on a lounge chair amid an array of what looked like peanut shells. A cocktail napkin stuck to his face flickered as he exhaled. Most of the crowd had dispersed with only the cleaning crew left behind, and he watched them clear away the dirty dishes and glasses and sweep the floor. He could hear a vacuum cleaner whir to life from somewhere inside the house. How Coop found people to clean at that hour in the morning he did not know. He swayed a bit as he stood outside and grabbed at the railing. He'd had several glasses of champagne and had stayed at the party far longer than he had anticipated. Cooper had disappeared upstairs about an hour earlier with a woman Gray felt sure had been on the cover of some fashion magazine in the recent past. He couldn't remember her name.

After the conversation with his old friends and the mention of Marilyn's death, he had planned a hasty exit, but Cooper wouldn't hear of it. He'd taken him and Gillian under his wing and had introduced them to everyone at the party, despite Gray's objections. Ultimately, he'd found himself with a few of his previous coworkers in the wee hours of the morning discussing recent developments in software technology and how best to position their company in order to adapt to the rapid changes. He had no idea how late it was. Gillian was nowhere in sight.

He headed across the porch and made his way back down the stairwell, ready to return home and fall into bed. He hated to admit it, but Cooper had been right. The party had helped to take his mind off his troubles. He'd forgotten the fun of socializing and even talking business in the midst of a raucous birthday party. Old habits died hard, it seemed.

Reaching the bottom of the stairs, he turned back toward home when he noticed a figure down by the beach. The moonlight filtered through the scattered clouds and he could make out a woman's silhouette. Then she turned and he saw her profile. It was Gillian Fletcher. Something within him caught, and he watched her stare out at the waves. He wondered what made her look so serious and why she hadn't left hours ago. Standing there, he saw her walk barefoot in the sand, holding her shoes, and he debated with himself. Should he go talk to her? He felt the urge, but he hesitated. The temptation nagged at him, but the risk was too great. He turned to go home but stopped again. What could it hurt, he thought, to just say hello?

Even though his brain told him to return to his house, he ignored it and walked down toward the beach. The breeze whipped his hair and he inhaled, smelling the ocean. When he got closer, he stopped. She must have sensed his presence because she turned and looked at him.

"Hi," he said.

"Hi."

"I thought you went home."

Her hair blew in her face and she pushed it back. "I almost did, but then I got caught up in some conversation with some of Cooper's neighbors. We talked about beach erosion and then it turned into a discussion about the storm and the bad weather they'd endured, and then they found out I was a reporter and it just went downhill from there."

He walked up next to her. "Sounds like it was going downhill well before that."

She nodded. "Yes. I think it was."

"So why are you out here now? Don't tell me you're walking home."

She smiled. "No. I drove. I just had a little too much champagne and was a bit tipsy. I thought it would be best to wait before I got behind the wheel."

"Smart."

"I thought so." She turned and looked up at the stars.

"Beautiful night," he said.

"It is."

He admired the reflection of the moonlight on the water. "So, did you end up having fun, despite the fact that you knew no one except me?"

She pushed another wind-blown lock of hair behind her ear. "I did actually. I enjoyed meeting your friends."

He smiled. "Sure you did."

"They seemed nice."

"You did have a lot of alcohol, didn't you?"

She studied the waves. "I could tell there was some tension. What's up between you and Kenny?"

He stilled for a second. "You're pretty perceptive."

"It's my job. Fran seemed a little out-of-sorts herself. You two have a history?"

He chuckled. "You don't beat around the bush, do you?"

"Just curious."

"Part of the job?"

"This is all off the record, of course."

"It is?"

"Yes, it is."

He put his hands in his pockets as he considered his answer. "Let's just say there's a lot of history between all of us. A lot of stories best left untold."

She hugged herself, and her shoes dangled by her hip. "You sure about that? Sometimes it's best to open the door on old wounds and let the fresh air in."

He took a deep breath of ocean air. "Or it's best to leave the closet door shut for good."

She paused. "If you say so. But if you ever change your mind about opening that door..."

A small crab skittered over the sand. "What? You want to hear all my old stories?"

"Why not? I think it would give some insight into the solitary man everyone wants to know about."

A soft groan escaped him. "Nobody wants to know about me."

"Yes, they do."

"No, they want to hear about the millionaire playboy. The guy who jet sets around the world and sleeps with super models."

"You mean Cooper?"

He laughed. "Yeah, I guess so."

"Funny. Nobody's beating down his door for an interview."

"That's because all you have to do is pick up the phone and ask him. It's a lot easier on the hands."

She half smiled. "Maybe."

"What do you think then? What do people want to know about me?"

She turned into the wind. "I think people are curious. They want to know what makes a man like you. Why does someone with the wild and crazy lifestyle, who has more money than he knows what to do with, suddenly pack it all in, disappear from the scene and become a recluse."

He shrugged. "I'm not a recluse. I just don't like to go out much."

"I just think," she said, "that there's more to you than meets the eye."

He stayed quiet but looked down as a wave rolled near his feet.

"And I'd love to get to know you better," she said. "I mean, your story, of course."

Her words made him look up, but it was her turn to stare off and he felt sure that if it hadn't been dark, he would have seen her blush.

His own skin began to warm, and he decided it was time to go home. "It's late," he said.

"What time is it?"

He looked at his watch. "Almost four."

"Four?" she asked. "Hell. I need to go."

He suddenly realized he didn't want her to leave. "How's your foot?"

"My foot?"

"Yes. You sliced your heel, remember?"

"Oh, that." She lifted her heel and looked at it. "It's much better, thanks."

"Good."

They stood for a few seconds and said nothing until Gray broke the quiet. "You okay to drive?"

"Yes. I'm much more clear-headed. The sea air helped."

He nodded. "It's good at that."

She stared for a few more seconds at the water before she turned toward him. "Well, it was nice meeting you, Grayson Steele."

The tone in her voice caught his attention. "That sounds final."

"It is. I'm going back tomorrow."

"Back? Back where?"

"Back home. I can't stay here forever. My editor's pissed enough at the hotel bill as it is."

"What? You're giving up so easily?"

She shrugged. "You've made it quite clear that you're not interested in an interview."

He didn't say anything as he considered her statement. "That's true. I have."

"So why should I stay?"

He couldn't help but meet her eyes then, and she didn't look away. Warning bells sounded and told him to let her go, that she needed to leave. But he couldn't ignore the other voice; the voice that wanted her to stay.

"You'll give me approval?" he heard himself ask.

"What?"

"You'll let me read the article first, and if I don't like it, you'll bury it?"

She stared in disbelief. "Are you saying?"

'You'll bury it if I don't like it?"

"I...I'd try and rewrite it first, based on your input."

"And if I still didn't like it, you wouldn't publish?"

"I...I...No. No, I wouldn't."

He stood there, not believing he was doing this. "You promise me?"

She nodded. "Yes, of course. I promise."

He hesitated again. "Okay," he said. "You've got your interview." He took his hands out of his pockets and began to walk toward his house.

"I...uh...when?"

He looked back. "Be at my place tomorrow. Six o'clock. I'll make dinner and we'll talk." He resumed walking. When she didn't respond, he turned back. "All right?" he asked.

She stood there wide-eyed. "I'll be there."

Her face reflected the moonlight, and she almost looked luminescent. He tried not to stare. "You okay getting back to your car?"

She nodded toward Cooper's house. "Yes. The valet drivers parked it out front. I'm fine."

"See you tomorrow then." He waved and walked away.

· · · • · • · · · ·

Gillian watched Grayson Steele leave as the shock wave of his acquiescence reverberated through her. Disbelief made her shake her head and she began to make her way back toward Cooper's house as Grayson disappeared into his. On the way back to her car, she couldn't help but think about what to do next. She'd been so focused on trying to get him to talk with her that now that he had agreed, she felt a little panicked. She'd taken a leap of faith when she'd told him she was leaving. She knew that if he still refused to speak with her, she would have lost her chance. But the gamble that her charms had made an impression on him had worked. He'd said yes.

She approached the house and took the side walkway that led to the front driveway. The outside lights were on, but the cacophony of departing people filing through the driveway an hour earlier had ceased. The valet parkers were gone, and the house was quiet. Her car was parked out front and when she approached and looked inside the driver's window, she saw the keys in the ignition.

Standing outside, she leaned against the car door. She thought for a moment and took a deep breath, trying to clear her head—not from the champagne—but from her own warring emotions. Was she doing the right thing? The decision to come here and meet Grayson Steele had been a difficult one. She'd wanted to talk to him for some time, but she had always felt that the timing was not right. Then, a week ago, she'd felt that sudden urge and knew then that it was time to at least meet him. After doing her research, she'd found him to be just as she expected. A tough nut to crack. He'd once been an easy interview, but now Grayson Steele's shell had hardened considerably. But she knew that once it softened, she'd find her way in. Now that she had, she wondered what to do next. His was a difficult case, but she'd handled difficult cases before.

Usually, she quickly assessed the situation, determined the best manner in which to approach which offered the highest likelihood of access, and then, once in place, finished her task and was gone within two to three days.

Grayson Steele had not been so simple. She'd already been here six days and was only just now wearing him down. But she'd succeeded at last. Now, if she could use her time wisely tomorrow, she might be able to complete her work and be on her way home within thirty-six hours. Forty-eight max.

Happy that she'd begun to make progress, she sighed when she considered that despite her success, she now had to deal with something she did not expect. Her attraction to him. She groaned. She hadn't planned for that. The moment she'd spoken to him on the beach, she'd felt the pull. It didn't hurt that he was a good-looking man. His dark hair, strong features, and dark blue eyes had turned several women's heads, but he had another appeal entirely. Something told her that once she pried her way past that gruff exterior that she'd find something soft and warm underneath. A shiver ran through her at the thought of discovering that hidden layer. Shaking her head to break from her thoughts, she realized the absurdity of that hope. Regardless of how she felt, she'd just have to deal with it and move on. Once she left, the attraction would fade. She considered leaving now, despite his agreement to speak with her, but she was so close, she couldn't turn back. Grayson Steele needed her help and she couldn't leave.

Lost in her thoughts, a nearby noise startled her and she looked up, expecting to see someone walk out onto the driveway, but she saw no one. The distant breaking of ocean waves was the only sound. Looking up at the façade of the house, her sixth sense began to tingle and the hair stood on the back of her neck. She looked at each window and then glanced around the driveway and back toward the walkway from where she'd come. There was nothing to see. The crickets chirped as she pulled the car door open and slid into her seat. Feeling uncomfortable, she quickly closed and locked the door. Continuing to look through the windshield, she still saw no one and had no idea what had her so spooked.

Rubbing at her tired eyes, she blamed the late hour and her overactive imagination. Her thoughts returning to her main objective, she thought back to the party and Grayson's strange group of friends and how they might be involved in his unusual circumstances. She knew what plagued him and it was no wonder he struggled. From what she'd learned, all the women he'd loved had died. His unique story had intrigued her and she'd found herself unable to ignore it, even wanting to help. She sighed when she realized that her desire to assist him could get her into trouble. But it was part of who she was. No matter what story she heard, she always felt the need to get involved, despite the objections of those closest to her. They knew she wouldn't be able to turn away when someone was in need, despite the risks. Thinking of Grayson Steele, she considered that perhaps his situation could be more difficult than any other story she'd handled. She could almost feel the weight of it press down on her.

Reaching for the ignition, she determined that she was too tired to think about the upcoming interview. Before she could start the car, though, a movement caught her eye. Looking out her passenger window, she saw what she thought was a shadow dart past the lawn near the walkway. Her heart began to hammer and she went still, studying the area, waiting to see if it moved again. She watched but saw nothing. The car was quiet, the only sound being her breathing.

A sudden rap on the driver's side window made her jump, and she jerked her head in the direction of the noise. Her heart slamming against her rib cage, she saw a man. She recognized him as a member of Cooper's staff. It was Franklin. He looked at her through the glass and she noticed he was holding the wrap she'd brought with her to the party. She stared back for a second but then started the ignition and rolled down the window.

He held the garment out to her. "Pardon me, ma'am. I didn't mean to startle you, but I believe you forgot this."

She took it from him and noticed her fingers trembled. "Thank you, Franklin."

"You're welcome."

"Don't you sleep?" she asked. "It'll be dawn soon."

"Mr. Stone pays me not to sleep, ma'am."

"I see."

"Have a nice night, Miss Fletcher."

"Goodnight." Closing the window, she watched him turn and make his way back up to the porch. Even at that hour, he wore a suit and tie. Her heart slowing, but her nerves still on edge, she looked back toward the area where she had seen the shadow but saw nothing. Blaming her paranoia on her fatigue, she shook her head to shake off her fears and headed back to her hotel.

CHAPTER FIVE

GRAYSON THREW THE STEAKS on the grill and listened to the satisfying sizzle. He'd sent his housekeeper, Martha, to the store that morning after she'd cleaned and had her pick up some food for dinner. Offering Gillian cereal for a meal seemed unwise, and the thought of a medium-rare tender steak made his mouth water. Martha had bought the potato salad and a vegetable because steaks were as far as he could go in the cooking department. He didn't open any wine, though. He considered this a business meeting and wine felt too informal.

As he closed the grill cover, he heard footsteps on his stairs and looked to see Cooper walking up on his porch.

"What are you up to?" Coop asked as he smelled the air. "What, are you grilling?" Max jumped up from his slumber on the deck, and Cooper patted him on the head.

"Your insight is impressive."

Cooper sat on a patio chair. "Thanks. When do we eat?"

"We are not eating anything."

Cooper sat forward. "Since when do you cook for yourself?"

"I don't."

Cooper's eyes widened. "Now I am intrigued. Who's coming over?"

"None of your business." Grayson waited for the expected response.

"You're kidding. A woman?"

Gray knew keeping anything from his friend was impossible. He sighed. "Yes. It's a woman."

"Outstanding." Cooper stood next to Gray. "Who?" He thought about it. "Oh, someone from the party? I knew you'd enjoy yourself. Was it Sheila? She was staring at you all night. You know she's a lingerie model?"

Gray rolled his eyes. "It's not Sheila."

"No?"

"No."

"Don't keep me in suspense, buddy. Throw me a bone here. It's got to be someone impressive. You never cook st— Wait a minute." He stared at Gray. "It's not Miss Fletcher, is it?" Gray didn't answer and Cooper smiled. "Holy shit. It is, isn't it?"

"I gave her the interview, that's all it is."

"The hell it is. You would never give an interview before. Why now?"

Gray lifted the grill cover and checked the steaks. He didn't answer Coop's question.

"Well, Don Juan? Why the sudden interest in telling your life story?"

Gray closed the grill and turned. Eyeing Cooper's smirk, he wished he could wipe it off his friend's face, but before he could answer, his doorbell rang.

"Oh, is that her?" asked Coop. "Let me answer."

"Cooper..." Before Gray could stop him, Cooper headed inside and Gray and Max followed. "Would you get the hell out of here?"

Coop reached the front door and opened it, but both men stopped when they saw Kenny at the door.

"Kenny?" asked Cooper. He looked back at Gray. "I'm assuming he's not your dinner guest? He's not very attractive."

"No, he isn't," said Gray, and realizing what he'd said, added. "I mean, he's not my guest." Kenny's visit surprised him. "What is it, Kenny?"

"Sorry to bother you," said Kenny. "I went to Coop's, but the staff said you were over here. Hope you don't mind." Standing stiffly on the front steps, he wore his uniform with his badge pinned to his pocket, his gun holstered at his side, and his hat on his head.

"Jesus, Kenny," Coop said. "You're looking serious. Is this an official visit?"

Kenny hesitated for a second. "I have a few questions about Marilyn. You mind if I come in?"

Gray felt his own posture turn rigid at the question. He'd managed to keep thoughts of Marilyn at bay while he thought of his upcoming dinner with Gillian. But now, his troubles resurfaced and he began to question his motives. What the hell was he doing tonight? Tempting fate?

He stepped back. "Sure. Come on in."

Kenny entered and they walked through the foyer and into the living room. They stood quietly for a moment while Kenny took off his hat and stared at it. Max trotted over and looked up, and Kenny reached down and ruffled his fur. "Hey, pooch."

"What's on your mind, Ken?" asked Cooper.

"Just give me a second," Gray said. "I've got steaks on the grill."

"Sure," said Kenny. Gray walked out to the back porch, checked the meat, and returned.

"Okay," he said. "Shoot."

Kenny looked solemn. "About Marilyn. You said you saw her body on the beach?"

Gray nodded. "Yes. I saw the scene from my porch. I went to see what was going on."

Kenny fiddled with the brim of his hat. "Either of you two know why she was in town?"

Cooper shook his head.

"No," said Gray. "She just said she was in town for a quick visit."

Kenny narrowed his eyes. "You saw her before she died?"

Coop looked over as Gray answered. "Yes. She came over here."

"She did? She came here?" asked Kenny.

"Yeah, she did." Anticipating Kenny's next question, Gray prepared himself for the reaction.

"When?"

"Is this important?" asked Coop.

"We just need to establish a timeline," said Kenny, still looking at Gray. "When?"

Gray sighed. "Three days earlier."

Kenny paused. "Before her death?

Gray hesitated, but finally answered. "Yes."

Kenny took a moment before he asked the next question. "You sleep with her?"

Cooper straightened. "What the hell kind of question is that?"

"Cooper...," said Gray.

"No, I want to know. What are you insinuating, Ken?"

Kenny set his jaw. "You know what I'm insinuating." He narrowed his eyes at Gray. "Did you?"

"Don't answer that," Cooper said.

"Yes. I did."

Kenny set his jaw. "You really are a son-of-a-bitch."

Cooper's face turned stony. "That's enough. Gray had nothing to do with her death and you know it."

Kenny spoke evenly but didn't hide his anger. "We all know what happens."

"Shit, Ken," said Coop. "Is this because of what happened in Mexico?"

"It's not just Mexico. What about the others?" He pointed at Gray. "The guy is poison."

Cooper's voice dropped and his cheeks went red. "You going to arrest him?" he asked. When Kenny didn't answer, he continued. "What? You afraid your friends will look at you like a fool when you bring him in because of a supposed curse?"

"Come on, Cooper," Gray said.

"Don't, Gray. Don't defend him." He walked up closer to Kenny. "I wonder why that is. I'll tell you. Because it's ludicrous. There is no curse, he's done nothing wrong, and you're a first-class jackass." Max woofed and made a low growl. "Even Max agrees."

Kenny fidgeted with his hat. "At least I call them as I see 'em." His eyes squinted. "You know full well that if he'd killed someone you cared about, you wouldn't be so quick to defend him."

Cooper expelled a gush of air. "Gray didn't kill anyone, you idiot. How about you get your head out of your ass and go out there and do some real police work. Or has the routine of island life made you soft, Kenny?"

Kenny stared but said nothing. He eyed Gray. "Don't you give shit about what's happening here?"

The wave of acrimony Gray felt from Kenny almost made Gray want to apologize, but he held back. "I've thought of nothing else since it happened. I didn't love her Kenny. I didn't think—"

"No, you didn't, did you?"

"For Christ's sake, Kenny," said Cooper. "If you don't have anything productive to offer, then get out of here."

The doorbell rang, interrupting the conversation.

"I think that's your cue," said Cooper, crossing his arms.

Kenny held his hat for a moment longer, but then placed it on his head. "I guess it is." He walked back toward the door and Cooper followed.

"Have a nice day, Kenny," said Coop. He opened the front door to see Gillian standing on the front steps. "Hello, Miss Fletcher," he said. "Please come in."

Kenny walked out the door and passed Gillian. He regarded her and noted the bottle of wine she held. "He's thought of nothing else but Marilyn since her death?" He huffed out a short breath. "Apparently, that's not the case, is it?"

"Go home, Kenny," said Coop. "Find something more substantial to dwell on other than a stupid curse."

Kenny remained on the steps, but he ignored Coop and addressed Gillian. "You should be careful."

"Excuse me?" she asked.

"Get out of here, Kenny. Give the man some peace."

Kenny looked back. "She deserves to know."

"Know what?"

Cooper reached to take Gillian's elbow. "Come on in, Miss Fletcher. Kenny is just making house-to-house calls regarding the storm watch. He's making sure everyone is safe." Kenny headed down the stairs, and Cooper waved at him. "Thanks, Ken. Appreciate the advice." Gillian walked inside and Cooper closed the door behind her.

"Everything okay?" she asked.

"Everything's fine."

"No. It's not." Gray had appeared after Cooper closed the door. "I'm sorry, Gillian. I have to cancel."

"What?" asked Gillian.

"No, he's not," said Cooper.

"Yes. I am."

"Gillian," asked Cooper, "would you mind waiting on the back porch for a moment? Gray and I have something to discuss."

"No, we don't."

"Yes, we do." Cooper eyed Gray as if daring him to argue, and Gray relented.

"Just for a moment," said Cooper to Gillian. "He'll be right out."

"You're sure?" asked Gillian. "If this is a bad time..."

"No, the timing is perfect. He can't wait to be interviewed. Don't worry."

She stood uncertain for a moment, but when Gray didn't stop her, she turned and walked through the house and out onto the patio with Max following her.

Gray watched her close the patio door. "She can't stay here," he said. "She has to leave."

"No, she doesn't. Don't let what Kenny said get to you. He's an idiot."

"He's right. I was careless."

"Stop it. Marilyn's death is not your fault. Ken's just hurting and hold-ing a grudge and he's using that to get back at you."

"It's an effective strategy."

"Don't let him succeed. You've got a lovely lady on your porch. Don't let him ruin that."

Gray pointed his finger. "It's an interview. That's it."

"So go be interviewed. Nobody dies after an interview."

"Not yet, anyway."

Cooper moaned. "Dammit, Gray. You were in a good mood before that asshole came in here and destroyed it. You want to talk to her, then go talk to her. Enjoy some conversation. You're not planning on sleeping with her, are you?"

"No, I'm not."

"So, what's the harm? Why send her away?"

"Because..."

"Because why?"

Gray didn't know how to answer. "She brought wine. Did you see that?"

"So?"

"So, maybe..."

Understanding dawned on Coop and his eyes widened. "Oh, you think she may want to sleep with you and you won't be able to resist?"

Gray tried to backtrack. "That's not what I mean."

"Yes it is. I know how you think. So just say 'no.'"

Gray had to concede that Cooper knew him too well. "Easy to say, but not so easy when you've had a few drinks and a beautiful woman is interested."

Cooper smiled. "I hate to tell you this buddy, but I don't think she's here for your body." He looked Gray over. "Although, you're actually well dressed, and you're wearing aftershave, which does make you quite desirable. Should I stay and defend you from her charms?"

"Would you shut up? I'm serious."

"Serious about what? Do you really think she's here to sleep with you? She's a journalist, not a groupie." He eyed his friend's worried look. "What is it? What are you trying so miserably to tell me?"

Gray shut his eyes before admitting what had been on his mind all day. "I like her. I invited her here to do the interview because she was going to leave otherwise. And now she's in my house, she's got wine, we're going to talk and..."

"You think one thing will lead to another."

"Yes," he sighed. "And, dammit, I'm wishing it could."

"So, let it."

Gray's eyes went wide. "I can't and you know it."

Cooper considered his friend's predicament. "Okay, so consider this."

Gray expelled a deep breath. "What?"

"If something does happen, we'll take precautions."

"What do you mean? Precautions?"

"Yes. Hell, we pay enough for our own security, or at least I do." He looked around Gray's house. "If you two hit it off, we'll hire protection for her."

Gray frowned. "Protection? Like a bodyguard?"

"Yes. Why not? You can afford it. I can find someone reliable. They can watch her like a hawk on day three. Once she gets past it, then you're in the clear. What do you think?"

The thought of it seemed silly at first, but the more Gray considered it, the more it made sense. "You think that would work?"

"Why wouldn't it?"

Gray continued to think it through. "It's not that bad an idea. You know someone who could do it?"

"Of course I do," said Cooper. He looked out the front window to see Gillian sitting out at the patio table. "But don't get your hopes up. I don't think you're getting lucky tonight. Miss Fletcher strikes me as a smart woman."

Gray narrowed his eyes at his friend but followed Coop's stare. "You're probably right." He paused. "I'm getting way ahead of myself, aren't I? What the hell am I thinking? She's here for an interview, and I've already got her in my bed." He shut his eyes. "Kenny's right. I am poison."

Cooper grunted. "Kenny's an ass, you are not poison, and you are not cursed. Just go out there and be your charming self. You do that, and she won't be able to resist you."

Gray's thoughts wouldn't stop swirling. "It's better that she leave, Coop. I can't get involved, especially if I like her."

Coop stepped forward and took his friend by the elbows. "Would you just take it one step at a time? Enjoy your meal and talk to her. If something happens, then we'll figure it out. If not, then you've worried for nothing. Unless, of course..."

"What?"

"She's a terrible writer, then people will think you're an imbecile, as well as coat yourself in insect poop. Not a good combination."

Gray shook his head. "I can live with that. I've dealt with worse."

Cooper threw up his hands. "Then what are you waiting for? Don't keep her hanging. Besides, the steaks will burn."

Gray swiveled his head toward the patio. "Oh, hell. The steaks."

"I'll see myself out. Have fun tonight."

"Hey," said Gray.

Cooper turned back. "What?"

"Thanks for the pep talk. I would have shoved her out the door after that conversation with Kenny."

"Anytime," said Coop. "Just let me know how it goes. Especially if..." He wiggled his eyebrows.

"I'm sorry I brought it up."

"I want details."

"Get lost. My steaks are burning."

Cooper left, and Grayson returned to the patio, praying that the evening would not be one he would come to regret.

CHAPTER SIX

GILLIAN SAT IN HER chair and watched the waves drift across the sand. While she waited, she pulled out her recorder and notebook. Max made himself comfortable on the lounge chair next to her. She set the bottle of wine on the table and again considered her interview strategy. She had a few ideas, but she knew that ultimately, it would all depend on Gray and how open he chose to be with her.

She glanced through the window and saw the two men talking. It seemed the encounter with Kenny had almost caused Gray to change his mind, and she gave silent thanks that Cooper appeared to be talking him off the ledge. But Gray's obvious reluctance caused her to reevaluate how to best start this conversation. Still watching, she saw Gray walk through the living area. The patio door slid open and he walked outside, opened the grill, and checked the steaks.

"Smells delicious," she said.

He took the steaks off the heat and placed them on a plate. "I hope you like them well done."

"That's fine with me."

"I prefer them a little rarer, but I was distracted."

He turned off the heat. "You're sure this is okay?" she asked. "We can reschedule."

He brought the steaks over and set them down on the table. "No. It's fine." He looked at the wine. "You want me to open this?"

She waved her hand. "No. Not now. Best to keep a clear head while we talk. Maybe later, though, in case you need something to drink after the interview."

Despite his somber mood, he smiled. "What? You planning on asking me the tough questions? I hope you're not expecting me to cry."

She smiled back. "That's not the plan, no. I'm hoping you might even enjoy the experience."

"If that happens, then we will open the wine. We'll have to drink to that."

"Let's hope for the best, then."

He moved back toward the patio door. "I'll be right back. I need to get the rest of the food and some plates."

"You want some help?"

He hesitated, but then agreed. "Sure. Why not?"

She followed him inside. He grabbed the potato salad and handed it to her and placed the broccoli dish in the microwave to warm it. He pulled out some dishes, silverware, and napkins. He filled two water glasses. The microwave dinged, and he took out the broccoli and placed it in a dish. She carried the items to the outside table and after a couple of trips, they had everything out and they sat down. She'd set the table, and he speared a steak with a fork and placed it on her plate.

"Dig in," he said.

"I will. Everything looks great. I hope you didn't go to too much trouble."

They both helped themselves to the food and started eating. "No," he said. "Martha went to the store for me. I can't take credit for the salad or broccoli. I can only take credit for the over-cooked steaks."

"They're fine." She took a bite. "It's very good."

"You're being kind. I would have taken them off sooner—"

"But Kenny interrupted you?" She decided her best route was to be direct. Making small talk would only prolong the inevitable.

Chewing a bite of food, he wiped his mouth with a napkin and sat back in his seat. "Yes. He had some questions about Marilyn."

"And why did that upset you?"

He took a sip of his water. "You mind if we talk about something else?" He eyed her recorder. "You want to start this interview of yours?"

Sensing his discomfort, she decided to begin with something easier. She could tell now that she'd have to go slow until he relaxed a little. "Sure. You ready?" She picked up her recorder and turned it on.

"Fire away," he said.

She placed the recorder between them. Her notebook sat open in front of her in case she wanted to take notes.

"All right," she said. "Tell me about yourself."

He stabbed at a piece of meat. "Tell you about myself?"

"Yes."

"That's a broad question."

"It is. But I'd like to hear your answer."

He popped the bite in his mouth and chewed for a moment. "Okay," he said, and then swallowed and took a sip of his water. "I was born Grayson Alexander Steele about fifty miles from here. My parents are Charlotte and Benjamin Steele. They divorced when I was eleven. I have no brothers or sisters. My childhood was typical. No major dramas other than the divorce. Mom remarried when I was in high school, and Dad married and divorced three more times until he died of a heart attack at the age of sixty-two. I went to private schools, excelled in math and science and graduated Summa Cum Laude from UCLA. My best friend and I started a business, which creates and sells affordable software programs designed to assist end users in anything ranging from website design, marketing a business, or management training. Within two years of starting it, we'd expanded globally and are now listed as one of the top one hundred fastest-growing companies in the nation. Don't ask me what our current rank is because I have no idea."

He poked his fork around on his plate and jabbed at a potato. "I used to live in the city but moved to the beach about three years ago. I used to be a socialite but prefer solitude now. I used to work out and eat healthy but now," he trailed off, "well, let's just say I exercise less and my food intake could be better." He popped the bite of potato salad into his mouth. "I have a dog named Max, who is my only and preferred companion. I've taken a leave of absence at work, which apparently has caused quite a bit of interest to the public, much to my surprise, and no, I don't sleep in animal skins, eat seashell dust, or rub roach dung on my face."

She made a face at him. "Roach dung?"

"Doesn't my skin look great?" When she didn't answer him, he said, "Never mind," without bothering to explain.

She stared for a second but then shook her head. "Okay, well, that was somewhat informative."

"Sorry. That's the extent of my life, basically."

"But you forgot something."

"What's that?" he asked, taking another bite of steak.

"Women," she said. "Surely there have been a few important ones in your life. Anyone special?"

He stopped mid-chew and looked at her. He finished his bite slowly and drank from his glass. "Please tell me," he finally said, "that this is not an article about my relationship status. The last thing I want right now is to see my picture plastered in some celebrity mag with me on the beach in a sweaty Speedo with the caption, 'Who's Grayson Steele's mystery woman?' Insect poop is bad enough."

"Insect poop?"

"Sorry. Inside joke."

She thought about his answer. "Do you wear Speedos?"

He shook his head. "No, I certainly don't."

"Then you have nothing to worry about."

He grabbed at his napkin and wiped his fingers. "I think you get my point."

"Yes, I do." She made a note on her paper. "But I think you get mine too. Has there ever been anyone special?"

He put his fork down and sat back as if debating whether to answer. "There was."

She paused. "You want to talk about her?"

He stared off at the waves. "Maybe we should open that wine."

She lightly tapped on her notepad. "Later. After I show you that this is not as bad as it seems."

"That boat has just sailed, Miss Fletcher."

"Has it? Why?" He didn't answer, but she didn't relent. "Obviously there's more drama in your life than you're leading me to believe."

"There are some things I'd..."

She waited for him to answer. "You'd what? You'd rather not talk about?" She mentally questioned if she was pushing too fast, but she felt the need to keep going. She doubted he'd ever been asked these questions before and now she waited to see if he would open up to her.

He pushed his dish back, although he still had food on his plate. She took a bite of her broccoli.

"I don't know," he said. "Maybe."

"You're not sure?"

He met her gaze. "You've done your homework, haven't you?"

"That's my job, but I don't know everything."

"No. You don't. Few people do."

"Who does?" She watched him stare off. "Remember, I won't print anything you don't agree to."

His shoulders dropped. "I know."

"So? Care to share?"

He leaned forward and put his elbows on the table. "There was someone special."

"Who?"

His finger traced the tabletop. "Her name was Angela. I met her at UCLA."

"What made her special?"

He smiled as he thought back. "Hard to say really. She had a lot of indefinable qualities." He laughed softly. "When we met, I didn't like her at all. She actually liked Cooper."

"Really?"

"Yes. We were members of a club called 'Computer Greeks.' Coop and I actually founded it."

"Catchy name."

He grinned. "Yeah, well, we were fraternity nerds, but we loved it. It was devoted to all things techy, not just computers. We actually had thirty members."

"Was Angela one of them?"

He glanced over at her. "She joined our senior year. She stood out like a sore thumb. We didn't exactly get beautiful women interested in science lining up to join our group. But when she showed up, I fell hard."

"I thought you didn't like her."

"I got over it."

"Love at first sight?"

"Maybe second sight. And more like lust."

"What happened?"

"She had a boyfriend at the time, but we rarely saw him. He was some jock who played every sport offered on campus. She came to all our events solo. And when she was there, she tended to linger with Cooper. He knew I liked her so he kept his distance. But since she hung out with Coop, she saw a lot of me too. We became friends." He stopped for a second, and she gave him the moment. "Anyway," he sighed, "the month before we graduated, she dumped her boyfriend. I felt sure she'd make a play for Cooper and I couldn't hide my misery. By then I was madly in love, but I'd never told her."

"Did Cooper like her?"

"Cooper liked all the girls. He wasn't big on commitment."

"So what happened?"

"The night after our graduation, we threw a big party. The whole damn campus was there, or at least it felt like it was." He paused. "She showed up. I had determined by then that I needed to tell her how I felt, or she'd go her way and I'd go mine and that would be it." He grabbed at his water glass and drank from it. "So I gathered my courage, knocked back a few shots of Jack Daniels, and approached her."

Gillian couldn't help but lean forward, eager to hear the story. "And?"

"Before I could say anything, she walked up and kissed me."

"She what?"

He smiled at the memory. "She said she'd been waiting for me to do that for six months, and she didn't want to wait anymore." He sat back. "Can you believe that?"

"Six months?" asked Gillian.

"Yes. All that time, she liked me and I had no idea."

"Better late than never, I suppose."

"I guess."

"What happened then?"

"I kissed her back, with great vigor."

"I'm sure."

"The next few days were pure bliss. I felt like an action hero on steroids. I'd gotten the girl, I'd graduated, and Cooper and I were going to make our fortune."

"Sounds like an amazing time. How long were you two together?"

He played with the rim of his water glass. "Three days."

"Excuse me?"

"She died in an automobile accident on her way to the grocery store."

Although Gillian knew the answer to her own question, his response was still hard to comprehend. She could hear the despair in his voice. She sighed and put her pencil down. "I'm sorry."

He didn't say anything, just stared vacantly at his glass, until he finally looked up. "So am I." He took a deep breath as if to shake off the ghosts of his past. "I think I'm going to open that wine."

She didn't argue. He went inside and came back with a bottle opener and two wineglasses. He popped the cork and served her and himself. She didn't drink any, but he took a large gulp of his.

"You okay?" she asked.

"Just great, Miss Fletcher. Any other questions?"

"Yes."

"Then by all means, continue."

She sat up in her seat. "All right. Tell me about your friends."

"My friends? What about them?"

"You all go back a ways. How long have you known them?"

"Cooper and I met in third grade."

"You two are close?"

"Like brothers."

"And the others?"

"Others?"

"Stuart, Kenny, Fran, Marilyn?"

He put his wineglass down. "I guess you could call us friends."

"Not a close-knit bunch?"

"We used to be."

She made a note on her paper. "What happened?"

He watched the waves. "Life. Life happened."

"What does that mean?"

He turned in his seat. "It just means that things change. People change."

She waited for him to say more, but he looked away.

"You all met in high school? Except for you and Cooper?"

He groaned. "Why do you want me to answer questions that you already know the answer to?"

"Because it's more interesting coming from you. Plus, as you said, I don't know everything."

He picked up his wine but didn't drink it. "Yes. We all met in high school."

"You hung out together?"

"Yeah. We were our parent's worst nightmares."

"Why?"

He chuckled. "We broke curfew, smoked pot, got drunk, skipped school."

"You got away with that?"

"For the most part. I still made straight As. So did Coop for that matter. Fran, Stuart, and Marilyn did fine. Joan—" He stopped.

"Who?"

He rubbed his eyes. "Joanie."

"Who's Joanie?"

"Another friend at the time."

"She was part of the group?"

"She was."

"Where is she now?"

He sat up, agitated. "What is all the interest in my friends? This is all old news. What kind of article are you writing, anyway? The life and times of Grayson Steele? Surely you can find a more interesting subject."

"Perhaps, but I don't want to talk to someone more interesting. I want to talk with you."

He blinked. "I'm not quite sure how to take that."

"You can think about it later," she said. "Tell me about Joanie."

"What about her? She was a friend in high school. We all hung out. What else is there to tell?"

"You started to say something. You and Coop made straight As. Fran, Stuart, and Marilyn did okay, but Joanie..."

He shifted in his seat. "Joanie was flunking out. She had a..."

"She had a what?"

"She had a more difficult time than the rest of us. Not that we were perfect, but we all managed our lives and had fun in the process. Her life, well, her life was more complicated."

"How so?"

He made a quiet groan but answered. "Her dad ran out when she was nine. Her mother was an alcoholic. Joanie skipped school more than the rest of us ever did. She did more drugs, drank more booze, slept all day and partied all night. We used to tease her about having a death wish."

"Did she?"

"At the time, we were just kidding around. But looking back now, I wonder..."

"What happened to her?"

He swirled the wine in his glass. "Did you know Fran and I were high-school sweethearts?"

Gillian noted the change in subject. "You were?" She wrote on her paper to come back to Joanie.

"Yes. I took her to the senior prom."

She tried to imagine him in a high school tux with a gaudy jacket and matching cummerbund. "Don't tell me. You were prom king and queen."

He laughed. "No. That was Cooper and his date..." He looked up to think. "What was her name? Julie something. Prettiest girl in school."

"Of course she was."

"And Coop was Mr. Popular."

"I don't doubt it."

"Those were good times."

"How long did you and Fran date?"

"We tried dating in college, but we went to separate schools. We broke up in our freshman year."

"You still friends after the break-up?"

He took a second before he answered. "Not at first, no. But it got better. Time heals, I guess. She went on to become an interior designer."

She studied him as he reflected on the past. "She and Stuart are together now?"

He stared off. "Sorry. What was the question?"

"Fran and Stuart are together now?"

"Yes. I guess so. Seems that way."

"Interesting," she said.

"What?"

"Where people end up."

"I guess so."

They sat quietly for a moment. A couple walked by on the beach below. They held hands as the woman laughed and the man put his arm around her. Gillian envied their contentment. She tapped her pen against her notebook. "So, tell me about Stuart."

"Stuart?"

"Yes. Was he a good friend?"

"Sure. We all were."

"What about after high school? You broke up with Fran. You went to college with Coop. What about Kenny and Stuart? Where'd they go?"

"Kenny stayed close to home. His family couldn't afford an expensive school. He went to community college and then went into the police academy." He stopped and chuckled.

"What?"

"I used to think that he had a crush on Fran. I always thought they'd end up together."

"Why did you think that?"

"Just the way he looked at her in high school. I thought that once I broke up with her, that he'd ask her out, but he never did."

"How do you know he didn't?"

"Huh?"

"Maybe he did, and she turned him down."

"Maybe. Who knows?"

"And Stuart? What did he do?"

"Stuart?" Gray settled in his seat, his tension seeming to ease. "He actually went to UCLA with Coop and I for a year but ended up transferring to a college in Boston. We almost went into business together."

"The three of you?"

"We talked about it."

"Why didn't you?"

"Stuart had different ideas. He wanted to invest more, start bigger, take more risks. Coop and I had a small idea, and we wanted to let it build over time. Stuart got impatient with us. By the time we graduated, he'd gone off on his own."

"What did he end up doing?"

Gray took a sip of his wine. "He started his own company. Went bankrupt in the first year. Then he started a second one, made it rich, but then lost it all. When he tried it a third time, he wanted Cooper and me to invest, but we turned him down."

"Really?"

He nodded. "Yes. Stu's a smart guy but doesn't know how to manage risk. He wasn't a good investment."

"How'd he handle that?"

"Not too well at first."

"I can imagine."

"He figured it out. He didn't really need us, anyway. He eventually found an investor, opened a chain of laundromats, and seems to be doing well."

She wrote in her book. "And what about Cooper?"

"What about him? There aren't too many secrets when it comes to Coop."

"I don't know about that."

"What does that mean?"

"I've heard some things."

"What?" His eyes widened. "Oh, that?" He laughed. "Contrary to popular belief, Cooper did not know that the woman at our Christmas party was a cross dresser."

His smile reached his eyes, and she felt her insides warm as his mood lightened. "That's not what I'm referring to."

"What are you referring to?"

"The rumors that you're the one with the business skills. That the company flourished because of you. That there's talk of stockholder dissatisfaction now that you're not on the scene to keep Cooper in check."

His smile faded. "That's a bunch of crap. The sole reason that we succeeded is because of Cooper, not me."

"It is?"

"I may have a head for business, but Cooper is the bread and butter. We would have failed a thousand times if Cooper hadn't been there to save our ass." His mood shifted, and he frowned. "You can call me the wonder boy if you want, but Coop deserves just as much credit as I do. And it's not fair to him if people are saying otherwise."

She didn't push any further, but chose another direction instead. "And what about you?"

"Me?"

"Yes. You graduated, lost Angela, but then somehow held it together to start a business. How'd you do it?"

He stood and groaned.

"You okay?"

"Just need to stretch my legs." He walked to the banister and rested his palms on it. She put her pen down and gave him a moment to collect himself. There were tougher questions ahead, and she figured he could use the break. A seagull swooped down, and she watched it fly away.

A few seconds passed, and he straightened. "What made you want to be a reporter?"

She crossed her arms. "No, you don't."

He tilted his head. "Don't what?"

"No changing the subject. We're not done." She waved at the chair. "You ready to continue?"

He chuckled. "You win. Where were we?" He returned to his seat.

"You were about to tell me how you pulled it together after Angela."

He picked up his wine. "Losing Angela changed everything for me. Because of what happened, I threw myself into my work. I fell apart for a little while, but then Cooper basically told me he was going it alone if I didn't snap out of it. I realized then that I was on the verge of losing more than just Angela. I was going to lose my whole future. So I recommitted. I spent long hours every day on the business, worked myself to the bone. Drove myself with the job, mostly because it kept my mind off of her." He paused. "Sometimes I think, if she hadn't died, would Coop and I have found the success we did?"

"It's an interesting question."

"One I'll never know the answer to."

"Things happen for a reason."

His face turned serious. "I hate it when people say that."

"Why?"

"Because I can only imagine what my life would be like now if she had lived. Could it have been that much worse?"

She considered her answer. "Probably not."

He didn't respond, but watched as the waves crashed against the shore. The sun was going down and the color of the water had turned a spectacular orangey-blue as the light shimmered on the sea.

"But since that didn't happen," she continued, "you became a successful millionaire. You had a penthouse in the city, threw lavish parties, traveled on private jets, drove a Porsche, and dated beautiful women."

He snorted. "Don't believe everything you read."

"What part of that isn't true?"

He hesitated. "All right. Most of that is true."

She looked around. "So how'd you end up here? It's a beautiful home, but why no more penthouse? You've got an SUV parked in your garage, no food in your pantry, and your only companion is a mutt named Max."

At the mention of his name, Max popped his head up. "Go back to sleep, Max," said Gray. "She's not talking to you." Max dropped his head and obliged.

"Well?" she asked.

"There's not really much to tell." He took a drink of his wine.

"Is it because of Erin?"

He choked and sputtered, grabbed at his napkin and wiped his mouth. "Shit."

CHAPTER SEVEN

"SO TELL ME ABOUT her."

He groaned audibly and rubbed his temples. "Isn't this interview over yet?"

"Not yet."

He poured himself some more wine. She took the first sip of hers.

"Erin." He pondered the name while looking into his wineglass. "I met her at some party. To be honest, I can't remember whose party or even where it was."

"She made an impression?"

"She did. She was drunk and made a pass at me. I turned her down because I was hot after some woman who'd just jumped out of a cake." He glanced over when Gillian's eyebrows raised. "Don't ask," he said. "Anyway, I found out later that she worked for Stone and Steele. I was her boss. I bumped into her in a conference room when she attended the same meeting as me. She avoided my look throughout the entire event, even though she was leading it."

"What was her job?"

"She was an accountant, working on the year-end financials. Boring stuff, but she was good at it."

"And what happened?"

"I bumped into her a few more times, but she kept refusing to talk to me. Finally, I asked her to get me some coffee. Called her 'honey' too. She didn't ignore me then. I think if laser beams could have emitted from eyeballs, they would have emitted from hers."

"I bet. What happened?"

"I apologized. Treated her to a cup of coffee, and we finally talked. She admitted how embarrassed she was by her behavior and lived in fear that I would fire her."

"Really?"

"Yes." He thought about it. "Jeez, if I fired all the women that made a pass at me..." He stopped. "Well, never mind."

Gillian smiled. "What happened after that?"

"I took her out a few times. We kept it quiet. She didn't want anyone to know she was dating the boss. Thought people would think that she was getting extra perks or something like that."

"Makes sense."

"I liked her, but she wouldn't let it be anything more than friendship. She didn't want it to get too serious. So, after a couple of months, I fired her."

"You what?"

"I fired her." He sipped his wine. "Don't worry. She went to work for a competitor getting paid just as much if not more. After about a month, I showed up at her door with a pizza. She was angry as hell at first, but she let me in and we talked and it finally dawned on her why I let her go."

"So she didn't have to worry about dating the boss."

"Right."

"She forgave you, then?"

"We never got around to eating the pizza."

She watched his face relax as he thought back. "So you succeeded as usual."

"I thought so." He stared at his wine.

"What do you mean?"

"I left on a business trip the next day. Two days later, I got the news."

"News?"

"She'd gone jogging. She'd collapsed. They couldn't revive her."

Gillian had known something had happened to Erin but hadn't known the details. "Are you joking?"

He took another gulp of his wine and finished the glass. "I wish I was."

"I..." She searched for words she couldn't find. "Gray..."

He smiled, but it didn't reach his eyes. "You seeing a pattern here?"

"What do you mean?"

"Three days."

"Three days?"

"Until they die." He reached for more wine. "Forget it." He refilled his glass. "It's the wine talking."

She didn't let him change the subject. "You think they die three days after..."

He put the wine back down. "After I sleep with them? Yeah. I do."

"But that's silly."

"Is it?"

"I admit," she said, "it's a bit coincidental."

"More than a bit."

"But are you saying this is your fault?"

"I am the common denominator."

"But you weren't even there when they died."

"I'm not physically present, but my relationship with them changes something."

"Changes what?"

"Changes circumstances. Turns the odds. Tempts fate."

"What are you saying?"

He sighed and stared off at the horizon. "Nothing. I'm talking too much."

She didn't let him off the hook. "Why do you think this is because of you?"

He laughed. "Are you serious?"

"I mean, I know they were with you three days before, but why do you think that is?"

"Why were they with me?"

"No, I mean why you?" She thought about her question and took another sip of her wine. "Why would this be happening?" He didn't answer her, but his look suggested something was on his mind. "What?" she asked. "Is there something that you're thinking?"

"Joanie."

Her eyebrows raised. "Joanie? From high school?"

He leaned forward and held his head. "Yeah."

"You never said what happened to her."

He lifted his head but didn't speak.

"What?" she asked. "What happened? Why do you think this has to do with her?"

A breeze lifted his napkin, and he grabbed at it and balled into up into his fist. "Three months before we graduated high school, we all went down to the beach. It was me, Coop with some girl he'd brought, Fran, Marilyn, Stu, Ken, and Joanie. We built a campfire. We got drunk, smoked some weed, and roasted marshmallows." He paused and Gillian noticed his tight grip on his glass. "We were up late. Coop disappeared with his date. Stuart and Kenny left with Marilyn to go to some other party. Fran and I made out on the beach, but then I passed out and Fran got pissed and left. I woke up face down in a dune. The campfire was dying out, but Joanie was still there. She was wrapped in a blanket and smoking a cigarette. I picked up an unfinished beer and drank what was left. I sat next to her, and we talked for about an hour."

He stopped for a second and ran a hand through his hair. Gillian didn't interrupt. "We were both drunk and before we knew it, we were making out. I stopped it, though, before it went too far and told her it was a bad idea. She laughed at me and told me she wasn't interested, anyway. I could barely keep my eyes open by then and asked her if she wanted me to walk her home. She said no. She didn't want to leave yet. I left her in front of the dying embers of the campfire. I didn't think anything of it because Joanie tended to hang out on her own, anyway. She didn't like to go home." He stopped and rubbed his chin. "That was the last time I saw her." His face fell at the memory.

"The last time?"

"She never made it back to her place. And it took her mother thirty-six hours before she reported her daughter missing. But once she did, the police started their search and met with all of us. I told them what happened. That I'd left her at the campfire at about 4 am and she was fine. They searched everywhere for her. We looked in all the places we thought she might hide. It wasn't the first time she'd taken off, so we thought she'd show, eventually."

"But she didn't?"

"Three days after I left her at the beach, they found her body on the shore."

Gillian slouched in her seat. "No."

"Her mother was devastated. This woman barely paid attention to her daughter when she was alive, but now that she was gone..." He shook his head.

"Did they figure out what happened?"

"The police believed she'd killed herself."

"They did?"

"I never really believed that, though."

"Why not?"

His sad gaze met Gillian's. "Because she wasn't that type of person. She always talked about how once she graduated, she was getting out of town and never coming back."

"Doesn't mean she wasn't depressed."

"Depressed maybe, but not suicidal."

"So what does she have to do with your current problem?"

He studied the table and didn't say anything. Gillian hoped he wouldn't declare an end to the conversation and walk off. But after a few seconds, he answered her. "The day of her funeral, her mother was distraught. We were all there, and she knew we'd been with her daughter the night she'd died. And she knew I was the last one to see her alive."

Gillian held her breath. "What did she do?"

"After the ceremony, she lost it. She was hysterical. She blamed all of us, but she pointed me out specifically. Said she wished for me the same pain that she felt. To know the pain of waiting three days to find out your loved one was dead. She said I would lose the ones I loved three days after I was intimate with them. Only the language she used was more colorful." He stared at Gillian, and his eyes looked haunted. "The woman was out of her head and likely drunk at her own daughter's funeral." He let go of a held breath. "I had nightmares for weeks after that. I kept seeing her pointing that bony finger at me."

The urge to comfort him almost made her reach out, but Gillian didn't move. "She was grieving her daughter's death. That can incite some odd behavior. She needed someone to vent her anger on."

"And she picked me."

"And you think that's why this is happening? You think she cursed you?"

He drew his hand over his face and into his hair. "I know it sounds crazy. Everybody tells me it's crazy. But it keeps happening."

"It's happened since Erin?"

"Yes."

"When?"

He looked at her glass. "Why aren't you drinking your wine?"

"Because I'm conducting an interview."

He looked at his own drink, now almost half empty. "I hate to drink alone."

"You need a little bolstering. This is crazy stuff."

"I'm glad you agree."

"So who else?"

He stood from his seat and leaned against the railing. He took a deep breath and turned to face her. "Two years ago. In Mexico."

"In Mexico?"

"Yes." The breeze caught his hair, and he turned into the wind. "I was a wreck after Erin. I went to work sporadically. I'd already bought the beach house, but after Erin, I sold the penthouse and the Porsche. When I wasn't staying in Coop's guest room, I came out here. I drank too much and slept with strangers." He paused, remembering. "I think I had my own death wish."

She made another note in her book. "The strangers didn't die?"

"No, the strangers didn't die, but I slowly was. I was miserable."

"How'd you end up in Mexico?"

He snickered. "Cooper, of course."

"What? Did he send you to rehab?"

He laughed, despite the serious topic. "Rehab? You think Cooper would send me to rehab?"

"What'd he do?"

"Cooper's answer to everything is to throw a party. That's not what he told me, though. He said that he was taking me on a trip to get away from it all. Said I needed to relax and get my mind off things. He wanted to take me to Mexico, where I could sit and try to find some peace."

"That's not what happened?"

"We got there, and I found he'd rented out half the damn hotel and invited just about everyone we knew, including everyone at the company."

"Expensive trip."

"He wrote it off as a corporate seminar. The only thing corporate about it was the occasional business talk in between golf swings and drink orders."

"Cooper knows how to have fun."

"He does. And, of course, he thought it would solve all my problems."

"It didn't?"

He reached over, picked up the bottle, and added more wine to his glass. "You want any of this?"

"I'm fine." She noticed that although he'd almost finished the bottle, he seemed unaffected.

He leaned back. "The resort was beautiful. I appreciated Coop's efforts, but the last thing I wanted was to socialize." He sipped his drink. "Fran came for a couple of days, but I barely saw her before she left. Stu had to cancel at the last minute. Kenny was coming a few days late. Marilyn was trying her luck as an actress and was doing a play, so she couldn't make it."

"So much for all your friends being there for you," she said.

He stared at his feet. "It was fine. I don't think they would have helped, anyway."

"So, what did you do?"

"The first day I just sat by the water with a margarita in my hand and watched the waves. I wondered what it would be like if a tsunami came and washed me away."

"You and everyone else that was there?"

"Not ideal, I know. But in my state of mind at the time, I wasn't thinking of anyone else."

"And the second day?"

"Same thing. I set up my lawn chair in the shade, ordered another margarita, and sat back and readied myself to do nothing." He sighed. "I had my eyes closed and was wishing I could just sleep forever when someone interrupted me."

"Who?"

"I looked up to see a woman standing by my chair."

"What did she want?"

"She asked if I was Grayson Steele. I told her 'no.' I closed my eyes and hoped she'd go away. She didn't."

"What did she do?"

He looked over at her. "Much like you, Miss Fletcher, she was persistent. She found her own lawn chair and sat next to me. I ignored her for about thirty minutes, but then I couldn't take it anymore. I asked her who she was."

"Who was she?"

"Her name was Amy. Coop had invited her. She grew up in the same town we did. She was getting her master's in psychology, and she thought I would be an interesting case study for her thesis."

"Which was?"

He smiled. "Something about people who achieve great success but can't handle all the pressure that comes with it."

"Really? She said that?"

"Yes. She did. Flattery wasn't her strong suit. I told her I wasn't interested."

"I can imagine. What happened then?"

"She asked me to go Bungee jumping with her."

"She what?"

"Yes. She said sometimes you just need to shock the hell out of your system to sort of reboot yourself. She suggested I try it. I had no idea what she knew about me or my past, but she told me it would be a rocket-ride to awesome." He grinned. "That's a direct quote."

"Did you do it?"

"I thought about what she said. I could either sit on that beach for the next six days nursing a margarita, or I could reboot myself. I figured, what the hell? At worse, the Bungee cord would break and I'd die and then I'd be out of my misery, anyway. Seemed like a win-win."

"So you really Bungee jumped?"

"She asked me to meet her that afternoon. I showed up, and she was ecstatic. She wanted to jump with me. I'm sure she thought I would chicken out, but I said okay and we did it together." Gillian saw his eyes light up. "Rocket-ride to awesome was an understatement."

"It was fun?"

"Thrilling and an incredible rush. After that, I learned Amy was an adrenaline junkie. Coop had set up all kinds of activities—from Bungee jumping to sky and scuba diving and swimming with the sharks. We did them all."

Gillian put down her pen. "You swam with sharks?"

"We were in a cage. They were harmless."

"Sure they were."

"By the third day, I was on a head trip. Thought I could do anything. Amy and I went cliff diving that day."

"Jeez."

"I was on an adrenaline high, or maybe like Joanie, it was the death wish." He paused, and Gillian did not interrupt. "After the cliff diving, I went back with Amy to her room. We were going to race dune buggies later that day. We were so hyped up after all we'd done that things got a little heated. I tried to pull back. I even told her that women I sleep with tend to die soon after. I think the risk of that excited her even more. I justified it by saying I didn't love her, so she wouldn't be in jeopardy."

"So you slept with her?"

He shut his eyes at the question. "I was so stupid," he said.

"I'm not judging you."

"You should." He moved to sit back down in his seat, his elbows on his knees.

"What happened?"

"The next two days we dune-buggied, rode motorcycles, and zip-lined. I stayed in emotional denial because I kept telling myself she was just a fling. We were just having fun."

"But it was more than that?"

"On the third day, I woke up in a panic. I knew then I'd been lying to myself. She was like a firecracker who'd managed to snap me back to life. I went looking for her, intent on keeping her by my side all damn day long, but she wasn't in her room. Her roommate told me she'd gone to the airport to pick up a friend who was going to join us for the weekend." He sat quietly before he continued. "I raced to find a taxi. I didn't know what I was going to do. She'd left thirty minutes earlier, but I had to do something. I headed out to the airport, but we got stuck in traffic." He stared at the deck. "I never got any farther."

Gillian waited. "Why not?"

"Because the traffic I was stuck in was because of a crime scene."

"No."

He cleared his throat and stared off. After a few seconds, he continued. "Amy shared a cab with a businessman who was also going to the airport. On the way, while they were stopped at a light, a motorcycle whizzed by and opened fire on the car. The driver, the businessman, and Amy were all killed."

Gillian gripped her pen. "My God."

"I know." Gray shut his eyes.

"But why? How?"

Gray opened his eyes. "The passenger Amy rode with? He was apparently involved with a Mexican drug cartel. He'd pissed somebody off and that was their retribution."

Gillian had no idea what to say. The two of them remained silent. The sun had descended, and the light was nearly gone.

"After that," he said, staring off, "I stopped going to work. I moved out here permanently. I avoid people, especially women. I stay here, thinking it will keep me sane. Sometimes I think it does, but most of the time..." He drained the rest of his wine.

"It doesn't?"

He huffed and rubbed his neck, but didn't answer her.

"And Kenny? What does this have to do with him?"

He looked up at her. "What?"

"I thought what happened in Mexico is what caused a rift between you and Kenny."

His eyes narrowed, and she wondered if the wine was finally hitting him, but then his face paled and he remembered. "That friend that Amy was picking up at the airport? It was Kenny. They knew each other. It's how Coop met Amy and why he invited her to the resort."

Kenny's anger toward Gray now made sense. "Were they more than just friends?"

"Maybe." He sighed. "I don't know. Maybe Kenny thought so."

She could understand Kenny's antipathy if that were true. "God..."

"Yeah." He finished his wine and put down the empty glass. "And that pretty much brings us full circle."

"Almost," she said.

"Almost?" he asked. His shoulders dropped. "Oh, you mean Marilyn."

"Something tells me you're blaming yourself for her, too."

"Hell." He put his head in his hands. "I am truly a monster."

"Before you start condemning yourself, what happened with Marilyn?"

He rubbed his face. "Why do you want to know? Haven't you heard enough?"

"You've gotten this far."

"Shit." He sat up. "Fine. She came over here three days before they found her body. She and I had a brief fling the summer after Angela died. It only lasted a couple of weeks. We both just needed the company. Afterward, she went her way, and I went mine. Nothing happened to her." He hesitated and shook his head. "So, when she showed up here, and we hadn't seen each other in so long, and she knew my history and we talked and we drank and..."

"I get the picture."

"I thought that since nothing had happened the first time..."

"That nothing would happen the second."

He groaned, frustrated. "I still don't get it. I liked Marilyn, but it wasn't the same as with Angela, Erin, or even Amy. I really thought she wouldn't be affected."

"Maybe there's something else you should consider."

He stared at her, and the look in his eyes conveyed the guilt he felt and the weight he carried. "Honestly, I don't really want to talk about this anymore. I think this interview is over." He stood and walked back to the railing, but then turned, kicked off his shoes, and headed down the stairs leading to the beach. Max jumped up from his slumber and followed him. Gillian watched him walk away and reached over and turned off the tape recorder, and closed her notepad. She thought for a few minutes before she stood. She put the recorder and pad in her purse, took off her sandals, picked up her wineglass, and headed down to the beach.

CHAPTER EIGHT

GRAY STOOD WITH HIS hands in his pockets and stared across the dark expanse of water. The only visible lights were from the line of homes along the shoreline and from distant ships flickering in the distance. The waves crashed harder than usual, as if to warn them that the Atlantic harbored its own impending curse. Gillian walked up and stood next to him but didn't say anything. She drank her wine and dug her toes into the sand. Max barked at a crab that ran along the water's edge.

"Did you get enough to eat?" he finally asked. "You didn't finish your dinner."

"I got distracted by our talk, but yes, I'm fine." She gazed at his profile. "You didn't eat much either."

He turned into the breeze. "Guess I was distracted too. I had plenty of wine, though."

"It helped you relax."

"I shouldn't have drunk that much."

"You talked about some difficult things. I don't blame you for needing a drink."

A wave rushed up and wet his toes. "Did you know?"

"Know what?"

"About this curse thing?"

She hesitated and sipped her wine before answering. "I knew you'd lost some special women in your life. I didn't know about Joanie or Amy, or Marilyn until I got here." She decided that was close enough to the truth.

"You going to write about this?"

She held his gaze. "What? That you think you've got a curse over your head and that you believe you're responsible for the deaths of four women?"

He kicked at the sand. "It's quite a story. It will sell a lot of magazines."

"No. I'm not going to write about that."

His eyebrows furrowed. "Really? What are you going to write about then? My charming wit and lousy cooking skills?"

She faced him. "I think you need to consider something."

He ran his hand through his wind tossed hair. "What is it that I haven't already considered?"

She took a deep breath. "That this isn't a curse, but something else entirely."

He chuckled as if he'd just been asked if he knew how to spell his last name. "You think I haven't wondered what else could cause this? I've questioned everything about me and these women for years, but I have no answers. I have no idea how or why this could be happening."

"I have a theory. I'm surprised you haven't thought of it."

He frowned. "Then by all means, Miss Fletcher, lay it on me."

"Don't you think that maybe someone wants you to think it's a curse?"

His lip crooked up. "Oh, that? The intruder in the woods theory? Somebody stalking my every move?"

"Why not?"

"That's ludicrous. Who would bother to go to all that effort? Nobody hates me enough to kill four women."

"How do you know?"

His jaw dropped. "How do I know? I think you've been watching too many crime dramas on TV."

"And I think you haven't watched enough."

He narrowed his eyes. "What do you mean?"

"Met many people with curses over their head recently?" she asked.

"What?"

"How many people do you know who walk around thinking they've got some kind of curse following them?"

"What are you talking about?"

"Exactly. You can't name any. Have you watched TV recently? Every other damn show is about some murder where a husband or wife offs the other. Nowadays, you can't seem to have a good fight over Thanksgiving dinner without somebody getting slaughtered with the family butcher knife."

"I think you're exaggerating."

"I am, but you get the gist."

"You really think some crazy person is stalking me?"

"Not just some crazy person."

That stopped him. "Who then?"

"Someone you know." She watched his reaction. "Someone close to you."

He stood and stared. "You mean like someone I know on the island or someone I worked with?"

"Someone closer. Someone who knows about the curse."

He turned and faced the ocean and shook his head. "That's crazy."

"Not if you think about it."

He threw out his hand. "That's what you think? That it's one of my friends...I mean, one of my close friends...that is doing this to me?"

"Yes." She'd suspected as much as he'd talked through his story, and the more he'd opened up, the more it made sense. She'd never encountered a situation like his before, but she always followed her gut, and her gut hadn't shut up since dinner, and it had nothing to do with the food.

He stared at the sky, but then pivoted and walked away. "That's the most absurd thing I've ever heard." He stopped and turned back. "Is that what you want to write about?" He set his jaw. "That one of my close friends is a murderer?"

"Gray. Listen to me..."

"That's it, isn't it?" He resumed his walk back to the house. "This meeting is over. You need to leave." He scanned the shoreline. "Max," he yelled. "Come on, boy." Max bounded up from the water's edge and caught up to Gray.

Gillian didn't let him off so easily. She knew she had to get him to see reason, or she'd never be able to help him. "Wait a minute!" she yelled back at him.

When he ignored her, she ran after him. He rinsed his feet and Max's at the shower and stomped up the stairs.

"Would you listen to me, please?" She tried to get his attention, but he refused to answer her. She quickly showered the sand off and headed up the stairs behind him. "I'm not going to write anything you don't want, remember?"

He whirled on her. "You better not write a single word about my friends. Do you understand?"

"Grayson Steele!" He stopped at the top of the stairs and she caught up to him. "Would you calm down long enough for me to talk?"

"We are done talking. I should have never agreed to this." He grabbed his dinner plate and brought it inside. She picked up hers and followed.

"Just wait a minute," she said. They walked inside, and she slid the door closed behind her.

"I can't believe you think that one of my friends..." He dropped his plate in the sink, leaned his palms against the counter, and hung his head.

She stopped and realized that the possibility of him being friends with a killer was hitting him. She held her plate, but then came up next to him and placed it in the sink along with his. She put her glass down on the counter.

Trying to think of what to say, she leaned her hip against the sink and faced him. "I know this theory is difficult to hear, but if you truly want to break free of this, you need to consider the possibility."

"I just..." He lifted his head. "I...God. I don't even know what to say."

"Sit down." She motioned toward his dining table. He sighed but didn't move. "I'll give you my reasoning. You can take it or leave it. But at least I'll have told you what I think. The rest will be up to you."

He hesitated, but then straightened and went to sit down. She sat next to him.

"Okay, Elliot Ness," he said. "Tell me what this theory is of yours."

She considered what to say, but now that he was listening, she didn't know where to start. "Bear with me," she said.

He grunted. "I don't promise anything."

She took a moment to gather her thoughts and give him some time to calm down. "Think about it," she finally said. "Just before you graduate from high school, one of your troubled friends disappears and winds up dead in a suspected suicide. Her grieving mother curses you in front of all your buddies and tells you the women you fall for and sleep with will die three days later."

"You're not telling me anything I don't already know."

"Well, think about it. Angela dies right after you graduate from college. Erin dies after you've become wealthy and successful, Amy dies while you're still coping with Erin's death, and now Marilyn dies."

"Is this supposed to be helping?"

"Just wait a second." She thought it through. "You said Kenny had a crush on Fran in high school."

"What? You think Kenny killed these women because he was pissed that I took Fran to the prom? God. Please tell me you've got something more to hang your hat on."

"Would you shut up and let me think?"

He held up his hands. "By all means, Lone Ranger."

She ignored him and thought back to what he had told her. "So suppose Kenny did try to ask Fran out after you broke it off? Maybe she did turn him down. Maybe because she was still in love with you."

"Oh, come on."

"So that gives Kenny and Fran a motive."

"A what?"

"Motive. Kenny's pissed because the woman he loves still loves you. Fran's pissed because she still loves you, but now you've met another woman and you only have eyes for Angela. Maybe she even knew about you kissing Joanie on the beach."

He stared at her, open-mouthed. "And what, Stu's mad because Coop and I are best friends and we didn't invite him to play during recess?"

She met his dubious gaze. "Maybe. Was he jealous of your friendship with Cooper? You told me you were all three going to go into business together, but then that changed."

"But that was no big deal," he said.

"Maybe to you it wasn't."

"Come on. Are you saying that one of them murdered Marilyn to get back at me?"

"They had the perfect set-up. They knew about the curse. They knew that would wreak havoc on you."

"Then why not the first time? Why didn't they kill her the first time we got together?"

"Think about it. It only lasted two weeks. Who knew about you two?"

He thought back. "Far as I know, just me, Cooper, and Marilyn."

"And when did you tell Coop?"

"I don't know. A week or two after it happened?"

"That's why. Once the three days had passed, you can't blame the curse. The opportunity is lost. But the second time..." She paused. "Who knew she was here?"

"Nobody. Unless she told someone."

"She obviously did, and it got her killed. Plus, if the killer is escalating, it just gives him the chance to dig the knife deeper. Whoever this is covers their tracks well."

"But we're talking about murder here."

"Depends on who's doing the talking. One man's murder is another man's opportunity."

His face fell. "That's morbid."

"But possible. People have done crazier things."

"Still…"

She voiced her other concern. "You have to think about Cooper, too."

He looked at her in shock. "What? There is no way in hell he would ever do this. I won't even go there."

"I'm just saying. You've always been the one to get the accolades. You're the brains and he's the pretty boy. It could get to someone after a while."

"Not Cooper. He's never had an issue with self-confidence."

"That you know of."

His voice rose. "I've known him since the third grade. He'd have to be a sociopath to get away with what you're suggesting."

She didn't answer, but just stared back at him.

"Oh, come on." He stood and paced. "Now you're telling me that my best friend, a man who is a brother to me, is a sociopath?"

She waved her hand. "I'm not telling you anything. I don't know any of these people. But because I don't, I can be more objective. And based on what I've seen since I've been here…"

He stopped pacing. "What?"

"I'd say that someone you think you can trust is stalking you."

His hands found and gripped the back of the chair he'd just stood from. After a few seconds passed, he chuckled. "Wow. You've been here, what, a week? And from one conversation, you've deduced that one of my close friends has murdered four women because of their hatred for me?"

"You said it yourself. People change."

"I wasn't talking about turning into a murderer."

"Who said anything about turning into one? Maybe they were from the start. This may go all the way back to Joanie."

The shock of her statement stunned him. "Shit. Now you've pegged one of them as a psychopath?"

"They murdered four people. What would you call it?"

"Insane."

"That works too."

"No. Not them. You."

She didn't back down from her theory. "Really? I give you a completely plausible explanation and you'd rather believe in a curse?" She stood. "You can stand there and look at me as if I'm the one who's lost their marbles, but at the end of the day, I can go home and live my life. I can look forward to one day getting married and having a family. I can go home and sleep at night. Can you?"

He didn't answer.

She gentled her tone. "I know this is difficult, but if you want your life back, you're going to have to take a hard look at the people in your circle and the role they play in it. If you want to be free of this supposed curse, then you need to take a leap of faith and assume it never existed to begin with."

His hands still gripped the chair and his face paled to the point where she began to wonder if he would fall if he let it go. She waited for him to respond, and she almost reached out and touched him. After a few seconds, he sighed and shook his head. "You're telling me that someone I've trusted since childhood may be the reason I've lost the women I've loved? That someone hates me so much that they're willing to go to these lengths to see me suffer?"

She hated to see the pain in his eyes. "Yes. That's what I'm saying."

Confusion clouded his features. "But if that's true, then why not just kill me and get it over with?"

She wondered about that herself, but she told him her suspicions. "Sometimes drawing it out is more fun. Obviously, it's been tormenting you for years."

He hung his head, but then dropped his hands and straightened. "It's been hell. There've been times when I thought..."

"What?" she asked, but he didn't answer. "When you thought what?"

His eyes conveyed his misery. "That it would be better if I wasn't around."

She knew what he meant. "Suicide?"

"It's crossed my mind more than once."

She fought the urge to take his hand. "Maybe that's exactly what they want. Maybe that's why your killer went after Marilyn. To push you closer to taking your own life."

He let go of a deep breath and walked to the couch and sat down. He held his head in his hands. "So if I consider this theory of yours..." He shut his eyes and rubbed his temples. "...then what do I do now?"

She empathized with him. The relief she'd felt at getting him to see the truth began to fade when she had to admit that she didn't know how to answer his question. She went to sit next to him on the couch. "I think you need to hire a..."

He popped his head up when she didn't finish her sentence. "What?" he asked. "Hire who?"

She didn't answer him because a possible solution to his predicament had popped into her mind. She stared off as she thought about it. It was crazy, but the idea had hit her hard in the chest, which told her it had merit, and the more she thought about it, the more she realized the wisdom of it. But if she did it, it meant staying three more days. The thought of spending more time with him appealed to her, but there were also drawbacks to staying longer. But she didn't stop to think about that. The extra time in one place would be risky, but she could figure that out.

"Gillian? You there? Hire who? A private investigator? What are they going to do?"

"No," she spoke quietly. "Not a P.I."

"Who then?"

She met his gaze. "Me."

"You? Hire you for what? You've already tortured me enough with your interview."

"Well, not hire me, but use me."

"What are you talking about?"

She stopped thinking about all the things that could go wrong with this plan and committed. "Let me spend the night with you tonight."

CHAPTER NINE

HE JUMPED OUT OF his seat as if something had shot at him from below. He stared at her like she was a sea monster. "Like hell I will. Look, I appreciate your willingness to help, but you sleeping with me is not the answer."

She stood, and he moved farther away. "Relax, Mr. Steele," she said. "I am not going to sleep with you."

He stopped. "You're not? I mean, what are you talking about? Why sleep over?"

"To make it look like I slept with you."

His eyes widened when he understood her plan. "You want to make it look like we slept together?"

"Yes. It's brilliant."

"You are insane. I have confirmation now."

"Would you think about this for a second? I'm here. We've had dinner. We've had a few drinks. We sit outside, enjoy the evening. We put on a little show. Then we come inside and go upstairs. The lights go out. Of course, I'll be in a guest room, but our bad guy won't know that. Then, we wait three days and see what happens."

He looked horrified. "That's a terrible idea."

"Why?"

"Because you want to get killed?"

"I won't get killed."

"How do you know that?"

"I'll have someone watch out for me."

"You will? Who?"

"You let me worry about that."

He shook his head. "No. I don't like this."

"You want to end this curse?"

"Yes. Of course, but not at your expense. Not at anyone's expense."

"I'll be fine. We know what to look for. Besides, what are the other options?"

He shot out his arms. "There's got to be another alternative."

"I can't think of any. Can you?"

"Damn it. This is crazy."

"But it will work."

He didn't move, and she knew he was considering it.

"Well?" she asked.

"Coop mentioned he could hire someone. I'd feel better if…"

"No. Cooper can't know. He's a suspect like everyone else."

He moved his hands to his hips. "Cooper didn't do anything."

"Then we'll all breathe a sigh of relief in three days when that's confirmed."

He hardened his features. "It will be confirmed." But when she didn't back down, he said, "Fine. So I'll tell him we slept together. But he can still hire someone to keep you safe."

"Assuming he's not the bad guy, then yes, I suppose so. But if he is…"

"Gillian, Cooper is not going to kill you."

She understood his need to believe in his friend. "All right. Let him hire someone then, if it helps with the story. But I'll have someone too. Just in case."

"You're sure you can trust them?"

"With my life."

He didn't ask who that could be, but he didn't dwell on it. "This is nuts. None of my friends are going to try to kill you. I can't believe we're considering this."

"Then if that's the case, my safety is secure. And if there really is a curse, then it won't kick in because we didn't do anything."

"What if it's someone else? Someone we haven't considered?"

"Then my protection will catch them, too. This is meant to catch whoever the guilty party is."

"And what if nothing happens?"

"Then we'll talk about that when the time comes, but for now, I think it's worth a shot. Don't you?"

He stood on the other side of the room from her, as if being near her would incite some sort of uncontrollable act he wanted to avoid.

"I'm still not sure." He took a shuddered breath. "If something happens to you, I don't know if I'll be able to recover."

"You? What about me?"

"You know what I mean. I won't be able to forgive myself for putting you at risk."

"I'm accepting the risk."

"But I'm going along with it."

She moved up closer to him, and he didn't back away.

"Believe me. I have no intention of dying anytime soon. But we have the edge here. The element of surprise. We just have to make it look real. If it looks faked, then we've lost our advantage."

His face shifted from fear to doubt. "You're sure? I mean, you better think this through."

The last thing she wanted to do was think about it. "I'll be fine. We're gonna catch this guy." He continued to look unconvinced. "Yes," she said to persuade him. "I'm sure."

He groaned, and shaking his head, he agreed. "I can't believe this." He rubbed his neck. "Okay. How do you want to do it?"

She smiled at the question, and he realized how it sounded. "Sorry. I mean, how do we make this look real?" He stared at the ceiling. "God help me," he said.

"Well," she looked around the room. She spotted her wineglass and walked into the kitchen to pick it up. "Open another bottle of wine."

"Another bottle?"

"We should make it look like we've been drinking."

"That shouldn't be hard." He walked to a wine refrigerator and pulled out a bottle. He found another opener and popped the cork. He filled her glass and grabbed a fresh one and filled it for himself.

"Pour half of the bottle out. Make it look like we've been drinking since we've been inside."

"Hell. You really think whoever this is, is paying that close of attention?"

"You never know. Better to be safe." She looked toward the patio door. "We need to go outside."

"Outside? Why?"

"Makes for a better show."

"What kind of show are you proposing? Why not just go upstairs and turn off the lights?"

"Because," she said. "Our bad guy may find it hard to believe that you'd actually sleep with me so soon after Marilyn. We have to convince him."

"And how do you propose we do that?"

She moved up close. "You'll have to make a pass at me. Act a little drunk."

He stepped back. "Wait a minute."

"What?"

"I'm not too comfortable with this."

"Why not? You wouldn't make a pass at me under other circumstances?"

"Maybe once this is over, we can discuss what I would and would not do with you under other conditions, but this is not one of those times."

"Listen, let's just go out there and talk, and we'll see what happens. Obviously, thinking about this is making you uncomfortable."

His mouth dropped open. "How can you be so calm about gaining the attention of a potential murderer?"

"If we catch this guy, then this is the story I want to write. How we caught the guy who stalked you for years."

"That's what you want to write about?"

"It's a hell of a story."

"And you're putting yourself right in the middle of it."

"It's what any good journalist would do."

"You're a lot braver than me."

"I better not be. I'm counting on you to get me through this."

He sighed and closed, and then reopened his eyes. "You would say that, wouldn't you?"

"Come on." She pulled on his arm. "Let's go."

He let himself be pulled toward the door. "What the hell are we doing?"

"You're Grayson Steele," she said, sliding the door open. "I think you know what you're doing. Especially when it comes to seducing a woman."

"Not when it comes to this. I hope you'll forgive me if I have performance issues later tonight."

"Don't worry. I'll be in the other room. You'll have to handle that one all on your own."

He made a face, but she had already moved out the open door and onto the patio, and he followed.

They stood outside and stared at each other. "You want to sit?" he finally asked her. "It's a great night to be outside."

"Sure," she said. She sat, and he took the seat next to her. She took a sip of her wine and set it on the table. "Feeling better now?" she asked. "Now that the interview is over?"

He sipped his drink. "Much better. Although it was just as bad as I thought it would be."

"I'm sorry to hear that." Gillian tried to relax and not think about what she was doing. She fidgeted in her seat and let him lead the conversation. "What?" she asked, when he kept staring.

Closing his eyes, he took a deep breath, let it out, and opened his eyes again. "Now that you know all about me, why don't you tell me a little about you?" She tensed, taking another sip of her wine. "What's the matter?" he asked after seeing her reaction. "Don't like being on the other end of the tape recorder?"

"There's not much to say," she said, studying her glass.

"I doubt that," he answered. He leaned in. "Come on, Miss Fletcher. Tell me all about yourself."

She smiled when she heard her own question directed back at her. She hadn't expected this, but she'd made it this far, and figured she could handle a few questions about herself without revealing too much. "Okay," she said. "You win."

"You bet I do."

She drank more of her wine, and he poured some more for both of them.

She started from the beginning, as he had. "I was born Gillian Margot Fletcher in a small town called Shepton just outside Phoenix, Arizona. My parents are Lillian and Carson Fletcher and they are still together."

"Impressive," said Gray.

"It's been years since they met, but they've only spent a sum total of..." she looked up to think about her answer. "Maybe eight years together? If my calculations are correct."

Grayson tipped his head. "That changes things. Why is that?"

She didn't know why she had told him. She could have easily said nothing, but something made her keep talking. "My dad travels."

"Military?" he asked.

She nodded. "Yes."

"You grew up in Phoenix?"

"For a short time. We didn't stay long, though."

"Lived all over the world?"

She tensed. "How'd you know that?"

He looked at her as if she'd had too much wine. "Military families tend to do that."

"Right. Yes, we did. We moved a lot."

"You have brothers and sisters?"

"I do. I have an older brother and sister."

"You're the baby?"

"I am."

"Explains a lot."

She knitted her brows. "Very funny." She took another sip of her wine. She began to gain a whole new appreciation for being on the other end of the interview.

"What made you want to be a journalist?"

"What?" She leaned over to pet Max, who slept by her feet.

"A journalist?" he asked. "Why are you one?"

"Oh, that. I guess I like to know about people. Help them."

"Help them? How do you help them as a journalist?"

She searched for a reasonable answer. "I've never been the kind of reporter that needs to be first on the scene or the one who uncovers government conspiracies. I'm much more interested in people and their stories. What makes them tick."

"And that helps them?"

She smiled and gazed out over the water. "I did a story once about a man who lived in poverty with his family. He worked three jobs and struggled to put food on the table. When his wife became pregnant with their third child, they made the agonizing choice to let an aunt raise the baby girl. They simply could not afford another mouth to feed. The aunt lived in another state, though and rarely visited. After a few years, the father managed to secure more stable employment, and he went looking for his daughter. When he got there, he learned that the aunt had moved away. He searched for years for his child, but without the money to hire someone to help, there was little he could do. On top of that, he'd heard rumors that the aunt was involved in shady business deals. The neighbors believed she'd left when she found herself in trouble with the wrong people. When I found him and talked to him, he blamed himself for his daughter's plight. His wife had died two years earlier and his sons were old enough to work and contribute to the family. All the father wanted was to find his child and bring her home."

Gillian took a moment and sipped her wine. Grayson said nothing and waited for her to continue.

"After hearing his story, I did a little digging. I knew a few people who could turn over dirt and find the worms, so to speak. I learned that the aunt had sold drugs out of her home. She'd been arrested a few times but always managed to avoid jail time. Apparently, though, she helped herself to the inventory, and her luck ran out. She disappeared one night and took her niece with her. After following several leads, I found the aunt in a disheveled hovel of an apartment. I called the father and told him, and he raced to meet her. Problem was, the daughter wasn't there. The aunt didn't have her. When we pressed her for information, she admitted that she'd left the child with one of her business associates who'd taken an interest in the girl."

"What?" asked Gray with disbelief. "She gave the child away?"

"She'd sold her."

"You're kidding."

"No. The father was enraged and called the police. They took the aunt in for questioning. It took a few weeks, but we finally learned the name of the man she'd sold her niece to. Long story short, a month later, the man found his daughter. She was living in a drug lord's home, and, after a raid in which authorities found bags of cocaine and money lining the halls of the house, the man was arrested and the girl was reunited with her father."

Gillian smiled at the memory. "I'd call that helping." She leaned back in her seat.

Her story seemed to relax him. "I would too," he said. "Did you do that story for *Lifestyle*? That doesn't sound like their sort of article."

"No." She scratched at the edge of the table. "That was before *Lifestyle*. I did some freelance work for a while."

"Who published it? I'd like to read it."

She looked up. "What?"

"Did you sell the article?"

She nodded. "Yeah, I did. To a small periodical in the South."

"Who?"

"It's called *Southern Style*. It was a few years ago. I don't even know if they're still in business." She studied her wine.

"I'll see if I can find it."

"It's not that big a deal."

He drank from his glass. "Don't sell yourself short, Miss Fletcher. You helped a father find his daughter. Sounds impressive to me."

She met his gaze, and his dark eyes held hers. "Thank you," she said.

"You're welcome. I'm just glad you write about more than cursed millionaire playboys."

She grinned. "You're my first," she answered. The intensity of their exchange inside the house faded, and the wine warmed her. "And hopefully the last."

His study of her made her nervous, and she finished the rest of her wine and stood, still holding her glass. Feeling his gaze on her, she began to second guess this plan of hers. Suddenly it felt way too personal, and she hoped she wasn't getting in too deep. She leaned on the railing and he picked up the wine bottle and emptied the rest of the contents into both of their glasses and moved to stand beside her. She wondered if he was also beginning to question the foolishness of their plan. Did they really think they could catch a killer?

If Grayson was nervous, then he didn't show it when he stood close and pressed up next to her. Feeling his nearness, she was surprised when her fears dimmed, and she found herself pressing back against him.

He leaned close and spoke into her ear. "You sure about this? You still have a chance to back out." His breath against her skin made her tingle. "I was enjoying our talk. Just sit back down if you want to stop."

She considered it and whispered back. "I don't want to stop." To emphasize her point, she leaned into him.

He sighed against her, and she thought she heard a muffled curse. He pulled back, his face serious.

"That wasn't so bad," she said.

"What?" he asked.

"My interview," she said.

"You call that an interview?" he asked. "I didn't even get to the tough questions."

Despite her sudden reluctance, Gillian determined to see this through. Her mind was telling her this was naïve, but she didn't listen. The desire to help him compelled her. And if it meant getting a little closer to him, then she didn't mind that either. She would deal with the repercussions three days from now, but for the moment, she ignored her nerves and enjoyed the feel of him against her. "And what would those be?"

He leaned in. "How do you feel about cursed men?"

She smiled. "I never met one I didn't like."

"Good." She could feel her face flush and he smiled. "You think you're tough enough to tempt fate?"

She felt the alcohol buzz through her. "Depends."

He brushed a lock of hair off her face. "Depends on what?"

Her breathing picked up, and she tried to slow it. "If the fate is worth the risk."

They locked eyes as she waited for his reply.

"And do you think I'm worth the risk?" he asked.

The conversation had lost its casual tone, and she knew he waited for an answer, despite the fact that this was only supposed to be for show.

"Based on what I know so far," she answered. "I think you are."

He kept his eyes on her, but then looked down at his glass. When he looked back, his posture relaxed. "Cheers," he said, holding up his wine-glass.

"To what?" she asked.

"To the end of the interview..." His eyes were darker than the night sky and they roved over her face, sending tingles through her. "...and the beginning of something else."

She clinked her glass against his and drank from it. She watched as he drained most of his. She decided to hell with it and drank most of hers, too. He took her glass and set it down on the table along with his and came back up next to her.

Feeling him against her again, she sucked in a breath. "I should go," she said.

"Probably," he said.

She didn't move. "I mean, if there really is a curse..."

He slowly exhaled. "Then we don't want to take any chances."

She moved up closer. "No." She brought her face up to his. "We don't." She could feel his body tense, but then just as quickly relax. She almost willed him to stay calm. He reached down and took her hand. His fingers trailed over hers, and it surprised her when soft tendrils of heat slid through her midsection and her body temperature soared.

He brought his other hand up and touched her jaw line. "You're a beautiful woman, Gillian Fletcher."

Steady breathing became impossible, and she wondered if they were playing anymore. She raised her free hand to his chest and felt him suck in a breath. "I really should go." Her insides churned.

He nodded. "Yes. You really should." He let go of the hand that held hers and slid it around her back, and pulled her close.

Her heart rate soared, and her body seemed to take on a mind of its own. She had not expected this reaction to him. "It would be utterly irresponsible for me to stay."

He lowered his head and his mouth lingered so close to hers that she could feel his breath on her lips. They stood that way for what felt like hours, and pulses of electricity shot through her. Gillian didn't know when it happened, but her arm had moved around him and her other hand had snaked its way up his shoulder. His hand on her face continued to stroke her skin and before she could prepare for his kiss, something sparked and she moved in just as he did, and their lips met. All thoughts of curses and killers vanished when she felt his warm lips move over hers. Whatever she'd expected to happen was dull compared to the feeling that shot through her when his mouth captured hers. Her arms tightened around him, and his hand on her cheek went to the back of her neck. The slow kiss picked up speed as he raked his lips over hers. Dropping all pretenses, she opened her mouth and touched her tongue to his. His breathing escalated along with hers, and the kiss deepened. The fire in her belly blazed hotter than she thought possible. Her reaction to him amazed her. She couldn't press herself close enough. He seemed to have no problem with it either, as his response felt just as eager. Pulling her in, Gray moved his hand down her back, and she moaned deep in her throat when he cupped her backside. Their mouths continued to explore, and all she wanted to do was feel his skin against hers.

The plan they'd concocted was forgotten as they moved against each other. He moved, and she shifted and felt all of him against her. Her breathing raced, as did his. When his lips raised, she moaned in dissatisfaction but gasped when she felt his mouth find the sensitive skin just below her ear. He nibbled and kissed her neck, and she dropped her head back. Her body seemed to move with no direction from her brain, and she arched against him. He moaned and let his hands travel over her; one dropped to her thigh. He pulled her leg up, and she wrapped it around him. He dragged his mouth up from her neck and jaw and then he was back at her lips and they kissed again. Something inside her let go and she couldn't stop herself from touching him. It was like she was on a speeding freight train with no brakes. She brought her hands down his back and found his shirt tail. She began to pull it up when he suddenly stopped and grabbed at her wrists. He spoke despite his heavy breathing. "We should bring this upstairs."

All she could do was nod, and he came back and met her eager lips again as she pressed her hands to his chest over his shirt. Her hands traveled up to his shoulders, and she wound them around his neck and pulled him closer. He groaned in his throat and broke away, grabbing her hand. "Come on." His eyes were stormy with desire. "Upstairs." All she could do was follow when he led her inside and shut the patio door. Max followed through his dog door. Switching off the lights as he moved, Gray led her to the staircase. Before she could clear her head, she was on the second floor. He took her to a room, and they stopped at the threshold.

Her heart was still beating so fast, she knew that if he took her into his bed, she wouldn't say no. He looked down at her with his own indecisive eyes.

"Jesus," was all he said. His lips found hers again in another hungry kiss, only now with no need to pretend. Her hands slipped under his shirttail, and he groaned when her fingers touched his skin. Pressing up against her, he guided her backward into the room. They continued to kiss while Gillian explored his stomach and chest. His hands gripped her back and waist, and she waited for him to unzip her dress, but her knees hit something solid and she fell backward onto a soft surface. Opening her eyes, she tried to clear the haze from her mind and realized she was in a dark bedroom. Gray stood over her as she lay on top of a bed, and their breathing was the only noise in the room other than the hammering of her heart. She waited for him to join her, and she almost reached out for him when he backed away.

"Good night, Miss Fletcher," he said, through a ragged breath. His eyes held hers for a brief second before he turned and walked out of the room.

CHAPTER TEN

THE COFFEE MACHINE BEEPED. Grayson grabbed for the pot and filled himself a full cup. He added his usual cream and sugar and sat down at the breakfast table. His head flared, and he rubbed his temples. The wine last night, paired with minimal sleep, had combined to give him a roaring headache. He drank from the cup and popped the lid off a bottle of aspirin he'd taken from the cabinet. He swallowed two pills and thought again about the previous evening. He couldn't stop thinking about Gillian Fletcher. His reaction to her had been startling and instantaneous. The minute their lips had touched, he'd devolved into a mindless mass of bone and muscle whose actions were driven based on taste and touch alone. He'd experienced lust before, but nothing like what he'd felt last night. He could still feel her body against his, his hands on her skin, and his lips slanted over hers. Angela, Erin, and Amy had all been memorable and wonderful, but Gillian lit up something inside of him he'd never known existed. And he wondered how much further it could go. Sliding his hand into his hair, he wondered how he'd stopped himself. Seeing her fall against the bed, her hair in disarray and her lips swollen, and knowing that she would have welcomed him if he'd joined her, it had taken every ounce of strength and fortitude he'd possessed to walk away.

The thought of the curse had been the catalyst to break through the sexual haze. If Gillian was wrong, if no one was out to murder his lovers, and there really was some elusive force that would culminate in her death in three days, then he couldn't take the risk. The vision of Marilyn lying in the sand with lifeless eyes staring back at him had pulled him back and out of Gillian's room. Now, as he sat at the table nursing his coffee, he debated his choice and knew he'd made the right one. Gillian may still be at risk, but at least he knew it would not be from any curse. The sensibility of their decision to play this "whodunit" game in the first place, though, was still up in the air.

"Good morning."

He stilled in his chair and turned, seeing her at the foot of the steps. She was barefoot and still wearing her dress from the previous night. Her hair was disheveled, and her puffy eyes suggested she'd slept about as well as he had. Her face was clean, though, so he realized she must have found the toiletries in the guest room and used them to wash off her makeup and brush her teeth. They were there in case his mom popped in for one of her rare visits.

"Good morning," he answered. They stared at each other for a few seconds, and he swore silently when he felt his body react to her again. "Coffee's on the counter. Help yourself." He turned away, hoping to control his reaction. He thought again about the previous night and berated himself for his lack of discipline.

"Thanks," she said. She walked into the kitchen and opened cabinets, looking for a cup. When she found one, she pulled it down and filled it and went to sit across from him. She avoided eye contact as she drank.

"How'd you sleep?" he asked.

She looked up then. "Terrible."

"Me too."

She put her cup down. "I...um..." She studied the table.

"What?" he asked.

"I...I want to apologize for last night. I don't know what came over me. I..." She stopped and her cheeks reddened.

He empathized with her. "Don't apologize. I didn't exactly hold back either."

"I didn't expect it to be so..."

His jaw clenched. "I know. It took me by surprise too."

She gripped her coffee cup. "Thank you for stopping. If you hadn't..."

"If I hadn't..." The room went quiet. He cleared his throat to break his train of thought. "We did, though, so let's not dwell on it."

She exhaled a deep breath. "I'm trying not to."

He couldn't help but smile. "Me too," he said, although the images in his head didn't disappear without effort. "So," he said. "What happens now with this little plan of yours?"

Her eyes focused, as if she'd just remembered the reason she was there to begin with. "Oh." She shook her head. "Well, we just wait and see, I guess."

"Wait and see?" he asked.

"I'm not really in any danger until day three."

"What do we do in the meantime? Just hang out and play Monopoly?"

She thought about it. "We still need to play the part if we really want to draw this person out."

"What do you mean?"

"We need to play the role of lovers. That's what seems to piss him or her off."

"That wasn't the case with Marilyn."

"Marilyn was different. You may not have been in love with her, but you two had a history. Not just with each other, but with the whole group, which is why it's likely your stalker is one of your friends."

"I'm still not convinced."

"Guess we'll find out soon enough."

"You need to contact your own friend."

"Who?"

"The person you say will watch out for you. You sure they know what they're doing?"

"Believe me, they know. What about Cooper?"

"What about him?"

"You can't tell him. He's got to think that...well, you know."

"He didn't do anything. He's not my stalker."

"Regardless, even if he isn't, we can't risk him spilling the beans about our plan. He tells someone, then that ends it. Better to keep this just between you and me until this is done."

He groaned and held his head. "I know. It makes sense. I just don't like lying to him."

"You can apologize later. I'm sure he'll understand."

"If we're lucky, maybe he'll head back to the city soon."

"You think he will?"

Gray thought about it. "After he learns you slept over?" He snorted. "No. I'll be lucky if I can keep him from sleeping on the couch."

"When will you tell him?"

"Tell him?" Gray gave her a surprised look. "I'm surprised he's not out on the patio knocking on the door. Your car's been out front all night. Believe me, he already knows."

As if on cue, the phone rang. "What'd I tell ya?" said Gray.

"You think it's him?"

He reached for his cell. "Of course."

"Don't say anything," she warned.

"I won't." He picked up the phone. "Hello?"

He heard his friend's voice on the line. "Good morning," said Cooper, sounding cheery. "You up?" He paused. "Or should I say, can you talk?"

"Morning, Cooper," Gray answered. "Yes. I can talk."

"Can I just say that you're either my hero or the stupidest man on earth."

"I think the latter might be accurate."

"You've definitely got cajones of steel, my friend."

Gray glanced at Gillian. He didn't like lying, but he knew Gillian was right. If this was going to work, it had to stay between the two of them.

"She there?" asked Cooper.

"Sitting across from me. Yes."

"Downstairs or upstairs?"

Gray rolled his eyes. "We're having coffee in the kitchen."

"You clothed?"

Gray sighed. "No, we're both sitting here in our birthday suits. Of course we're clothed. Why?"

"Just checking before I knock."

Just then there was a banging on the back door and they both turned to see Cooper standing on the deck, cell phone in hand. He waved at them through the glass.

Grayson hung up the phone. "You ready for this?"

"Don't have much of a choice, do I?"

"If our little show last night didn't attract the right attention, then the next best way is to get our dalliance out there in the open."

"And Cooper won't be able to keep his mouth shut, will he?"

"Not about this, he won't. He'll make it his personal mission to ensure you stay alive and prove there's no curse."

"I'm all for that," she said, preparing herself. "Then, by all means, let him in."

Grayson stood and walked to the back door. He flipped the lock, and Cooper opened it. He picked up a bag at his feet. "This must have been left outside." He held Gillian's purse with her notebook and recorder. He walked inside and handed it to Gray. "Guess you were otherwise occupied."

"Thanks," said Gray. "Come on in," he said, but Copper had already stepped inside. He made his way to the kitchen. "Good morning, Miss Fletcher." He pulled a mug from a cabinet and helped himself to some coffee.

"Good morning, Cooper," she said. Gray returned to the table and sat.

Cooper carried his coffee and took the seat beside her. "I hope you don't mind me popping in," he smiled. "I'm just so curious about the interview." He smiled. "How did it go?"

Gillian caught Gray's eyes. "The interview went very well, thanks," she said.

"I take it he answered your questions?"

"Every one of them."

"Really?" He leaned forward. "Did you reveal all your secrets?"

Gray drank from his coffee. He decided not to delay this conversation. "She knows, if that's what you're asking."

Cooper's eyes widened. He raised his cup to Gillian. "Then I admire your courage," he said. "You decided after one interview that he's worth the risk?"

Gillian raised a brow. "Not that what happened last night is any of your business, but I think the curse is nonsense and I'm sure I'll still be alive three, four, and many more days after last night. And yes." She reached over and rested her fingers over Gray's. "I think he's worth the risk." She glanced back at Cooper. "Don't you?"

Cooper paused as if sizing her up. Coming to his own decision, he sat back in his seat. "I'll call someone today," he said.

"Call who?" she asked.

"Someone to keep an eye on you," said Cooper.

"What for?"

"Because, my dear. We're going to make sure that you get from day three to four intact." He flicked a finger toward Gray. "We're going to prove to him that there is no curse."

"This person is reliable?" asked Gray.

"One of the best," said Cooper.

"What, I'm going to have a bodyguard?" asked Gillian.

Cooper rested an elbow on the table. "Since you find my friend here so desirable, then yes, for the next three days, consider yourself Fort Knox."

"I only need to be watched on day three."

"I like to be thorough."

She played along. "You really think it's necessary?"

Cooper shrugged. "That's up to him."

Gray didn't hesitate. "Yes. I think it's necessary."

"He should have an easy job," said Gillian. "All I'm going to do is sit in my hotel room and work on the article."

"No," said Gray.

"No?" asked Gillian and Cooper at the same time.

Gray didn't want her outside of his house, and he didn't stop to think about it. "I want you to stay here."

"What?" asked Gillian. She hadn't expected this.

"I think he wants to keep you in his sights, Miss Fletcher," said Cooper. His mouth turned up. "Among other things."

Grayson ignored Cooper. "I don't want you in that hotel room by yourself." That much was true. "I want to know you're safe."

"But I will be safe."

Grayson moved his hand and put it over hers. "Just humor me, okay?" he asked. "I'll feel a lot better if you stay close for the next three days."

She held his look and blushed. The boundary between real and pretend seemed hazy. "I just need to get my things from the room and check out. I can be back here this afternoon." She checked the clock on the wall. "In fact, I should go soon. My editor is going to want to hear from me."

"You go straight to the hotel, clean up, pack your stuff, checkout, and come back," said Gray. "Don't dawdle." He thought about it. "In fact, I'll come with you."

"Nonsense." She took the last sip of coffee and stood. "You're worrying too much. I'll be fine. Besides," she looked at Cooper. "I'll have protection, right?"

Cooper pulled out his cell. "Within the hour." He stood and went to make his phone call.

Gillian picked up her purse, found her shoes, and slipped them on as Gray walked with her to the front door. "Give me ten minutes," he said.

She put her hand on his wrist. "Relax. Remember, if the curse is to be blamed, then nothing will happen until day three. Going to the hotel and back is not an issue."

"I want to go with you."

"It's better you stay. Talk to Cooper. Keep up the story."

He hesitated, but then nodded his head. "All right. But I'll feel better when you're back."

"You're sure you want me to stay here?" she asked. "I mean, it'll be easier to get to me if I'm alone."

"No killer in their right mind, especially one who knows me, would believe for one second I would let you walk around unprotected. Especially if I..."

"If you what?" she asked.

He debated how to answer. "We have to make it look like I'm falling for you, right? Well, that won't play if I let you go back to an empty hotel room and leave you vulnerable."

She nodded. "You know, you're getting pretty good at this sleuth thing. You're going to come off as Perry Mason in this article."

He smiled, but still looked anxious. "You get through the third day and you can call me Donald Duck for all I care."

She smiled and stepped up close to Gray, who was all too aware that Cooper was watching. "I'll be back soon," she said. Leaning in, she kissed him. He hadn't expected it, but he didn't show it as his surprise disappeared and he kissed her back. They held the kiss for a few seconds before she pulled away.

He watched her walk down the front steps, get into her car, and leave.

CHAPTER ELEVEN

GRAY BARELY HAD THE door shut before Cooper spoke. "Do you know what the hell you're doing?"

Gray returned to the kitchen and sat back at the table. He rested his forehead in his hand. "I have no idea what I'm doing." That answer, he felt, was mostly true.

"You want to tell me how this happened?"

"No," Gray said, sitting up. "I don't."

"Don't hold back on me, buddy. You can't imagine my shock this morning when I go outside for a run and see her car still out front."

"Since when do you run?"

"Since this morning. It's great for the lungs, as well as spying on your friends."

Gray huffed. "I need to call the realtor. It's time for me to move."

"Hey, I'm not saying this isn't a good thing. She's hot."

"Cooper..."

"Wait. Let me finish. She's hot. She's smart. She's got a job, and I think she likes you."

His mind returned to the passionate kiss on the porch. "After last night, I'd say she does."

"I'm just curious, though. What made you go through with it? I mean after what happened with Marilyn, I figured you'd turn down a young, half-dressed Sophia Loren whispering in your ear all the dirty things she wanted to do to you."

"Believe me, I hadn't planned on this."

"What changed your mind? Was it the booze? You opened that bottle of wine, didn't you?"

Grayson didn't know whether Cooper was his best friend or worst enemy. He knew he would not let up until he got the information he wanted. "I opened it. The interview..." He thought back. "Well, I told her about Angela, Erin, and Amy."

"No shit. No wonder you opened the wine. How'd she take it?"

"Like you." Gray sipped his coffee. "Doesn't believe in any curse."

"Is she going to write about it?"

Gray considered his answer. He couldn't tell Cooper what Gillian planned for her article. "I don't know. Maybe," he said.

"You okay with that?"

"I don't know. She won't print it unless I give approval, so we'll see what she comes up with."

"And then what happened?"

Gray shot him an irritated glance. "You don't give up do you?"

"How long have you known me?"

Grayson conceded. "Point taken."

"Thank you. And then what happened?"

"After the interview, we went down to the beach. We both had wine then. We argued about the validity of the curse."

"That sounds like you and me."

"Yes. But I wouldn't be convinced."

"I know."

"We came back up to the house. Drank more wine. Started talking instead of interviewing. She told me a little about herself." His conversation with her replayed in his mind, and he recalled the easy feel of it. "Anyway, we were on the balcony, and she was close, and she mentioned leaving, and then we were kissing." He groaned and closed his eyes. "I don't know what happened, but suddenly we were all over each other."

Cooper shook his head. "I didn't think I would ever say this," he pointed his finger at Grayson, "but you're Batman."

Gray opened his eyes. "More like the Joker. I can't believe I've done this again."

"Don't be so hard on yourself. She went into this with her eyes wide open." Cooper thought for a second. "You mind if I ask you a question?"

"What?"

"Do you trust her?"

"What do you mean?"

"Like you said. She's a reporter. You barely know her. How do you know she's not just sniffing out a juicy story about the playboy recluse who's living under a curse? She gets you into bed and then writes about how she did it. It'd make a hell of a headline."

Gray leaned in with his elbows on the table. "If there's not a curse, and she's alive and well in four days, then I'll deal with the article, whatever it is."

"Never mind the article. It's you I'm thinking of."

"Me? Why?"

"You're falling for her."

Gray grunted, but Cooper continued. "If she writes shit about you, approval or not, it's you who's gonna take the hard hit." He paused. "And that may be worse than any supposed curse."

Cooper's words sunk in, and Gray understood his concern. "I guess I'll just have to take that chance."

Cooper's face tightened. "If that's what she does to you, then God help her if I get a hold of her. She'll be lucky to write a story about beetle dung and its anti-aging properties."

· · • • • • • · · ·

Gillian packed her bag and looked around the room. She had showered and made the necessary phone calls. She'd explained where she was and had spent the next half hour arguing over the situation, her decision, and the potential repercussions. In the end, she hadn't backed down, and they'd conceded the three extra days. They had little choice. Their only other option would have been to drag her back home against her will, but past attempts at that had all proven unsuccessful, so they were left only with Gillian's stubborn insistence to see this through.

She zipped her bag, slung her purse over her shoulder, and pulled her tote with her laptop up next to her suitcase. She'd checked out fifteen minutes earlier and paid the bill. She stood for a moment as she pondered the next few days at Grayson's. Her mind had not stilled since waking that morning, and she found it difficult to focus. The thought of being so close to him over the ensuing seventy-two hours made her heart skip. The curse seemed a distant worry compared to what it would be like when she had to move on and leave Grayson Steele behind. She'd not mentioned her feelings to those she'd called and hoped she'd managed to keep them concealed. If they believed she was personally involved, then they probably would drag her away kicking and screaming. An image of Grayson smiling at her appeared in her head at the same time as a bright yellow caution sign flared and Gray's face faded. Her stomach clenched when she realized it was a sign to heed. Usually, she paid attention to those signs. But, despite the warning, she made up her mind to continue, picked up her bags, and left the hotel.

CHAPTER TWELVE

GILLIAN SAT AT HER laptop and typed. She paused for a moment to think and then resumed her typing. She was glad for the distraction. It was her second day at the house, and the energy required to keep her distance from the man who offered her the safety of his home far outweighed any energy expended worrying about any impending threat against her life. Her mind drifted as she thought again about last night. In order to keep up appearances, they'd spent a good part of the day inside, although they'd kept their distance from each other, as if the slightest touch would re-engage the spark from their first night together. She'd worked on her computer, and he'd read a book, or at least tried to. After a while, they both felt cabin fever, and he invited her out with him and Max for a little Frisbee catch. She welcomed the opportunity. They spent the next two hours walking and playing with Max. They talked, threw sticks to the dog who bounded through the water to chase them, and threw the Frisbee. The calm weather, despite the heavy waves, made the storm watch posted seem futile, as if they were speaking to a bored audience. They held hands on the way back to make it look like they were a couple, but the action had made her uncomfortable—this game was going to cost her more than she was prepared to give. She worked hard to control her escalating emotions. She had no idea what it was that made her react to him that way. She understood her attraction to him but had to believe that it would pass. It was not uncommon to develop an attachment to someone during a story, especially one as dramatic as his. But as time went by, the attraction only increased. And by the amount of energy she felt coming from him, she felt confident that his emotions were just as turbulent. The moment they'd returned to the house, he'd dropped her hand and offered to make dinner. Since the man did not cook, she knew he'd needed an outlet to use as a distraction.

He'd made spaghetti but did not open any wine. They sat at the dining table and ate a quiet meal. They'd talked a little about the plan and the car out front with a man inside it watching the house. The protection she'd arranged was also in place. When he asked where that protection was, she could only tell him she didn't know. His reaction had been less than ideal, but she'd assured him that if she didn't know where her protection was, then neither did the killer. The answer appeared to satisfy him long enough for them to clean the dishes.

Afterward, they went upstairs and to their separate rooms. They both knew it was better not to re-enact another kissing scene on the porch and, to anyone observing, it would seem as if they'd retired upstairs after their meal. Since neither of them had slept well the first night, going to bed early had seemed like a good idea. Although, she thought, as she took her fingers off the laptop keyboard, she hadn't slept any better the second night.

Now, as she stared at the screen, she wished it was already day three, just so she could think of something else other than him.

"How's the writing going?" His unexpected voice startled her. "Sorry," he said. "Didn't mean to scare you."

"It's okay. Guess I was just concentrating."

"Can I read any of it?" He came up behind her, and she closed her laptop.

"Nope. Not until I'm done."

"Not even a page?"

"No. Sorry. I'm not a writer who shares. Nobody reads anything until I've got it all down."

"You can't write too much until we see what happens tomorrow."

"I can get a head start."

"I guess." He paced behind her chair.

"Relax. Everything is going to be fine."

"Sorry. As we get closer, I'm getting more restless."

She tapped her computer. "You know. I'm thinking we need to get out tomorrow. Not hang out in the house."

"What for?"

"It makes it easier for someone to get to me."

"We don't want anyone to get to you."

"We don't want anyone to succeed in getting to me. There's a difference. But if we're going to catch him, we have to give him access."

He moaned. "This is ridiculous." He stopped pacing. "I can't believe we're talking about someone trying to kill you."

"It is a little surreal, isn't it? I admit, it makes me a little nervous."

"Does it?" he asked. "I can't tell. You look as cool as a winter breeze."

"Looks can be deceiving."

He sat down beside her. "You still want to go through with this?"

A whisper of doubt crept up her spine, but she pushed it back. "Yes. Of course. We've gotten this far. It's silly to stop now."

He leaned close. "You know you can stop if you want. You won't get any argument from me."

"I know. But I'm not backing out."

"If you change your mind—"

"I won't."

He stopped questioning her and tried to change the subject. "So, you enjoying your stay at Grayson manor?"

She smiled. "It's quiet, but the company's good."

He relaxed at her comment. "I'm glad I'm entertaining."

"I was talking about Max."

He narrowed his eyes. "Funny."

"Sorry. You walked right into that one."

"I did." He paused and looked at his watch. "You hungry?"

"Not just yet. But soon."

"Good, because we've been invited to dinner."

"We have? By whom?"

"Cooper. He wants us to come over."

"Really?"

"You all right with that? I can decline if you want."

She didn't see a reason not to go. In fact, a night out of the house without the need to avoid each other sounded appealing. "No. I don't mind. Who will be there?"

"Not sure exactly. I think Fran and Stu are still in town. I doubt Kenny will attend."

She hesitated. "You realize we'll likely be having dinner with your stalker."

He hung his head. "You would have to say that, wouldn't you?"

"Sorry. I'm not saying it to upset you."

He raised his head. "I know." He chewed his thumb. "But now I'm not so hungry."

"Would you rather stay here and cook?"

That got his attention. "God, no. I'd rather have an expensive catered meal with my stalker than subject myself and you to another one of my meals."

"Your food has been fine."

"Overcooked steaks and undercooked spaghetti. Delicious."

"You're overly critical."

"Maybe. But admit it, an overpriced meal served by someone else with some good wine sounds good, doesn't it?"

"I admit, it does." She stopped when she considered another issue. "I think it's a good idea to go. If one of your friends is your bad guy, then what better way to draw them out? But, it begs the question..."

"What question?"

"How do you want to play it?"

"Play it?" He looked unsure. "Oh, you mean us?"

"Yes." She held her breath. She didn't know how she would get through a meal with him with his hand on her thigh, or with them touching throughout the visit.

"I think we play it cool," he said. "They know me too well. I'm not the kind of guy who flaunts his girlfriend at a dinner party. That's Coop's style. I say we just go and get something to eat. Have some light conversation and then leave."

She almost breathed an audible sigh of relief. "And what about the curse?"

"What do you mean?"

"They all know about it. Cooper has likely filled them in on us. It might come up."

"We'll deal with it if we need to. Until then, let's just enjoy our meal. God knows what's going to happen tomorrow, and I'd like to be able to get out of here and not dwell on it tonight. That's probably why Cooper planned this."

She could feel his worry and couldn't disagree. They could both use the distraction. "Okay. Then let's go have dinner."

He nodded his head. "We'll leave in an hour."

"I'll be ready."

·•·•••·••··

Sixty minutes later, they stepped out of the back door and closed it behind them. Max popped his head out the dog door. "No, Max," said Gray. "You're staying here. Go back inside." Max gave a tilt of his head as they walked down the stairs, but then retreated into the house.

"Poor Max," said Gillian. "Coop wouldn't want him to come?"

"Have you seen Coop's house? It's no place for a scruffy dog with wet, sandy paws who needs a bath."

"I can't argue with that," said Gillian.

They walked down the pathway that led to Cooper's home. The sun was going down, and the sunset lit up the sky with hues of orange, yellow, and pink. They admired the view. "It's beautiful, isn't it?" asked Gillian.

"It is," said Gray, although his mind wondered just where they'd be in twenty-four hours. He could only hope that they would both be able to admire the sunset again. He shook his head and tried not to dwell on morbid thoughts. They reached Coop's stairs and walked up. He couldn't help but notice how the light reflected on Gillian's skin. She wore a long, loose dress with a fitted top and spaghetti straps. Her shoulders looked soft and supple, and he imagined what it would feel like to kiss them. He groaned silently. Between potential murder scenarios and the beautiful woman he was pretending to sleep with, he didn't know if he'd get through another day of this. He could only give silent thanks that this charade would be over tomorrow.

Gray and Gillian walked up onto the deck. "There they are," said Cooper. He sat on his white outside living room couch with a drink in his hand, and Fran sat with him. "Come on over, you two."

Gillian and Gray made their way over and sat down. A server appeared out of nowhere. "What will you two have?" asked Cooper.

"Glass of white wine, please," said Gillian.

"Vodka tonic," said Gray. He hadn't touched the hard stuff since Marilyn's death, but he felt the distinct need for it now. The server disappeared with their orders. Gillian sat next to Cooper and Gray next to Fran. The warm summer breeze blew, and Gray allowed himself to relax. He didn't know how this evening would play out, but he decided he would do his best to enjoy it. He glanced at Gillian who appeared to be doing the same.

"Where's Stu?" asked Gray.

Fran had sat quietly at their arrival. "Upstairs. On the phone. He'll be down in a minute."

"How long are you two staying?" asked Gray.

"Stu has to leave tonight. He's opening a new location next week, and he's got some sort of equipment crisis. I'm leaving tomorrow night. I have to get back to my own work."

"Gray tells me you're an interior designer," said Gillian. "Where do you work?"

"I'm at Templeton Designs, in Manhattan."

"Sounds impressive. Do you do residential or commercial?" she asked.

"Residential."

"Fran helped design this place," said Coop. "And she just finished Sydney's Marquis's pad on the upper west side."

"Who?" Gray asked.

"She's the actress and singer. She won a Golden Globe this year," said Gillian.

"You know your celebrities," said Fran.

"I'm a fan."

Fran eyed her. "Read all the gossip mags, do you?"

Gray met Gillian's gaze. The drinks arrived and the subject thankfully changed. Gillian took her glass of wine and sipped from it.

A voice from inside the house caught their attention. "Thanks, Jenkins." Stu stepped outside as he grabbed a drink from a waiter. "Sorry I'm late." He sat on the other side of Fran. "Did I miss anything?"

"We just got here," said Grayson.

Stuart slung his arm behind Fran. "Good." He nodded at Gillian. "Nice to see you again."

"You too. Fran says you're about to open another location?"

Stuart sipped his drink. "She did, huh?" He smiled. "Yeah. It's my ninth. It always comes with its headaches, though." He looked at his watch. "I'm catching the last flight out tonight."

"Ninth location?" asked Gray. "That's great, Stu."

A server arrived and placed a tray of nuts, veggies, and a side of hummus on the table. Stuart reached for a cashew. "Well, it ain't Stone and Steele, but it's a start."

"It's more than a start, Stuart," said Cooper. "You've always had a head for business."

Stuart's eyebrows arched. "Really? Since when have you thought that?"

Cooper grabbed some peanuts. "We've always thought that."

Grayson chimed in. "You've opened nine locations. You don't do that without knowing what you're doing."

Stuart shot back his drink. "And to think I did it without any help from you two." He dropped his empty glass on the table. "Jenkins!" he yelled. "I'll have another."

Cooper and Gray made eye contact but didn't say anything.

"Stuart," Fran said. "Slow it down."

Stuart raised his arm off the back of the couch and leaned forward. He sighed. "Sorry." He raised his head. "I'm just stressed. Don't mean to take it out on you guys."

"Don't worry about it," said Cooper. "This night is about having some fun and letting our hair down." He took a breath and let it out. "It seems we could all use it."

Gray nodded. "Agreed."

Footsteps on the deck stairs made them all look toward the noise. "Hey, you're here," Cooper said to an arriving couple. "Come on over." A man and woman of similar age stepped on to the patio and approached. Cooper stood. "Greg, Sandy, this is Gillian Fletcher." Gillian stood and greeted the new arrivals. "And this is Grayson Steele." Gray shook hands with them. "And you remember Stu and Fran?"

Stu waved, and Fran nodded. "Hey, Greg," said Stu.

"Stuart," said Greg. He looked at Gray. "I don't suppose you remember me." He sat down on a white patio chair, and Sandy took a seat beside him.

Grayson searched his memory. "Sorry. I can't place it. Have we met?"

"Try high school," said Cooper.

"High school?" asked Gray.

Stuart grunted, and Fran elbowed him.

"I'm Greg Huffy." He gave the server his drink request. "But you might better remember me as H cube."

A faint memory flashed in Grayson's mind of a skinny kid with a high-pitched, whiny laugh. The memory flared when he recalled that they'd nicknamed the kid Hairy Hyena Huffy when they'd noticed in gym class he had hair on his back. The name had morphed into H cubed, and by the time they'd become seniors, simply to H cube. He shut his eyes at the memory. "Yes, I remember," he said. "How are you?" He felt his cheeks warm with embarrassment.

"Greg has a house half a mile from here," said Cooper. "Can you believe that?" He took a swig of his drink. "He came to the party the other night. I couldn't believe it was him."

"Neither can I," said Gray. He found himself tongue-tied. "About the nickname..."

"H cube," said Stuart.

Greg eyed Stuart, but then addressed Grayson. "Forget it. That was years ago." He popped a piece of broccoli in his mouth.

Grayson caught Gillian's eye. This dinner party was becoming more interesting as the players revealed themselves. Her look suggested she thought the same thing. "So," he said, sipping his drink. "How long have you lived out here?"

"We don't live here. It's just a summer house. Sandy and I spend most of our time in Manhattan."

"We have a townhome in Chelsea," said Sandy. "I love the city. Don't you?" She had a southern twang.

"Yes," said Gillian. "But the beach is lovely, too."

"Yes," Fran said. "I'm sure you've enjoyed Gray's house for the short time you've been here." Her facial expression remained passive. Gillian stayed quiet.

"You're right about that," said Sandy. "The beach is beautiful." She touched Greg's knee. "When I can get him away from work, we try to get down here to relax."

"What is it you do, Greg?" Gillian asked.

"Be careful," said Fran. "She's a reporter. Don't spill any secrets."

Greg smiled. "I'll keep that in mind. I'm in commercial real estate. I buy and sell properties all along the Atlantic coast."

"That's fantastic," Cooper said.

"Really?" asked Stuart. Jenkins brought him another drink and Stuart took a sip. "You must own a lot of it."

"Well, I own some, but it's not as exciting as Stone and Steele Enterprises," he said. "You two have made quite a name for yourselves."

"We were lucky," said Gray.

"The hell we were. You and I worked our asses off to get where we are," said Cooper.

"But you climbed fast," said Greg. "Most never get that far." He dunked a carrot in the hummus. "I'd call that luck."

"Luck is only persistence disguised," Gray said. He glanced at Stuart. "Looks like we were all lucky." Stuart didn't say anything.

Greg smiled at Sandy and took her hand. "I know I was. I've been blessed."

Fran scoffed under her breath. "Haven't we all..." She waved down a server and requested another drink.

"So, you two still keep in touch with everyone?" asked Greg. "I saw Ken at the party. Is he coming tonight?"

"I invited him," said Cooper.

"You did?" Gray asked.

"Yes. I figured we should at least try to reconcile. We've known each other too long to hold grudges." He flagged down Jenkins for another drink.

"Somehow, I doubt he sees it that way," said Gray.

"What?" said Fran. She finished the remnants of her wine. "You three lovebirds have a fight?"

Stuart chuckled.

Nobody answered her until Cooper spoke. "He's still pissed with Gray. Plus, we had a slight disagreement over Marilyn."

"Marilyn?" asked Greg. "Marilyn Horn? I remember her."

"She was hard to forget," said Cooper.

"Developed early, as I recall," said Greg.

Cooper grinned. "Yes. She did."

Greg reached for another carrot. "How is she?"

Nobody answered, and Fran took advantage of the ensuing silence. "She's dead."

Greg stopped in mid-chew. "She's what?"

"Oh, my," Sandy said. "What happened?"

"Drowned," said Fran. "Right, Gray?" Jenkins brought a wine bottle and refreshed her drink.

"Come on, Fran," Cooper said. "Maybe you should hold off on the booze, huh?" Fran shot him an annoyed look but kept her mouth shut. Cooper answered Greg. "She drowned not far from here. Coroner ruled it accidental."

Gray tried to relax the grip on his glass. "He did?"

"Yeah, he did," said Stuart.

"Ridiculous," said Fran under her breath. She sipped her drink.

"Yes," said Cooper. "Kenny called and told me this morning. She had alcohol in her system. That's when I told him to come by tonight if he wanted."

"Hell...I didn't know," said Gray.

Cooper leaned forward. "What? Were you expecting it to be murder?"

"I'm sure he was," said Stuart. He chewed a stuffed mushroom.

"Come on, Gray," said Cooper. "We all know Marilyn had troubles."

"I know," said Gray. He didn't want to dwell on Marilyn's death or his possible role in it. "You think Ken will come over?"

"Don't worry about it. I'd be surprised if he did. But he was apologetic on the phone. Said he may have overreacted when he talked to you."

"Poor Marilyn," Greg said. "She was so young."

"I guess that's why we should all live to the fullest while we still can," said Sandy. "You just never know when your time's up."

"Sometimes you do," said Fran. She swirled her wine. Gray felt the hairs stand up on his skin, and he could see Gillian tense.

"When do we eat, Coop? I'm starving," asked Gray. He tried to assure Gillian with his eyes.

"Good question. If you'll excuse me, I'll go check on our progress." He directed a pointed stare toward Fran. "Why don't you join me, Fran?"

"What for?" she asked. "Maria's in there. William too. You've got plenty of help."

"Maybe he wants your recipe for bitch soup," said Stu flatly.

Fran glared at him. "Shut up, Stuart."

Cooper held out his hand. "I insist." She hesitated but stood, put her hand in his, and walked into the house with him. The mood lightened the moment she left.

"So," said Gillian, looking at Sandy, "tell me where you're from. I detect a Southern accent." The two women began an easy conversation about Sandy's Texas roots as Gray and Greg discussed the political climate and the time passed. Stuart chimed in as well and they managed to maintain a polite conversation. It wasn't long before Cooper came out and announced that dinner was ready and asked them to join him at the dining table. They all stood and went inside. Gillian took a seat next to Gray, with Sandy, Greg, and Fran across from them, and Stuart and Cooper at the ends of the table.

Their drinks were refilled and Cooper made a toast to friendship, and then the servers appeared with the various courses. The first was a light consommé soup, then a dinner salad served with pecans and apples and a light wildflower dressing. The main course was a tender rack of lamb with mint jelly, followed by a delicious dessert of crème brûlee. At the end of the meal, Gillian held her belly, exclaiming the food had been excellent. Gray was pleased they had all managed to talk without any mention of death or curses. Fran had even held her end of the light conversation without shooting a single malevolent look at Gillian. Fran and Sandy had discussed various styles of design, and Cooper, Stuart, and Greg had talked of potential opportunities in the real estate market. Gray and Gillian listened and contributed their own insights into the ongoing dialogue.

Dessert finished and the conversation ebbing, Cooper stood. "How about we move outside for a little after dinner drink?"

"I don't know how I can eat or drink another thing, Cooper," said Gillian. Their drinks had been refreshed throughout the meal, and it was obvious the group was feeling the effects. Stuart was telling a bawdy joke to Greg, and Sandy giggled when she rose from her chair. Fran swayed slightly as she stood, and Gillian's face was flushed from the alcohol. Grayson felt a little hazy, and he laughed at Stuart's joke. Only Cooper seemed unfazed, other than his raised voice when he spoke.

"Ah, Miss Fletcher," said Cooper. "No meal is complete without a nice dessert wine to finish it off. Right, Gray?"

Gray smiled in agreement. "He's right, Gillian. And Cooper only buys the best. It's worth a sip or two."

They walked out onto the patio and sat.

"I can remember when you two were less discriminating," said Fran. She smiled and wobbled as she took her seat, grabbing the armrest for support.

"Me too," said Stuart. He slapped Grayson on the back.

"All of us were," Cooper said, smiling. Jenkins brought him a glass of dark liquid and he took it. "We'd buy the cheapest stuff and drink it behind the bleachers after the football games." He raised his drink. "Thanks, Jenkins."

Jenkins nodded and served the others.

"Drink it and smoke it," said Fran.

"Don't remind me," said Grayson, taking his glass of port wine.

"I miss those days," Stuart said. "We had a hell of a lot of fun."

"You guys were always considered the cool kids," said Greg. He took Sandy's hand. "Everybody wanted to be you."

"They did?" asked Gray. "What was so special about us?" The breeze picked up, and he took a deep breath. It helped to clear his head. "We were just a bunch of dumb high school kids."

"You really don't know, do you?" Greg asked.

The doorbell rang, but nobody acknowledged it. They knew Cooper's staff would answer.

"Know what?" asked Fran.

"You guys were idolized in school. Everyone wanted to hang out with you. You did everything everyone told us not to do and got away with it. You never got in trouble and you still excelled in school. Other kids either loved or hated you."

"I was idolized in high school?" asked Stuart, leaning forward. "That's news to me. I thought everybody hated us."

Grayson listened to Greg's revelations in surprise. "Which one were you? Did you love us or hate us?"

Greg stared at the port wine he'd been given. "People called me H cube for three years because of you guys." He sipped his drink. "What do you think?"

Nobody responded.

Stuart broke the silence. "Come on, Greg. So you got pegged with a lousy nickname. Hell, Charlie Brant called me needle-dick for two years."

"Until you yanked his drawers down in front of the cheerleading squad," said Coop.

"Then we all knew who the true needle-dick was." Stuart chuckled and the others couldn't help but smile.

"At least you were able to exact some revenge," said Greg, and the group quieted.

"Hell," said Cooper, fiddling with his glass. "I had no idea we were such assholes."

"Who was an asshole?"

They looked up to see Kenny standing at the door to the patio. Franklin stood with him. "I hope you don't mind, Mr. Stone," said Franklin. "He said he was invited."

"I thought you were done for the day, Franklin."

"Just finishing up some last-minute paperwork, sir."

"Then come join us for an after-dinner drink. And yes, I invited Kenny." He patted the seat next to him. "Come on over, Ken. Have a seat. Pull up a chair, Franklin."

"No, sir. I should be going."

"It's late, Frank. It's an hour's drive back. Just stay here tonight. I've got plenty of room."

"That would be imposing, Mr. Stone."

"Sit down and shut up, would you?"

"Yeah, Frank. Sit down and shut up," said Kenny. He sat down heavily next to Cooper. They all looked at him in disbelief.

"Are you drunk, Ken?" asked Fran.

Kenny shook his head. "No way. Just had a few beers down at Smiley's." He grabbed an offered glass of port and slugged it back.

"You might want to take your time with that," Cooper said. "You might actually taste it if you do."

"Tastes just fine," said Ken. He stared back at Franklin. "Grab a chair, Gallagher. Sit your butt down."

Franklin's face carried the distinct look of distaste at Kenny's reference toward him, but he turned and found a chair and sat. A server offered

Franklin some port, and he took it. Cooper introduced the new guests to everyone, and Kenny squinted at Greg and blurted out. "H Cube? Is that you?"

"Shit," said Grayson. He grimaced. "Sorry, Greg."

"Hey. Don't apologize. Some things never change."

"He doesn't mean anything by it," said Fran. "He's drunk."

Greg was not appeased. "I guess that excuses everything, doesn't it?"

Kenny couldn't seem to sit still. "What's your problem, H?" He reached up and accepted another drink from a passing server.

"Shut up, Kenny," said Gray.

Kenny looked over as if he had just noticed Grayson. "Like I need a lecture from you, Steele."

"Kenny, pull it together. I thought we were past this," said Cooper.

"Past what, Coop?" He waved his hand and his drink spilled. Port wine splattered on the white couch. "How you and your best friend over here can shit on all the rest of us and get away with it?"

Franklin put his drink down and stood.

"Calm down, Kenny," said Fran. "Nobody likes a drunk and disorderly police officer."

"Oh, come on, Fran," said Kenny, standing as well. "How can you sit there and act so sweet, when all the while this fool is sitting in that damn house of his drooling all over some new tramp."

"Wait a minute," said Gray. He stood at the same time as Cooper. Gillian stayed quiet.

"Take it easy, Kenny," said Stuart, sitting forward. "You're getting everyone all riled up."

Kenny took another slug of what remained in his glass.

"You've had enough," Fran said.

"I'm just getting started." He eyed Fran. "You're just pissed because I said it and you didn't."

"You need to leave, Ken," said Cooper. "Now."

Kenny put his empty glass down. "Fine. I'll leave. But you should know something." He turned and faced Gillian, but pointed at Gray. "That man is going to get you killed. You won't live long enough to see the moon rise tomorrow."

"Kenny!" said Gray.

Kenny leaned in toward Gillian and almost lost his balance, but Franklin was there in an instant and grabbed him at the same time as Cooper, and they hauled him back and away from Gillian.

"That's enough," said Cooper. "You're leaving." He and Franklin both pulled him off the deck and back into the house.

Stuart watched them remove Kenny. "This is one hell of a party," he said. He looked at his watch. "I'm almost sad I have to leave."

Gray moved over and sat next to Gillian. "You okay?" he asked.

Her eyes were wide, but she nodded. "I'm fine," she said. "He's just drunk."

"He's an ass. He never should have said that to you."

"What was he talking about?" asked Sandy. "Why would he say you would kill her?"

"It's nothing," said Gray. "Just some ugly history between us."

"That and the curse," said Fran. She took a healthy slug of her drink.

Stuart swore under his breath. "You're really going to bring that up?"

"Curse?" Greg asked.

Grayson muffled his own expletive. Gillian reached over and took his hand. He squeezed her fingers in return.

Fran stared at their entwined fingers. "Yes. Don't you know? Grayson is cursed."

"That's ridiculous, Fran, and you know it," said Gillian.

Fran scoffed. "Let's hope so, for your sake."

"What curse?" asked Greg.

"You remember Joanie?" asked Fran.

Gray moaned and rubbed his face. "Come on, Fran."

"Joanie? From high school? Who committed suicide?"

"Yes. Her mother cursed Gray at the funeral."

"What?" Sandy asked. Her eyes widened. "That's silly."

"Exactly," said Gillian. "It's absurd."

"But true," said Stuart. He chuckled nervously. "I remember that clear as day. That woman scared the hell out of me."

"I heard something about that, but I didn't believe it," said Greg. "As I remember, Joanie's mom was known to be a bit unstable."

"Well, whatever she did worked," said Fran.

Cooper came back onto the patio. "What worked?"

"Where's Kenny?" asked Gray.

"Franklin is driving him home." He looked at his guests. "I apologize for my friend's outburst. Especially you, Miss Fletcher. He's been dealing with a lot lately." Seeing Gray next to Gillian, he sat down in Gray's unoccupied seat.

"I hope he's okay," said Sandy.

"He'll be fine. So, what are we so ardently discussing?" He grabbed at a handful of nuts left over from earlier and popped one into his mouth.

"Fran's telling us that Gray here is cursed," Sandy said.

Cooper stopped chewing. He dropped the nuts on the table and wiped his hands. "Jesus H. Christ, Fran. Don't you think you could take one night off from being a stone-cold bitch?"

Stuart looked up. "Oh, boy."

Fran's lips tightened. "You think you could take one night off from being his supposed sainted protector?" She sat forward in her seat. "Why don't you tell him the truth?"

"What are you talking about?" asked Cooper.

"You're not the devoted best friend you pretend to be. I know what you're planning. You want him out. Out of the business. Out of everything."

"What the hell are you saying?" Cooper's voice rose.

"Stu told me everything."

Stuart put a hand on her elbow. "Fran."

Fran ignored him and pulled her elbow away. "He told me how you were fed up with Gray's drama. Tired of all the attention he always gets. Even when he disappears, people want to know where he is. They want to know when he's coming back, who he's seeing, who's handling the business. It's always about him, and you're sick of it."

"Fran..." Cooper warned, his face stony. "You don't know what you're talking about."

"I think I do. You just don't have the balls to tell him."

Cooper stood and shot back. "Just like you don't have the balls to tell him you're still in love with him?"

Fran's face went white, and she stood. "You are a piece of shit, you know that."

"I call 'em as I see 'em. And you aren't exactly sewage-free yourself."

Fran slammed her almost empty glass down on the table. "Say whatever you want. I don't care anymore." She aimed a stony glare at Gillian. "Good luck tomorrow, sweetheart. You're gonna need it." Before she left, she caught Grayson's wide eyes. "And you. You deserve everything you get." She turned and left the patio, disappearing from view as everyone sat in stunned silence.

Stuart placed the remains of his port on the table and rose from the couch. "I think that's my cue." He nodded at Cooper. "Thanks for a lovely evening."

Cooper remained where he stood. His eyes looked like shards of ice. "Feel free to take her with you."

Stuart walked toward the door but glanced back. "I think I'd rather be called needle-dick again."

Cooper sighed and closed his eyes. Some of the tension seemed to drain from his shoulders. "Did you say that to Fran? About me?"

Stuart shrugged. "I may have been a little inebriated at the time. And she may have exaggerated a bit."

Cooper shook his head. "Have a pleasant trip, Stu."

"I will." He swiveled toward Gillian. "And contrary to what you may be thinking, I hope everything goes well tomorrow." He pointed between her and Gray. "You two look good together."

"Thanks, Stuart," said Gillian. "It was nice to see you."

"Good night, Stu," said Gray. Stuart waved and disappeared into the house.

Greg finally spoke. "You throw a great party."

Sandy squeezed his fingers. "You never told me you had such lovely friends in high school."

Greg smiled. "Let's be honest, honey. These people were never my friends."

Cooper stared off, but after a few seconds acknowledged the group. "I apologize everybody." He sat and held his head in his hands. "This has been a disaster."

Gray released a pent-up breath. "You could say that."

"Gray," said Cooper. "I hope you don't believe any of that."

Gray studied his friend's stricken face. "Is it true?"

"Of course it isn't." Cooper sat up. "I admit. I may have had a few drunk nights where I might have bitched about a few things, but that's all it was. Just venting." He looked at Gillian. "I apologize again for what Fran and Kenny said."

"Is what she said accurate?" Sandy asked. "About a curse?"

"No, of course not. Gray's just had a few tough breaks in his life. He's lost people he loved." He picked up his drink and finished it. "And some people want to blame a stupid curse for things that are just hard to understand or explain."

"I know how that can be," said Greg. "When the unexpected happens, you'll find any explanation, no matter how bizarre."

Sandy's face turned sad. "You mean your half-sister?" she asked. "That was a tragedy."

Gillian took advantage of the change in subject. "What happened?"

Greg hung his head. "She died unexpectedly a few years ago."

"Shocked all of us," said Sandy. "Such a sweet girl. She and Greg were very close."

Greg clasped his hands together. "You may have known her. She used to work for Stone and Steele."

"No kidding?" asked Cooper. "Who was she?"

"Her name was Erin. She worked as an accountant at your firm. She went out for a jog one day and never made it back. She collapsed and died in Central Park."

Gray choked on his port. He coughed and tried to catch his breath. "Excuse me," he said with a cracked voice. He smacked his chest with his hand, and, still coughing, walked into the house.

He heard Sandy and Cooper speak from behind him.

"Is he okay?" asked Sandy.

Then Cooper's voice. "You said her name was Erin?"

Gray walked into the guest bathroom, still coughing, and flipped on the faucet. Gillian followed him in a few seconds later. "You all right?"

He ran water over his face and took a deep breath before he rose and grabbed a hand towel. "Did you hear that?" he asked. "Erin?" He held the towel against his eyes as if trying to purge the memories. "He's Erin's half-brother? Is that what he said?"

Gillian nodded. "That's what he said."

"Son of a…" He dropped the towel and stared at himself in the mirror. His face was a pasty white. "How is that possible?"

She cocked an eyebrow. "Coincidence?"

He watched her through the mirror. "You believe that?"

"Not really. Do you?"

He hesitated. "What the hell should I believe?"

She stared for a second. "That your suspect list just got a little bigger."

He took his eyes off hers and regarded his reflection. "Shit."

CHAPTER THIRTEEN

MAX POKED HIS HEAD out the dog door and barked. "It's just us, Max," said Gray, stepping up onto his patio behind Gillian. Max darted out and jumped up to greet them. Entering the house, Gray walked into the kitchen and dumped some dog food into a bowl. "Here you go." He ruffled Max's fur. "Hope you enjoy dinner more than we did."

They'd left the party not long after Gray had returned from the bathroom. Gillian had offered the excuse of having to be up early to meet a deadline, and they'd said their goodbyes. The dinner now over, Gray returned the bag of dog food to the pantry as Gillian leaned back against the kitchen counter.

"Interesting evening," she said.

He cocked his head at her. "You think?"

"What are your thoughts about Greg Huffy?"

He made a snort under his breath. "A man I haven't seen in years, who hated us in high school because we tagged him with an awful nickname, all of a sudden, shows up at Coop's dinner party?"

"He seems like a nice guy. So does his wife."

He huffed. "They do, but still, what are the odds?" He shook his head. "No. His involvement in any of this doesn't gel. So we were jerks in high school. I can't imagine this guy has been stalking me for years because of a nickname. Besides, he certainly wouldn't kill his half-sister. That makes no sense." He watched Max eat. "He may have good reason to dislike me, but not kill the women in my life."

Gillian didn't disagree. "Okay. So probably not Greg. But you certainly can't rule out Kenny."

"I suppose it's possible. But he's a cop."

"So? All the easier for him to make it look accidental." She pulled up a chair from the breakfast table and sat. "And Fran. She's a possibility. She certainly doesn't hide her malice towards me."

He rubbed his neck. "I suspected Fran may have still had a thing for me. I just didn't realize how deep it went, or how angry she was."

"She definitely seemed a bit irrational. And she loves throwing the curse in your face."

"I noticed."

"And..."

"And what?"

"Cooper," she said. He sighed and looked away. "You can't ignore what Fran said. That he harbors some sort of resentment toward you."

"That doesn't mean he's a killer." He scoffed. "I get it can be annoying when someone else gets the credit when you're doing all the work, but that doesn't make him a murderer."

Gillian didn't push the issue. "And there's still Stu."

He raised a brow. "He's leaving for Boston. You think he can kill you from there?"

"Who says he's going to Boston? You want to take his word for it? Or Fran's for that matter? Hell, the two of them could be working together. Besides that, who says they couldn't hire someone?"

Gray pushed off the counter in annoyance. "This is ridiculous." He strode into the living room.

"What?"

"That we're even thinking about this. That we think any of them could do this or even hire someone to do it." He paced behind the couch.

"It sounds crazy, I know."

"Crazy? It's beyond crazy." He stopped and his face dropped.

"What?" asked Gillian. "What is it?"

"You know, if we're being thorough, then there's someone else you should consider."

"Who?"

"A pretty obvious possibility. Me."

She stilled. "You?"

He threw out his hands. "Yes. Me. If you're going to suspect my friends, you should suspect me too. I mean, I am the common denominator in all this. How do you know I'm not some psychopath who kills the women he sleeps with?"

She stared openmouthed. "Are you?"

Her lack of concern bewildered him. "No," he said.

"Good. Now, can we get serious, please?" She stood and walked around the side of the couch and sat down. "We've got to think about tomorrow." She looked at her watch. "Which is not far off, by the way."

Gray moved to sit beside her. "But how do you know?" he asked.

"How do I know what?"

"How do you know I'm not a killer? Why do you have such blind faith in me? Other than the interview, you hardly know me."

She thought about how to answer. "Because," she said. "I just do." Without thinking about it, she reached and took his hand. "I wouldn't be here if I thought otherwise."

He looked down at her fingers entwined with his. "And why are you here?" He squeezed her hand. "Why are you risking your life for me?"

She swallowed, and her face warmed. "You know why." She took a breath. "I want the story. I want to catch a killer."

Her answer didn't satisfy him. His thumb traced over the back of her hand. "And that's all? That's the only reason? You show up on my doorstep, hassling me for an interview, and what..." He calculated the time in his mind. "...a week later, you're debating with me who might want to kill you because of me?"

The movement of his thumb distracted her, and she had to make herself think. "Reporters are known to risk their lives for a story."

He took a deep breath and expelled it. "Maybe in a war zone, but this..."

His proximity began to affect her, but she didn't back away. "But what?" His touch sent shivers up her arm.

His blue eyes turned the color of the ocean at night. "I'm just a guy, Gillian. Yeah, maybe I've got a little notoriety and I've made some money, but who cares?" He leaned closer. "You hear my story and suddenly you're ready to jump in, headfirst, when I could be just as dangerous as the rest?"

She couldn't stop looking at him. "I told you. You're not dangerous."

His smile made her heart thump. "I'm not?" He pulled her hand, bringing her closer. "I think, Miss Fletcher, that in this moment..." His eyes scanned her face and focused on her mouth. "...I am very dangerous."

She didn't pull away when his lips came down over hers. Immediately, the energy spawned from their first kiss reignited. Eager to feel what they'd felt before, the kiss quickly turned hungry. His mouth opened, and she welcomed the feel of him against her. As the intensity grew, he moved forward and pushed her back against the couch cushions. She let go of his hand to pull him closer. He slid his fingers behind her neck, slanted his lips over hers, and probed her mouth with his tongue, letting it dart in and rub over hers. Her breathing deepened, and she slid farther down the couch. The kiss grew hotter, and she moaned in his mouth. He lifted himself and shifted, and then he was above her. His lips grazed a fiery trail to her neck, and she felt his other hand slide up the curve of her waist and she tried to breathe when she felt his fingers cup her breast over the fabric of her dress. She gasped and arched and slid her leg up over his; she wrapped it around his lower body. She writhed against him, and he pressed into her. She heard him groan, and his mouth burned a path along her neck as she clutched at him. Reaching down, he found the edge of her dress. His palm touched her leg, and he dragged his hot fingers up from her knee to her thigh. He traced his lips along her jawline and then his mouth was back on hers, capturing her again as his hand moved higher. Desperate to touch him, she pulled his shirttail out of his pants and reached under his shirt. The passion between them escalating fast, they both barely heard the house phone ring.

They continued to kiss as the haze that enveloped them drowned out all other stimuli. The ringing persisted, though, and it finally penetrated the fog. Gray pulled up with a muffled curse. The interruption allowed Gillian some respite, and she collected her thoughts long enough to make her brain work. "Maybe you should get that," she said through a ragged breath. She reluctantly let go of his shirt.

Looking down at her, he blinked and came back from the edge. He pulled his hand back, and she almost audibly groaned. "Damn it," he said. "I'm sorry." She wasn't sure if he was sorry he had to stop or sorry that he'd started this in the first place. The phone continued to ring, and he stood and picked it up.

"What?" he asked. He took a breath to collect himself. "Oh, hey Coop." He listened for a moment. Gillian sat up on the couch and pulled her dress down. "No," he said, shutting his eyes. "You're not interrupting anything." He turned and rested his arm against the wall and hung his head. "Don't worry about it. I know." His breath began to return to its normal rhythm. "Tomorrow?" He raised his head. "I'm not going anywhere." He looked at Gillian. "I'm sticking like glue." He listened again. "No. That's fine." He brought his hand up and he pinched the bridge of his nose. "Yes. I will. I'll call in the morning. Okay, Coop." He paused again. "No. I know you didn't." He dropped his hand to his hip. "Okay. First thing. Thanks. Goodnight." He hung up the phone.

"Anything important?" she asked. Her body still tingled from his touch, but she tried not to show it.

His eyes raked over her and, for a moment, he appeared to consider picking up where he left off. "He, uh, wanted to apologize again about tonight. About what Fran said." He leaned back against the wall. "And he wanted to ask about tomorrow."

"Tomorrow?"

"He wants your protection closer. He wants me to call when we're up in the morning and he'll have Travis join us in the house."

"Travis?"

"He's one of the guys who's been sitting in the car out front the last two days. Cooper wants him to shadow you tomorrow."

"Shadow me? You mean not leave my side?"

"Yes."

"That's going to make it hard for someone to get close."

"Isn't that the point?"

"The point is to catch this guy. Not scare him off."

Gray took a deep breath and exhaled. He pushed off the counter and walked back toward the couch, but didn't sit. "Listen. I realize your need to solve this thing, but please be reasonable. I'm not going to let you go for a walk down the beach unescorted and getting in the car and driving anywhere is out of the question. Besides, the killer, if there's a killer, knows I'm going to be vigilant. He's not going to let—"

Gillian finished the sentence. "—some bodyguard stop him from getting to me?"

He sighed. "Not if he wants to keep blaming the curse."

She considered that. "So, he'll find a way to separate me from you and Travis."

Gray sat, but in the chair across from her. "I don't know. Maybe. Probably." He wrung his hands together. "You promise me something." He narrowed his eyes at her. "Do not go off on your own tomorrow in some stupid attempt to draw this guy out, you understand? You do that, then you'll have to deal with me. You got it?"

She smiled, but shivered at the same time and rubbed her shoulders. As much as she wanted to find the person responsible for making Gray's life hell, she also didn't want to die doing it. The magnitude of what she might face tomorrow suddenly made her nervous, and the thought of being anywhere alone was the last thing she wanted. The possibility that this guy would try to get to her despite Gray and a bodyguard made this plan lose its allure. "Okay. I hear you," she said. "No heroics. I promise."

"Damn right," he said. He saw her tense up. "You okay?"

"Yes. I guess the weight of what might happen is hitting me." She met his gaze. "Guess I'm a little scared all of a sudden."

He paused at her revelation. "I know. So am I." She could tell he wanted to sit beside her, but he stayed where he was. "You going to be okay tonight?"

She studied her hands. "What do you mean? Am I going to sleep much? I doubt it."

"Me either." He made a soft smile. "I'd offer to sleep next to you, but I doubt that would lead to any rest."

She lifted her head. "Maybe that wouldn't be such a bad thing." She heard herself say the words but couldn't believe she'd said them. She'd never been so forward.

She swore she heard him groan under his breath. "Believe me," he said, "if you made one move toward me right now, I'd carry you upstairs and take your mind off of things. But," he stopped, "if I do that, then we'll have that much more on our minds tomorrow. Plus, if nothing happens and we don't catch a killer, then we'll have to wait three more days to see if a curse really does kick in." His eyes moved over her. "It's better to wait. If we catch this guy and you're alive and well and willing, then you and I, Miss Fletcher, will have some celebrating to do."

The thought of sharing his bed made Gillian ache to reach out to him, but his logic made sense. She could certainly wait twenty-four hours. She shook her head. What was making her so eager?

"Unless, of course..." he started to say.

"Unless what?"

"You plan on leaving." He leaned forward in his seat. "I mean, you'll have your story. There will be no need to pretend anymore. There'll be no need to stay."

They held a shared gaze, and she knew he was right. If she stayed, then she jumped into murky waters. But the thought of leaving him seemed impossible. He'd wiggled his way into her heart, and she knew there was something about him that beckoned her. She'd come to help him with his problem, but this assignment had become much more than that. She didn't know how she would handle it, but at that moment, she didn't care. She stood from the couch and walked up to him. He sat back as if he feared she was actually going to act on her desire. Instead, she squatted down in front of him.

She paused for a moment and then put her hand over his. "If we end up catching this guy and nullifying this curse, then I hope you don't mind if I stick around for a while." She squeezed his fingers. She couldn't promise any more than that, but she owed it to him and herself to see where it led. Grayson Steele had a purpose in her life, and she had to determine what it was. She leaned in and gave him a quick kiss, but pulled back before it could lead to more. His hand found her waist, but she caught it and held it.

"Tomorrow," she said.

He let go of a sigh and agreed. "Tomorrow, Miss Fletcher." He gripped her fingers. "You and I have a date."

They stared for a few seconds until she moved back. He shook his head as if to clear his mind. "So," he said. He stood and so did she. "Since neither one of us is going to sleep tonight..." He walked over to a cabinet against the wall, slid open a drawer, and pulled out a remote. He slid the cabinet doors back to reveal a flat screen TV. "Care to watch a movie?"

CHAPTER FOURTEEN

GOING TO BED AFTER 2 am, their restless sleep had them both back downstairs by 7. Gray poured the coffee for both of them, and they both said little as they struggled to clear their foggy heads. Gillian wore a loose t-shirt and pajama pants, and Gray thought she looked just as sexy as she had in the spaghetti strap dress. The memory of kissing her neck made him shut his eyes and he tried not to think about it.

"Something wrong?" asked Gillian.

He opened his eyes. "What?"

"You look like you're in pain."

"It's nothing. It'll pass. Hopefully, by tomorrow, I'll be cured."

She took a sip of her coffee and looked at the clock on the wall. "Think we should call Travis?"

He reached for the phone and a pad of paper on the counter. "Good idea." He dialed a number. Gillian listened as he spoke briefly and then hung up. "He'll be up in a few minutes." He thought for a second. "Your guy? He's still around?"

"Yes. He's still around."

"He keeps a low profile."

Gillian nodded her head. "He does." She tried to think of something else. "You hungry?" she asked.

"Not really. You?"

"Not at all. My stomach's in knots."

She sipped her coffee and bounced her knee up and down. "You okay?" he asked.

"I'll be better when this is over."

"Still want to go through with it?"

"I don't think I have a choice. We can't exactly go out there, wave our hands, and announce 'Just kidding. We never slept together.' Somehow, I think the killer wouldn't buy it."

"We certainly gave him ample opportunity to believe we did sleep together."

Her eyes shifted as if she thought back. "Yeah. We did."

He reached over and took her hand. "Don't worry. Everything will be fine. By this time tomorrow, the killer will be revealed and you and I..." He stopped, and she held his gaze. They sat that way and their fingers moved over each other's.

The doorbell rang, and they both jumped. He tried to calm himself and stood from the chair. "I'll get it."

"Okay."

He walked through the foyer and checked through the peephole. A large man in a dark suit stood outside the door. It was Travis, Cooper's hired protection. Gray opened the door and let him in.

"Good morning, sir," said Travis. Despite his wide shoulders and tree trunk legs, he carried himself with a graceful ease. "Is Miss Fletcher awake?"

"She's in the kitchen. And call me Gray."

Travis followed Grayson through the entry and back toward the kitchen where Gillian sat.

"Good morning, ma'am. I'm Travis." He held out his hand, and she shook it. "You and I are going to be hanging out today. I hope you don't mind."

"Believe me, Travis," she said. "You're a sight for sore eyes."

Grayson tried not to reveal his own worry. "We have reason to believe that someone I know may try to harm her."

Travis nodded "Mr. Stone filled me in. Said to stick close and keep an eye on her. He didn't say anything about who it might be though."

"Let's just say Gillian and I have our reasons and that Cooper is not aware of our suspicions."

Travis's brow furrowed. "Is there someone specific I need to be aware of?"

"No," said Gray. "Not yet anyway."

Gillian stood. "I'm going to get dressed. If I'm going to be a target, I should be dressed appropriately."

"I'm coming with you," said Travis.

She stared back, surprised. "Thanks, Travis, but I don't think you need to help me put on my clothes."

He smiled. "No, ma'am. But as your security, I will follow you and check your room to assure that you are the only one in it, and I will dutifully stand outside while you dress."

"You really do plan on shadowing me, don't you?"

"All day."

She looked back at Gray.

"That's what I'm paying him for," he said.

"Okay," she said. "Then let's go, Travis."

"Yes, ma'am."

· · · · ● · ● · · · ·

Three hours later, Gillian paced the living room. Travis stood in the corner looking out the window while Gray stood in front of the open refrigerator, staring at nothing. He shut the door. "I don't know why I'm looking in here. I'm not even hungry." He'd scrambled some eggs earlier, but they'd each only managed a few bites.

He walked into the living area to see Gillian moving anxiously behind the couch. "This is silly," she said.

"What's silly?" asked Gray.

"This. This standing around and doing nothing. If this is what we end up doing all day, then we've accomplished nothing."

Travis shifted his stance. "Excuse me, but wouldn't that be a good thing?"

Both Gray and Gillian ignored him. "Listen," said Gray. "It's only been three hours. The day is still young."

"What could possibly happen? We're holed up in here like ground-hogs."

"What would you rather do?" he asked.

She stopped and crossed her arms. "I wish I knew."

Gray understood her frustration. He felt stuck between the need to find the killer and the need to keep Gillian safe. The problem was, they couldn't have one without losing the other. It was a challenging position to be in, and he found himself wanting to pace right alongside her.

"You two sound like you want something to happen," said Travis.

Gray opened his mouth to answer when a banging on the back patio door interrupted him. Max barked and jumped from his seat by the couch. The commotion drew them all toward the noise and they saw Maria, Cooper's cook and housekeeper, standing on the deck, pounding on the glass.

Gray unlocked the door and opened it. Maria spoke frantically and grabbed Gray's arms. "Mr. Steele. Mr. Steele. Help. We need help. I can't...I can't...they're asleep. They won't wake up." She pulled on him and her words ran together like a jumbled scrabble board and Gray couldn't understand her.

"Maria. Maria. Calm down." He tried to get her inside, but she pulled away.

"What's the matter?" asked Gillian.

Maria tried to catch her breath. She gripped and pulled at Gray's hands. "Fire. Mr. Steele! There's a fire." She choked on a sob. "I can't get them out! Please. Help."

Gray stared as the magnitude of her words penetrated. "Cooper?" he asked. "The house is on fire?"

"Oh my god," said Gillian.

"Yes. Please," said Maria, almost shrieking. "We have to hurry!"

Gray turned, pointed at Gillian, and spoke to Travis. "You keep her inside," he said. He looked at Gillian. "Don't leave this house." He followed Maria out to the deck.

Gillian was right behind him. "No. You can't go by yourself. You'll need help."

"I don't have time to argue with you," Gray shot back. "Go back inside."

Gillian refused. "I am not going to sit inside this house while people die in a burning house." She yelled at Travis. "Come on. We'll need your help."

Gray gave up trying to stop her. He raced down the stairs and the moment he reached the bottom, he could see heavy black smoke rising into the sky. He prayed Maria was wrong and that Cooper and Fran were not still inside. The four of them ran for the house and raced up the steps to Cooper's patio, with Max behind them, barking at their heels. Reaching the deck, they watched smoke billow from the upstairs windows. Gray saw William, an older man who occasionally cooked for Cooper, standing on the deck.

"William," Gray said, grabbing at the man's elbow. "Where's Fran? Where's Cooper?" A window on the second floor shattered and flames could be seen licking up a set of curtains.

William wrung his hands as if he wished he were twenty years younger and twenty pounds lighter. "They're still inside, Mr. Steele."

"What?" Gray asked.

"We couldn't wake them up. We called nine-one-one."

Gray stared at the house in shock as the smoke searched for exits and made lazy trails upward to escape confinement. He pointed at Gillian. "Stay here." He ran for the door.

She ignored him though and followed, with Travis and Max behind her. "Gray. You can't get them out by yourself. You need help."

"I can't risk you too," he said, stopping beside the pool. Something shattered, and he looked back toward the home.

"All due respect, sir," said Travis, "But she's correct. We need to get everyone out and we need to do it now. I'll keep an eye on her, but at the moment, she's okay and your friends are not."

Gray knew that this fire was not an accident, but he didn't have the luxury of time to think about it. "Damn it." He knew Travis was right. He needed help. "Find something to put over your mouths. Stay low." He searched for Max. "Stay!" Max looked dissatisfied, but sat at Gray's command.

The three of them crossed the rest of the patio and entered the smoky living room. The thick air burned Gray's eyes and the smell of burned plastic, upholstery, and wood assaulted his senses. A stack of cloth napkins sat atop the nearby kitchen counter and Gray ran and grabbed three. He flipped on the sink and held them under the faucet to wet them. He handed one to Gillian and one to Travis, and kept one for himself. They each held the cloth to their mouths and breathed into it. Despite the barrier, Gray couldn't stop himself from coughing as the smoke intensified. More popping sounded, and then something else shattered from above. The smoke continued to grow until the room felt claustrophobic. Gray started up the stairs, but stopped when he saw a figure at the top. He rushed up to meet Fran as she descended. She coughed heavily, and Gray grabbed her.

The noise from the fire grew, and he had to yell to be heard. "Fran?" he asked. "Where's Cooper?"

"Upstairs," she yelled back. "I tried to wake him." She coughed and couldn't continue. She tried to walk down the stairs, but stumbled.

"Travis," said Gray. "Take her. Get her out. Take Gillian with you." He coughed again into the napkin.

"No, Gray," said Gillian.

Gray pushed her back. "I can get Cooper on my own. I want you out of here. Go!" He charged up the stairs and disappeared into the smoke.

Travis took Fran by the waist and assisted her down the stairs. Gillian coughed and headed upward.

Travis stopped her. "Let him be. He can't be worried about you and save Cooper at the same time. Let's get out of here."

Flames engulfed the ceiling and licked at the walls. Gillian took one last look upstairs before she turned and followed Travis. At the bottom of the staircase, they turned to leave, when another figure emerged from a hallway that led to a downstairs guestroom. Gillian almost walked right by when she heard the strangled voice. "Here. I'm here." She recognized Franklin Gallagher, Cooper's employee. He held the wall for support but slid to his knees as the smoke overcame him.

"Travis! Wait." She turned and headed to Franklin's side. Travis stopped and Fran turned as well. She managed to hold herself upright and pushed away from Travis.

"Go," said Fran. "I can make it out from here." She coughed and bent low and made her way out through the back of the house.

"Travis, hurry!" Gillian held her breath and attempted to help Frank up, but she didn't have the strength. Travis reached her, stooped, and pulled Franklin's arm up and around his shoulder and hauled him up. Franklin coughed but stood, and Travis began to walk him out of the house. Unable to hold the wet cloth to his face, Travis coughed, but held on to Franklin. They walked through the smoke-filled living area and Gillian glanced back to see if she could see Gray when she saw Max bound through the room, barking as if on the trail of a taunting squirrel.

"Max!" she yelled, but he zipped by her and ran toward the back of the house.

"Come on," yelled Travis. "We have to get out of here."

"But Max!" She turned to follow the dog, hoping to see him.

"Leave him," yelled Travis. "We've got to go." He struggled to hold Franklin, who slumped against him.

"You go," said Gillian. She coughed into the cloth. "Get him outside. I'll be right behind you." She didn't wait for his response and turned and ran into the back hallway, yelling for Max.

She heard Travis yell her name, but she ignored him. She ran down the short hallway, screaming for the dog. The smoke was less intense in the hall, but the longer she looked, the heavier it became. The napkin helped less and less as her lungs burned and her eyes stung. Hearing barking, she headed into the room farthest down the hall. A loud crash made her turn just as Max bounded out of a guest room, yapping wildly. He stopped briefly, looked back, and resumed barking. Gillian reached for him, grabbed him by the collar, and bent to pick him up when something heavy dropped over her face. She released Max and grabbed at the material, but was pulled backward. The fabric tightened over her mouth and eyes; she couldn't breathe. Grasping at the cloth but unable to pull it away, she panicked. She tried to scream, but the sound of the fire and fabric over her mouth muffled the sound. Whoever held the gag over her face yanked her backward, and she stumbled. Max continued to bark, but his barking faded as the gag tightened. Her fear spiked. Her legs buckled, and she fell. The combination of the smoke, lack of air, and her struggle sapped her strength. Making one last desperate attempt to free herself, she flailed and pulled at the gag, but the cloth held. Unable to escape, her limbs became heavy, the noise turned into a flat hum, and she lost consciousness.

CHAPTER FIFTEEN

GRAY FELT HIS way along the walls to Cooper's room, holding the wet napkin against his nose and mouth. The smoke was as thick as a muddy stream and he had to move on almost touch alone. He found and entered the room and closed the door to help prevent the smoke from worsening. Cooper was on the bed, eyes closed as if enjoying a peaceful sleep.

"Cooper?" He felt for a pulse and found a steady beat. He listened for breathing and could feel the warmth of Cooper's breath against his cheek. He grabbed him by the shoulder and shook him, but Cooper remained unresponsive. More popping and shattering sounded outside the door, and Gray knew they didn't have much time. Coughing, he ran into the bathroom and re-wet the napkin and tied it around his face. He raced back to the bed and tried one last time to wake Cooper with no success. His burning lungs protesting, he leaned over, gripped Cooper by the arms, and pulled him up over his shoulder. Struggling to stand, he almost fell, but he managed to hold himself upright. Once Gray felt balanced, he hefted Cooper up higher and got his friend's torso over his shoulder with his legs hanging in front. A moment of dizziness made Gray hesitate at the door, but it passed just as another coughing jag hit him. Standing at the door, he took a deep breath despite the coughing, opened the door, and stepped into the hallway. The smoke filled the house, and he couldn't see anything. He turned toward the stairs and had to be careful not to fall down them. His eyes burned, and he blinked to try to clear them. Getting air into his lungs became harder and harder, and the napkin over his face felt like a piece of gauze. He choked on the smoke but pushed forward. The fire roared, and the ceiling was in flames and he hoped it would hold until he could get Cooper out. Reaching the bottom of the stairs, the heat almost made him turn back, but he made himself run through the living room. He stepped over debris and chunks of burned wood as pieces of the ceiling fell from above. He made it to the back door and out onto the patio and almost ran into Travis, who was heading back inside.

"Don't, Travis," he yelled with a rough voice. "I'm here. Help me with Cooper." He got as far as he could before he felt his legs buckle. Travis grabbed Cooper and helped ease him down before Gray dropped him. A fit of coughing hit Gray again, and he fell to his knees.

Fran kneeled next to Cooper. Maria and William stood close, their faces raw with fear. Maria cried silently.

"Oh god. Is he okay?" Fran asked.

Sirens wailed in the distance. Travis sought Franklin, who sat on the deck coughing. "You," he said, pointing at Franklin. Franklin bobbed his head up. "Go meet the firefighters. Tell them where we are. We have one more in the house."

Franklin nodded. He stood slowly, but gaining his balance, he left the patio.

"Who?" asked Gray. He sucked in the fresh air and tried to slow his breath.

Travis stood. "Gillian. She went back in."

Gray, despite his soot covered face, turned white. "She what?" He looked back toward the house. "She's still inside?"

"Max ran into the house. She went after him. She went down the back hall." He wiped at the sweat that ran down his cheek. "I'm going back in."

"Oh god," said Fran who shook Cooper. Sirens blared as help approached. "He's not breathing." She slapped his cheeks. "Cooper. Cooper." She looked up at Gray with frantic eyes and spoke in a rush. "Gray, he's not breathing."

Travis and Gray shared a look. "You take care of him," Gray said. "I'll find her." He didn't stop to wait for Travis's agreement. He pulled the grimy cloth off his neck and re-wet it in the pool to wrap it back around his face. Stepping back toward the house, he prayed he could find Gillian in time. Nearing the back door, Gray heard barking and saw Max bound out of the house, dirty but uninjured. He ran over to Gray, but Gray didn't acknowledge him. Doing his best to fill his lungs with as much clean air as he could, Gray ran back into the living area and faced the blaze of smoke and heat. The downstairs walls were burning, and the furniture began to ignite as burning embers fell down from above. He raced to the back hallway, calling Gillian's name but getting no response. The smoke was less intense in that area of the house and it was easier to breathe, but it still felt like he had a five alarm fire in his lungs. He checked the guest rooms. He looked in closets and bathrooms, but there was no sign of her. Panic welled up. The longer he looked, the thicker the smoke became until he felt himself weakening. The heat burned his lungs and breathing became painful, but he refused to leave. His fear roared through him just as the fire did the house. This can't be happening, he thought.

He retraced his steps. He couldn't lose her. Not this way. He'd bring her out or die trying. After rechecking the hallway and rooms, he had no idea where else to look. Upstairs was no longer an option. He screamed her name, but his hoarse voice barely carried over the noise of the inferno. The toxic mix in the air made him dizzy. Coughing, he reached for the wall. His vision swam, and he began to go to his knees when he felt a firm hand on his shoulder. It grabbed him and hauled him up. The smoke was so thick now, he could hardly see and he couldn't stop coughing. His body felt like a brick, and he was so disoriented he didn't stop to think who was braving this toxic hell with him. He closed his watery eyes and felt something cover his face.

"Breathe," was the only word he heard. He did what the voice said and gulped in air, feeling fresh oxygen reach his lungs. He opened his eyes and saw a filmy mask. His brain cleared, and he realized it was an oxygen mask. Despite his coughing, he inhaled two more deep breaths. Feeling some of his strength return, Gray focused and could make out a man standing next to him. Assessing him, Gray could see the stranger was well over six feet tall and the muscles in the man's arms bulged as he supported Gray. The man did not have a mask, but he seemed unaffected by the heavy smoke. After Gray managed a few more inhales and exhales, he heard the man speak again.

"Take a deep breath and follow me."

He did as he was told and sucked in a breath of clean air before the mask was removed from his face. The man walked into the smoke and Gray followed him back into the kitchen. The heat was intense, and he held up his arms in a futile attempt to block the fiery assault on his senses. The man entered the hallway that led to the garage and approached a closed door next to the side entry. He raised a powerful leg and kicked out, connecting with the closed door near the doorknob. The door cracked and gave way. The man moved aside and Gray looked into the room. Gillian was lying on the floor of a small closet, unconscious.

"Get her out of here," said the unknown figure, who then disappeared into the smoke. Gray didn't hesitate. He dropped beside her and pulled her up into his arms. The smoke filled the room as he rushed out, carrying her. The kitchen became the only viable path left to him. The living room was now ablaze, and the fire engulfed the house. Gray heard a loud crack but didn't look back. He ran toward the back of the home, through the kitchen, and out through the door. Taking a quick glance behind him, he stared in shock as the ceiling caved in and fire consumed the room he'd just left. He didn't stop to think about it as he made his way back to the others. Reaching them, he saw Travis leaning over Cooper, giving him a rescue breath. Fran kneeled next to them, wringing her hands.

Gray laid Gillian on the ground. He took her pulse and found it weak but steady. He dropped his ear to her mouth, but felt nothing. There was no breath against his skin. "Gillian…" He tried to rouse her, but she didn't move. "No," he said. "Don't do this."

Cooper coughed and sucked in some air. Gray heard it, but his attention was on Gillian. He heard Fran sob in relief as Cooper began to breathe on his own.

"Gillian?" he repeated. He shook her limp body.

He heard Fran speak. "Gray?"

"God, no. Come on, Gillian." He tilted her chin up and pinched her nose. He covered her mouth with his own and breathed into her lungs. He gave two breaths before he had to stop and cough, his own lungs burning from the smoke he'd inhaled. As soon as he could, though, he dropped back down and gave Gillian two more breaths. She didn't respond.

"Come on, Gillian." It wasn't his voice, but Travis's. Gray continued to put air into her lungs while Fran, Maria, and William hung back and clung to each other. In between breaths, Gray checked her pulse again. There was a steady but weak heartbeat, but she still wasn't breathing on her own. Travis sat next to him, ready to help if Gray needed a reprieve, but Gray didn't stop. He kept giving Gillian mouth-to-mouth, telling himself with every breath that she wouldn't die. She would live. Death was not an option.

Footsteps pounded nearby and firefighters arrived on deck. One dropped next to Gray. "Sir, let us help." One of them felt for Gillian's pulse as Gray continued to breathe for her. "Sir," said the firefighter. "Stop."

Gray didn't see or hear anything. Tears blinded him, and he didn't know whether to blame the smoke or his fear. He felt a hand tug on his arm, but he pulled away, refusing to leave. Preparing to give her another breath, he stopped when he heard her emit a weak gasp. He watched, waiting, and saw her begin to breathe. His trembling fingers cupped her face, and she coughed. The relief that coursed through him briefly erased the fire in his lungs, but another coughing fit brought it back. He reached for her but was pulled back as an EMT put an oxygen mask over her face. He looked to see a firefighter in full gear standing beside him.

"She's okay," he said. "She's breathing. We have EMTs on the scene to help." He continued to hold Gray's arm. "Sir, is there anyone else inside?"

Gray tried to focus on his words, but all he could do was watch Gillian. Although she was still unconscious, the color returned to her soot-stained face. He took her hand and gave silent thanks.

When the firefighter got no response from Gray, he looked around at the group. "Is anyone still inside?"

"No," said Fran, clutching Maria's hand. "Everyone's out."

The haze in Gray's mind began to clear, and he swiveled his head toward the firefighter. "There was a man," he said. His voice was hoarse, and he coughed again.

The firefighter kneeled next to him. "A man? What man?"

"Inside the house. I thought he was one of you guys."

The firefighter looked puzzled. "No sir. None of my guys are inside yet. Are you saying someone is still in the house?"

Gray surveyed what was left of Cooper's home. If there was anyone still inside, then there was little hope that he still lived. "I don't know where he went. He helped me find her." He coughed again, and the EMT offered him an oxygen mask.

The firefighter stood and pulled a walky-talky from his side. He spoke into it, but Gray couldn't hear the response. The firefighter turned and addressed the group of survivors. "Ambulance is on its way. We'll get you all to the hospital." Firefighters ran onto the porch, aiming hoses that blasted the burning house with water. Before leaving, the firefighter turned back. "You guys are lucky to be alive," he said. He spoke into the two-way radio again and walked away.

CHAPTER SIXTEEN

ARRIVING AT THE HOSPITAL, everything seemed to happen at once. All of them suffered from smoke inhalation, but Cooper and Gillian had suffered the worst. After initial exams, the doctors cleared Travis and Fran. After completing tests on Gray and Franklin, the doctors wanted them to stay overnight for observation, but both declined. They left the emergency room, and Franklin checked in with Fran in Cooper's room and made the necessary phone calls to business associates and insurance companies. Gray sat in the waiting room while doctors completed their tests on Gillian.

Now, three hours after arguing with the doctors regarding his discharge, Grayson sat in Gillian's hospital room. Tests completed, she lay unconscious in her bed. An IV stand stood beside her and the room was quiet other than the occasional sounds from the hallway as people strode by the open door. A monitor recorded her heart rate and oxygen levels. Her tests had revealed nothing ominous and doctors believed she would wake soon. Travis stood outside, choosing to continue his protection duty.

Cooper remained unconscious in his own room on another floor. Initial tests had not determined what had prevented him from waking, nor what had kept Fran and Franklin from waking sooner. Gray had not yet been to Cooper's room, but Fran had agreed to notify him if Cooper regained consciousness.

Sitting in his chair, Grayson watched Gillian. His eyes still burned, his voice was hoarse, and his lungs felt like he had cotton stuffed in them, but the coughing had eased. They'd given him drops for his eyes and aspirin for his headache and had recommended that he rest, but he couldn't. He had no plans to leave. Maria and William had brought him and Travis fresh clothes, and Gray and Travis had been able to shower and change. His weary body ached, but he knew he wouldn't be able to relax until she opened her eyes. He worried about Cooper too, but the doctors had found nothing serious and they expected his friend to make a full recovery.

He sat and hung his head, considering how close it had come. He rubbed his throbbing temples. Now that the adrenaline had dissipated, his whole body complained from the stress of the morning. He looked out the window and saw the cloudy skies. The expected storm had stalled at sea and now seemed to bide its time, as if deciding when and where to make its mark.

Gray felt his lungs spasm, and he coughed. Although the effects of the smoke had subsided, the doctors said it would take several days to recover.

He heard a noise behind him and turned to see Ken standing at the door. He was in uniform and was holding his hat in his hand. Gray said nothing, mainly because he couldn't muster the energy to speak.

"You mind if I come in?" Kenny asked.

Gray turned back toward Gillian. "No. That's fine," he said roughly.

Kenny entered and placed his hat on the nearby tray table. "How is she?"

"She's okay, considering. Just waiting for her to come around." Kenny walked up and stood beside Gray's chair.

"Have you seen Cooper?" Gray asked.

Kenny sighed. "Yeah. I just came from his room. He still hasn't come around."

Gray sat back in his seat and closed his eyes and thought again of how terrified he'd been when he'd realized Gillian wasn't breathing. He voiced his anxious thoughts. "It was so close, Kenny." He paused. "Both Cooper and Gillian..." He couldn't finish the sentence.

Kenny pulled up another chair and sat down. "The way I hear it, you came pretty close yourself. Doctor says you should be in bed too."

Gray opened his eyes. "I'm fine. Me lying in a bed doesn't fix anything."

Kenny stayed quiet. "Who's the guy out front?"

"That's Travis."

"Who's Travis?"

"The guy I hired to watch out for Gillian."

Kenny's eyes widened. "Why would you hire a—" He stopped. "Oh, never mind. Sorry I asked."

"Didn't do her much good, did it?"

"She's alive, isn't she?"

He sighed. "Day's not over yet."

Kenny nodded and changed the subject. "About the other night...I said some things..."

Kenny's outburst from the previous evening seemed a distant memory. "Forget it," Gray said.

Kenny stared at the floor. "I know you and I have our differences, but I was an asshole." He scuffed his foot on the ground. "I'm sorry." When Gray didn't answer, he waved at Gillian. "And I shouldn't have talked to her the way I did. She didn't deserve that."

"No, she didn't."

Kenny didn't offer any more explanation than that, and Gray didn't expect any more. They both remained quiet as Gillian continued to sleep.

"I know it's early," said Gray, breaking the silence. "But is there a theory about what started the fire?"

Kenny shifted in his seat and didn't answer.

"What? Do you know something?"

Kenny exhaled. "It is early, but it looks like the fire was intentional."

"What?" Gray blinked his dry eyes. "Who would want to burn down Cooper's house?"

"We don't know. We also suspect that Fran, Franklin, and Cooper were drugged."

"Drugged? Is that why Cooper never woke up?"

"And why Maria couldn't wake Fran and Franklin. William says they tried to rouse them but couldn't do it. Fran and Franklin have no memory of that. All they can remember is waking up to smoke-filled rooms. We've taken blood samples from all of them. We should know soon enough."

"Then why didn't Cooper wake up too?"

"We can only suspect he was exposed to more of the drug than they were."

Gray didn't understand. "You think someone wanted to kill Coop?"

"I don't know. It's too early to say. There's a lot more to sift through before we come to any conclusions." He rubbed his neck. "For all we know, Fran or Franklin could have been the target." He pointed toward Gray. "Or even you."

"Me?"

"They knew you'd come to help."

Ken's comment pierced Gray's fogginess, and the events of the morning finally began to make sense. Everything had happened so fast that he hadn't been able to sit long enough to put it all together, but now the pieces fit and he knew exactly what had happened. "What about her?" he asked, nodding at Gillian.

"What about her?" Kenny asked.

Gray moaned. "Don't act like you don't know what I'm talking about. Think about it, Kenny. It's the third day."

Kenny's face broke into a sad grin. "Listen. I know what you're thinking. And I'm partly to blame. I've been angry about Amy, and I used you as an excuse. I let my feelings..." He paused and sighed. "Anyway, I contributed to this curse garbage. I can't deny that. But now, I have to put my cop hat on."

"So put it on, Kenny. Can't you see the writing on the wall?"

Kenny's face hardened. "Come on, Grayson. You think some nut burned down Coop's house and almost killed three people to get to Gillian? Because you slept with her three days ago?"

"Kenny," said Gray, trying not to lose his patience. "Think about it. I've had four women die on me already for that very reason. Don't you think this is too big of a coincidence?"

Kenny shook his head. "I realize that you're dealing with a lot here, but if somebody wanted to get to her, there are easier ways. They could have popped her with a bullet the minute she left the house."

"Not if you want to make it look like some stupid curse is to blame."

"So," asked Kenny. "Your theory is that some weirdo is killing your girlfriends? All in some vain attempt to get to you?"

"God, Kenny. Don't you think it makes sense?"

Kenny made an annoying chuckle. "You hired protection for her. Your man was there the whole time. You think this criminal mastermind was lying in wait for her, inside a burning house?"

Grayson scowled. "I'm not saying he planned for that. Maybe he just got lucky. Maybe, in all the confusion, he was just waiting for an opportunity."

Kenny scoffed. "You really think the world revolves around you, don't you? Even this fire?" He snorted. "You really are something else."

Gray attempted to hold his temper, but the events of the day were wearing him down. "I'm just trying to offer a plausible theory. Look who's lying in a hospital bed. Hell, I found her in a locked closet."

Kenny raised his hand. "She ran after Max. She got lost in the smoke, couldn't find her way out, and she hid in the closet. That's one hell of a killer to plan all that."

Exhausted, Gray didn't have the strength to argue. "Forget it. I should know better than to talk to you about this. Shit." He blinked his tired eyes. "I could have found her with her throat slit and a note on her chest with the killer's confession on it, and you'd still blame the damn dog."

Kenny turned rigid in his seat and gripped the armrest. He aimed a stony look at Gray. "Why don't you go f—"

"Kenny." The sound of his name stopped him. Gray turned to glimpse Fran at the door. She looked frail and small. "Now is not the time."

Kenny's shoulders shrank. Visibly restraining himself from finishing his sentence, he stood as Fran entered the room. She walked up to the other side of Gray's chair.

"How's Cooper?" Kenny asked.

"Still out," she said. "Maybe you should go sit with him."

Kenny hesitated, but then nodded and moved toward the tray table. "I've got a few phone calls to make." He picked up his hat. "Then I'll go look in on him." He put his hat on.

"Thanks, Kenny," said Fran.

Kenny walked toward the door, but stopped before leaving. "I probably shouldn't say this..."

"What?" Fran asked.

Kenny grabbed his belt buckle and hesitated for a moment before speaking. "We're looking for Greg Huffy. We want to bring him in for questioning."

Gray perked up at that.

"Greg Huffy?" asked Fran.

"What for?" asked Gray.

Kenny paused. "Everyone at the dinner last night is a suspect. Maria told us she'd caught Huffy snooping around the house after he'd excused himself to use the restroom. I made a few phone calls. He doesn't own any home on the coast. Records show that the house he's staying in is up for sale. It's not his place."

"You're kidding," said Fran. "He said he was some real estate big wig."

"Oh, he's into real estate, all right. But from what we can tell so far, it's shady real estate. Guy's got money, but it's likely investors' money."

"You're sure about this?" asked Gray.

"Like I said, it's still early, but it looks like he targeted Cooper to invest in one of his scams."

Gray considered this new information. "A scam is one thing. Doesn't mean he burned the house down."

Kenny hesitated at the door, as if debating about sharing something else. "You left the party before Greg, didn't you?"

Gray thought back. "Yes. Greg and Sandy were still there when we left. Why?"

Kenny squeezed his belt. "According to Maria, Cooper and Greg got into it before Greg left. Something about a deal gone bad. Maria didn't know what it was about."

Gray's jaw dropped. "What are you saying, Kenny?"

Kenny took a second, but finally spoke. "I'm saying, Grayson, that you haven't been at the reins of Stone and Steele for a while now. And maybe you don't have all the information you think you do." He let go of his belt buckle and rested his hand on the doorframe. "You and Cooper may be friends, but it's been a while since you've been partners." Kenny's face was tight with tension. "And when it comes to a motive for this crime, I'd call that a lead. Not some curse that's been haunting you for years. That runs a distant second, no matter who's in a hospital bed."

The two men held a strained look, and getting no response from Gray, Kenny dropped his hand from the doorframe and walked out of the room.

· · · · · · · · · · ·

The room was quiet after Kenny left, and Fran sat in the chair Kenny had just vacated. She glanced at Gray. "You need anything?"

Gray stared off. "He really hates me, doesn't he?"

Fran reached over and patted his hand. "He doesn't hate you. He just doesn't like you very much." She regarded Gillian. "Any change?"

Gray shook his head. "No. Nothing."

Fran turned in her seat. "You really think she was the target?"

He hadn't realized she'd heard his discussion with Kenny. "It's the third day, and she ends up almost dying in a house fire. Seems slightly coincidental."

"Then why not burn your house down?"

"What?"

"If your theory is correct, then why not target you? Why Cooper?"

He thought about it. It was a logical question. Suddenly, nothing made sense anymore. "I don't know."

To her credit, Fran offered no argument. "Have you contacted her family?" she asked.

Gray popped his head up. "No. I don't know how to reach them."

He must have looked lost because Fran took pity on him. "I'm heading out for a bit to get cleaned up. Franklin got me a nearby hotel room and even found an assistant to go buy me some clothes and toiletries. I'm going to take a very long and hot shower." She squeezed his hand. "After that, I'll see if I can find any relatives or contact info for her."

Gray appreciated her willingness to help. "Thanks, Fran. I appreciate it. Has Stu heard?"

"He's flying back tonight."

Gray nodded, and his focus returned to Gillian.

After a moment of quiet, Fran spoke. "You really like her, don't you?"

The question took him by surprise, and he sighed. "More than I was willing to admit." He glanced back at Fran. "Does that bother you?"

Fran averted her eyes. "I'm not the one that matters. You are." She patted his hand again. "Despite what Kenny says, she almost died today. And like you said. It's day three and the day's not over."

Her answer sent a shiver of worry through him, and he had to ask the obvious. "Do you think someone is out to hurt me by targeting the women in my life?"

She looked sad, and her gaze found his. Gray saw the pain behind them. "It doesn't matter what I believe. All I know is that I care about you. And

I don't want you to get hurt." Her face clouded, and she swallowed. She spoke roughly. "I hate to admit it...but what Cooper said was true."

As much as it pained him, Gray knew he couldn't tell her what she wanted to hear. "Fran..."

She didn't let the moment linger. She stood and smoothed her shirt. "I'm going to go."

"Fran," he said again, but she avoided his look.

"I'll be back soon. Call me if anything changes."

Before he could respond, she fled the room.

CHAPTER SEVENTEEN

MUFFLED VOICES EMERGED FROM the silence and words began to penetrate and make sense. She couldn't hear everything, but the dullness slowly diminished. She knew she was lying down, covered and warm. The voices grew louder, and her alertness heightened. The words "hospital," "tests" and then "sleeping" infiltrated the tiny crack of consciousness. The voices faded and the urge to drift back down into slumber returned until a catch in her airway blocked her throat and she coughed. The cough made her chest ache, and she came fully awake. Gillian opened her eyes and blinked. Despite her blurry vision, she could make out a man above her. Blinking several more times, she heard someone say her name. She shifted in the bed, and a hand came down and rested on her arm. She stilled, but coughed again.

"Gillian? Can you hear me?" Her brain registered the sound, and she attempted to concentrate. After several seconds, her eyes cleared, and she could see the man. It was Grayson, standing over her with a worried expression. "There you are," he said. "You awake?"

She stared for several seconds, trying to understand where she was. Her throat and eyes were dry, her lungs burned, and her head ached. She opened her mouth to say something, but nothing emerged.

"You're in the hospital," said Gray. He reached down and took her hand. "You're okay."

The word hospital penetrated, but it made no sense. Thinking back, all she could remember was sitting in Gray's house. After that, her mind was blank. She wanted to sit up, but the effort required to do so felt monumental.

"Take it easy," said Gray, when he saw her feeble struggle to move. He found the controls and lifted her bed into a more upright position. The bed raised, and she closed her eyes and tried to sift through her memory banks.

"Better?" she heard him ask, and she opened her eyes.

One broken word escaped. "Water?"

He disappeared and returned, holding a large, covered, plastic jug with a straw. He held it up to her, and she took a long sip and felt the coolness relieve the brittleness of her throat. Finally beginning to understand, she sighed when another round of coughing hit her. Her nose itched, and she reached to pull off the oxygen tube, but he stopped her.

"Leave it on," he said. "You need it."

Nodding, she dropped her hand, and he offered her more water. Her awareness continued to increase until she could see and hear him clearly.

"Hey. You back with me?" he asked.

She cleared her throat. "What happened?" she said, although her voice sounded no better than her body felt.

He sat on the bed next to her. "Fire. Cooper's house. Do you remember?"

An image of smoke broke through her haze and then the sound of popping wood, shattering glass, and blazing heat pierced her memory, and she opened her eyes wide. "Cooper?" she asked.

"Okay," he said. "Everyone's okay."

Another memory surfaced. "Max? Where's Max?"

Gray smiled. "William took him back to the house. He's fine." He looked at his watch. "He's probably wondering where we all are. It's rare for me to be gone this long."

Relieved to know that everyone was alive, she relaxed. Her senses still felt dull and fuzzy, but they were slowly returning to normal. "What happened?"

He sighed, and she blinked again when her vision swam. "You ran in after Max but didn't come back out. I found you in a back closet, unconscious. Got you out just in time." She had no memory beyond running through a smoke-filled hallway and yelling Max's name. "You weren't breathing," he continued. "I had to give you mouth-to-mouth. Scared the hell out of me."

His hand squeezed hers. "You pulled me out?"

"Yes, after I found you. You somehow ended up in a back closet." He paused. "There was a man. He told me where to find you. I have no idea where he came from."

She shrugged. "Guess I have a guardian angel."

He raised a brow. "Somehow I think it was more than that."

She didn't answer directly. "Maybe."

Frown lines creased his forehead.

"What?" she asked.

"Gillian," he said with concern. "Whoever it was, I don't know if he made it out. By the time I carried you to safety, the house was ablaze. I never saw him leave."

Seeing he was upset, she remained calm and squeezed his hand. "I'm not worried about it. You shouldn't either."

"Gillian..." he said, as if she denied the truth. A sudden wave of fatigue hit her and her eyelids drifted down, but she forced them open. "Hey. You look tired. Go back to sleep." He found the controls and lowered the bed.

"I'm fine," she said, but her limbs felt heavy, and her eyelids seemed to have a mind of their own. Something in the back of her mind flickered as if she'd forgotten something, and if she hadn't been so weary, she would have searched for what gnawed at her, but her energy waned, and she knew she needed to rest.

"I'll be here," he said. "The doctor will come by again to check on you. The initial tests didn't show anything serious, but they'll probably want you to stay overnight."

"I don't want to stay overnight." Her eyelids drifted again, but she held them up.

"Rest, and then we'll talk about it." The bed went flat, and he reached over and placed his palm on her head and traced his thumb over her forehead. "I'm going to check in on Cooper while you sleep, but I'll be back. Travis is outside the door. He'll keep an eye on you."

"Travis?"

"Yes," he smiled. "Big guy, dominant, security-oriented? He's watching out for you."

"Okay," she said. She yawned and her eyes closed as she coughed again. As soon as it passed, though, she relaxed and peeked her eyes open. "Thank you."

"For what?"

"For...saving my life," she whispered. She held his gaze for a moment, but then her eyes shut.

She didn't hear him quietly answer back as his fingers stroked her face. "You're welcome."

· · · • · · • • · · ·

Gray pushed the door open to Cooper's room. The first person he saw was Franklin, sitting at a small table near a couch with a phone pressed to his ear. He spoke quietly, but looked up and waved Gray into the room. Cooper lay in bed, looking peaceful as if he slept at the Four Seasons hotel.

Gray pulled up a chair and sat as Franklin hung up the phone.

"How are you, sir?" he asked. He stood from the table and walked to the bedside across from Gray.

"I'm fine. Coughing is better. How about you?"

"Much improved. Thank you for asking. I think after a good night's sleep, I'll be back up to full speed."

Gray nodded. "Don't push yourself too hard, Frank. Doctor said to take it easy."

The phone in Franklin's hand vibrated, and he stared at it but declined the call. "I've never been one to take it easy, Mr. Steele. I'm more of a 'do it now, or don't do it' fellow. I don't like unfinished business."

Grayson pointed at the phone Franklin held. "You're actually getting phone reception in here?"

Franklin glanced at his cell. "Actually, yes. I am. Is that unusual?"

Gray shrugged. "Hospitals are notorious for bad cell reception."

"Perhaps I'm just lucky, sir."

Gray considered that. "I think we all are."

Franklin nodded. "Quite right, sir." He looked down at Cooper. "Quite right."

"Has he come around at all?" asked Grayson.

"He stirred for a few moments, not too long ago. I thought he would wake, but then he quieted." His phone buzzed again, but he didn't answer. "How is Miss Fletcher?"

"She woke up just before I came in here."

"She did? That's good news."

"She's still a little out of it. She fell back asleep, so I came in to check on him."

"You should rest up yourself, sir." Franklin's eyes noted Gray's tired features. "If you don't mind me saying so, you look like you could use it."

Gray rubbed his face. "I'm fine. I'll be better when Coop wakes up, and I know he and Gillian are all right."

"They are, sir. As you said, we were all very lucky." He paused. "I saw Mr. McDougal. Is there any indication of how this happened?"

Gray shook his head. "They think it was intentional." Franklin's eyes widened. "Don't have much more information than that, though. And they brought Greg Huffy in for questioning."

"Intentional? But who would do such a thing? And why are they speaking to Mr. Huffy?"

Gray tried to get comfortable in the chair. "Apparently, Mr. Huffy is not who he says he is." He glanced at Franklin. "Maria told Kenny that Greg and Coop had an argument last night after Gillian and I left. Did Cooper say anything to you about it?"

Franklin thought about it. "No, sir. I came back to the house after dropping off Mr. McDougal at his home. It was quiet though, when I returned." He cocked his head. "Do you think Mr. Stone had a prior business arrangement with Mr. Huffy?"

Gray shrugged. "I don't know, Frank. I don't know." He watched Cooper sleep. "I've distanced myself from the business lately. Cooper and I haven't really talked much about it."

"I wouldn't worry too much about it, sir. I've worked with Mr. Stone long enough to know that he is a smart man. He wouldn't do anything ill advised."

Gray felt surprise and relief, as if he'd needed the reminder. "You're right. I guess I'm just feeling out of the loop."

"Isn't that what you wanted, sir?"

The direct question was unexpected. "Well, yes. I guess so." He wondered just how far out of the loop he was. He started to say something else when Cooper moved in the bed. When Cooper's lids fluttered, Gray leaned over the bed.

"Cooper? You awake?"

Cooper's eyes became slits, and then he blinked. "Mr. Stone?" asked Franklin.

Cooper came awake, and he took in the room and its occupants. He cleared his throat and attempted to speak. "Something tells me I'm not in Kansas anymore." His voice cracked, but it sounded strong.

"Try a hospital bed, partner," said Gray. "How do you feel?"

He coughed and his eyes opened wider. "Like I've been sleeping under a sumo wrestler." His arm moved up, and he tried to push back the blankets. "My head is killing me." He squinted his eyes closed. "What happened?"

Gray and Franklin eyed each other over the bed. "Cooper," said Gray.

Cooper cracked his eyes back open. "What? Did I have a heart attack or something? God. I knew it. The doctor told me to lay off the fries."

"It's not the fries, buddy. There was a fire."

Whatever dullness remained in Cooper evaporated. 'What?" he asked. His head lifted. "A fire? Where?"

"Your house, sir," said Franklin.

"My what?"

"Your house, Coop. It's a total loss."

Cooper could only stare as he tried to take in the news. He tried to sit up. "Oh god. Fran. Is she okay?"

"Take it easy," said Gray. He put a hand on his friend's shoulder. "Everyone's okay. We got everybody out."

"Jesus," said Cooper, laying back in bed. He stared around the room. "Why am I in a hospital?"

"Because you wouldn't wake up. I had to haul you out of the house."

Cooper's eyes narrowed. "What? You took me out?"

"He did, sir," said Franklin. "He saved your life."

Cooper took a second to digest Franklin's information. "Great," he said. He freed his hand from the sheets and shifted carefully on the bed with a moan. "Now I'm going to have to buy you dinner, aren't I?"

"Some place expensive," said Gray.

"I would expect so." He blinked again. "No one else was hurt?"

Gray didn't answer, but Franklin did. "Miss Fletcher is in the hospital also, sir."

Cooper's eyes rounded. "Miss Fletcher? Gillian? What the hell for?" He stared at Gray. "What happened?"

A wave of fatigue hit Gray, but he pushed it back. "Maria alerted us you were in trouble. When we got to the house, you, Fran, and Franklin were still inside. The place was engulfed in smoke. I ran upstairs to get you. Fran came down on her own, and Travis got her out. Franklin woke up and got himself out. Apparently, Gillian saw Max run inside and followed him. After I got you safely away, we realized Gillian was still in the house. I ran in after her and found her just in time." He paused as he remembered giving Gillian rescue breaths. "We got you both out, but neither one of you was breathing."

"Not breathing?" asked Cooper. "I wasn't breathing?" He rested his head back and his hands gripped the sheets. "God. Please tell me you didn't give me mouth-to mouth."

Gray smiled. "No. I rescued Gillian."

"Thank God," said Cooper.

Gray enjoyed saying the rest. "Travis got that duty."

Cooper's head shot up. "Travis? Who the hell is Travis?"

Gray couldn't help but savor the look on Cooper's face. "The security we hired for Gillian."

"Shit," said Cooper. His face drooped. "At least tell me he's attractive."

"He's a nice-looking man, sir," said Franklin. "You could do worse."

Cooper dropped his head back on the pillow. "Thanks, Frank."

"Of course, sir."

Cooper stilled and looked over at Gray. "Is she all right?"

The brief flare of humor dissipated, and the mood turned serious again. "Yes. She's fine. She's conscious but sleeping."

Cooper nodded, but didn't say anything. Franklin's phone buzzed again, and he looked down at it. "I should take this."

"You keeping the clowns in the car, Franklin?" asked Cooper.

"I'm trying, sir. A few are doing their best to escape, though." He answered the phone. "I'll step outside." He exited the room and Cooper and Gray were left alone.

Cooper shifted again in the bed and looked uncomfortable. "Can you move this up?"

"Sure." Gray found the controls and raised the bed. He found the water next to Coop's bed and offered him some. Cooper sucked it down and handed it back to him.

"Thanks," he said. He stared pointedly at Gray. "So tell me..."

Gray put the water down. "Tell you what?"

Cooper saw through Gray's attempt at avoidance. "Don't play stupid, Grayson. There's more to this story. I didn't just happen to sleep through a fire and Gillian didn't get lost looking for your dog." He waited, but Gray avoided his eyes. "Spill it, Cochise."

"Nobody knows how the fire started," said Gray. His body language conveyed his discomfort when he couldn't seem to sit still. "Kenny says it was intentional, though."

"You think?" Cooper shook his head. "What are the odds my house burns down on the day your girlfriend is supposed to die?"

"We don't know if that's the reason, Coop."

"It's pretty coincidental."

"It's pretty elaborate, too. Kenny thinks you, Fran, and Franklin were drugged."

"Drugged? Is that why I didn't wake up and why my brain feels like your mom's cream pea soup was poured in my ears?"

"Yes. The doctor took blood samples to see if they could find anything in your system. Fran and Frank eventually woke up, but you didn't."

"So, what does that mean?"

"Not sure. Probably that you got more of the drug than they did."

"A lot more, apparently."

Grayson nodded. "Kenny thinks you were the target. Or maybe even Fran or me."

"Kenny's an idiot."

Gray shrugged. "You can't be sure. Maybe someone does want you dead."

"Who the hell wants me dead? I'm way more fun alive."

Gray stretched his neck. "They want to question Greg Huffy."

Cooper widened his eyes. "They what? Greg?"

"Maria said he was snooping around the house last night. She told Kenny that you and Greg had an argument after Gillian and I left. Plus, he lied about the house he owned."

Cooper made a snorting noise. "I knew it. That guy had something to hide."

"Did you know about Erin being his sister?"

"No. That was a surprise. But it makes sense. It's probably how he knew about us and our business."

Grayson lifted a brow. "Why did you think he was hiding something?"

Cooper tilted his head toward Gray. "He'd been bugging me about investing in the renovation down on the boardwalk."

"The boardwalk?"

"Yes. You know that commercial area down by the beach on the north side? All the restaurants and retail? They've been wanting to renovate but don't have the funds. They want to add residential. Build condos and a hotel. Update the shops and infrastructure. Make it a tourist trap and bring in more consumers." He stopped as he thought back. "Greg contacted me six months ago. Asked to have a meeting."

"Really?"

"Yes. We met. Talked about it. I told him no."

"Why not?"

"I didn't like it. It didn't feel right." He chuckled.

"What?"

"We used to hang out under that boardwalk. Remember?"

Gray smiled. "It's where I smoked my first cigarette."

"The pack I stole from my dad."

"I know."

Cooper grinned. "I made out with Elizabeth Zinser under that deck."

"You did?"

"Yes. I told you. I was about to get to third base when the tide came in and she freaked out because a crab ran over her foot. It killed the mood."

"Fran and I went down there once," said Gray.

"You did?"

"Yeah. We got past third base, though."

"You always did have all the luck."

Grayson asked the obvious. "So why not renovate? It sounds like a good idea."

"It's not about the renovation. I think that area could use a makeover. But Greg wanted the big money. He saw dollar signs when he talked about the residential plans. He wanted to redevelop the area." He sighed. "I didn't want all that. The place is just as it should be. Why tear it all down and start over?"

"So you're sentimental?"

Cooper smiled. "Maybe. But sometimes it's just nice to hold on to your roots. Besides, something about it smelled funny. I mean, that place doesn't need me. Any savvy investor could jump in and take over."

"Not just any savvy investor. An investor with deep pockets, who can handle the risk."

"True. But I'm not the only one out there."

"And you didn't buy Greg's story?"

"Not that I didn't buy it, but I didn't get the impression he was telling me everything."

"So what happened after you told him no?"

"He kept calling, and I kept putting him off. I finally talked to him about six weeks ago. He told me that things were moving fast. That he had other investors in place. If we could make an initial down payment, we could get the ball rolling. He sent me blueprints and financial reports and predicted a return on investment. He made it sound like a goldmine."

"But you didn't go for it."

"I did a little checking of my own. I had someone do some digging on this boardwalk project. Two weeks ago, I learned that Huffy had stretched the truth. The land around the area is mired in litigation as to who actually owns it. It's no wonder no one has sunk any money into it. I didn't plan on confronting him about it, but then he sent me an email and he said he'd be staying on the island for a while and could we get in touch. So, I invited him to the party."

"Why not just tell him what you knew?"

"Because the guy pissed me off. He wanted to bug me again? Fine. But I was going to make him suffer through it."

"Is that what happened last night?"

"We never got a chance to talk at the birthday party. He wanted to meet, so I invited him to the dinner. He threw me, though, when he brought his wife. It's why I wanted you and Gillian there. It helped to calm the waters and keep the evening relaxed."

"But after we left..."

"After you left, he asked Sandy to wait in the car. He started in, but before he could get two sentences out, I let him have it with what I knew. He left pissed. Called me a few unpleasant names. Said he would prove me wrong, and I'd learn the hard way."

Grayson straightened. "Don't you think that's motive?"

Cooper tucked a hand beneath his pillow. "Guys like Huffy don't burn people's houses down. They spit fire and brimstone, but then disappear and bug someone else when they don't get what they want. You don't make any money when you're sitting in a jail cell. I suspect he and Sandy would have cleared out by now if Kenny hadn't found them first."

"Greg could be some sort of psychopath for all you know."

"Greg? A psychopath? I doubt it. He might be good at scamming people, but he'd be lousy at killing them. He doesn't lack empathy. He just saves it all for himself. If it doesn't serve him in some way, then he's not going to do it. And killing me does not serve him. It only creates more problems, which he's got enough of already."

Grayson listened to Cooper and smiled.

"What?" asked Cooper.

"I'd forgotten how good you are at reading people."

"Well," said Cooper, shifting his head against the pillow. "You haven't been around a lot." He stared at the ceiling. "You've had other things on your mind besides me."

Gray heard the reserve in Cooper's voice. "I guess so," he said, and he began to realize the ramifications of his absence. Thinking about it, he chose to be honest. "I know I haven't been the greatest friend lately."

"That's not what I mean. I'm not blaming you for anything."

"I know. But I've been so wrapped up in my problems that I've left you holding the bag."

"I can handle it."

"It's a multimillion-dollar gig, Coop. Hell, even when I was there with you, I was working eighty-hour weeks."

"Gray, I didn't mean for this to start a conversation about us. I get it. What's happened to you would have destroyed me."

"What has happened to me should not have added to your burden. I left you to handle everything."

"And I'm handling it just fine. I may have made a few glitches here and there without you to bounce around my decisions with, but we've done okay."

"You've done more than okay."

"Some may disagree."

"Screw them."

"I'd rather not. I've already kissed Travis. That's as far as I'm willing to go." He glanced back at Gray with a smirk.

"When I get past this," said Gray, "and I figure out what's going on with me. I promise I'll be back."

Cooper didn't argue. "And what is going on with you?"

Gray considered how to answer. "Where do you want me to start?"

Cooper shifted toward Gray. "Let's start with Miss Fletcher. What's up with you two?"

Gray hesitated, but decided he needed to confide in his friend. He knew in his gut that Cooper would never hurt him or Gillian, and he certainly wouldn't burn his own house down.

He took a deep breath and told Cooper the truth. "After our interview the other night, Gillian came up with a theory."

"What theory?"

Gray felt stupid saying it. "She thinks someone I know is killing the women I love." He waited for Cooper's reaction. When Cooper didn't say anything, he spoke up. "What? You think it's crazy, don't you?"

Cooper didn't seem fazed. "On the contrary. I've wondered the same thing myself."

Gray couldn't believe it. "You what?"

"I don't believe in curses, Gray. I never did. You know that."

"Why didn't you say something?"

"It's not the kind of thing that comes up in conversation. Besides, it's hard to prove. And it's so spread out. I mean, Angela was in college for God's sake. And then Erin was years later. And even after Amy, it didn't seem possible. But Marilyn..." He paused. "Marilyn made me wonder."

"It doesn't make any sense."

"No, it doesn't. But since when does a killer make sense?"

"I mean, we're talking about someone hating me so much that they've been following me for years and they're close enough to me to murder the most important people in my life. Who would do that?"

"I bet Miss Fletcher has some ideas."

Gray clasped his hands together. "She does."

"Who?" asked Cooper. When Gray looked away, he voiced his suspicion. "Me? Was I on the list?"

Gray shut his eyes. "Yes. So are Fran, Stu, and Kenny. And now I suppose Greg Huffy."

"Greg Huffy?" Coop asked. "The rest I can understand. But Huffy?"

"His half-sister is Erin."

Cooper's eyebrows arched. "And you think he's been following you since high school?"

"We didn't exactly make his life easy. We hung an awful nickname on him. He told us he hated us."

"Because of a nickname? That's one nasty grudge."

"Then he shows up the night before the third day. And then your house catches fire?"

"I see the connection." Grayson's gaze studied the floor. "Am I still on the list?"

Grayson hung his head even more. "You were never on my list, Coop. You were on Gillian's, though."

"Why? Because she thought I might hold some grudge against you for being the wonder boy?"

Gray's shoulders shrunk. "Something like that, yeah."

"Let me put your mind at ease. I actually like that you're the wonder boy and I'm not. It takes some of the pressure off. Oh, and just so you know, I'm not killing your girlfriends."

"Cooper...I know that."

"Good. Then let's discuss who it could be."

Gray's head came up. "Are you serious?"

"Fran. What about her?"

"Cooper…"

"It has to be one of us from high school. It's the most logical conclusion. We all know about what happened with Joanie and the curse. Plus, we've all known each other long enough to hate each other's guts, no matter what we may have shared together."

"Fran almost died in the fire."

"You said she walked out on her own. Did you wake her?"

"No."

"So she drugs me and Franklin. She sets fire to the house. She waits long enough to make it look like she's a victim, too. Then hightails it out of there."

"That's ridiculous. Number one, she waited a damn long time to get out. Two, she was outside when Gillian ran in. She had no way of predicting that would happen."

"Maybe she sent Max into the house."

"What are you talking about?"

"How hard would it be? The dog's barking. You're still inside. All she'd have to do is encourage him. He would have run inside to save you."

"He also could have killed us. If he'd run up the stairs, I could have tripped over him or dropped you to save him."

"You'd drop me to save the dog?"

Gray took his time to wonder about it.

"Well?"

"I'm thinking," said Gray.

Cooper scrunched his face. "Funny guy."

Gray smiled. "This supposed plan to send in the dog is thin at best."

"I admit. It's a long shot. And sloppy."

"And why do all this in the first place? Just because she still loves me?"

Cooper's eyes softened. "You know it wrecked her when you broke up with her."

Grayson threw up his hand. "We were freshmen in college, Cooper, living on separate coasts."

"I'm not defending her, but I think she always hoped that after college…"

"What? That we'd hook up again?"

"And then you met Angela."

"And I dashed her hopes? Is that what you're saying?"

"She was at that party, you know."

"What party?"

"College graduation. The one where Angela walked up and kissed you."

"She was?" asked Gray.

"Yes. She wanted to see you. I think she would have tried to rekindle the relationship, but then she witnessed the kiss."

"Wait a minute. She saw it?"

"Yes," said Coop. "Angela kissed you in the kitchen, as I recall."

"I thought it was the dining room."

"Whatever. Anyway, Fran hadn't seen you yet. The timing couldn't have been worse. I looked up from the poker game I was playing and saw Fran just as Angela walked up and made her move."

"I didn't know that."

"I never told you. Fran left the party not long after. She tried to play it off, but I could tell it hurt."

"And you think it was bad enough to target Angela?"

"I'm just saying. It's a motive. Maybe it made her mad enough to want to keep you from finding love with anyone."

"But how did she know about Erin? Or Amy?"

"We were all back on the east coast by then. Maybe she had someone watching you. And she went on that trip to Mexico with us."

Gray recalled seeing little of Fran during that trip. "Well, she certainly wouldn't kill her friend. Not Marilyn."

"Really? Her friend sleeps with the man she wants? Maybe that's enough straw to knock that camel over."

"I don't think she'd burn down your house, Coop. Like you said. It's sloppy."

"But it almost worked. It got Gillian out of your house."

Grayson thought about his earlier conversation with Fran. "She mentioned something to me. Something that made sense."

"What?"

"Why not burn my house down?"

"You mean instead of mine?"

"Yes. It's a good question."

"Probably because she could end up killing you instead. Plus, we had security watching the house. Makes it hard for an arsonist to do their job."

"I could have died in your house just as easily."

"Maybe. Maybe not."

"No." Gray shook his head. "Fran may be long suffering and ill-requited, but I don't think she's a murderer. My money is on Ken."

"Ken? Why Ken? Other than he takes his job a little too seriously."

"He holds a grudge against me. There's no doubt of that."

"Yes, but that's because of Amy. Doesn't explain Angela or Erin."

"It does if he liked Fran."

Cooper pushed up on the bed. "What? You think he liked Fran? You never told me that."

"I think I did."

"No. You didn't."

"It's just a hunch. I expected him to ask her out after Fran and I broke up."

"Did he?"

"Don't know."

"So you think he liked Fran, but Fran liked you. She comes out west to express her feelings, and he follows. He sees her heartbreak, maybe tries to console her, but she denies him. He's pissed at you for hurting her and goes after Angela."

"That is all pure conjecture," said Gray. "Plus, why go after Angela? Why not get rid of me? I'm the one he hates."

"Because getting rid of you only makes her want you more."

Gray's eyes widened in appreciation. "You know," said Gray. "Maybe you missed your calling. You should have been a detective."

Cooper's expression didn't change. "Maybe, but I met this awkward, nerdy kid in third grade and took pity on him. We became friends, and the rest is history."

Gray chuckled. "I think you forget who the awkward, nerdy kid was."

Coop didn't argue. "Getting back to the point, we have to think like the killer in order to find him."

"So Ken takes care of Angela. But why Erin? Why Amy?"

"Because Fran is still hung up on you. And every time you fall for someone, you hurt Fran. It's his way of making you pay."

"He'd kill his own friend, though? He and Amy were close. Maybe closer than we know."

"If he liked her, and she ended up with you, all the more reason for him to hate you."

Gray shook his head at the idea. "Shit. I don't know what to think."

"And don't forget about Stu. He supposedly left town, but maybe he didn't."

"Stu? I didn't think he hated me." He sighed and rubbed his face. "But hell, why not? Everybody else does."

"He was pissed at both of us, remember?"

"I know he was upset about our plans after college."

"Right. He wanted to go one way, but we went another. He ended coming back east and doing his own thing."

"He was at that graduation party, too."

"Yeah. He was, wasn't he?"

"He was hitting on our neighbor."

"That's right. Rosalee." Cooper remembered. "She was cute."

"So he's pissed that we've left him out, so he kills Angela?"

"Maybe he plans on hurting us both. He just targets you first because he saw the opportunity."

"Maybe it's his way of separating us?" asked Gray.

"You mean stopping us from going into business?" Cooper considered that. "It's possible. It almost worked too. It took you a while to get back on your feet." He narrowed his eyes. "Wait a minute."

"What?"

"Not long after Angela died, and we'd moved back, he approached me."

Gray sat up with interest. "He did?"

"He asked if I needed help. Offered to jump in and take your place for a while."

"You're kidding."

"No. Said something about how it would be good to give you some time to recover. And to not push you too hard." He looked up. "He offered to partner with me."

Gray's eyebrows raised. "I didn't know any of this. What did you tell him?"

"That I already had a partner. That you would be back when you were ready."

"How did he take it?"

"You know Stu. He shrugged and smiled. Acted like it was no big deal."

"So all this time he's killing my girlfriends to get me out of the way? Including Marilyn?"

"If he's desperate and angry enough, sure, why not?"

"That seems farfetched."

"Of course it does, but we have to think about what this person wants. And it seems they want to drive you over the edge. I think that's what got Marilyn killed."

"What do you mean?"

"Up until Marilyn, you'd been locked up in that house for a while, not seeing anyone. You'd distanced yourself from the business and from all of us. The killer had you on the ropes. At the same time, though, you weren't homeless and destitute. You were down, but not out."

"And then Marilyn shows up on my doorstep."

"Right. You let her in and you two rekindle things. Friend or no friend, now your stalker is pissed. He's escalating."

Gray thought about his time with Marilyn. "Damn it."

"Now is not the time to judge yourself. Marilyn's death made him show his hand. We're wise to his existence. And he's taking more risks."

"Marilyn dies because I dared to show a spark of life?"

"It sucks, but it may also be the trigger that brings this guy out into the open, helps solve this curse thing, and gives you your life back."

Gray shut his eyes to block the memories. "I'd rather have her alive."

"I know you would, buddy. But that's not going to happen. We work with what we've got."

"Shit."

"And hellfire. I agree," said Cooper. "So let's get back to Stu. Him not being at the house makes him a prime suspect."

"It almost seems too obvious. He would be the perfect one to pin this on. Plus, why would he put everyone else in the house at risk?"

"Interesting thought. But let's assume it's him."

Gray humored Cooper. "Fine. So he's knocking off my love interests to get into the business?"

"Yes."

"Why? Does he want to get closer to you?" Gray widened his eyes in mock excitement. "Maybe it's you he wants, and I'm in the way." He thought of another possibility. "Maybe he's carried a torch for you all this time." He couldn't help but smile at his theory.

"Would you shut up?"

"You are a good-looking man."

"I admit, I'm a great catch, but Stu doesn't stand a chance. Besides, he looks lousy in heels."

"How do you know?"

Cooper rewarded him with a not-so-kind gesture, and Gray appreciated the humor. The subject was becoming too serious, and he needed to relax. He rubbed at his shoulders to ease his tension.

"You look like shit," said Coop. "What did the doctors tell you?"

"You should take a gander in the mirror. And they said I'm fine." As if on cue, he felt the urge to cough, and he couldn't suppress it.

Copper eyes narrowed. "Yeah, you sound fine. You haul me out and then save Gillian. How much smoke did you inhale in the meantime?"

Gray managed to stop coughing. "Don't worry about me. I'm okay."

"Something tells me I'm not the only one that should be in a hospital bed."

"I'm fine, Cooper. I just need a good night's sleep." He made an effort to appear better than he felt, but he knew Cooper could see through it.

"Just how much sleep have you been getting?"

Grayson frowned. "What are you talking about?"

"The lovely Miss Fletcher. You two have been cozy since she spent the night."

Grayson opened his mouth, but then closed it. Cooper raised a brow. "Gray?"

When Gray didn't answer, Cooper stilled, and he voiced his suspicions. "You didn't sleep with her, did you?"

Gray met Cooper's gaze. He hesitated, but couldn't lie. "No," he sighed. "I didn't."

"Son-of-a-bitch," said Coop. He slapped the bed and winced at the movement. "You two were faking?"

Gray tried to hide his discomfort. "Yes." He thought of Gillian and remembered trailing his hand up her thigh. "It's not for lack of interest, though." He groaned. "It's been a long three days."

"What for? Why pretend?" Cooper stopped when he realized the reason. "You wanted to draw this guy out, didn't you?"

Gray let out of a gush of air. "It was Gillian's idea. She wanted to be the bait."

Coop let out a low whistle. "I have a whole new respect for Miss Fletcher."

"She's unique."

"That she is," said Coop. "You really didn't sleep with her?"

Gray couldn't suppress a groan. "Believe me. We came close. But if I'm going to break this curse, then I've got to take the offensive."

"And she's willing?"

"She wants the story."

Cooper's eyes widened. "Ah. I see. That would be quite a tale. Still, it's a lot to risk for an article."

"Don't I know it." Gray stood with anxious energy. He walked to the foot of the bed. "And it almost got her killed. And she's still not safe."

"Travis is with her, right?"

"Yes. He is."

"She's in a hospital. People are all over the place. She'll be fine."

Gray couldn't hide his doubt. "Tell me that at midnight." He paced and coughed again. For a moment, he felt dizzy, and he reached out and leaned on the wall.

"Hey," said Cooper. "Sit back down before you fall over on me."

The vertigo passed, and Grayson realized what he was doing. If he didn't calm down, he would be of no use to anyone. He took a deep breath, sat back in the chair, and shut his eyes. Feeling Cooper's stare, he cracked his eyes open.

"What?" he asked.

"So, what happens after this is over?"

"What do you mean?"

"I mean, after you catch a killer and Gillian gets her story? Does she ride off into the sunset?"

"I..." Grayson felt an unexpected constriction in his gut and he didn't know how to answer. "I'm..."

"Grayson?" Cooper's eyes softened. "Oh, man."

That got Gray's attention. "What?"

"This is serious, isn't it?"

"Serious? What do you mean?" Gray fiddled with the bedsheet that hung over the side of Cooper's bed.

Cooper voiced his hunch. "Are you in love with her?"

Gray smiled and shook his head. "No. Don't be silly. I hardly know her." His hand explored the lowered bedrail.

"I've seen this look before."

Gray gripped a section of the rail. A flurry of emotion fluttered through him. "I'm not in love with her. I can't be."

"Why not?" asked Cooper. He turned toward Gray. "You have a tendency to fall hard and fast."

Gray observed his knuckles turn white as he wrapped his fingers around the metal of the bed frame. "Because if I do, and I lose her, Coop," he looked up at his friend with anxious eyes, "I won't make it back. Not this time."

CHAPTER EIGHTEEN

SMOKE FILLED HER LUNGS and burned her throat. The thick air and the sharp smell of burning wire, wood, and plastic made her head throb and her eyes water. Searching the rooms, she checked every corner, but she was lost in a burning haze of hell. The flames danced and intensified, igniting the curtains and furniture. The ceiling began to crumble, and the floor began to melt beneath her feet. Desperate, she lunged for the door, eager to escape. Reaching it, she grabbed the knob with outstretched fingers. The door opened, and she saw Max barking at her. Fresh air rushed in and she inhaled, frantic to rid her lungs of the acrid smoke. Mere steps from freedom, her exit was halted when a heavy, cloying cloth draped over her face. Her sight went dark, and the sound and the smell of the fire was muffled. She sought to free herself, but was yanked from behind and pulled back into the spitting inferno. Mustering her last bit of strength, she used her last breath to scream.

Gillian's eyelids shot open. They darted around, expecting to see smoke and fire, but she saw only her quiet hospital room. Her heart thumped, and she blinked to clear her eyes. The room was empty other than the furniture and the medical equipment next to her bed. The dream fading, her heart began to slow, and she adjusted to her surroundings. Listening, she heard only the subdued murmurings of conversations in the hallway and the soft footfalls of people walking by her door. As she studied the room, she saw her IV stand beside her and the window, where partially open blinds allowed soft sunlight to drift in. She was alone, but she remembered

Grayson sitting with her earlier. A vague memory reminded her he was likely with Cooper. She had no idea what time it was. Seeing a clock on the wall, she saw it was almost 4 pm. After all she'd been through that day, she couldn't believe that it was still afternoon. She felt like she'd slept twenty-four hours.

Moving slowly, she pushed up and looked for the controls to raise her position in the bed. Seeing the water jug on a tray, she reached for it despite her achy muscles and took a long draw from the straw. Her lungs felt like she'd been breathing sand, but she could inhale and exhale with ease. She thought back to that morning and visions of Cooper's burning house flashed in her head. Her mind clearing, she shivered, recalling the popping glass and wood, the heated air, the billowing smoke, her search for Max, her yelling when she...

She froze mid-breath, holding her water jug. Staring off, she recalled searching for Max and finding him, but then something had covered her face. Her stomach dropped. Someone had been in the house. Whoever it was had draped something over her face. She'd been pulled backward, and she'd fought to free herself, but the unknown assailant had tightened his grip, and she'd fallen.

Fear bubbled up, and she placed the water back on the table. She thought of Grayson and knew she had to tell him. Someone had tried to kill her. Her theory had been correct. Someone was killing Gray's lovers. She shook her head to clear her muddled brain and attempted to think. Who could it have been? There was no way to know. She needed to talk to Gray. Her eyes darted back to the clock, and her heart raced when it occurred to her that this day was not over. Whoever this was would likely try again. That thought alone urged her to move. She pulled the oxygen tube from beneath her nose and began to slide the bed sheets off to stand when she remembered Travis. Gray had told her he was outside the door.

She sat up in the bed. "Travis?" She was grateful the door was open.

She was relieved when he peered into the room. "Miss Fletcher?" he asked, coming in. "You okay?"

She exhaled a held breath, but her lungs protested, and she coughed. "Yes, Travis. I'm fine."

"You had us pretty worried. You should not have gone after the dog."

More images of searching for Max flashed through her mind. "In hindsight, perhaps it was not the smartest thing I've ever done."

He stood next to her bed. "Maybe next time, let me handle the heroics."

"You'll get no argument from me." She tried to remember her earlier conversation with Gray. "Everyone else got out okay?"

Travis nodded his head. "Yes. Everyone's fine. Including Max." He crossed his arms. "You and Cooper, though, gave us a scare."

She could feel the fabric over her face and almost reached to pull it off. "Gray got me out?"

"He did. He found you in a closet. He rescued you just in time."

Gray had told her he'd given her mouth-to-mouth. She could only imagine how terrified he must have been.

"You're very lucky, Miss Fletcher."

She stared back at him. "So far..." She continued to think. "Travis?"

"Ma'am?"

"Where is Mr. Steele now?"

"He's with Mr. Stone. He's been unconscious since they brought him in."

Gillian made up her mind. She pulled the bed sheets back. "I need to go see him."

"Ma'am?" asked Travis. "I don't think that's a good idea. You're supposed to be resting." He moved to stop her.

"Travis," she said, looking for a wheelchair, but not seeing one. "This is not over. Someone tried to kill me in that house." Her feet touched the floor, and she put her weight on them, but dizziness made her sit back on the bed.

"Hold on there, Miss Fletcher." Travis reached out to help her. "What are you talking about?"

There was a knock on the door, and both of them looked toward the sound. A man stood at the entrance to her room with a wheelchair in tow. He looked at a paper in his hand.

"Gillian Fletcher?"

She stared at the man and wondered how to get a hold of the wheelchair he held. She knew she wouldn't be strong enough to walk to Cooper's room. "Yes. That's me."

He dropped the paper. "Radiology is ready for you. They've been backed up. They asked me to come get you."

"Radiology?" asked Travis.

"Chest X-ray. I'm Perry. I work as an intern on this floor. They just called down and asked me to bring you up." He swung the wheelchair into the room. "You ready? Your chariot awaits."

She tried to think of a way to get the chair and find Grayson, but her mind couldn't form a plan. The only thing she could think of was to get the X-ray done and hope Gray would either return or she'd have them take her to Cooper's room after her tests. She nodded at Travis.

"Is it okay if he comes with me?"

"No sweat off my nose," answered Perry.

She stood. "How long will this take?" Travis helped her into the chair.

"Not long." He pulled her IV stand over, and she grabbed hold of the pole to roll it alongside her. "Hopefully, they'll take you in as soon as you get up there."

Perry wheeled her out the door, and Travis walked beside them. A doctor and nurse walked by and Gillian peered into rooms as they passed open doors, seeing a few occupied beds and others that were empty. Somewhere in a distant room, a machine alarm beeped and Gillian watched two nurses converse at a nursing station in the central part of the floor. One talked on the phone and the other spoke to a young woman in pink scrubs, who pushed a cart that carried magazines and books. They reached the elevator, and Perry pushed the up button.

"What floor is Radiology?" asked Travis.

A loud clang startled all of them and Gillian looked over to see a metal tray clatter against the hard floor. The entire floor seemed to pause as they looked to see the source of the noise.

"Are you Perry?" Gillian heard a new voice behind her, but she continued to watch as a frazzled nurse bent to pick up the tray. Plastic cups and cutlery had spilled along with the tray, and the nurse stooped to pick them up.

"Yes?" she heard Perry say.

"I'm Stevens, from Radiology. Is this Miss Fletcher?"

"Yes, it is," she heard Travis answer.

"Sorry," said Stevens. "We've been swamped upstairs. I just now made it down." There was a rustle of paper. "I can take her up."

The nurse gathered the fallen items as a man in green scrubs stopped to help her. Gillian watched as he handed her the tray.

"Cool," said Perry. "Thanks." Gillian's attention drifted from the nurse, and she listened to the remaining conversation.

"Thanks, Perry."

"She's all yours."

The elevator pinged, the doors opened, and Gillian's wheelchair was pushed inside. It turned, and she faced the closing doors. "We'll get you taken care of as soon as possible, Miss Fletcher," said Stevens from behind her. "Sorry for the wait. It's been a crazy day."

You could say that again, thought Gillian to herself.

"What floor?" asked Travis.

"Twelve. Thanks."

A woman joined them in the elevator just before the doors closed and she hit the button for the sixth floor. They rode up quietly. Thinking of finding and talking to Gray, Gillian tapped her foot. She felt her nervousness rise, and she looked up at Travis for reassurance. He saw her and smiled, as if he knew she needed it. The elevator stopped at six and the woman stepped out and the doors closed again.

"How long does a chest X-ray usually take?" asked Travis.

"Oh, not too long," said Stevens. "Should all be over in no time."

Gillian watched the number twelve illuminate, and the elevator slowed and stopped. The doors opened, and she was pushed forward out onto the floor. She noticed the difference immediately.

"What the hell?" asked Travis.

The floor was completely empty. No one was there. Rooms sat silent and the nurse's station stood vacant and somber, like a phone booth in a world of cell phones.

"Oh, damn," Gillian heard Stevens behind her. "Did I do this again?"

"What is this?" she asked. "Where are we?" She heard the elevator shut behind them. The silence unnerved her. Down the hall, she could see an empty wheelchair and a solitary tray table, both awaiting non-existent patients, and she suddenly felt as she were in the middle of some post-apocalyptic movie where everyone had died and they were the only survivors.

"This floor is due to start renovations. They closed it last week. I keep forgetting."

"How about we find the right floor," said Travis.

Gillian sensed the immediate shift in the air around her. Her heart slammed against her chest. Something was wrong. "Travis?" She gripped at the rails on her chair.

Stevens spoke. "How about you hit the floor instead?"

Gillian heard a faint thump, and a strangled gasp. She turned to see Travis with his hand gripping his neck. Blood trickled through his fingers. She jumped from her chair and watched Travis drop to his knees. Blood oozed from his neck, ran down his chest, and dripped and splattered onto the floor.

"Travis!" she yelled. She dropped next to him. The IV stand dragged behind her, and she felt it pull on her arm.

Travis said nothing, but he stared wide-eyed in terror at her before his eyes dulled and he collapsed and fell to the ground, the blood beginning to pool beneath him.

"No." She tried to put pressure on the wound, but the blood came too fast. "Travis…"

Frantic, she searched for anything to staunch the flow of blood. There was nothing, though. The only thing she saw was the technician Stevens, who stood motionless beside her wheelchair. Her gaze met his, and she froze in shock when she saw who looked back.

CHAPTER NINETEEN

"WE'RE NOT GOING TO let that happen."

Gray stared up from his white knuckles. "I should go back." Seeing Cooper's worry, he wanted to change the subject. "I don't want to leave her for too long."

"You don't think she's safe?" asked Cooper. "She's got hospital staff and Travis with her. There are no cars, solitary jogs, or drug dealers in sight."

Grayson let go of the rail. He tried not to think the worst. "If this guy wants to get to her, I don't think being in a hospital will stop him. Hell, he tried to burn your house down."

Cooper nodded. "I agree with you there. If that's what he did, he's determined." Cooper laid back on his pillow. "Something's bothering me, though."

Gray felt relief that the conversation had shifted back to his stalker. He wasn't ready to deal with his feelings for Gillian. "What?"

"The house. Burning it down is risky. And there's no way to know it would even work."

"You mean if his goal is to go after Gillian?"

"Yes. There's no way to assume she would run inside and risk her life. What happened to her is likely pure accident."

"Then why do it?"

Cooper wondered. "What does he gain if he wants to get to her?"

Gray began to put the pieces together, and he gripped the bed rail again. "I think you already said it. The house wasn't meant to kill her."

"What do you mean?"

Gray's mind raced. His conclusions made sense. "It was just a distraction."

"A distraction?"

"Yes. Like you said. To get her out of my house. Maybe the fact that she got hurt was just dumb luck on the murderer's part."

"You mean by setting fire to my place, he knew you'd come to help, and she'd likely follow?"

"And if you ended up in the hospital, we'd come too."

"Giving him an opportunity to get to her."

"Jesus...," said Gray. He stood, ready to leave the room.

"Hold on there. Relax for a second. It may have got her out of the house, but our bad guy probably didn't plan on her being a patient, being checked on by staff, with a bodyguard outside her door. Coming after her now seems unlikely."

"I know, but..."

"Keep in mind. This distraction theory is thin," said Cooper. "Surely there's a better way to get you two out of the house without killing me."

Gray had to admit that was true. "Then maybe he did plan to get to her through the fire if an opportunity showed itself. But if it didn't..."

"Then he would still have the chance at the hospital."

"Hell," said Gray. "I'm going to check on her."

Before he could leave, the hospital door opened, and a nurse walked in. Seeing her, both men's jaws dropped. She wore a traditional nurse's uniform, cut snugly to emphasize her narrow waist and ample bosom. The skirt ended at mid-thigh. White sheer hose hugged her long, shapely legs, elongated even further by white high-heeled pumps on her feet. The outfit outlined her perfectly proportioned hour-glass shape. A traditional nursing cap sat atop her head, pinned over amber-colored hair that was pulled into a loose, wavy bun, and tendrils of hair softly framed her face. Gray could recall no other nurse he'd seen looking like this one. Most of them wore scrubs and looked fatigued after being on their feet all day. He continued to study her, as did Cooper. The front of her uniform was zipped low and both men's eyes naturally found and followed her revealing cleavage.

"Hello," she said. Her soft, deep voice was like silk against skin. She approached the bed. Both men stared in silence, their previous conversation forgotten. Her almond-shaped green eyes were emphasized by dark liner and her red lipstick amplified her pouty, full lips. Rosy blush dusted her striking cheekbones. Her skin seemed to luminesce in the light, and she moved with a lithe grace. "My name is Eve."

Cooper shifted in the bed and found his tongue. "Hello, Eve." She approached his bedside, and Gray stepped back to give her room. "Please tell me you're my nurse."

She smiled seductively and her gaze traveled over Cooper. "Makes not breathing seem worth it, doesn't it?" Her voice vibrated the air like a sultry jazz song, and Gray felt fairly certain Jessica Rabbit had just walked into the room.

Cooper went speechless, and Gray could only stare as she turned, giving him the same appraisal she'd given Cooper.

"Not bad," she said. He felt himself blush like a school kid. "You're just her type."

He tried to form a thought. "Excuse me?"

She gave him a quick smile and her pearly white teeth gleamed behind her lipstick. "You might want to check in on Gillian, Gray."

Her use of his name surprised him. "You know Gillian?" He tensed. "Is she okay?" He moved toward the door to leave.

Her smile dropped, and she seemed to lose focus as her eyes stared off at some distant point. After a second, her attention returned. "You need to hurry. Floor twelve."

He stopped as he grabbed the door handle. "What?"

"You heard me," she said, more urgently. "Floor twelve. Go now."

He ran out of the room.

· · · · · · · · · ·

Gray rushed down the hallway, Eve's voice rattling in his head. Floor twelve? Why would he need to go to the twelfth floor? He headed down the corridor, moving fast. He found the stairs and headed down, grateful that Gillian's room was just below Cooper's. Accessing her floor, he passed the elevator and considered going up to the twelfth floor, but he thought it made more sense to check her room first. He turned the corner, and his heart lurched when he didn't see Travis. He told himself that Travis must be in the room with her, and he picked up his pace. He almost skidded as he took the turn fast and froze when he saw her empty bed. It took a second for him to adjust to her absence before he finally broke out of his trance and ran toward the nurse's station.

"Excuse me," he asked a nurse who studied a chart. He made the quick observation that her uniform in no way resembled Eve's. "Where is Gillian Fletcher?"

She looked up from her chart. "Who?"

He tried not to show impatience. "Gillian Fletcher. She's not in her room. Where is she?"

Her face scrunched. "What room?"

His frustration mounting, he answered her. "Two-one-eight."

The nurse dropped the chart and moved to a laptop and rapidly typed the keys. "I don't know. You sure she just didn't go for a walk?"

"A walk?" Gray fought the urge to yell. "Why the hell would she go for a walk? She almost suffocated from smoke inhalation."

"I'm sorry, sir. I'm sure she's nearby."

Another nurse approached from behind the counter. "What's the problem?" She was older and carried the air of authority. Her nametag read Janet. She looked at Gray like a mother protecting her cub.

"You have a missing patient and I'd like to know where she is. She's not in her room."

"Her name?"

He rolled his eyes. "Gillian Fletcher. They brought her in this morning. She was under observation. Where is she?"

The nurse dropped low to look at the same laptop. "She's not scheduled for any tests. She should be in her room."

Gray felt his patience dissolve. "I know that." His fingers gripped at the counter. "But she's not."

Janet's own impatience began to show. "I'm sure there's no need to worry. Maybe she felt the need to get up and move around a little." Gray stifled the urge to argue when a man walked by in purple scrubs, whistling a tune.

"Perry?" asked Janet.

The man stopped and approached the counter. "What's up?"

"Have you seen one of our patients..." She looked at the computer screen. "...a Miss Gillian Fletcher, by chance, as you made your rounds?"

"Sure."

Gray swiveled toward Perry. "Where?"

"Radiology called. Said they could take her."

"Radiology?" asked Gray.

The nurse looked at the computer and typed some more. "For what purpose?"

"Chest X-ray," answered Perry.

"Chest X-ray?" asked Gray. "She had that this morning." He tried to get a look at the computer screen. "Did the doctor order another one?"

Janet shook her head. "Not that I can see."

"Then why the hell did they show up?" asked Gray. He looked at Perry. "Where did you take her?"

"I didn't."

"You didn't?"

"No. I was about to wheel her up when Radiology came down and got her."

The nurse raised her head. "Radiology came and got her?"

"Yeah. Some guy named Stevens."

The nurse studied the screen. "That makes no sense."

"Why not?" asked Gray. His heart rate doubled.

"Because there's no record of any Gillian Fletcher needing a chest X-ray other than the one she received this morning." She typed some keys. "You said someone came and got her?"

"Yup. He took her up in the elevator. She had some big guy go with her."

"Elevator?" asked Gray, and he felt his face lose color. He stopped and thought. "What floor is Radiology?"

"Four," said Perry.

"Shit," answered Gray. He spoke to Janet. "What's on the twelfth floor?"

"Nothing," said Perry, answering for the nurse. "Well, there's something. It was closed for renovations last week. It's dead as a tomb up there." He grinned at Janet. "Kinda spooky if you ask me. Why do you want to know?" He spoke only to dead air, though. Gray had disappeared down the hall.

CHAPTER TWENTY

GILLIAN STARED IN shock.

"Surprised?" asked the man in front of her.

She continued to look for anything she could use to staunch the flow of blood from Travis's neck. She couldn't find anything, though. The floor appeared empty of supplies.

She tried to stay calm, but her voice betrayed her. "What do you think you're doing?"

"I'm taking care of business." His hand moved, and she caught sight of the knife he held; the tip smeared red with blood. She stiffened, and her heart leapt into her throat. Her stomach shriveled in panic.

"Stuart..."

"You knew, didn't you?"

His cold eyes moved over her, and chills broke out on her skin. She willed herself to stay calm and hoped to keep him talking. "Knew what?"

"Knew you were at risk. How could you not?" He slapped the flat side of the knife against his leg. He wore green scrubs and Travis's blood on the knife stained the fabric. She tried not to look.

"I don't believe in curses," she said.

He grinned. "Why not?"

"Because it's stupid. Nobody dies from a curse." She rose from Travis's side and wiped her bloody hands on her hospital gown. She realized that the only way to save herself and Travis was to buy time and hope someone would come looking for her.

His grin dropped. "Of course they don't. But it came in handy." He looked at Travis with no change in expression, as if he stared at a broken piece of plastic. "Just goes to show you how stupid he is." His attention returned to Gillian. "Something I've known all along."

"Who?" Her breathing had quickened.

He tilted his head at her. "Come on, Miss Fletcher. You know who I'm talking about. Don't play coy with me." The knife smacked again.

"Grayson?" She swallowed, and her throat stuck together.

He smiled. His lips spread thin and his teeth glimmered in the fluorescent light. His eyes, no longer hiding his madness, offered a flat, almost dead gaze. How had she missed it before?

"Yes. Grayson. You're new boyfriend." He moved the knife to his other hand and began to walk. She tensed, ready to run, but he didn't approach her. He stopped at her wheelchair and rested his hand which held the knife against the back of it. "Tell me. Was three days with him worth it?"

She mustered all her courage to stand and talk with him when her mind screamed at her to get away. "Why are you doing this?"

He rolled the wheelchair back and forth. "Why not?"

"You killed the others?"

He laughed, and she stifled the urge to cry. "What do you think?"

She didn't know how to answer.

"Come on, Miss Fletcher. You're a smart lady. Tell me what you think."

She bit her lip to try to focus herself. "Yes. You killed them. But I don't know why."

"Why would I kill them?" His gaze traveled upward. "Hmmm."

She looked around her for anything she might use against him. The hall looked barren, though, and her hopes sank.

"It's a fair question," he said. "I've never had a chance to explain myself before. The others, well, we never had the chance to talk."

She said nothing and wrung her hands together. She thought of Gray and prayed she'd find a way out of this. She knew he would return to her room soon and wonder where she was.

"He won't find you," said Stuart, as if reading her mind. "No one will." His eyes scoured the surrounding area. "This floor is closed. By the time they look for you here, it will all be over."

She clenched her jaw. "I still want to know why."

His fingers moved over the knife handle, as if he enjoyed the feel of it in his hands. "This is going to be different for me." He shifted his grip on the handle so that the blade pointed downward. "I've always killed fast and easy." He chuckled. "You, on the other hand, will be quite different."

"Stuart..."

"Maybe this time he'll take me seriously."

"What do you mean?"

"He's always gotten everything he ever wanted."

"What? What does he have that you don't?"

The knife slapped again against his leg, and she tried not to focus on it. She wanted him to talk.

His lip curled. "Don't compare me to him. He's been a spoiled, rich kid from the start. He's had the upbringing, the friends, the popularity, the grades, the looks, the money, the women, and the success. Everything falls at his feet." A vein throbbed in his neck. "I'm the only one who's shown him what suffering is." His body stood rigid and his knuckles bunched from his grip on the knife. "Somebody had to."

Gillian stood her ground, determined to keep her fear at bay. If she planned to survive, she'd have to outsmart or delay him. "What for?" she asked. "What did he do that made you resort to this?"

He took a moment to consider his answer. "Did he tell you about us? In high school?"

She nodded her head. "Yes."

"He told you about Joanie?"

"Yes. She committed suicide."

His unexpected laughter made her jump, and the sound echoed down the halls. "She didn't commit suicide. I killed her."

Her face conveyed her shock. "You what?"

"She was the first. Not Angela."

"But why?"

His face turned dark, and she could feel the anger build in him. "Because she liked him. She'd always liked him. She just never told him."

Gillian sensed his desire to vent, and she remained quiet.

"He was with Fran and never knew how Joanie felt. I tried to tell her he wasn't interested. That he didn't deserve her, but she wouldn't listen." His eyes strayed as he remembered, and Gillian suspected the reason for his rage.

"You liked Joanie, didn't you?"

He whipped his head back toward her. "I only wanted her to understand that she was wasting her time, but she was so stupid." He paused for a moment. "I saw them together that last night."

"Saw who?"

"Her and Grayson. At the campfire on the beach. She made out with him. It was disgusting." His posture straightened and his outrage rippled through him. "I was out of eyesight. They never saw me." He slapped the knife again, and the tip came close to poking his leg. "I watched them paw at each other. But then he backed off. Just like I knew he would. He stumbled home and left her there all alone, pining away for him. I watched and waited, and when she got up to go home, I approached her."

His eyes wandered; he seemed distracted. Gillian said nothing, and within seconds, his attention returned. "We argued. I told her what I thought. That she was weak, wanting someone who could never please her, never satisfy her. Not the way a real man could."

"Stuart..." Gillian whispered his name before her throat closed up. She didn't want to hear what came next.

"I tried to tell her, to show her." The knife moved and the bloodstain on his scrubs widened as the blade slid over the fabric. "She fought me." He looked at her with blank eyes. "Can you believe that? I could have given her everything she wanted, but she pushed me away. Called me pathetic. Said she wouldn't touch me even if I had the money or the looks." His face hardened. "The more she pushed, the harder I fought. She screamed, and I put my hand over her mouth and nose."

Gillian stood rooted to her spot. She wanted to scream, too, but she kept her emotions shielded.

"It didn't take that long. It wasn't as hard as I thought it would be."

"Oh god," said Gillian.

"Afterward, I dumped her body down by an alcove near the water. I knew the tide would come in and maybe wash her out. They found her three days later. Nobody ever knew it was me." His mind returned from the past. "And then her mother made that scene at the funeral. I couldn't believe it. It was as if destiny had smiled down on me. All eyes were on Grayson, not me. I felt exhilarated."

Gillian shook her head in disbelief. "You killed her, Stuart."

He nodded back. "Yes."

"She didn't deserve that."

"I freed her. She was a wreck anyway. Considering the path she was on, she would have died young, regardless."

"You don't know that."

He turned angry. "Don't tell me what I do and do not know, Gillian. You're just as stupid as the rest of them."

She froze at his outburst, but he made no move toward her. "The rest of them?" she asked. "You mean Angela, Erin, and Amy?"

"Yes. All of them deserved what they got. They needed to be free from him and his curse. I helped them figure that out."

The pool of blood below Travis slowly expanded. She felt the warmth of it as it reached her toes and she stepped back. The IV stand pulled with her, the tube that connected her to the bag stretching between her and the pole. She realized that if she ran, she would have to yank the needle from the back of her hand in order to free herself from the bag. Without thinking about it, her fingers found and traced the tape just below her wrist, which held the needle in place.

"His curse?" she asked. "But there is no curse."

He rolled his eyes as if he was talking to a child. "That's not the curse I mean. I'm talking about what he does to people. How he uses them."

"How does he use people?"

He chuckled softly, but didn't smile. "He's done it since I've known him. He used Fran until he didn't need her anymore. Then he threw her away."

Gillian shook her head. "They dated in high school, then they went to college and broke up. It happens all the time." She didn't know if arguing with him helped her or not, but she had few other options.

"No. He dumped her because she didn't serve his purpose anymore." His voice rose. "I watched them. Fran was one of the prettiest girls in school. Everybody liked her and all the boys wanted her, and he paraded her around like a trophy."

She wondered why that bothered him. "Did you like her too, Stuart?"

"That is not the point!" he yelled, and she jumped. The knife moved in his hand, and the blade faced forward again. She felt the urge to step away, but she forced herself not to move.

"He is a parasite. He takes what he wants and leaves only scraps behind. He deserves to know pain."

She could barely get her next words out. "Why Angela?"

He narrowed his eyes, as if he knew she stalled him, but the need to brag about his victories compelled him forward. "He did the same thing with her. He paraded her in front of Fran. Used her to show how desirable he was. He would have dumped her eventually too, when he didn't need her anymore."

"He loved her."

"He doesn't know how to love, Gillian. When are you going to learn?"

"You caused the car accident?"

He smiled, and the hair on her skin rose. "Not that difficult, really. Just the right push from behind at the right time. Plus, a little adjustment to her brake fluid. It worked beautifully." He stared off, but then his gaze returned to hers. "They always underestimated me."

"Who?"

"Grayson and Cooper. They thought they shit gold. They sat on their thrones and expected me to be their vassal." The flare of anger engulfed the hallway. "They had no idea what I was capable of."

"Cooper...why not him? Why only target Gray?"

"Cooper? Because he's a vain, vapid, worthless idiot. He parades women around, but he knows he's doing it. He doesn't pretend. Women, and men for that matter, know he's an ass right from the beginning. I can respect that much about him. His shortcoming is Grayson. He's fooled by him." He slapped the knife again against his bloody scrubs. "Plus, he didn't have the added benefit of being cursed by Joanie's mother."

Gillian fought to stay centered. She kept the air moving in and out of her lungs as calmly as she could, but she could feel her body tremble. "But you wanted to work with them, didn't you?"

The knife smacked harder and the tip of it bit into his skin, but he didn't react. "They needed me. Cooper knew it. But I know Grayson talked him out of it. Cooper's always been blind to Gray's manipulations. After Angela, I thought Gray had learned his lesson, but he wedged his way back in, so I had to show him again."

"Erin?"

"I had a few inside sources at Stone and Steele. I knew he liked her, but she was smart and kept her distance. At least at first. Then Grayson did what he does best. Used his power to manipulate her. Got her fired." His anger fueled, and he clenched his jaw. "And she fell for it. Just like they all do. He fired her, and she let him into her bed. He got what he wanted again."

He winced as blood seeped through his scrubs from his leg. He stared hard at her. "I bumped into Erin on her run three days later. Injected her with some medication I can't pronounce. I found it through some back channels when I visited some country in South America. It's great stuff if you're sick. Not so great if you're healthy. It can stop the heart during physical exertion. It worked very well."

Gillian didn't know how to react. "God..."

"I thought that would do it." He held the knife still. "I thought he would learn. It almost worked. He bowed out of sight. Stayed home a lot. Began to realize that he wasn't the great and powerful Steele. But then Cooper planned that trip..."

"To Mexico."

He stared off again. "I'd been invited, but I begged off. What they didn't know was that I was there the whole time. I watched from a distance. Saw the parties, the wasted money, and the debauchery. It was pitiful. And all to cheer Grayson up. It made me ill."

"He was grieving..."

"The only thing he grieved was the loss of control. He would have used Erin too."

Gillian could only stand and listen. She knew nothing she said would permeate his madness.

"I hoped he would take his own life. It would be the one act of courage from him I could respect. I watched him on that beach and waited, and I thought it might happen, but then she showed up, and it made him believe again."

"Amy?"

"Stupid bitch. She should have known better. She saw a simpering fool and took pity on him."

"She wanted to help. She was a good person."

"Shut up!" His voice echoed down the hall, and it took everything she had to stay rooted in place. "You don't know anything. You're just as pathetic."

"Stuart…" she whispered. "Please…" She didn't continue because he'd stopped listening. His mind had traveled back to his time in Mexico.

"I watched the two of them. They spent all their time together. Bungee jumping, skydiving, hang-gliding. And like some damn snail, he came out of his shell. And despite everything, he let it happen again, and she didn't stop him, even though she knew. She knew the risk. They were laughing at me. Mocking me." The knife sliced again, and this time he made an audible groan. Gillian's eyes watered with fear.

"He tried to stop the inevitable, but he underestimated me again. The good news is that Mexico was easy. All I had to do was pay someone to spray that cab with a hail of gunfire. It was just pure damn luck she shared a taxi with a suspected drug lord. It goes to show you that God was on my side." He let his hand and the knife relax. "I think God hates him, too."

Gillian forced herself to think. She had to expect that Gray was looking for her by now. "Amy's death almost destroyed him. Why wasn't that enough?"

"Almost," he said. "I reveled in my success. He'd been defeated. He'd left work, sold his penthouse, drank himself to sleep, and avoided women like the plague. All I had to do was wait."

"For what?"

"For him to end it. By then, that's all that would satisfy me. I waited to hear the news. That he'd shot or drowned himself. I knew it would happen, eventually. Fran still wanted him, even though she and I were together by then. I could feel it. The mention of his name made her eyes light up. She had no idea what she had right in front of her. I gave her everything…and she still wanted him."

Gillian wiped a tear that had trickled down her face; he noticed. "Are you scared, Gillian?"

She saw no reason to lie. "Yes."

"You should be."

His gaze made her frantic to keep him talking. "And then Marilyn happened," she said, and relief flooded her when that faraway gaze returned, and his eyes drifted off.

"Marilyn..." he said. "She threw a kink into the plan. I heard Fran on the phone with her. Talking about sex. From Fran's reaction, I knew it was about Gray. She had that same stupid look on her face she gets when she's thinking about him. It's pathetic." He paused and smacked the knife again. "Fran told me how Marilyn gave into him. Let him use her." The knife slapped harder. "My plan was to meet her..." He stopped and stared vacantly.

Gillian felt her remaining color drain from her face. Gillian remembered seeing the body on the beach the day she'd met Gray. She shook her head in disbelief. "Why Stuart?"

He shook his head, and his attention returned. "Her death should have ended it," he said. He spoke casually, as if Marilyn's murder was of no more concern than driving a friend's car. "I waited for him to take his own life." He raised the knife and studied it, seeming surprised by the blood on the blade. But then he looked back at Gillian. His face turned stony and his casual air evaporated. "But then you showed up."

Stuart took a step forward, and she took a step back. The IV stand rolled along the floor as the tube between her and the bag stretched taut.

Her mind raced to think. "Stuart...listen..."

He raised the hand with the knife and whipped out and sliced through the IV tube, cutting it cleanly in half. She jumped, and a whelp of panic erupted from her throat. The IV tube hung limply from the stand, and fluid dripped into a puddle on the floor.

"You wanted an interview, right?" He took a few more steps forward; she retreated.

"Let me explain..." Her tongue felt as dry as the air she breathed.

"Explain what?" he asked. "How do you explain what you did with him? How you let him touch you, paw at you, when you knew. You knew you would die." He smacked the knife against the palm of his opposite hand.

She rushed to tell him the truth. "I didn't sleep with him."

He stopped his advance. "You what?"

Her heart slammed so hard, she had to force herself to speak. "It was an act. I...we never slept together."

His mind seemed to drift, but then his eyes narrowed, and he stared hard at her. "You suspected, didn't you?"

Her voice shook when she answered. "I suspected someone was stalking him. Someone he knew." Another tear escaped, but she let it roll down her cheek.

"You were trying to catch me?"

"I...I..." she fought to find the right words. "I didn't believe in a curse. It made sense that it was deliberate."

He dropped the hand holding the knife back down to his side. "So, you're smarter than I gave you credit for. I wondered if, or when, someone might begin to suspect. I'm surprised it took as long as it did."

She tried to still her shaking hands. "You covered your tracks well. You're a wise man."

He smiled as he recognized her attempt to appease his ego. "You're much smarter than the rest of them."

"But you can't get away with this. They'll know."

"Know what? That you were slaughtered in a hospital corridor by a madman? So what?"

"Stuart...they'll find you."

Her observation had no effect on him, and he cocked his head. "Tell me something..." He let the thought hang in the air. "You said you didn't sleep with him...but you want to, don't you?"

The question took her by surprise. "What?"

His lips turned upward in a sneer. "Do you want him? Does your body respond to his? I saw you two kiss. You lust for him, don't you?"

She could feel the emotional charge the question spawned in him. "I..." She struggled to answer. "I just want the story."

"Oh," he said, moving closer, his eyes darkening, "you want much more than that, Miss Fletcher."

"Stuart...don't do this." She backed up and held up her hand. "They'll know. They'll find you."

"No," he said. He shifted the knife in his hand and held it as if he were ready to stab a piece of meat. "They'll find you. In bits and pieces. And I..." he said, stepping away from Travis and closer to her, "...was never here."

The scream in her throat would not emerge, and when his forward progress picked up speed, she turned and ran.

CHAPTER TWENTY-ONE

GRAY HIT THE UP button outside the elevators. When neither door opened, he slapped at them again. He searched the area and saw the door to the stairwell. He ran for it when he heard the elevator ding. He moved back to the door, and when it opened, he waited as an elderly couple emerged, and then he jumped on and hit the button for the twelfth floor. The doors began to close when a hand appeared and the doors stopped and retracted. Grayson cursed at the lost time when he saw who stood outside the elevator.

"Perry?"

"Is everything okay?" asked the intern.

"I don't have time to explain. I'm in a hurry."

"You're Grayson Steele, aren't you?"

Grayson almost moaned audibly. "I don't have time for small talk or autographs. I have to find Gillian."

Perry hopped into the elevator, and Grayson protested. "What are you doing?"

"I'm going to help you find her." He saw the number twelve highlighted on the panel. "Radiology is on the fourth floor."

"That's not where I'm headed." Gray watched the doors close.

"What's the interest in the twelfth floor? No one is up there."

"Listen, Perry," said Gray, trying not to yell. "I have reason to believe that Miss Fletcher needs help. So whatever we find up there, I need you to stay calm and do whatever needs to be done. I may need you to contact the police."

"Police?" Perry looked uncertain. "Why?"

"Like I said, I don't have time to explain. I didn't ask you to join me, but you're here, so there's no turning back now." He hit the number twelve button as if it would make the elevator move faster. "If something happens, just take care of Gillian for me, all right?"

"I don't understand, Mr. Steele. Just what exactly do you expect to find up there?"

Grayson didn't know how to answer. He stared at the floor buttons as they lit up with the ascending elevator. Nine, ten, and then eleven. "Trouble," he finally said. "Trouble."

· · · · ● · ● · · · ·

Her bare feet flew over the hard floor. All of her fatigue and dizziness evaporated as she raced down the hall. Panicked, she imagined him gaining on her. She made herself glance back, terrified but desperate to know how close he came to reaching her with his bloody knife. She almost stopped when she saw him rise from the floor down the hall, his scrubs stained with blood. The IV stand was in his way, and he shoved it into the wall. It hit hard and fell over, clanging against the ground. Within a split second, she surmised he had slipped and fallen in Travis's blood. Seeing his look of fury and feeling the rage pulse from him, she rounded the corner, and he disappeared from view. Breathing fast, she searched for a place to hide as tears ran down her face.

She raced through the corridor, looking into the empty rooms, knowing none of them offered her a safe place to conceal herself. Running from him would not work for long. She could already feel herself tiring, as if her body had already run a marathon, and the need to flee sapped the little energy that remained. Adrenaline fueled her, though, and she continued to move, continually watching behind her to see if he was there. She rounded another corner and, for a moment, terror almost froze her in her tracks when she imagined running into him, but he wasn't there. Her eyes searched for any avenue of escape. She found the stairwell door and rushed toward it, only to have her relief dashed when it would not open.

She jumped when she heard Stuart's voice echo through the halls. "You can't escape, Miss Fletcher. I've made sure of that. I'll reach you soon enough. There's nowhere for you to go."

She couldn't tell where the sound came from. Her fingers shaking, she tried the stairwell door again, but it didn't budge. She pushed away and headed back into the hall, but stopped when she saw a closet. The door stood partially ajar. She raced over to it and peered inside. The room contained supplies. Cleaning products sat on shelves and a broom and mop rested against the back wall. There were scrub brushes, containers of bleach and window cleaner, along with paper towels and spray bottles. The light was off, and she ducked inside. There was ample room for her to squat down and hide in the corner behind the door. She left the door open, figuring it would look too obvious if the door were closed. It also allowed soft light to filter in, and when her eyes adjusted, she could see clearly. She listened and waited, hearing her heart pound and feeling cold sweat pop out on her skin. She made herself take long, deep breaths and tried to regain control of her frantic state. Her body shook with adrenaline and fear. She sat for several minutes and heard nothing. She prayed that her absence from below had been noticed and that Gray was looking for her.

As she sat in the quiet, half-lit room, her fingers traced the tape on the back of her hand that still covered the needle from her IV. Without thinking, she pulled at the tape and removed the needle. The puncture began to bleed, and she grabbed a paper towel to blot the blood. If she had to defend herself, she didn't need anything encumbering her ability to fight back. Holding the towel against her skin, she studied the items around her. Several products were arranged on a shelf nearby and she read the names on each. One of the items was a spray bottle, likely bought in a grocery or drug store, since it was plain and white. She noticed a handwritten word on the side of the bottle. It read, "Bleach."

She stared at it, and then picked it up, holding it in her hand. She closed her eyes and, taking a deep breath, said a silent prayer for help.

Several minutes passed when she thought she heard a footstep. Opening her eyes, she listened. The quiet lingered, as if the hallways anticipated the looming end to this showdown. The footstep came again, and she strained to hear. She startled when she heard a voice, much closer to her than she expected.

"Gillian..."

She gripped the bottle and froze in mid-breath, frightened that he would hear the air moving in and out of her lungs.

The footsteps in the hall moved closer, and a shadow moved past the door. Her heart beat so fast, she feared it would reveal her location. Her mind whirled as she considered what she would do if he found her.

The shadow continued on, and she heard the steps fade. She felt a small measure of relief when the door didn't move and her hiding place was not revealed. She quickly realized, though, that she couldn't stay there. If she were found, she would have nowhere to run. He would return and she had to be gone when he did. If she could get to the elevator, then maybe she could get downstairs and find help. Her ears listened for any other sounds, but she heard nothing. Terrified, but determined to escape, she made herself stand and held her breath, convinced that if she didn't, the sound would reveal her.

She waited for several seconds, and when nothing happened, she took a tentative step out from behind the door. Peering into the hallway, she saw nothing. Shaking and sweaty, she pushed on the door and it swung open silently. She wished she could stay frozen in place until help arrived, but she knew she had to move. With careful and quiet steps, she stepped into the hallway and almost cried in relief when she saw no one staring back at her. She turned and tiptoed in the opposite direction of where the shadow had moved, still holding the bottle in her hand. She looked into rooms and tried to decide where to hide next when his voice stopped her in her tracks.

"There you are," he said. She whirled as he entered the hallway. "I wondered how long you'd wait in the closet."

Her throat closed, and she could barely breathe. She walked backward.

He stepped toward her and held the knife in front of him. "You're not going anywhere. You can only run for so long." His eyes were blank and cold, and she expected to see them roll back and turn white like a shark ready to attack.

She had a brief thought of trying to talk to him again, but that vanished when he picked up speed, and she turned and fled. He didn't fall this time, though; he was close behind her. She raced down the corridor, never looking back. Feeling him near, she pushed herself as fast as she could go, her breathing coming in short, shallow gasps. Her heart hammered and her side burned from exertion. She turned a corner and had no idea where she was or where to find the elevator, but all hope was dashed when she felt a hand on her back. Pure terror seized her and then he was on her. Her legs buckled, and she went down hard to the ground.

·········

The elevator dinged, and the doors opened. Grayson stepped out onto the floor, and Perry followed. Travis's inert form was the first thing they saw.

"Oh my god," said Perry. The blood beneath Travis had spread out into a wide circle. Perry stepped into it and squatted next to Travis's unconscious form.

Gray couldn't believe the scene in front of him. He looked for Gillian but saw only Travis, the empty wheelchair, and the IV stand lying flat on the ground, the tube hanging listlessly. He watched Perry check for Travis's pulse and his fear shot skyward. "How is he?"

Perry put pressure on the wound to staunch the flow of blood. "He's still alive, but not for long if he doesn't get some help." He searched around him. "You see anything I can put against the wound?"

Gray looked around. An empty nurse's station stood behind him, and he peered behind it. He saw a pair of scrubs on a lower shelf. He grabbed them and threw them at Perry, who caught them and held them against Travis's neck.

"Call down for help," said Perry.

Gray tried to focus on the immediate scene, but he was torn by his need to find Gillian. The floor was quiet, but he knew she had to be nearby.

"I've got to look for Gillian."

Perry used what little authority he could muster and spoke harshly. "He's going to die if we don't get him some medical attention."

Despite his worry for Gillian, Perry's tone got him moving. "Where's the phone?" asked Gray.

"Check the station. It should still work."

Gray, still searching the floor as if Gillian would appear out of nowhere, scanned the desk and breathed a sigh of relief when he saw a phone on the opposite side of the work area. He picked it up and heard a dial tone.

"What number?" he asked.

He never heard Perry's answer. A woman's bloodcurdling scream reverberated through the halls and his skin went ice cold. Forgetting Travis, he dropped the phone and ran.

· · • • • • • • · ·

Gillian went down hard, hitting the cold hospital floor. A heavy weight pressed down on her, and she fought to gain leverage, but the fall took the breath from her, and her strength was waning. Stuart pulled on her legs and a surge of adrenaline made her fight back and kick out. He grunted when her foot connected with his neck. She pushed away, but he grabbed at her ankle and wouldn't let go. She flailed and fought harder. She remembered the bottle in her hand and when he dragged her back toward him, she lifted it and sprayed him in the face. Cursing, he shut his eyes and let her go. He reached up and wiped his face, but in his maddened state, the bleach appeared to have little effect. As she attempted to scoot away, he lunged and grabbed her again. She reared up and aimed the bleach, but he lashed out with his empty hand and slapped at her fingers. The bottle was knocked out of her grip, and it skittered across the floor. Eyes watering, he blinked to clear them. She kicked out again and was rewarded with a grunt of pain as she connected with his midsection. She turned, got to her hands and knees, and crawled to escape. The hard surface bruised her, but she kept going, trying to put some distance between them. A sharp pain sliced through her upper arm and she pulled back in shock. Blood oozed from her shoulder, and she watched as the knife's momentum from Stuart's swing carried it into the floor, creating a deep nick in the surface. He'd barely missed her. Seeing him raise the knife once more, she turned to defend herself. Desperate to deter him, her throat finally opened, and her scream of desperation erupted and sliced through the air. Her feet fought for purchase, and she pushed back, but it felt as if she moved through molasses. She managed to gain some distance from him, but she froze in terror when he reached out, gripped her ankle, and yanked her back again.

·········

Gray rushed through the hallways, headed toward the scream. He didn't know at first which way to run, since the echo bounced through the vacant halls, but he continued to hear her cries of struggle, as if the scream had opened up a vent, and he used it to lead him toward her.

"Gillian!" he yelled. He raced to find her, searching walkways and empty rooms.

Another scream ripped through the vacant floor, and he listened, trying to determine a direction, and he turned down another hall. He saw nothing, but then another corridor intersected and he ran, rounded the corner, and came to a cold stop. Breathing hard, his skin prickled when he took in the scene in front of him. Stuart held Gillian against him, a knife at her throat. She was gasping and digging her fingers into the arm that held the knife. Her bare legs were kicking at the floor, and she was fighting to pull away. Blood trickled down her arm. When Grayson came into view, she saw him and cried out, but Stuart's hold on her prevented her escape. She whimpered, and Grayson saw tears streak down her face. Seeing him, she stopped fighting, although her body betrayed her when she shook with fear.

Gray tried to think, but his mind went blank. Stuart stared back at him and grinned. His maniacal look told Gray his friend had descended into madness. Stuart's rapid breathing ruffled Gillian's hair and when he saw Gray, he yanked Gillian hard up against him. Gillian winced when the knife creased her throat.

He reached out his hand. "Stuart," he said. "Don't."

Stuart attempted to catch his breath. He sat up taller and pulled Gillian up with him. She moaned in protest.

Gray's heart constricted. He gentled his voice. "Stuart. Stop. Don't hurt her."

Stuart studied him. "Hello, Gray. You're early. I'm not quite done here." He tightened his hold, and Gillian sucked in a breath. "Miss Fletcher and I have some unfinished business."

Gray's heart ached to see her terror-filled eyes. "It's me you want, Stuart. Kill me, not her."

Stuart appeared to appraise his situation and his breathing slowed. "I'll kill you all right," he said. "In my own way. You'll suffer. I'll make you watch her die." He lurched up and attempted to stand, taking Gillian with him. She groaned at the hold he had on her neck, but her feet found secure footing and she stood with him. She held Gray's gaze, and he mustered every ounce of strength to convey calm assurance to her.

Gray searched for a way to talk to the man who'd caused him so much pain. "Listen to me," said Gray. He stepped forward and Stuart stepped back, his hold still securely around Gillian. "This is not her fault. Whatever anger you have or grudge you hold, blame me, not her." He took another step forward. "Just let her go."

"I'm not going to do that." He continued to pull Gillian back. "I know where this leads. I'll kill you both."

Gray told him the truth and hoped it wouldn't backfire. "You can't escape this. No matter what happens, they'll know it was you. You have to stop. Just let her go. You can use me as a hostage."

Stuart erupted. "I don't want a hostage!" Gray almost took a step backward and Gillian clenched her eyes shut, as if expecting the fatal blow. Stuart's voice quieted. "I just want you to suffer."

Gray softened his own voice. "Why?" he asked, trying to keep Stuart talking. "What did I do?"

Stuart's eyes narrowed, and if hatred had form, Gray felt certain he would have seen it conform to Stuart's shape. "You're just like him."

Grayson remained calm, although his insides quivered. "Just like who?"

Stuart cackled as if the last fringes of his mind had begun to unravel. "My father."

Gray didn't understand. "Your father?"

Stuart spat onto the floor, and Gillian's eyes flared wide, and she grimaced. "He was an arrogant, selfish bastard. Wealthy, successful, unfaithful. I was never good enough for him. Told me I was worthless. That I should be more like that Steele kid. The one with all the charisma."

"Stuart," Gray's eyes widened. A brief memory flickered of Stuart's father from their high school years. Stuart had never spoken highly of the man. "I'm sorry." He wanted to move closer, but he didn't want to tip Stuart over the edge. "I didn't know."

Stuart's face dripped with wrath. "Of course you didn't. No one did. No one ever taught that man a lesson. Not even my mother, who stood by like the simpering coward she was, letting him use her, until I took care of it for her." He tightened his hold on Gillian's neck and she gasped. A trickle of blood dripped down her neck.

Gray fought to keep his voice even. "What are you saying?" He did his best to stay focused on Stuart. "What happened to your father?"

"I destroyed him," he yelled. He stepped back farther and bumped into the wall when he reached the end of the corridor. His demeanor relaxed. "Just the way I'm going to destroy you."

Gray searched for the right words. "Destroying me won't help." He raised his arms in surrender. "But I'm here. Right now." He flicked his eyes to Gillian's in a vain attempt to communicate, but he doubted if she got the message. "You want to hurt me? Go ahead. Kill me. Take me, Stuart. Not her."

For a quiet moment, Stuart appeared to consider his offer, but then his eyes shifted again and the dark wave of malice he exuded magnified.

"You think you're so smart, don't you?" He tilted his head toward Gillian. "I know what you want me to do. You think I'm stupid."

Stuart was unraveling, but Gray didn't know how to stop it. "I don't think you're stupid."

"Yes, you do." Stuart's knuckles turned white against the knife handle. Gray stepped forward in desperation. "Stuart...stop."

"I want you to watch." Stuart pressed back against the wall, and Gillian clenched. "Watch as I take her away from you. And she dies in your arms."

··········

As Stuart spoke, Gillian, despite her trembling, held still. She hated her vulnerability. Grimacing, she anticipated the sharp slice of cold metal against her skin. The intensity of the fear that coursed through her as she prepared to die brought her life into pinpoint focus. She thought of her family and ached to tell them how much she loved them. She prayed for Gray and sent out a silent apology for all that had gone wrong. She heard the conversation between Gray and Stuart, but their voices barely registered. Gripping Stuart's arm, she prepared for the worst. And when they bumped against the wall and he raised the knife, she closed her eyes and waited. Preparing to feel the sharp blade slice into her, she was surprised when she felt a slight release of the pressure of Stuart's arm against her neck. Cracking her eyelids open, she saw Gray but also caught sight of movement to her left. She tracked the unexpected shape from her peripheral vision and felt an acute moment of shock when a figure emerged from around a wall down the hallway. Her eyes shifted in that direction, and she saw who it was. The figure held a gun and stood ready to use it. The overwhelming need to survive surged through her and, trusting her instincts, she relaxed her hold on Stuart's forearm. As Stuart raised the knife, she felt his grip loosen along with hers, and a kernel of hope raced through her.

Everything seemed to move in slow motion. Grayson yelled, "No!" and she brought her elbow up and then down hard into Stuart's mid-section. The punch to his gut gave her enough leverage to drop low and away as a shot rang out and the noise deafened her. She fell to the ground, preparing again to feel the sharp edge of the knife rip at her flesh, but she felt nothing. Hands wrapped around her and pulled her back. Fearing another attack from Stuart, she fought and pushed against them, but the sound of her name pierced her fog of fear.

"Gillian, it's me. It's Gray."

She stopped her struggle and focused her eyes. Grayson was holding her at arm's length, and an overwhelming sense of relief engulfed her.

Breathing rapidly, she trembled in shock. Her aching muscles wouldn't move, but her eyes darted, and she searched for Stuart.

"It's okay," said Gray. "It's over." She followed his gaze. Stuart lay unmoving on the ground, an ugly wound in his head. Blood splattered the walls in an ugly, thick, asymmetric pattern. A man stood over him, holding his fingers to Stuart's neck. He straightened and shook his head. Hands shaking, he holstered his gun.

"Kenny," said Gray, breathless.

Kenny blinked, his face pale. "He's dead," he said. "You're safe now, Miss Fletcher." Despite his shock, he remained composed and professional. "Will you two be okay while I go get some help?"

Grayson nodded. "We'll be okay." His voice quivered. Kenny slowly stepped away from the body and left the scene.

Gillian met Gray's gaze, and she finally allowed the last reserves of terror to dissolve and let her arms relax. Tears threatened to fall, and she shook from the effects of the attack. Blood coursed down her arm, but she felt nothing. Her body seemed to shrink, and Gray pulled her inward and wrapped his arms around her. She let herself be held as he rocked and soothed her. "It's over. I've got you."

Hearing his words, she buried her face into his neck, wrapped herself around him, and let go, crying hot tears of relief.

CHAPTER TWENTY-TWO

HEARING THE SHOWER RUN, Gray closed the door to his bathroom. He'd returned home with Gillian a short time ago. She'd been quiet and sullen, and when he'd tried to talk to her, she did not engage. Both were numb from exhaustion, so he couldn't fault her for not wanting to have a conversation.

Max trotted up and Gray stooped over and patted him on the head. The dog had greeted them when they'd returned and had been under Gray's feet ever since. He ruffled the dog's fur.

Max sniffed him and barked. "It's all right, Max," said Gray. "Everything's fine." He didn't know if he spoke to the dog or himself.

He picked up his cell phone. Cooper had called earlier and Gray needed to call him back. The scene had been utter chaos at the hospital, and he'd had little time to explain the situation to his friend. The media had been alerted and had waited outside the building to get whatever news or interview they could find. Police filled the hallways, and the entire twelfth floor had become a crime scene. Perry had become an overnight hero when he detailed his account of saving Travis's life, although the man hired to protect Gillian was still in critical condition with a tentative prognosis.

He hit the call button and listened as it rang on the other end. Cooper picked up on the second ring.

"Hey," said Cooper. "You okay?"

Grayson groaned with fatigue and rubbed his face. "Depends on your definition of okay."

"What the hell happened? This place is a madhouse. I've had two reporters try to sneak into my room and Franklin's had to throw them out."

"You haven't heard?"

"It's all over the news, and I'm trying to believe it. Stuart tried to kill Gillian?"

Gray clenched his eyes at the memory of the knife at Gillian's neck. "He's my stalker, Coop." Not trusting his balance, he found a chair and sat down. "He killed all of them, including Joanie. And he almost killed Gillian."

"Holy shit, Gray." Silence ensued as Gray waited for Cooper to assimilate the news. "It was him all along?"

Gray rested his elbows on his knees. The shower continued to run, and he listened to the comforting sound of the spray. "All along."

"I don't know what to say. How's Gillian?"

"She's coping. The doctor wanted her to stay overnight, but she refused. With all the craziness at the hospital, it's probably for the best, anyway."

"Did she get hurt?"

"She's got stitches in her upper arm, and bumps and bruises, plus the damage from the smoke inhalation, but she'll be fine. Tests were all negative."

"That's great. I'm glad she's okay. How are you?"

Gray didn't know how to answer. "Physically, I'm exhausted, but I'll survive."

"What about mentally?"

He waited before he answered. "That may take some time."

Cooper took his own pause. "I hear you. You need anything?"

"Just a hot shower and a very long sleep." A thought occurred to him. "How's Fran? Does she know?"

"I've been trying to reach her. Hell, if she's watching the news, she knows."

"Damn..." He hated the idea of her learning about Stuart from the TV. "Keep trying, would you?"

"You know I will. I heard Travis is touch-n-go."

"He lost a lot of blood, but he's still alive. They transfused him, but the doctor says his vitals are strong, so they're hopeful."

"Jesus, Gray." There was a hesitation on the line. "Is it true that Kenny took Stuart down?"

Gray, despite his attempt to avoid it, saw the image of Stuart falling and blood splattering clearly in his mind. "He shot Stuart in the head. Saved Gillian's life. Likely mine too."

"Shit..." Grayson heard Cooper take a breath. "How did he find you?"

Gray remembered asking the same question at the hospital after Gillian gave her statement. "Said he'd received a phone call, telling him to return to the hospital. That you had regained consciousness and wanted to talk to him. When he arrived, some big guy stopped him. Told him that Gillian was in trouble on the twelfth floor. He headed up and heard the ruckus."

"Some guy? Who was he?"

"Kenny didn't know and didn't see him afterwards. I asked him to describe him."

"And?"

"The description matches the man in the fire who told me where to find Gillian."

"The man in the fire? What man?"

Gray sighed with fatigue. "I didn't get a chance to tell you. There was a man in your house. When I went in to look for Gillian, I couldn't find her. A man showed up, threw a mask on my face, and showed me where she was. If it wasn't for him, well..."

"And you never saw him afterward?"

"No."

"Really? That's interesting."

Gray caught the tone in Cooper's voice. "What? Do you know something?"

"Just that sexy Eve disappeared as well. I've been asking about her and no one knows who she is."

Grayson remembered her well. He tried to put the pieces together, but his mind would not function.

"Guess Miss Fletcher has some guardian angels," said Cooper. Grayson didn't answer. He fought to keep his eyes open. "Hey," he heard Cooper say. "You there?"

The shower shut off, and he sat up in his seat and stifled a yawn. "Yeah. I'm here."

"Do me a favor and go get some shuteye. Did you close your front gate?"

"The moment I pulled in." He and Gillian had managed to sneak out the back of the hospital without the press knowing, but Gray knew it was only a matter of time before they found him at his house.

"Good. Call me tomorrow. They're supposed to spring me in the morning."

"Okay."

"And Gray?"

"Yeah, Coop?"

"I'm glad it's over, and that you and Gillian are safe."

Gray smiled into the phone and gave his own silent prayer of gratitude. "Thanks, Coop. Me too." He wanted to say more, but the words wouldn't form.

"Go get some rest."

"I will. Good night."

"Good night."

He hung up the phone and turned it off. The last thing he needed was some reporter calling him at 3 am and waking him up. He didn't think they had his cell number, but if they tried hard enough, he knew they would get it, eventually.

He stood and stretched. He walked up to the bathroom door and listened. When they had come home earlier, neither of them was hungry and without thinking, they'd walked straight upstairs. Gillian had headed toward her room, but Gray had stopped her. He sensed her distress and knew she felt vulnerable. Without thinking twice, he guided her into his room. He turned on the shower and sat her down on the toilet seat. He went into her room and found a nightgown and robe and her toothbrush. He came back into the bathroom and laid out her items on the countertop. They'd wrapped her bandage in waterproof tape, and he told her to take her time.

Saying nothing, she'd watched him leave, and he'd left her in there while he made his phone call. Now, he knocked softly on the door. "You all right?" he asked.

He heard a soft rustling sound and imagined her drying herself with a towel. "Yes," she answered. "I'll be out in a minute."

"No hurry." He waited at the door to be sure she was okay and then returned to his seat and tried to fathom the events of the day. Max sat down at his feet and cocked his head.

After a few minutes, the door opened. She stood in a white nightgown, and her wet hair sat in gentle waves on her back and shoulders. A bandage was wrapped around the upper part of her arm. He stood and saw the signs of fatigue on her face. She looked like she could drop where she stood.

"Shower's all yours," she said and walked toward the door.

"Where are you going?" he asked.

"To my room," she said.

"Not tonight." He moved over to the side of his bed. When he'd realized that he and Gillian would be coming back to the house that evening, he'd called his housekeeper. He wanted to return to a presentable home and fresh sheets.

Her eyes questioned him when he lifted the covers. "Sleep," he said. "That's what we both need right now." She nodded, but stayed rooted to her spot. "And I don't know about you," he continued, "but I don't want to sleep alone tonight."

The impact of his words reached her. "Me either," she said, and she walked over, slid into the bed, and he covered her. Max jumped up as well and curled into a ball at the foot of the mattress.

"I'm going to take a shower," he said. She nodded against the pillow, but her head popped up when he walked away.

"You'll stay with me?" she asked. Worry reflected in her eyes.

He moved back to the bed and took her hand that lay above the covers. "I'll be right here." She rested her head back down, and he pulled the blankets up. "Now go to sleep."

She closed her eyes, and he watched her finally relax. After he was sure she rested, he grabbed a towel and took his own shower. The hot spray wiped away the hours of stress and the remnants of their confrontation with Stuart. He stepped from the stall and dried himself, feeling his mental weight diminish and his body unwind. After whipping the towel through his hair, he decided he was too tired to dry it. He threw on some clean pajamas and stepped out of the bathroom.

Looking at the bed, he saw Gillian had left the lamp on, but she had turned on her side and moved further over, giving him room. He watched her sleep for a few brief seconds, but then reached down and flipped off the light. He raised the bed sheets and slipped in between them and almost sighed out loud in relief. Max popped his head up and watched as if to ensure that both adults were where they should be and then dropped his head back down.

Gray laid his head on the pillow. Seeing Gillian sleeping next to him, he wondered if she was still awake. He turned sideways and stared at her back. His eyelids began to drift and his body slowly succumbed to fatigue, but before he surrendered to slumber, he moved up closer to her and, without thinking, placed his hand on her waist. His eyelids opened slightly when he felt her fingers on his, pulling him closer. And as she moved back toward him, he curled up against her and fell fast asleep.

CHAPTER TWENTY-THREE

THE CRY OF SEAGULLS woke him, and he cracked his eyes open to see murky light filtering through the blinds. He had no idea what time it was. His last memory was of waking at 4 am to use the bathroom. He'd stumbled through the dark, hardly coherent, used the facilities, and returned to the bed, snuggling up to Gillian as he had before, and falling right back to sleep. Now, blinking the slumber from his eyes, he tried to focus and saw Gillian across from him. She'd moved and now faced him. Her eyes were open, and she was watching him. He stared back and admired her in the dusty light. The fatigue she'd exhibited the night before had lifted, and her eyes were vivid and no longer red-rimmed. She said nothing as she lay against the pillows. The blanket was pulled up to her shoulder, and he felt warm underneath the blankets. He had no intention of approaching her. The ordeal she'd been through the previous day would require time for her to recover, and he didn't want to confuse her even more or take advantage of any emotional pitfalls.

Since she continued to stare and he felt himself react, he broke the silence. "Good morning. How do you feel?"

She didn't answer, but only continued to watch him with her attentive eyes.

"Gillian?"

She answered with only one syllable. "Shhh."

"What?" he whispered.

"Don't talk."

He did as she asked and wondered why she wanted the silence. But as he continued to lie there unmoving, he felt an almost imperceptible energy in the air, and then she turned in the bed. Holding his breath, he watched her move her arms beneath the covers, reach low, and pull up from below, and his whole body shivered when he watched her wriggle her nightgown up, lift it over her head, and throw it on the ground. The covers still hid her, but now he knew she wore nothing beneath them. His breathing seemed to short circuit, and he tried to speak, but he could only say her name.

"Gillian..."

She gave him the same response. "Shhh. Don't talk." She turned back to her side in the bed and watched him again, but did not move.

He held her gaze and tried to grasp what to do next. She'd fired the first shot, and she'd hit her target. Now it was his turn to make the next move. He wanted to say something, but she wouldn't let him. When he thought about what to tell her, he realized he didn't know. Words seemed useless, and he wondered if she thought the same. After all they'd been through, maybe action was the next best step.

Making up his mind, he followed her lead and rolled onto his back. He pulled off his pajama top and dropped it to the floor. Then he reached down and pulled his bottoms off as well, and they followed the top to the ground. Then he turned in the bed and looked back at her. He took a deep breath to calm his heart. He'd fired the return volley and now he waited to see what she'd do.

He didn't have to wait long. Moving with sinewy precision, she moved across the bed. Placing her hand on his shoulder, she pushed him onto his back and her leg moved over him. Sliding her body over his, she straddled him, her body laying completely on top of him.

His heart slammed hard into his chest when he felt her soft skin glide over his and it took every ounce of restraint he had not to touch her. But he let her be the aggressor, and although his breathing picked up and he ached to kiss her, he held back. By the twinkle in her eye, he knew she wanted to torment him, and he decided to let her.

She moved her hand over his chest, and her touch tingled on his skin. Watching her, he could see her eyes rove over his face and chest, as if savoring him. He wondered how much longer he could hold out when she pushed up and lifted her torso. Her knees came up to his waist as she sat astride him, and he got a full view of her magnificent body. He let his gaze rove over her beautiful skin and narrow waist, up her ribcage to her full breasts, sexy shoulders, and long neck, and he moaned. His breath caught in his throat, and his whole body reacted to her. He gripped at the sheets to keep from touching her.

A movement on the edge of the bed caught his eye, and he saw Max poke his head up. He managed a steady breath and spoke. "Downstairs, Max."

The dog cocked his head. Gillian looked behind her, and Gray saw her smile. The dog looked back at her, but then seemed to get the message when he stood and jumped to the floor. Leaving the room, his nails clicked against the wooden floor as he trotted down the stairs.

Gillian turned back and their eyes met. For a moment, she looked uncertain, and Gray wondered if she'd changed her mind. He didn't move.

Finally, she spoke. "Do you have something?"

It dawned on him then. "Oh, hell." He glanced toward his nightstand. "Yes. In the drawer." He reached for it, but she stopped him.

She smiled again and something shot through him; he couldn't stop looking at her. "We'll get it in a minute." Her gaze lingered on his chest and then lowered. Heat bloomed through his body when she moved her fingers over his belly. Breathing became difficult, and he froze when she moved her fingers lower. Letting out a shuddered breath, he almost grabbed and pulled her back down, but she moved and took his hands in hers and brought them to her knees, encouraging him. He let her guide his touch. With her hands over his, he caressed his fingers over her skin, trailing them up her thighs. As they moved higher, he heard her take a breath.

Roaming his hands up her legs, he slid them up to her hips, and he cupped her buttocks. She ground her lower body into his, and he gasped at the sensation of her moving against him. Looking down, she let her gaze follow their hands as he moved them up to her ribcage. He lightly touched a scar beneath her breast, and she moaned. The sound of her excitement drove him forward, and he lifted his torso and pressed his upper body against hers. She dropped her hands, and he moved his upward until they found and cupped her breasts and she arched against him.

"Grayson," he heard her whisper. He felt her hands on his back, and they traveled up to his shoulders until he felt them in his hair. She arched farther and at her direction, he leaned forward, and his lips touched the sensitive skin of her breast. He moved his hands behind her waist and pulled her close. Sliding his mouth to her nipple, he felt and heard the shockwave move through her when he tasted it. He let his tongue and lips continue their ministrations and by the sound of her breathing and the hands in his hair, he knew his touch drove her wild and he reveled in pleasing her.

He slid his mouth up from her breasts and his lips explored her neck. He kissed the crease inflicted by Stuart's knife. She tensed, but his soothing touch relaxed her, and his hands caressed her, and he felt her return fully to his touch.

Imagining all the things he wanted to do to her, he almost lost his train of thought when she boldly slipped her hand down between their bodies. Audibly groaning, he grabbed her wrist when he felt her touch him. Things were moving fast enough, and he wanted to slow it down and enjoy every inch of her. Holding her hand, he let his lips travel to the opposite side of her neck, and he tasted her salty skin as she rocked against him. He let go of her hand, wrapped his arms around her, and let his torso drop back down to the bed, taking her with him. Back on top of him, with her body pressed into his, their eyes met. Desperate for her, he moved his hands up and into her hair. Pulling her down, he met her lips in a fiery kiss. Their mouths moved hungrily as they each sought to deepen the connection. Holding her against him, he rolled, pinning her beneath him. They continued to kiss, but now he moved his body against hers, as she had done to him. She gasped in his mouth, and he silenced her with his tongue, sliding it over hers. She matched his movements with her own. His mouth slanted over hers and he remembered their kiss on the patio, the heat of it. He thrilled in the fact that this time he didn't need to stop. That he could taste her and touch her and satisfy her completely. Their rapid breath intermingled and, continuing to kiss him, she wrapped her arms and legs around him. Feeling her urge him forward, he lifted his mouth from her lips.

"Gillian," he said in a breathless whisper, and he tried to focus on speaking.

Her hazy eyes found his, and she attempted to adjust to the unexpected pause. "I know. It's in the drawer. I'll get it."

She began to move, but he stopped her. "Not that."

Her hands moved on his back and then went lower. He made the effort to not be distracted. "What?" she asked.

"Listen to me," he said.

Staring at his lips, she lifted her head, and they kissed again, their tongues exploring and mouths searching, before she pulled back. "I'm trying to," she said, trying to catch her breath. "What is it?"

Her sexy gaze made him melt, and he couldn't help but drop and kiss her swollen lips once more. He ravaged her mouth before he made himself still with monumental will and spoke once more. "This is not a one-time thing for me."

She quieted and listened.

"I don't want this to be over before we start." She blinked back at him. "This is the real deal. You write your story, but I want you to stay." He held motionless and waited for her reaction. Her hands trailed up his torso and shoulders, and she cupped his face in her hands and kissed him gently.

"Screw the story. I want you. I've always wanted you, from the first moment I saw you."

He stilled, letting her words penetrate. Looking into her eyes, all his doubts evaporated, and he captured her lips again in a searing kiss. She wrapped herself around him and met his need with her own yearning desire.

Dragging his lips off of hers, he said breathlessly, "We need to get to that drawer."

And as he prepared to join her body to his, he realized that for the first time in years, he could enjoy and bask in the sheer pleasure of making love to a woman without fear. Smiling and ready for her after accessing the nightstand, he reached down between them and touched her intimately. She moaned and arched into him.

"Get ready, sweetheart," he said. "It's gonna be a good day."

···•·•·•···

Hours later, Grayson turned on his cell phone. He had twenty-eight messages. He turned it back off and smiled at Gillian, who lay next to him with her head on his arm.

"Don't you think you should listen to them?" she asked.

"No."

"Why not?"

"Because I know who it is. It's reporters. They want me to comment on what happened."

"It's probably Cooper too. And what about your mom?"

Grayson groaned. He hadn't thought about his mother hearing the news. "I'll talk to them later." He admired the shape of her under the sheet draping over her from her hip down. "I'd rather focus on you."

"We've been focusing on each other all day," she said, grinning.

"Not all day. We got some lunch."

"I thought that was dinner."

"Depends on what time it is."

"What time is it?" she asked.

"I have no idea."

She moved in the bed, and he felt his body respond to her again. He'd never felt such a powerful attraction to a woman before. The sight of her and the way she reacted to him gave him chills. Even when he thought he was spent, all she had to do was touch him and he'd answered with no delay.

Her body had acted as hungry as his. When he'd thought she'd dozed, she'd surprised him when she suddenly awoke and reached for him again, eager for his touch. He felt lured in by her, as if she wiggled on a hook and he was a starving fish. Her smile, her scent, the way her fingers and lips brushed over his skin in just the right places drove him mad with lust. He didn't want it to end.

Looking out the window, he saw the dimming light. When they'd eaten earlier, he'd noticed the clouds and the billowing wind. The skies warned of the impending storm. With all the activity of the last few days, he'd paid little attention to the weather and wondered when, or if, the storm would reach land. For all he knew, a hurricane could be on its way.

All thoughts of storms vanished though, as he raised his hand and brushed a strand of hair from Gillian's face. "You sleepy?" he asked.

"No."

"You want to get up?"

"No."

"You want to talk?"

"No."

He made a face at her. "Then what else could we possibly do?"

Her eyes drifted up, and she stared at his mouth. "I have an idea."

He grinned. "What?"

"I noticed you've got a mighty big bathtub in there."

His grin became a frown. "That's not the answer I was expecting."

She smiled, moved her leg, and her toe grazed his ankle. "Want to take a bath with me?"

Her touch made him shiver, and he reached his own foot out to meet hers. He moved it against her instep and imagined her in a tub full of bubbles. "How hot do you like the water?"

Her eyes met his. "Hot," she said.

"Hot?" He slid up close to her. "How hot?"

She leaned in and kissed him. He met her kiss with equal urgency before she pulled back. "Very hot," she said in a whisper.

Looking at her, he debated forgoing the tub, knowing she wouldn't say no. But the thought of sitting in the bathtub with her while water caressed and dripped down her skin gave him chills. He pushed up and out of the bed. "Your wish is my command."

· · · · • · • · · ·

Jets whirring, the bubbles popped and spilled over the side of the tub. Gray sat on one end and Gillian on the other. They'd covered her bandage with a waterproof covering, and she insisted it didn't hurt, although he didn't believe her. Her foot moved over his thigh, and he took her toes in his hand and massaged them. She visibly relaxed and leaned her head back.

"Feel good?" he asked.

"Mmmm..." she said. "Very."

He didn't want to spoil the mood, but he wanted to ask her a question. "You doing all right?"

Her eyes peered back at him. "I'm naked in a tub with you. I'm doing just fine."

His hands kneaded her heel. "That's not what I mean."

He felt her tense up as he moved his fingers up to her calf. "Gillian?"

"I don't want to talk about it."

"You sure?" Her finger traced the mark on her throat where the knife had left a scab. "Yesterday was pretty terrifying."

She pulled her foot out of his grasp and sat up. "Can we talk about something else?"

He nodded. "We can if you want." He waited, but she didn't say anything. "It's just that you could have been killed yesterday. I don't think something as intense as that should be swept under the rug."

Crossing her arms, she leaned back again. She didn't look at him.

"You risked your life for me."

Her gaze met his. "Does that bother you?" she asked.

It was his turn to sit up. He reached out of the tub and turned off the jets. The room went quiet. "Your damn right it bothers me. What we did was stupid."

"It worked, didn't it?"

"At a pretty high price, though."

"Are you saying you'd rather be back where you were?"

"No, I'm not saying that."

"Then what?"

"He almost killed you."

"But he didn't."

He couldn't understand her lack of emotion. "Doesn't that upset you?"

Her face displayed the first hint of fear. "Of course it does. He scared me to death."

"You shouldn't have done it."

"Why not?"

"It was too big of a risk."

She played with a bubble. "Great reward comes with great risk."

"I should have never agreed to it."

"Are you saying you feel guilty?"

"Hell, yes. I do."

"You think you weren't worth the risk?"

"Was it worth losing you? No."

"And if I hadn't done it, would we be here right now? Would we have ever had a chance to be together?"

He conceded her point. "I can't argue with that. But if it had gone the other way…"

"But it didn't."

"But if it had, I would have never forgiven myself."

"But it didn't, so…"

"So?" he asked.

"So." She swatted at the bubbles. "What do we do now? Keep reliving the past?"

"What do you mean?"

Her hand fell back into the water, and her fear turned to frustration. "You have your life back, Gray. Yes, it was ugly. Yes, he almost killed me. Yes, I questioned my sanity when he had the knife at my neck. But none of that matters now."

"I think it does."

"Only if you let it."

Gray thought back. "How am I supposed to get that visual out of my head—of him holding you, threatening you?"

"Grayson, you're free now. Don't let him continue to haunt you."

He sat back against the tub, and the tension from yesterday returned. "If he'd hurt you—"

"But he didn't."

"Are you really as calm as you're acting? Because I'm having a hard time with it and I'm not the one who was attacked."

"I'm dealing with it."

"Don't do it alone."

"I'll be fine."

"Gillian." He lifted his torso and leaned up close to her. "Please don't be brave with me. If you're upset, tell me."

She stayed quiet, but then she rose up and brought her face close to his. The suds compressed between them. "Listen." She spoke quietly and traced her fingers down his bicep nervously. "I'll admit I'm a little freaked out by what happened. I thought..." When she paused, Grayson found her other hand under the water and squeezed it. "I thought he was going to kill me." Her eyes filled, and he grabbed her knees and pulled her closer. Her legs wrapped around his waist, and he held her against him. "And in that moment, when he raised the knife, I..."

"You what?"

"I thought of my family and how upset they'd be."

He felt her tremble, but didn't interrupt. "And I thought of all the things I'd never do, and I felt regret."

A tear slipped down her cheek, and she wiped it away. "But you know what I didn't think about?"

"What?"

"You."

He didn't know what to say.

"I didn't blame you. I didn't entertain one thought of regret about the decision to find the man responsible for the horrific crimes he'd committed. I knew that no matter if I lived or died, that we had succeeded. We had found him, and you'd never have to live in fear again, and neither would the women you loved."

Her words surprised him. "Why would you sacrifice yourself for me? Do you know me that well?"

She cupped his face with her hand. "I know you better than you think I do."

"You do?"

"Yes, I do."

"How?" Her openness and her proximity made his heart, as well as other parts, warm.

She looked away. "Let's just say I have my ways."

He sighed and brushed his nose against hers. "That's right. I keep forgetting you're a nosy reporter."

Her posture relaxed as he trailed his hands over her legs, and she sighed. "I'm good at finding things out. Remember that."

He moved his mouth close to hers but didn't kiss her. "And what if I have more secrets up my sleeve?" he asked.

She stared off again. "We all have secrets."

Her tone piqued his interest. "Do you have secrets?"

Her gaze darted back to his, and he caught her shift of discomfort. "Me?" she asked. She moved her hand to his shoulder. "What if I did?"

He let his hands travel to her back, and he rubbed her tense muscles. Leaning in, he whispered into her ear. "After all you've done for me, you'd have to be a terrorist preparing to torture me before I could ever be upset by it."

Her head popped up. "You're sure about that?"

He sensed her hesitation. "Are you trying to tell me something?"

"It's just that..."

"What?"

She stared at her fingers. "I haven't told you everything about me."

"How could you? You haven't exactly had the chance. We've both been a little preoccupied."

Her hand on his shoulder slid to his chest, and her eyes followed it. "There are things you should know."

He had an idea what that might be. "Is this about the man and woman who helped us find you?"

He felt her stiffen. "What?" she asked.

He didn't let her off the hook. "You know what I'm talking about. The man in the fire who told me you were in the closet and who also directed

Kenny to the twelfth floor. The nurse in Cooper's room." He tried to catch her eye. "You want to tell me about them?"

Her fingers trailed over his chest, and he wondered if she was deliberately trying to distract him. "I told you I had someone watching out for me."

He raised an eyebrow. "You want to share any more than that?"

She hesitated. "Not right now." She finally met his look. "I'm just not sure how to explain it." Her eyes turned sad. "Is that okay?"

Not wanting to upset her, he chose not to push further. "If this is the secret you don't want to tell me about," he moved his hands up and brushed the hair off her shoulders, "then tell me when you're ready." Her shoulders dropped. "But you know you can tell me anything. You won't scare me off."

She took a deep breath and exhaled. "You don't know that."

"Are they bad?"

Her face furrowed. "Bad?"

"Your secrets." He pulled her body closer to his. "You're not a danger to me, are you?" He leaned in and kissed her neck below her ear.

"No," she said. He heard her breathing deepen.

He trailed his tongue and lips down to the nape of her neck and traced his fingers along her waist. "You're not filming this, are you? Planning on selling a sex tape?"

She giggled, and he felt her relax. "No."

"You weren't a man once, were you? Had a sex change?"

Her muscles softened as he moved his fingers down and trailed them over her lower back. He moved his tongue and lips up her neck and to her chin.

"No. No sex change," she said. She arched against him.

He loved teasing her with his touch. "Are you planning on marrying me, using my body, spending all my money, and leaving me with nothing?"

She pulled back then and stared at him with stormy eyes. "Maybe," she said. She squeezed her legs and rocked against him. "Especially the part about using your body."

He sucked in a breath and stared at her beautiful face. "I have no problem with that." He dropped his mouth and his lips found and slanted over hers. She wrapped her limbs around him. Moving against each other, the bathwater sloshed against the sides of the tub. And as the water slowly cooled, and the bubbles popped and dissipated, they both surrendered to their unrelenting need for each other.

CHAPTER TWENTY-FOUR

GILLIAN STIRRED IN THE bed. Stretching, she reached for Gray but found nothing but his pillow. She cracked her eyelids open and saw the empty space beside her. She pushed up and eyed the note on the sheets.

"Making breakfast. Come join me, sleepyhead," it read. Smiling, she stretched again in delight as she thought back over the past twenty-four hours.

After their shared bath, they'd made their way back to the bed and had wasted no more time talking about Stuart or her secrets. They'd focused only on giving each other the maximum amount of pleasure possible. She smiled at the memories, and her cheeks flushed. The smell of coffee made her wonder if perhaps she could sneak up on him downstairs. Her mind imagined all the fun things they could do on the kitchen table or the living room couch.

She sat up in bed and wondered what had happened to her. Somewhere between the return trip from the hospital and waking up in Gray's bed the next morning, her usual low-key manner had disappeared. A powerful sexual urge had coursed through her, and despite their active time together, she still felt as if she'd never touched him.

She stood and took a few minutes to clean up. Seeing one of Gray's shirts, she threw it on and pulled on a pair of yoga pants. She checked her image in the mirror. The pants elongated her legs, and the oversized shirt gave her a sexy appeal. She debated leaving the pants off and greeting him downstairs with nothing on but his shirt, but decided against it when the thought of him sliding her pants down her legs made her belly flip. She ran a brush through her hair and headed out of the bedroom and down the stairs. It was quiet, and she almost said his name when she heard other voices in the house. At the bottom of the stairs, she stopped. A woman's and then a man's voice emitted from the kitchen. Recognizing them as belonging to Cooper and Fran, she continued into the den, glad that she had worn pants and disappointed that she'd have to wait to get Grayson on the kitchen table.

Seeing them in the kitchen, she paused. Max ran over and greeted her. Fran and Cooper stood at the breakfast table while Grayson sat in one of the chairs. Her laptop was open in front of him. He looked pale, as if the screen he studied had sucked the color from him. The conversation ended when she entered the room and three pairs of eyes studied her.

Max wagged his tail at her feet, but she ignored him when she felt the wave of enmity wash over her. She couldn't pinpoint where it came from until she saw Fran, and the look in her eyes left nothing to the imagination. Gillian ignored her though and focused her gaze on Gray, who did not acknowledge her. A chill went through her.

"Good morning," she said when no one said anything.

"Morning," said Cooper. His stint in the hospital appeared to have had few lingering effects. He looked as if he'd just stepped off the beach after a long walk on the shore. His face held a solemn expression which Gillian could not interpret.

Fran said nothing, and her face was flat, but Gray's reaction worried her most. He continued to sit at the table, staring at her computer, as if he'd just been given the key to hell, and he'd unknowingly unlocked the door.

She tried to understand the unexpected signals directed at her. "What's the matter?" she finally asked.

"What's the matter?" asked Fran. Her arms had been crossed, but now she uncrossed them. She held a small maroon notebook and dropped it on the table. It hit with a satisfying thunk, and Gillian saw Gray jump at the sound. She recognized the notebook, and her hair stood on the back of her neck.

"What are you doing with my address book?" she asked.

Fran stared for a second before she answered. Neither Cooper nor Gray spoke.

"I tried to contact your family," said Fran. "Since you were in the hospital, I thought they might like to know where you were and that you were all right."

Gillian stared dumbly at her. "You went through my things?" She could feel the color drain from her face.

Fran's demeanor hardened. "I did. I found your book. Thought I might be able to contact someone you knew."

Gillian didn't know what to say. She looked at Gray, but he stared off, no longer looking at the computer screen.

"Your little book didn't help much. For some reason, you have names listed but no numbers. I find that interesting. Who keeps an address book with no numbers, or addresses for that matter?"

Gillian tried to think. "I have a good memory." That much was true. She could remember numbers with ease.

"Really? I'm impressed." She crossed her arms again. "When I couldn't find a number to call, I contacted *Lifestyle* magazine."

Gillian's stomach turned, and she prepared for what she knew was coming.

"You want to explain to us," said Fran, as if she relished in her revelation, "why the hell they've never heard of you?"

Fran and Cooper both watched her, and Gray finally looked at her.

The unexpected revelation made her head spin. "I..." she struggled to explain, but couldn't find the words. "I'm..."

"You're what?" asked Fran. "Not a reporter?"

Fran's eyes narrowed in anger, and Gillian almost stepped backward. She finally admitted the truth. "No. I'm not."

"I don't understand," Cooper said. "Why pretend to be one?"

Her gaze sought Grayson's, but he wouldn't look back.

"I'll tell you why," said Fran. "Because she used it to get close to Gray. To get him to tell her about him."

"That doesn't make sense, Fran. If she's not a reporter, then what's the point?"

"Because she's worse than a reporter," Fran spoke with venomous outrage. "She's a source."

Gillian couldn't keep track. Her head spun as she sought to gain control of what was quickly devolving. She considered how to explain it without making it sound any worse than it already was.

"I'm a what?" she asked Fran.

Her outrage growing, Fran gripped the back of a chair. "When I realized you'd been lying, I came back to that address book of yours. You have some interesting names in there."

Gillian felt her own anger rise. "You had no right to do that. That's personal information."

"Not anymore, it isn't." Her grip turned white on the chair.

"Fran," said Cooper. "Relax. Give her a chance to explain."

"Explain what?" Fran grabbed the notebook and waved it at Gillian. "Explain why you have Jeremiah Horn's name in here? And Ernest DeMille's?"

Gillian recognized the first name, but not the second. She tried to speak, but Fran hadn't finished.

"Oh, and I found a few Fletcher names in your book. I can only assume they're the names of your family." She flipped through the book, and Gillian stifled the urge to walk up and yank it out of her hand. "You mind telling us how there's no record of..." She found a page in the book and read from it. "A Royce Fletcher or Eve Fletcher..." She slammed the book shut. "Or a Carson or Lillian Fletcher living in Shepton, Arizona."

Gillian's eyes flicked back to Gray. She wondered when he'd told Fran her history.

"And you know what's even stranger?" asked Fran.

"Fran, come on," said Cooper. "Give her a break."

"Shut up, Cooper," said Fran without her gaze leaving Gillian's.

Gillian didn't answer. The energy in the room came at her with such intensity that she found it almost hard to breathe.

"That there is no Shepton, Arizona." She slammed the book back down on the table, but this time Gray didn't jump. "You want to explain that?"

Gillian didn't address her. All she could do was watch Gray and hope for an opportunity to explain. "Gray?" she asked.

Fran erupted. "Don't you dare talk to him. Haven't you done enough?"

"I haven't done anything."

"Really? You haven't lied?"

Gillian didn't know how to get through to them. "I did. But I had good reasons."

"What?" Fran asked. "Please enlighten us."

Gillian didn't want to talk to Fran. She wanted to get Gray to look at her, but she knew she'd have to think fast. "I came to help."

"Really? How sweet of you. Is that what you did for Jeremiah Horn?"

Gillian nodded. "Yes. I helped him too. But that's none of your business."

Fran ignored her outburst. "Jeremiah Horn was a prominent businessman. He was on track for being *Time's* Man of the Year. Until someone leaked a story about him. A story that cost him everything. His wife and family. His career."

"That's not true," said Gillian. She remembered Jeremiah fondly and knew the true reason for his downfall.

"It is true. A magazine article came out, exposing him and his secrets. As a result, he was forced to leave his successful life behind and he lost everything."

"I remember that story coming out," said Cooper. "He had a male lover. A man he'd known for years."

"Exactly," said Fran. "And some gossip mag outed him. Spilled secrets and published photos. They had an inside source. A source who I'm sure was paid very well."

Gillian almost laughed at their assumption. "And you think that was me?"

Fran narrowed her eyes. "Horn's name is in your book. So is Ernest DeMille's."

Gillian didn't understand. "Who is Ernest DeMille?"

Fran sneered. "The man who wrote the article that exposed Horn."

"What?" asked Gillian. "I don't know him." She thought back to the time when she'd helped Jeremiah. She'd felt the same need from him that she'd felt from Gray. The man was on the verge of despair, living a life he didn't want with no idea of how to escape it. She'd posed as a reporter for him, too, and during her interview with him, she'd used her skills to get him to open up. He'd lived a secret life for years, posing as the man everyone wanted him to be. A prominent figure in the community, a wealthy industrialist, and well-known in the press. He'd often been asked to throw his hat into the political ring.

What the world didn't know was that he led a secret life. He'd loved one man for years. After their interview and his ultimate confession to her, she'd stayed close and promised him she'd keep silent. She knew that in time, she'd convince him to confront his demons. He'd chosen an un-orthodox method of coming out by contacting a gossip magazine. He'd been the source of his own story. Once the story was out, he changed everything. He'd divorced and left public life behind. He put the business behind him, and the last she'd heard was that he now lived a happy and quiet life with his husband on a ranch in Wyoming. It was what he'd always wanted, and Gillian had helped him find the courage to do it.

"Then how come his name is in your book?" Fran asked.

Gillian could only shake her head in confusion. She couldn't answer that question. "I don't know."

"Don't give me that crap. You're lying."

"No, I'm not."

"I called him," said Fran.

"You what?"

"I called him."

"You called who?"

"Ernest DeMille."

"You called him?"

Her eyes turned hard, and she looked and felt like a lioness stalking her prey. "He confirmed you were his source."

"He what?" Gillian shook her head in shock. "That's not possible."

"Apparently, it is." She cocked her head. "And he can hardly wait for any more information you have on Grayson."

"That's a lie."

"I'm sure that's what you want Gray to believe."

"I am not some inside source for any gossip magazine."

"I'll tell you what you are. You're disgusting."

"Fran..." Gray spoke for the first time. His voice was barely above a whisper. "Stop."

Fran swiveled toward him. "She's lying to you, Gray."

"Fran," said Cooper, putting his hand on her arm. "We should go."

"Go?" asked Fran. "And leave her here with him?"

"Yes. They need to talk."

"He needs to kick her out. And now, before she can do any more damage."

Cooper looked at Gray. "You want us to stay?"

Gray finally drifted back from his far-off gaze. "You should go."

"Gray," said Fran. "You can't trust her."

"Come on, Fran," said Cooper. "Leave him be."

"It's okay, Fran. Just go with Cooper."

Fran stared in disbelief. Cooper pulled her toward the back patio door. "We'll go back to the hotel," said Cooper. He gave a sad glance toward Gillian before looking back at Gray. "You call me later."

Gray nodded his head. "I will."

Fran looked back at Gillian. "You do anything to hurt him and I swear, you'll wish you'd never set foot on this island. I don't care what you did for him. As far as I'm concerned, you're a con artist and a leech."

"That's enough, Fran," said Gray. "Cooper..."

"We're going." He pulled Fran out the back door and closed it behind him.

The silence in the house pressed down on Gillian when the door shut. Gray continued to sit at the table, unmoving. Max, apparently tired of waiting for Gillian to notice him, trotted over to Gray and sat at his feet.

Gillian waited for him to say something, but when he didn't, she attempted to explain. "Gray, listen..."

"How long?"

She shook her head. "What?"

He continued to stare at the screen. "How long have you been after me?"

"After you?"

"After my story? When did you find out?"

His questions confused her, but she tried to reach him. "Gray, I didn't want your story. I..."

He whipped his face in her direction and the anger she felt from him and heard in his voice made her jump. "How long have you known?"

She attempted to sound calm. "Known what?"

His jaw clenched, and he narrowed his eyes. "My story. My curse. You knew about it before you ever met me, didn't you?"

"Gray, I..."

"Didn't you?!"

She told him the truth. "Yes. I knew."

"Why did you lie to me?"

"I can explain everything."

"What the hell do you want from me?"

Her hands whipped out. "I don't want anything from you."

"Why are you here?"

"Because I want to be. I want to be with you."

He slapped his hand on the table. "Don't lie to me."

"I'm not lying."

"Did you already tell them about me?"

"I told you. I'm not a source."

"But you're not a reporter, either?"

She winced. "No, I'm not."

Agitated, he stood from his seat and paced. "What exactly am I supposed to believe?"

"Let me explain." She wrung her hands together. "Please."

He stopped and stared hard at her. "By all means. I can only hope what you're going to tell me is true."

She nodded her head. "It is. I'll tell you everything."

He crossed his arms and waited.

She considered where to begin. "I knew about you. I knew you needed help."

"How?"

She wasn't ready to explain that part yet. "I'll get to that. But for now, let me just say that I didn't come for a story. I came for you."

"What the hell are you talking about?"

"I knew you were in trouble. I knew you were suffering. I showed up to help you."

"To help me?" He looked doubtfully at her. "Really? What are you, some sort of angel of mercy?"

"No, I'm not an angel. I'm just sensitive to certain things. I became aware of your situation about six weeks ago. I tried to ignore it, but I couldn't. I did some research into your background. I learned about the deaths of the women in your life. I came down to see you and meet you. I didn't intend to stay, but after we met on the beach, I knew I couldn't leave. You were in a bad place."

"Who the hell are you?"

"Please believe me, Gray."

"How the hell did you know I was in a bad place, huh? What are you, a mind reader?"

She considered how to respond. "I just know things."

He cocked his head at her. "And you knew I needed help." He snorted. "How the hell do you expect me to believe that?"

"Because it's true."

"Maybe it was true, but you knew it because of your research. Of course I was depressed. The women in my life were dying. How hard is that leap? You expect me to believe you knew it otherwise?"

"Gray, I know this is hard to understand..."

"Hard to understand?" His voice rose, and she tried not to react. "Why would I find it hard when you've already admitted that you're a liar?"

She felt the pain of his verbal assault, but kept going. "That morning on the porch," she said.

Her diversion made him hesitate. His eyes narrowed. "The porch? What morning?"

"When I cut my heel. I knew what you were thinking."

He seemed surprised. "What was I thinking?"

"You were considering suicide."

His jaw dropped open, but his composure returned quickly. "What are you talking about?"

"You were thinking of walking out into the waves and not coming back."

He didn't react, and she tried to read him, but his emotions ran too high, and all she felt was a jumble of erratic energy.

"How the hell do you know that?"

She hoped maybe she had reached him. "I told you. I know things."

"You knew I wanted to die?"

"Yes."

He hesitated. "And what? You felt sorry for me? So you made up some excuse to get close to me?"

"I told you. I knew you were in pain. I had to help. You called to me."

His brows furrowed. "I what?"

She hadn't meant to say that much, but now that she had, she questioned how much further she should go. "I felt you. You called to me."

"You want to explain that one? 'Cause last I checked, I don't recall picking up the phone and dialing your number."

"That's not the kind of call I mean."

He shook his head and dropped his hands to his hips. "What exactly do you mean?"

"It's...it's what I do."

"It's what you do? For who?"

"For anyone I feel called to help."

He chuckled, but didn't look amused. His hand came up, and he squeezed his temples. "I don't understand."

Her mind raced to think of how best to explain. She had to get through to him, but she didn't know how to do it without telling him everything. "Grayson, listen. I've helped a lot of people. Not just you. Jeremiah Horn was much like you, only for different reasons. He lived a life he didn't want. His whole life was a lie. All the trappings of success made him miserable. He wanted to leave it all behind. I felt his misery and pain and I couldn't ignore it."

His face was as flat as a statue's. "You pretend to be a reporter with him, too?"

She didn't let his anger affect her. "I did."

"You're just a regular Bob Woodward, aren't you?"

She ignored him again. "Posing as a reporter gives me a reason to ask questions, to get to the heart of something faster. I can't help unless I can get you to open up. I have to be able to connect in order to relax your defenses. Once I do that, then I can find the way to the answer."

"The answer?"

"Yes. To help you find a solution, a way back from the brink."

He frowned. "And you did this with Horn?"

"Yes, I did."

"And with me?"

"Yes."

He hesitated again before he asked the next question. "And if Horn hadn't been gay, would you have slept with him too?"

His words were like a slap to her face. Her skin prickled in shock. "No, of course not. What happened with you—"

He didn't let her finish. "And what about that man and his daughter? The one you helped find?"

She tried to keep up with the change in subject. "Who?"

His irritation rose again. "The man who gave up his daughter, remember? To the aunt who gave the child away. Did you feel his pain, too?"

She remembered. "Yes, I did."

"And what did you tell me? That you wrote an article about it? That's not true either, is it?"

She looked at the ground. "The story is true, but I never wrote an article."

"No, of course you didn't. Just like you didn't sell Horn's story to a tabloid. Just like you're not selling mine, either."

Her body shook at the thought of it. "I never sold anyone's story."

"Demille's name is in the book, Gillian. He knows you! How do you explain that?"

She threw out her hand. "I don't know why his name is in the book, Gray. I don't know the man. Unless..." Her mind came up with a possible explanation.

"Unless what?"

"Fran had the book."

His eyes reflected his understanding. "What are you saying? That she wrote his name in there?"

"Maybe. It's no secret she doesn't like me."

He grunted in disbelief. "You lie to me and now you're trying to tell me you're being framed?"

"I'm trying to offer an explanation."

His posture went rigid. He moved to the laptop and swiveled it toward her so she could read the screen.

"You want to explain something?" he yelled. "Explain this."

She stared at the screen, and it felt like a bucket of ice had dropped on her head. It appeared to be an article on a news site. The headline read in bold print, "Lovers Killed by Playboy's Curse." She could make out the name of the writer. It was Ernest Demille.

She felt frozen in place. "Gray, I..."

He slammed the screen shut. "You what?"

"I had nothing to do with that."

"How much did they pay you?"

Her own anger swirled. "Nothing. I didn't do that. I didn't tell anyone."

"What were you writing the whole time you were staying in my house, before the fire? You told me you were writing the article."

Her mind flew back. "I was journaling."

He scowled. "Journaling?"

"It wasn't an article. I was simply journaling about my experiences, my feelings, my emotions. It helps me when I'm working with someone. Sometimes dealing with another person's pain affects me and I've learned that it helps to write it down. It helps clear my head and clear blockages. That's all it is, though."

"Stop lying!"

"I'm not lying!"

He kicked out at the chair; it slid across the floor and hit the wall with a crack. They both breathed hard, trying to rein in their emotions. Gray turned and faced the wall, and she waited to see what he would do. She felt the tears in her eyes, but she wouldn't let them fall.

When he seemed to gain control of his emotions, he turned back to face her. "Tell me the truth."

She was at a loss for words. She didn't know what he wanted to hear.

He seemed to understand her confusion, and his eyes softened. "Just tell me, Gillian. You say you came to help me? I can't deny that you did. You risked your life for me. But why lie? Why lie about your family? About where you're from? Something doesn't add up here. Who were the man and woman who helped you? Why are you really here?"

She felt his struggle. She'd had no plans to tell him about her situation, but she knew she'd come to a point where she no longer had a choice. If she wanted him, she'd have to tell him everything. But to tell him could mean losing him, anyway. She sighed and prayed she was doing the right thing.

Her hands clenched, she pushed forward. "There are things about me that are different."

"What things?"

"I'm..." She searched for the right words. "I'm different. So are my brother and sister."

He acted surprised. "Your brother and sister? Were they the ones who helped you?"

"Yes."

He seemed to relax as she talked. "Okay. Why are you different?"

"I'm not supposed to say."

His shoulders bunched. "Why not?"

"It's been advised that I...we...not tell anyone about us."

"Who advised you?"

Her nerves frayed, and her fingers would have trembled if her hands weren't clasped together. She knew she should stop, but she wanted him to understand. There was a connection between the two of them she knew meant something, and she didn't want to keep secrets from him. She was just as scared to tell him the truth, though. "My dad."

"Your dad?"

"Yes."

"Why can't you tell anyone?"

"Because...who I am could cause problems."

"Your dad told you this?"

"Yes."

"Your dad that's in the military?"

She'd forgotten she'd told him that. She bit her lip.

"He's not in the military, is he?"

She tried to stay calm, but her heart hammered. "He is, but not in the one you think."

His face reflected his confusion. "Is he from another country?"

She swallowed. "No. Not another country."

She could feel his uncertainty. "Then where?"

She clenched her jaw. She stared at him and considered just walking out the door and never looking back. It's what her family would expect her to do. But she couldn't do it. She made her vocal cords respond. "He's...he's from another planet."

She waited as her words hit him. He did exactly what she expected. He laughed. "Oh, come on, Gillian." His face froze when he saw she was serious. "You don't expect me to believe that, do you?"

She took a deep breath and released it. "No, I don't. Doesn't mean it's not true."

He continued to stare at her wide-eyed. "Do you honestly expect me to believe that your dad is from another planet?"

She shifted nervously. She knew how big of a risk this was, but she kept going. She'd jumped in and now she had to convince him. "He visited many years ago. Long story short, he met my mom. They fell in love. She got pregnant and had triplets. Royce, Eve, and me. Dad disappeared after the birth. We saw him every few years. I don't remember how or when I knew I was different, but I was. He finally told us who we were three years ago. He came back because we were all about to go through a transformation. He called it a Shift. He had to tell us who we were then. He couldn't keep it a secret anymore. Things were about to change for us, and we had to go into hiding."

Her body was a bundle of nerves, and the words rushed out of her. "All three of us were very ill. I don't remember much about it other than I felt like hell. When we finally got through it, we realized things were different. We could do, feel, and sense things we'd never experienced before. Royce is very strong and can move objects with his mind and cloak himself. Eve can read objects and animals. I am intuitive and empathic and can read people. We all have various abilities, which we've all tried to adjust to over the last few years. And because of who we are, we have to be careful. If anyone were to know we existed, we could be at risk."

She stopped her explanation and waited for him to respond, but all he did was stand and stare at her. She waited him out, intent on giving him time to adjust to what she'd said. She watched as his wide eyes narrowed and his posture shrank, and she felt him close up like a snail in his shell.

"Get out," he said.

His response scared her. "Gray. Please. You have to believe me."

He stood like a stone in the room. "I want you to leave. You've said enough."

She took a step toward him, but he backed off. "Don't do this."

His face constricted, and his voice rose. "Don't do what? You're standing there telling me that your father is some sort of alien who came down here and slept with a woman and had three alien children?" He shot his hands out. "What am I supposed to say to that?" A wave of outrage projected from him. "Your father is a nutcase, Gillian. He did a number on you and your family, and sadly, you believed him."

"Gray..."

He wouldn't let her speak. "And you show up in my life thinking you're going to save me from my demons by telling me this crazy story about how you have abilities, which is how you know things about me. You tell me you're a reporter when you're not. You say you're not a source, but an article comes out about me, anyway. A man's name is in your book that you say shouldn't be there." He shook his head at her. "What am I supposed to believe, Gillian? That you're telling the truth or that you're lying to me to protect yourself, thinking I'm stupid enough to believe this ridiculous story?"

Her emotions were swirling. She fought back tears, but one escaped and trickled down her cheek to be wiped away. "I'm telling the truth."

He appeared unaffected by her pain. "I don't know what you're doing. I wish I did." He paused, as if trying to decide what to do next. "All I know is that you came into my life, and I fell for you. You rid me of my curse. I'm grateful for that. But now..."

"What?"

He swallowed. "Now I wonder why."

A sob threatened to erupt, but she bit it back. "Grayson..."

"Why risk yourself for a man you hardly know?"

"I know you."

"Was it part of the story? Was that the plan all along?"

She shook her head in confusion, and she swiped at another tear. "What are you talking about?"

"The curse wasn't enough? You thought you could get paid more if you risked yourself in the process and caught the killer?"

She shook her head. "No!"

"And now, to add insult to injury, you're adding that you're some sort of gifted alien that found and helped me? Is that the next headline? Playboy Curse Ended by Benevolent Extraterrestrial?"

The shock of his assumptions rippled through her. "That's ridiculous. I never..."

His body shook with fury. "This whole thing is ridiculous!" he yelled at her and she jumped. "You're in so deep you don't know how to get out. You're lying, Gillian! This whole thing is one big joke on me. Well, guess what? Joke's over. Get your stuff and get out of my house."

Her tears ran down her face. "Gray...please."

He ignored her. "Now." He stood frozen, watching her cry. "I'll wait on the porch. You know the way out." He walked to the back door, his body looking wooden. He reached the door and turned back. "If you're still here when I come back, I'll call Kenny and have you removed from the property." He stepped out onto the porch and slammed the door shut behind him.

Gillian stood like a paralyzed animal in the room. Tears dripped down her cheeks and trailed down her neck. Max sat up and stared at her. His head moved between the back door and her, as if he debated which side to take. Finally, he stood and trotted to his dog door and slipped through it, apparently choosing to stick with the hand that fed him. A sob escaped her, and she covered her mouth with her hand. Her frozen body shook, and she forced herself to break free from her trance-like state. She took a first step, and once she did, she found she couldn't move fast enough. She ran upstairs, grabbed her things, and stuffed them in her overnight bag. She went back downstairs, threw her laptop and notebooks in her workbag, found her purse, and flipped it over her shoulder. Nose running and wiping at her face, she walked to the front door, opened it, and left.

CHAPTER TWENTY-FIVE

THE RAIN SPLATTERED AGAINST the windowpane, the hard drops sounding like pellets of tiny stones as they hit the clear surface. Gray stared out over the water, watching the large waves hit and crash on the shore. The storm was finally moving inland. Many had left the island, knowing that most low-lying areas would flood and that any beachfront property could suffer potential damage from the wind and storm surge. He had no intention of leaving, though. If the storm ended up taking his house and washing him away, then it would be a relief. It would end the nightmare of the last two days where he'd done nothing but think of her.

He turned from the window and sat down at his breakfast table. As he'd done countless times already, he thought back to his confrontation with Gillian. The story she'd told him clattered through his brain, and he clenched his eyes shut at the memory. The anger built again, but at the same time, he remembered her face. Tears had streamed down her cheeks as if she'd actually believed what she'd told him. His emotions raged at the memory of her standing there, lying to him. An untouched glass of water sat on the table; he picked it up and threw it. The water sprayed out and the sound of the glass shattering against the wall gave him a momentary sense of satisfaction, but it didn't last and his despondent state returned.

After she'd left, he'd tried to drink himself into a stupor, but the liquor had not had the desired effect. He'd ended up in the bathroom, ridding himself of the alcohol but without the benefit of the drunken haze he'd hoped for. His body, for some reason, rejected the attempt at numbing himself, and all he'd done is made himself sick.

He thought of their time together after the hospital. The feel of her soft skin against his, her boisterous laugh, her assertiveness in bed, how she'd said his name when he'd touched and aroused her, the sounds she'd made as he'd moved against her, her cries of pleasure when they'd both found release in each other's arms.

He shook his head, trying to clear it, but his body responded to the memories and he cursed himself for thinking of her.

Thinking of the curse, he considered that today was the third day after they'd slept together. Some part of him gave thanks that he no longer had to worry about her safety. She'd given him that much. But at what price? He felt just as miserable now that she was gone. He wondered again if he'd done the right thing, but then angrily chastised himself. Her betrayal could not be forgiven. Maybe she had unwittingly fallen in love with him, but that could not make up for her lies, and he couldn't forgive her, no matter how much he missed her.

The phone rang, startling him. He read the display and saw Cooper's name. He'd avoided all phone calls since Gillian had left. He'd talked to Cooper only once, only to tell him he didn't want to talk about it and to leave him alone for a while. Cooper had given him the space but apparently didn't want to wait any longer. It was the third time he'd called that day. Gray sighed and reluctantly answered it.

"Hello?"

Cooper's cheery voice greeted him. "There you are. I was beginning to think you'd gone for a swim in these waves with no plans to return."

Gray shut his eyes and thought of Gillian again. "No. I'm still on dry land."

"You okay?"

Gray could hear the worry in Coop's voice despite his attempts at levity. "I've been better."

There was silence on the line before Cooper spoke again. "You want to talk about it?"

Gray sighed. "What's to talk about?"

"Oh, I don't know," said Cooper. "Maybe the fact that you threw the woman you love out of the house?"

"I'm not in love with her."

"Yes, you are."

Gray pinched the bridge of his nose. "Maybe I was, but it's over now."

"You sure about that?"

The statement surprised Gray. "What do you mean? You think I should gloss over the fact that she's been lying to me? And the fact that she sold my story to some slimy gossip magazine?"

Cooper didn't answer at first, but Gray knew the wheels were turning. "The article wasn't that bad," he said.

"Excuse me?"

"It's not any worse than any of the other stupid shit they've printed about you. It's not *Time* magazine."

Grayson couldn't hide his shock. "Cooper, what are you saying? Are you taking her side?"

"No, I'm on your side. But I saw you with her and you were happy. If there's a chance that you two could patch things up, then I'm all for it."

Grayson had not told him about the other side of Gillian's story. "That's not going to happen."

"You're angry right now. That's understandable. But that will fade in time."

"I can't go back to her."

"I admit what she did sucked, but I saw the way she looked at you when you two were together. No matter what her initial motives were, she fell for you. She loves you."

Gray shut his eyes. "Stop it, Cooper."

"Stop what?"

"Stop trying to fix it."

Cooper didn't back down. "I'm telling you what I think. I'm your friend. That's my right. I've known you too long. You're stubborn and proud, but that won't last and it sure as hell won't keep you warm at night. You're finally free of this damn curse and you've found a woman you love. You're pissed. I get it. But at some point, you're going to look back at this moment with either remorse or gratitude, and I'd rather it be gratitude."

Gray listened and didn't know what to say. Could he get over it? Maybe if she hadn't told him she was the daughter of an alien visitor. Perhaps he could have found a way around her lies. At the heart of it all, he felt that her motives were genuine, and she had wanted to help. He couldn't help but remember Stuart with his knife at Gillian's throat. Nobody risks that without a very good reason. He shook his head in frustration when he realized what he was doing. He knew what her reason was—a bigger payday. He cursed himself for defending her. "She's not who you think she is."

Cooper kept trying. "How bad can she be? Do you really think you can't trust her? You actually think she was the source?"

Gray perked up. "You think she wasn't?"

"Come on, Gray. How hard would it be to get that story? You told me yourself that all she had to do was a little research in order to learn that your girlfriends had died. The story was there the whole time. She was just the first one determined enough to look for it. If she could do it, then so could someone else. She wasn't the only one who knew the story, either."

Gray sat straight at that. "Are you saying that one of our group may have leaked it?"

"I'm not saying they did it deliberately. Hell, we were all at my party. We'd all had a lot to drink. Maybe someone opened their mouth to the wrong person."

"I doubt it," said Gray. "Besides, it doesn't explain Demille's name in her book, or how he knows her. I'd call that a smoking gun."

"Maybe." Cooper's tone suggested doubt.

"What does that mean?" asked Gray.

"What if she's telling the truth?"

Grayson's jaw dropped. "Do you think she's telling the truth?"

"What if she is?"

"Cooper..."

"I think she is."

Gray snorted in disbelief. "You can't be serious."

Cooper took a second before he asked his next question. "How long have you known me?"

The inquiry took Gray off guard. "What are you talking about?"

Cooper insisted. "How long have you known me?"

Gray's shoulders shrunk, and he tried to sound less defensive. "A long time."

"Have I ever steered you wrong?"

Gray thought back through their years of friendship. He had to admit his friend had always had a reliable radar when it came to people they could trust. It had served them well in their business, and Grayson could remember more than once when Cooper had warned him to back off from certain people, men and women alike.

He didn't answer.

"Gray?"

Gray grunted. "Okay, so you may have helped me out in the past."

Cooper's voice rose. "May have? I warned you about that lousy assistant of yours, Martha, didn't I? And Brimford, the doorman who was stealing from you? Oh, and let's not forget about Gloria. Did you honestly think that a woman who jumps out of cakes could step in as your legal counsel?"

Grayson remembered that incident. "She had a law degree."

"From the University of Barbados, you idiot."

Grayson couldn't argue with him. "All right. I get your point."

"The only point here is the one on top of your head."

Gray shook his head and tried to get back on the subject. "So, if I'm stupid enough to go along with this theory of yours, and Gillian didn't know Demille, then how is his name in her book? How come he knows her?"

"That I can't answer."

Grayson groaned. "Why do I talk to you?"

"Because I'm the only thread you've got to sanity right now. And you need me."

Grayson couldn't deny that. "It doesn't add up."

"So do some of your own investigating. She's done all of her homework on you. Why don't you do some on her?"

The idea took him by surprise. "You mean check out her story?"

He could hear Cooper sigh on the line. "No, I mean call the papers and tell them how mean she was to you." Gray could picture the look of impatience on Cooper's face. "Yes, that's exactly what I mean. Fran did some digging. Why can't you? You gonna let her be your only source of info? You know she'd love to see Gillian out of the picture. Are you going to trust her word over Gillian's?"

For the first time since Gillian left, he felt a flare of hope. Maybe Gillian was telling the truth. Maybe there was another reason why Demille's name was in her book. Just as quickly, though, he thought about her other story. The one about her father. How in the hell would he research that?

He considered Cooper's idea. What could it hurt to do a little digging? "Does Nelson still work at the firm?"

"Our in-house investigator?" said Cooper. "Now you're talking. You want me to call him?"

Grayson hesitated. Visions of Gillian naked in his bed made him shiver, and he answered before he could talk himself out of it. "No, I'll call him. Give me his number."

He made up his mind that, before he made any more assumptions, he would find out all he could about Miss Gillian Fletcher.

· · · • · · • · · ·

At the other end of the island, Gillian stared out her hotel window, hearing the patter against the glass as the rain fell in a downpour. She'd returned to her room at the hotel after her argument with Grayson and had not left since. She'd shut her phone off and had ordered room service, but ate little.

She studied her reflection in the rain-spattered glass and made out her blurry features. Her eyes were puffy, and her nose was red. She'd showered that morning after finally getting upright. She'd been buried under the covers for two solid days, rising only to answer the door to room service or to use the bathroom. Her depression consumed her. The look in Gray's eyes when she'd told him who she was would not leave her mind. Dismay, disbelief, anger, and betrayal had all been conveyed through his look, and she'd felt every one of them like a spear in her chest. He hadn't believed her. Worse, he'd thought she was crazy. She'd endured some difficult periods in her life, but this was the worst.

She recalled the times she'd said goodbye to her father, knowing that every time she did so meant it might be the last. The recent separation between her and her siblings had also been excruciating. They'd all been so close growing up. But after their Shift, their father warned them not to spend too much time together. Their shared abilities and combined energy could attract the wrong people, and so they'd had to separate and spend much of their time apart, although they talked often on the phone.

It was at that time that she'd begun to answer the calls for help. It had been an outlet for her—a way to connect with the world in a way that made her feel useful and needed. And the results were the best part of the job. The people she'd helped had found their way to happier and fuller lives.

It gave her a sense of purpose and duty, and the more she did it, despite her family's objections, the more important it became to her. She'd not planned for Grayson Steele, though. He'd been just another person who'd popped onto her radar screen. When her brother had advised her to lay low for a while, she'd almost ignored Gray's call. She'd been told that it was best to take a break in between assignments to ensure her own safety. Her brother believed the longer she remained in the open, the more at risk she became. But Grayson's call was insistent, and the more she ignored it, the stronger it grew. Then she'd gone to the beach at the crime scene. After that, she knew she could not walk away. She thought back to that day and wondered if that had been the moment she'd fallen in love with him.

She shook her head and pushed back another round of tears. Sitting on the bed, she dressed herself and checked the time. Her plane was due to leave in three hours, although she suspected that because of the weather, it would be delayed. The wind whipped against the window, and she could hear the crash of the surf. Due to the storm, most of the hotel was empty. Her bag sat on the floor, only partially packed. Her mind drifted, and it occurred to her that today was day three. It was the third day since the morning she'd woken up next to Gray and found herself pulled by some force she still didn't understand. She still felt it in her bones, and his absence was agonizing. It was as if her body had a mind of its own and no amount of conflict would convince it otherwise.

She smiled sadly when she realized the irony of her situation. She'd set out and succeeded at her task, but now she felt more miserable than ever. She'd saved him from his curse but now found herself embroiled in her own, knowing that because of who she was, she could never have the man she loved.

Despite her attempts to stop crying, another tear escaped and trickled down her face. Her phone sat by her bedside, and she considered turning it on. She no doubt had messages. Her mother certainly would have called and likely Eve too. She knew Royce would be furious; she wasn't ready to have that conversation. It would be wise to let them know, though, that she was okay. They probably knew what had happened. And if they didn't, they would know soon.

A knock on the door startled her, and she wiped her cheek. Grabbing a tissue, she blew her nose when the knock came again. She reached out to see if she could pick up who it might be, but she felt nothing familiar. Standing up from the bed, she faced the door, and the knock came again.

She cleared her throat. "Who is it?"

A male voice responded. "Concierge, ma'am. The phones are down. We're trying to contact all our guests."

She relaxed and caught a brief glimpse of her reflection in the glass of a framed picture on the wall. Eyes still puffy and nose red, she reluctantly walked to the door and opened it.

CHAPTER TWENTY-SIX

THE PHONE RANG, AND Gray picked it up. "Hello?"

"Gray? It's Nelson."

"That was fast. I only called you two hours ago."

"You and Coop hired me for a reason."

"Now I remember why. Did you learn anything?"

"A few things. Initial search shows no city called Shepton in AZ."

"I know that much, Nelson."

"But there is a Sheldon."

"Sheldon?"

"Yes."

"So? Why look at Sheldon?"

Nelson grunted on the phone, and Gray heard a shuffling of papers. "Because, in my experience, people who are trying to hide something, if they're smart, stick as close to the truth as they can."

"Did you find something in Sheldon?"

"Triplets."

"What?"

"Triplets. Royce, Eve, and Gillian Fletcher. Birth certificate shows they were all born at the local hospital on May 3rd. Mother is Lillian. Father is Carson."

Gray sat up. "You found them?"

"Yup."

Gray sighed. "She wasn't lying about her family. That's something, at least."

"Sure as shit is."

"Anything else?" asked Gray.

"Can't find anything about this Carson Fletcher yet. I'm still looking though. Mom used to work as a teacher at the local high school. After she gave birth, though, she dropped out of sight."

"Did they move?"

"Probably. Don't know where. It's going to take some more digging."

"I figured. I'm surprised you found out this much so soon."

"There's more."

Gray listened as Nelson bit into what sounded like an apple and made chewing noises. "Did you get a hold of Demille?" he asked.

"I did."

"What did he say?"

"Said he had a source."

Grayson deflated. He braced to hear whatever Nelson had to say. "Who?"

"He wouldn't tell me."

"Damn. Did you do what I asked?"

"Yup. I offered him money."

"He didn't budge?"

"Nope. Said he was protecting his informant."

Gray groaned. "Well, it was worth a shot."

"Something interesting though."

"What?"

"He kept referring to the source as a 'he.'"

Gray held still. "A 'he?'"

"Yup."

"You think he did it on purpose?" Gray asked. "To throw you off?"

"Demille?" asked Nelson. "Guy's an idiot. He'd fall off a flat surface. He didn't think twice about it. I'd bet money his source is male."

Something bloomed in Gray, and his heart thumped. "You're sure about that?"

"Hundred percent. I've been doing this too long."

Gray rested his forehead in his hand. "Thanks, Nelson."

"Oh, but I'm not done. I'm just getting to the good part."

Gray popped his head up. "What do you mean?" Gray heard him take another bite and more chewing ensued.

"That birth certificate," said Nelson.

"What about it?" asked Gray.

"Had a doctor's name on it."

"Yeah. So?"

"I called him."

Gray stilled. "You did? Did you get a hold of him?"

"Damn straight. He works in Phoenix now, but I tracked him down."

"No shit. What did he say?"

"He was a little hesitant at first. Didn't want to talk about his patients."

"Did you convince him?"

"He was more open to the offer of monetary reward than Demille."

"Excellent."

"Agreed."

"What did he say? Did he remember them?"

Gray heard a drawer slam shut. "Oh, he remembered them all right."

"He did?"

Nelson's voice pitched lower, as if he didn't want anyone else to hear. "Said it was like nothing he'd ever seen before."

"What was like nothing he'd seen before?"

"The birth. The delivery."

"The birth? Why?"

There was a brief silence on the line before Nelson spoke again. "Said there were complications."

"What complications?"

"Baby one came out fine. It was a boy. Baby two did okay, but the mom was showing signs of weakness and blood loss."

"Baby two?"

He heard more paper rustling. "Yeah. According to the cert, the second child's name was Eve."

"Okay," said Gray. "What happened then?"

"This is where he wanted to stop talking, but I added a few more Ben Franklins to keep him going."

"Good. What did he say?"

"Apparently, dad was in the delivery room. When baby three...I believe her name was..." Gray heard more rustling, "Gillian. Yeah. Right. Gillian. She had the cord wrapped around her neck. Baby was in distress."

Gray bounced his knee. "What happened?"

"Problem was, mom was in distress too. She'd started to bleed out."

"Shit."

"Exactly. Doc had his hands full. He handed baby Gillian to a nurse to deal with the cord and he tried to stop mom's bleeding. She went into shock, though, and her heart stopped. He performed CPR and brought her back. Meanwhile, the nurse had got the cord off baby Gillian's neck, but the baby was blue and unresponsive."

"What?"

"He tried to resuscitate her, but it was too late."

"Excuse me?" asked Gray.

"Gillian died."

Gray's mind went blank. "She what?"

"According to the doctor, the baby died, and mom wasn't much better."

"That can't be right, Nelson. You've missed something."

"Let me finish. The dad was distraught. Asked the doctor and nurses to leave."

"Leave where?" asked Gray.

"The delivery room. The doc agreed to give him a few minutes with his baby girl. They took the other two babies and put them in incubators, made sure mom was stable, and left baby Gillian in his arms. They stepped out for just a few minutes."

Grayson felt the hair rise on his skin. "What happened then?"

"Said there was some sort of electrical surge. The lights on the floor dimmed and then went out. But they flicked back on just as fast. At the same time, the doc said he saw a flash of light come from inside the delivery room."

"A flash of light?"

"Yeah. He ran back in and couldn't believe what he saw."

Grayson gripped the phone. "What did he see?"

"Dad was holding baby Gillian, who was alive and well."

"Wait a minute. What are you saying?"

"This is the doctor's story," said Nelson. "Not mine."

"Are you saying the baby was dead, but then it wasn't?"

"Yes. And the mom was sitting up in bed, looking healthier than the doctor."

Gray didn't know what to think. "You believe him?"

"Hey. If you want me to check out the doc's back story, I can. But he sounded pretty coherent and reliable. Doesn't mean he was stable back then, though. He may have been on some acid trip for all we know."

Grayson stared off. Gillian's words rippled through him. *He's from another planet.* "Yeah," he said. "I hear you."

"So now you know what I know. Take it or leave it."

Gray sat back and tried to make sense of the story. "Thanks."

"You want me to keep digging? See if I can find more info on dad?"

Grayson somehow knew that whatever research Nelson did, he would find nothing. "No," he said. "That's good for now."

"I'm here if you need me. Just don't forget to pay me."

Grayson chuckled. "You're worth every penny, Nelson."

"That's what all the girls say."

Grayson heard Nelson laugh just as the line went dead. He put the phone down and stared, trying to think. Had the man actually healed his wife and brought his newborn daughter back to life? He scoffed at himself. Was he really buying into Gillian's story? How could he? In all likelihood, Gillian had been alive the whole time and dad had just given her one swift slap on the back. And mom had perhaps not been as bad off as the doctor suggested. He shook his head at the thought. The whole thing was preposterous.

A gust of wind shook the windows. Max popped his head up from his slumber on the floor and woofed.

Gray looked down at him. "What's wrong, boy?"

Max jumped up and barked fervently just as the doorbell rang. Gray had not seen him that animated since he'd been a puppy. Frowning at his dog, he stood and walked to the front hall, wondering who would be at his door in this weather. The remaining reporters standing outside his gate hoping to get a photo or a comment had dispersed when the rain had begun to fall. He stood at the door, waiting to see if whoever it was would leave, when three loud bangs sounded against the wood and Grayson jumped. Max barked harder.

Before he could even react, the bolt on his entry slid into the open position, the knob turned, and the door flew open. Two figures stood at the entrance, male and female, the wind whipping at their backs. Their hair and clothes were dripping wet, and they both looked as if they'd been waiting outside for hours.

Gray reached for his cell phone, preparing to call for help, but when he put it up to his ear, it was dead. He looked at the display. The batteries, which had been recently charged, were now dead. He watched as the two people entered his home and shut the door behind them. As soon as the door closed, Max went quiet, and so did the house. The only thing that could be heard was the rain on the roof and the howling of the wind. The intruders stared at him, and Grayson didn't move. The man was huge, easily six foot four or more. His biceps almost split his slim cut long-sleeved shirt and his chest and shoulders bunched as water trickled down his face. The woman was smaller, but her clothes were just as tight. She wore snug jeans that sat low on her waist and a tight, low cut V-neck shirt. The jacket she wore was zipped up to just below her breasts, emphasizing her narrow waist and ample cleavage. Water dripped from her neckline and down the front of her shirt. Gray recognized her auburn hair, almond eyes, high cheekbones, and alabaster skin. It was Nurse Eve, and the big man was undoubtedly her brother, Royce—the man who had directed Gray in the fire and Kenny in the hospital. Speechless, Gray realized Gillian's siblings were standing in his front foyer.

Royce finally broke the quiet. "Where is she?"

Gray attempted to think. "Who?"

Royce made an irritated face and spoke to Eve. "I told you he was an idiot."

Eve stood staring at Gray, but she answered her brother. "It's not me you have to convince."

Gray finally pulled his thoughts together. "Gillian?"

The sound of his sister's name irritated Royce even more. He walked right up to Grayson, arms crossed. Gray tried not to be intimidated. "Is she here, Steele?"

Gray looked up at the man that loomed over him. "No," he answered. "She's not."

Royce didn't seem convinced. He scrutinized Gray, and his face looked as hard as Gray's granite countertops. "You slept with her, didn't you?"

Gray hadn't expected that question, but didn't have to answer it because Eve stepped in first. "Whoa, there, Royce. Let's watch the questions. What Gillian does with this man is none of your business."

Royce's voice boomed. "None of my business! You know the repercussions if he's—"

Eve was unfazed by his anger. "I know the repercussions. You don't have to remind me. But it's unavoidable. At some point, it was going to happen."

"Damn it, Eve. We...she has to be more careful."

"This is Gillian, Royce. Since when is she careful?"

Confused, Grayson finally spoke when he had the chance. "You two want to tell me what the hell is going on here?" They both turned. For the first time, he saw the worry on their faces. "What's wrong?"

Royce hesitated, as if debating whether to answer, but then he turned away. "Let's go. He can't help us."

Gray felt something cold crawl through his stomach. "What's wrong?" he asked again. "Where's Gillian?"

Eve addressed her brother. "We can't go. We don't know where else to look. He likely knows who took her."

Grayson's alarms sounded. "Took her? Did someone take Gillian?"

They both continued to ignore him. "We have to be cautious," said Royce to Eve.

"If we keep being cautious. We could lose her. If she's in the wrong hands..."

Royce's granite face softened. "If she's in the wrong hands, he sure as hell can't help." He nodded his head in Grayson's direction.

Gray felt his impatience rise. "Is someone going to fill me in here? Where the hell is Gillian? Is she in trouble?"

"That's not the point," said Eve to Royce. "We need to find her first. She's been hanging out with him. If someone's been watching her, then he likely knows who it is."

"Watching her?" asked Gray. "Who the hell is watching her? And why are Gillian's brother and sister in my house?"

His knowledge of who they were got their attention. "You know who we are?" asked Royce.

Gray almost backed away again at his intense gaze. "You're Royce and Eve. She told me about you."

Royce's face turned dark. "Dammit. When I find her, I'm going to wring her neck."

"No, you're not," said Eve. She spoke to Gray. "What else did she tell you?"

Gray realized they were all still standing in the foyer. "Why don't we move into the den? We can talk there." He walked away and waited. They stood for a few seconds, but then followed him.

Once in the den, none of them sat. "What else did she tell you?" asked Eve again.

Gray debated how much to say. "She told me she had siblings. I knew she had someone looking out for her." He looked at Royce. "You were in the fire and told me where to find Gillian. You also told Kenny where to go in the hospital." He eyed Eve. "You were Cooper's nurse. Told me to go to the twelfth floor."

"So you get a gold star," said Royce. "But I want to know what else she said, and what happened after the hospital. Why isn't she here?"

"What happened?" asked Eve.

Gray debated whether to tell them everything, but he sensed it was important to be upfront with them. "After the hospital, she stayed here with me."

"Did you take advantage of her?" asked Royce, taking a step forward. "After all she did for you, I'll kick you through a wall if you hurt her."

Gray stood his ground. "No. I did not take advantage of her. She was as willing as me, if not more so."

Royce and Eve exchanged glances. "What happened then?" asked Eve.

Gray's confidence deflated. "I found out who she really was."

"What?" asked Eve.

Royce's brows furrowed.

"She's not a reporter. Everything she told me was a lie. The place she was born didn't exist. The magazine she said she worked for didn't know her. The name of a reporter who printed my story was in her address book. I thought she was a source, getting paid to get the details, and the reporter confirmed it."

They both stared with wide eyes. "That's what she told you?" asked Eve.

Gray spoke before he thought. "That, and that she was from another planet. Or at least her dad was."

Royce and Eve made no reaction except to stand there.

"I didn't believe her, of course," he added. "It's completely ridiculous. I..." He remembered Gillian's stricken face as she stood in his den.

"You what?" asked Royce, his voice deepening.

"I..." Gray felt the first pangs of guilt and pushed them back. "I kicked her out."

"You what?" Eve asked. She stepped closer.

"You kicked her out?" Royce's muscles bunched even more. "How was she when she left?"

Gray swallowed. "She was crying."

Royce moved fast across the room and grabbed Gray by the throat. He shoved him backward until Gray hit the wall hard behind him. Royce held him by the neck and squeezed hard enough to constrict his air flow. "I'm going to kill you, Steele."

"Royce!" shouted Eve. She ran up to the two men. "Stop it. Let him go."

Gray gripped Royce's wrist to ease the hold the man had on his neck, but it felt like moving hardened concrete. He struggled to pull air into his lungs.

"Royce!" Eve shouted again, and Royce finally eased off. He let go, and Gray bent over, sucked in a deep breath, and rubbed at his neck.

"You bastard," said Royce. "Gilli couldn't betray anyone if she tried. She came to help you, risked her life twice for you, and you think she's some vermin's source?" Royce stepped back as Gray tried to recover. "What the hell does she see in you? I swear to God, if Eve wasn't here right now and Gilli didn't love you, I'd take you outside and drown you."

Gray pulled himself up after regaining his composure. Seeing Royce's angry face, he spoke roughly. "I know what she did for me. And I love her too. You think I wanted to kick her out?" He waited and took another breath to calm himself. "But it's the alien thing that did it for me. She thinks your father is from another planet. She thinks all three of you have special abilities. It's why she says she showed up here in the first place. That I called to her, and she answered." He dropped his hand from his neck. "What am I supposed to do with that? It's crazy. She's bought into this whole story, and she thinks it's true."

Royce stared at him and then at Eve. He backed off and walked away. Gray stepped back from the wall. "I didn't want to hurt her. But I was so angry. I thought she was lying to me. Maybe I could have gotten past that, but then when the alien thing came up..."

"Sit down," said Royce.

Gray stopped where he stood. He had no interest in sitting. "What?"

"I said sit down," repeated Royce. He made eye contact with Eve briefly before looking back at Gray.

"I don't want to sit down. I want to know what the hell is going on. Why are you here? Where is Gillian?"

The energy in the room electrified, and a heaviness filled the air when the couch suddenly slid from its location near the fireplace and right into the back of Gray's legs, causing him to fall backwards onto it.

"I said sit down," said Royce.

Everything went silent as Gray froze and looked at the couch, and then back to where it had been. Eve remained quiet. He tried to comprehend how the couch had moved on its own. "What the hell?" he asked. He looked back at Gillian's siblings. "How did...?" Gillian's words rang in his ears. *Royce is very strong. He can move objects.*

"Listen," said Eve, eyeing Royce for confirmation. "Gillian told you the truth. We are who she said." She paused, as if considering her next words. "We're unique."

Gray barely heard her. "How did this couch move?" he asked. Max jumped up next to him and sat beside him, unfazed. He'd been quiet since the front door had closed. The coffee table slid next and worked its way up to the couch, untouched. Gray stared in shock.

"The same way that moved," Royce said.

Gray's mind wouldn't work.

Eve came up next to him. "We are, in fact, the children of a man from a planet called Eudora, Gray. Gilli told the truth. We all have abilities. It's how I know you're wearing red boxer briefs right now."

Gray dropped his jaw. "What?" he asked. "How do you know that?"

"Because Max told me. He saw you get dressed. He also prefers the wet food you used to give him. Not the dry."

Max cocked his head at him as if to say, *Finally...*

Gray shook his head, and Gillian's voice popped into his head again. *Eve can read objects and animals.* He couldn't absorb it. "What are you telling me?"

Eve crossed her arms. "I'm telling you that Gillian didn't lie to you. Well, except for being a reporter. But she wasn't anyone's source and she can indeed read people. Most people, at least. We're all still getting our bearings as to what exactly we are all capable of."

Gray tried to stand but felt woozy and sat back down again. "I don't believe this." It was all he could think to say.

Royce stepped up next to Eve. "Well, you better start believing because if what we think is true, we don't have much time."

Gray lifted his head. "Time for what?"

Royce stared soberly at him. "To save our sister's life."

CHAPTER TWENTY-SEVEN

A BOOM OF THUNDER penetrated Gillian's senses. The vibration pulsed through the hard ground. The sounds around her began to shift from a ringing in her ears into recognizable noises. The rain pounded on the roof and the whiny sound of wind whistled through a crack or an opening somewhere nearby. Her head throbbed, and she opened her eyes but closed them just as quickly when the hazy light felt blinding and everything looked out of focus. Cold seeped into her bones, and she realized her clothes were wet. A groan escaped her when she moved her head and a flash of pain traveled down her back. Her midsection flared with heat. She had no idea where she was nor how she had got there. Her fingers felt the chill from the floor, and she opened her eyes again long enough to see that she appeared to be lying on polished concrete. Another crack of thunder made her head ache; she shut her eyes once more. She tried to think back to the last thing she could remember. The hotel. She'd been in the hotel and someone had knocked on the door. A brief flash echoed through her mind of her reaching for the doorknob and then everything went blank. The rain came down harder outside. She wondered if she was dreaming. Another attempt at movement made her groan again.

The sound of footsteps caused her to open her eyes. Her vision was still blurry, but she could make out the shape of what looked like a man approaching her. He sat down in a metal chair beside her. It squeaked when it took his weight. Knowing she was in trouble, her heart began to thump. This man had taken her and now she was lying on the ground in a strange place, unable to move, and hurting from head to toe. She made no effort to speak, and she blinked again to clear her vision.

The man, seeing her awake, spoke. "Welcome back, Miss Fletcher. How are you feeling?"

Gillian recognized the voice, but her muddled head couldn't place it. Although she wanted to move, she was too scared to try.

"I'm sure you're wondering where you are and why I'm here." She heard the creak of the chair as he sat back. "I'm happy to answer any questions you may have."

Talking seemed like a monumental effort. Her midsection flared, and she bit back another moan.

"The pain will pass. I had to hit you with a major jolt, I'm afraid. I couldn't risk you fighting back and making a scene. I was unsure of how strong you might be." The chair creaked again. "Thankfully, you're still new at this. Guess good ol' dad hasn't had the chance to teach you."

At the mention of her father, she stirred and tried to push up, but she had no strength. Her head pulsed in time with her heartbeat, and she took a deep breath to calm herself.

The man kept talking. "I can tell you are curious. Wondering who I am, are you?"

She swallowed and tried to speak but it came out as a whisper. "What do you want?" Her vision spun. She still couldn't see him clearly.

"I'll tell you what I want. I want you, your brother, and your sister." She saw his blurry form lean in toward her. "I have to admit. You three were smart to stay away from each other. I expected this to be any easy job, but you made it a fun challenge."

She tried to shift into a more comfortable position, but it hurt to move. "But I figured if I found one of you, then I'd find the other two." He paused. "I'd hoped that after the whole hospital scene and subsequent chaos that you would go home and lead me right to your siblings. But no, you had to go back with that egomaniac Steele. Of course, I understood what was happening between you and him. It's not your fault really. But it just made me have to wait even longer."

He stood from his seat and leaned over her. "I'm a patient person, but I have my limits. And then it occurred to me." He paused again. "What if I waited till the third day after your fling with Steele? How fitting would that be?"

Gillian's mind felt like mud.

"What if the woman he loved, despite the whole debacle with Stuart, died anyway on the third day?" She heard him chuckle. "I thought that would be the perfect ending to this irritating story."

Understanding began to slowly trickle past her foggy state. This man planned to kill her.

"Of course, it helped that he kicked you out. My ploy to get him to doubt you worked very well. Perfectly, in fact."

As her mind continued to clear, she began to put some pieces together. "You were the source."

"Yes. I was. After I looked through your address book, it was easy to set you up. I just added Demille's name and made a phone call. Gave him plenty of money to keep his mouth shut and tell a little white lie. Humans are very easy to manipulate."

Her body, despite its soreness, reacted to his use of the word "humans." She understood its implications. "Who are you?" she whispered.

He sat back down. His energy was as calm as a tree on a windless day. "I'm a Red-line, Gillian. Just like you."

Gillian blinked and wished her vision would clear, but all she could make out were blurred shapes and circles that made up his face.

"A what?"

"Oh, come now. Surely dad told you." Reaching down, he lifted her shirt. She attempted to push him away, but he swatted her hands away as if they were ants on a picnic table. "You have the mark," he said as his fingers trailed over the red scar on her skin over her ribcage. It was a highly sensitive area, and his touch sent a jolt through her as she jerked away from him.

The movement sent another wave of pain though her body, and he laughed. "Sorry," he said. "Didn't mean to make you squirm." He sat back and seemed to study her. "You see, Gillian, you are a special case. You're part human. You're a rare breed." He sighed. "Unfortunately, for you, it's a breed that needs to be eradicated."

Her breathing had picked up. Her vision began to improve, and he began to come into focus. "Why?" she asked.

"Because," he said, "you're dad broke a lot of rules coming down here. He slept with a human and had children with her. Three Red-line children with human DNA." He stared off. "That is against the law. Red-lines do not cross breed with other species. We were never meant to. Now, I realize we may occasionally swim in other waters, so to speak, but precautions must be taken to prevent unnecessary offspring. Your father was not careful." He sighed as he reflected. "He thought no one would find out, but he was wrong." He grunted. "You see, it's my job to filter out mutants and half-breeds, to prevent the dilution of our kind. Those on our planet no longer abide those that don't measure up to our unique standards."

Gillian's body slowly began to recover. Her aches and pains diminished and the heat in her belly began to recede. Her mind raced to think of a way to escape this man, but she knew her opportunities were few.

"It's a big job," he continued. "But somebody's got to do it." He watched her uncurl. "Did you know there were others like you on this planet? Well, not exactly like you. They're Gray-Lines. They came a long time ago." When he realized she probably didn't understand, he explained. "Gray-Lines are also Eudoran, although they lack the abilities and sensitivities of a Red-Line. They're a sort of half-breed themselves, I suppose. We just ignore them though. They'll die out soon enough." He spoke with interest. "There's actually a community of them not far from here."

She had no idea what he was talking about.

He sighed. "Yes. When I'm finished here, I've got to head up there. Apparently, there's another half-human Red-Line among them. Some sort of crossbreed experiment, I suspect. Not unlike your family. Such a shame. I plan to take care of her too."

She shivered at the thought of him hurting someone else. She had to find a way out of this. Her head still hurt, but she tried to pull herself together. She heard his chair scrape against the floor.

"But once that job is done, it's back to Eudora for me, where I plan to find a nice, sandy beach to relax for a while."

Gillian squirmed. Her mind wouldn't still. "Why?"

He rested an ankle on a knee. "Why?" he asked. "I'll tell you why." His voice dropped low and Gillian's skin prickled as her body sensed his anger. "Because I can't abide rule breaking. And my brother is a damn rule-breaker. He's done it his whole life, and people think he's charming because of it. Not after this though. As soon as I'm done here, I'm going to expose him for the fraud he is, and if I play my cards right, he'll be exposed and exiled in front of the Grand Council while I sit and watch. But before I do that, I plan to make him suffer. I'm going to tell him how I found you and your brother and sister. How I used you as bait to lure them and how they came to save you. And when they did, I killed each of you, and listened as you cried for mercy. And then I'll watch when the guilt of leaving you unprotected and ill-prepared destroys him." He smiled. "I'm going to revel in his downfall."

His words stunned her. This man, who was apparently her uncle, planned on killing her entire family. "They won't come for me," she said with a shaky breath. Her eyes began to focus and his features began to take on a clearer shape.

He grinned down at her. "Oh, yes they will. I left a few clues. Their love for you will bring them. Granted, I'd expected to get to them before this, but I commend them for holding back. I waited at the hospital, but they managed to keep their distance and stay separated. This time though, they'll come."

Fear rippled through her. "Please don't do this. They're my family."

He leaned back down and studied her face. "Don't take it personally. Look at it this way. At least you got your night with Steele. Based on what I've heard, female Red-Lines are adventurous when they Bind with their mate. I'm sure it was no different with you. You can think of him when I send you to your grave."

His words didn't make sense, but she forgot about them when she blinked and her sight returned. His features came into crisp view and her eyes widened when she saw who sat in the chair.

· · · • • · • · · ·

Gray stared in disbelief. "What do you mean?" He tried to make sense of Royce's words. "Stuart's dead. Who else would want to hurt Gillian?"

Royce grimaced with impatience. "This isn't about you, Steele. This goes way beyond that."

"What?" Gray gripped a pillow on the couch. "I don't get any of this. You two walk in here, tell me Gillian's in trouble, and now you tell me that she was telling the truth. That all three of you are the product of an alien father?"

"We don't have time to explain," yelled Royce.

"Listen," said Eve, trying to calm the situation. "I know you've had a lot thrown at you, but Royce is right. We are running out of time. Has Gillian been in touch with you since you last saw her?"

Despite the moving furniture and the fact that Eve apparently conversed with his dog, Gray tried to answer. "No, I haven't heard from her."

"Can you call her?" asked Eve.

"We tried that," said Royce. "Her phone is turned off."

Eve groaned in frustration. "So we try again."

Gray looked at the phone he still held. "I'd call, but my phone is dead."

Eve reached out and lightly touched his cell with her fingers. The display lit up, and he felt it buzz in his hands.

"Try it now."

His eyes widened. He started to say something but then changed his mind. Shaking his head, he punched some numbers and lifted the phone to his ear. It went straight to voicemail.

He lowered the phone. "No luck."

Royce began to pace. "Where would she go?"

Eve sighed. "She went to the hotel. We traced her that far."

"Dammit. I never should have let her out of my sight."

"It's not your fault," said Eve. "We can't stay together. We thought she was safe."

They regarded Gray. He stared back in surprise. "You thought she was with me."

Eve looked solemn. "Yes." She sat down in a chair next to Gray. "I tried to reach her yesterday, but she didn't answer. I gave her the benefit of the doubt. She'd been through a lot, and I didn't want to interrupt." She gave him a knowing glance. "But when she still didn't answer as of this morning, my warning bells went off. It's not like her to disappear for a long period of time. We've all agreed to check in at regular intervals. She's late by twenty-four hours."

Gray took a deep breath. "Since this has nothing to do with me, then I'm assuming this has to do with you?"

Gray heard Royce groan in annoyance.

"Yes," said Eve. "We have reason to believe that someone is targeting us."

"Who?" Gray asked.

Royce's patience snapped. "Who do you think? We just told you who we are. We're different."

Gray tried not to get angry. "I don't understand what you mean. Let's remember for one brief second that I'm new to this party. I'm going to ask for some latitude here in order to adjust to the fact that I'm the only human in the room. Accepting that, hard as it may be, does not mean I understand your situation, so please stop assuming that I do."

Royce stopped pacing. Eve broke the quiet. "Gray," she said. "Royce, Gillian, and I are a combination of human and Eudoran DNA."

"Eu... what?" asked Gray.

"Eudoran. Our father is from Eudora. He travels here when he can, but it's rare when we get to see him. When he told us who we were, we were naturally just as skeptical. But, when we realized what was happening and what we could do, we had no choice but to believe him. He told us though, that because of who we are, we are at risk."

Gray tried to suspend his disbelief. "Why?"

"Because we are half human. Our father told us that those in his society do not take lightly to those of his kind having children outside the bloodline, which he did. He felt confident that we would be safe as children, but when we grew up, we went through a change..." She stopped as if she struggled to explain.

"A Shift?" asked Gray.

Eve's eyebrows rose. "Gilli told you?"

"She mentioned it."

Eve nodded her head. "The Shift changed us. We became aware of our true nature. We could do things we couldn't do before. It was a scary time for us. Everything changed."

She went silent, and Royce continued for her. "Our father told us of the danger we could be in. As triplets, we garner enough force that could attract unwanted attention. He asked us to separate. Spend less time together. He stayed long enough to ensure we were back on our feet and stable, but then he was gone again. After he left, we did as he asked. We went our separate ways. Eve and I," he looked at his sister, "we have tougher skins. Eve is a social chameleon. She can fit in wherever she goes and does not lack confidence. I like to move around but am comfortable on my own. But Gilli—"

"Gilli's different," interrupted Eve. "It was hard for her. It took her longer to adjust, and when we separated, she was lonely. We spent little time with our mother because we didn't want to put her at risk either. At first, Gilli spent much of her time alone."

"A lot of that was due to the fact that she's an empath," Royce said. "She can feel the feelings and emotions of others. It was difficult for her to go out in public. Until she learned to control it and rein it in, she had to stay away."

Eve continued. "Once she learned though, she began to feel people's need. And she began to differentiate between those who could use her help and those that couldn't. Before we knew it, she started to go out and search for these people. Once she honed it further, she could pinpoint exactly who needed her help and where they were. We were sort of in awe of her."

Royce grunted. "She took too many risks though."

"We all took risks," said Eve. "Especially at the beginning."

"She's still taking them though," Royce said.

"We can't ask her to live in a box."

Royce's anger bubbled up. "I think we could ask her to not put her life on the line for some cursed bozo. Is that too much to ask?"

"Bozo?" asked Gray.

Eve ignored the insult to Gray and kept talking. "The problem is that if we stay out in the open too long, it's possible for us to be found."

"Found? But who is looking for you?"

Royce and Eve exchanged glances. "Anyone who thinks we should be eliminated," said Eve. "We're not considered true..." She looked away as she thought and asked Royce. "What did he call us?"

"Red-Lines," answered Royce. "We're not considered true Red-Lines. We're an aberration. And if anyone were to come looking, they would eliminate us."

Gray felt himself shiver. "Eliminate you?"

"Yes," Eve said.

Gray could only stare dumbfounded. "And you think someone came looking? And found Gillian?"

Royce and Eve said nothing, and Gray knew they were worried. He felt his own insides constrict. "And what if he has?"

Royce met his stare. "He'll use her as bait."

"Bait?"

"Yes," said Eve. "He'll want all three of us. He's counting on us coming for her."

"And he's right," said Royce. "We will."

The information coming at Gray made his head swim. Someone was holding Gillian hostage? Someone who wanted her and her family dead? "Do you have any idea who it could be?" he asked.

"Do you think we'd be here if we knew that?" asked Royce.

"I thought you guys were sensitive. Can't you pick up on him?"

"Not if he's like us," said Eve.

"Like you?"

"Another Red-Line," said Royce. "Only not the half-human kind." His tone turned serious. "He could easily hide from us."

Gray considered that. "You mean someone else from this planet of yours..."

"Eudora," added Eve.

"Whatever," said Gray. "He's come here to get rid of all three of you because he considers you to be some sort of mixed breed?"

"Yes," said Royce.

"Exactly," said Eve.

Gray didn't know what to think. Was he dealing with three crazy people? He couldn't deny the couch moving and Eve's knowledge of the color of his underwear, but could there be another explanation? Could they be conning him in some way? If they were, then he couldn't understand why. Why make up this crazy story? They didn't want money. He didn't think gossip magazines would pay that much to make up this kind of story. Besides, what reader would believe it anyway? And the ones that did were likely quacks already. The story was completely irrational, but beneath all the insanity, he could tell that these two cared for Gillian and were scared. He could see that much. And if she was in trouble, then he had to help her. She'd done that much for him. He set reason aside and decided he could worry about alien visitors later. Right now, they needed to focus on finding Gillian.

"How can I help?" he asked. "Where can we look?"

Eve seemed relieved that he'd chosen to assist them. She sat forward in her seat. "Is there anyone you think might have been suspicious? Anyone who seemed out of place? Somebody who may have shown an unusual interest in her?"

Gray thought back but no one came to mind. "No. Not that I recall."

"Think," said Royce. "I know all the attention was on you and your problems, but try to think of something that might have been off. It may have been something small or just slightly out of place."

Gray tried to think of anything that might meet that criteria but had no success. "I don't know."

Royce grunted and glanced toward Eve. "I told you this was a waste of time."

Just then, Gray's phone rang.

"Is it her?" asked Eve.

"No," said Gray, raising the phone to his ear. "It's Kenny." He answered it. "Hello?"

"Gray?" said Kenny. "It's Ken. You got a second?"

Gray looked at his houseguests. "A quick one. What is it?"

"Is Gillian there?"

The question startled him. "No. Why?"

"Something interesting we found. We got some more information on Marilyn."

"Marilyn?" Gray was confused. "I thought that case was closed. You think Stuart drowned her."

"She did drown, but we just talked to a friend of hers. She'd called looking for Marilyn. When I gave her the news, she couldn't believe it. She told me that she'd talked to Marilyn."

"Talked to her?" asked Gray. "When?"

"The day she died."

"What?" asked Gray. "What did she say?"

"She said Marilyn was going out to meet someone down by the beach. Her friend pressed for more info. Apparently, she was meeting a man."

"A man? What man?"

"I was guessing Stuart. Based on Gillian's statement, we assumed Stuart killed Marilyn."

"It's the logical conclusion."

"I agree. But I've been doing some checking."

"What checking?" asked Gray.

"Stuart's whereabouts on the day Marilyn died," Kenny said. "According to the coroner, she died sometime between 8 pm and midnight."

"So, what's the issue? She meets with Stuart, and he kills her for sleeping with me."

"That's just it," said Kenny. "I checked the flight records. Stuart flew into the city around 6 pm. He met up with Fran and Cooper and they had dinner. Then he and Fran drove out to the island. The staff said they didn't get in until close to ten o'clock and they went up to bed soon after."

Gray tried to follow. "Did Stuart sneak out to meet her?"

"Maybe, but that's not the point."

Gray felt the stares of his houseguests. He needed to wrap up the conversation. "What is the point, Ken?"

"Marilyn's friend. She was talking to Marilyn as Marilyn was heading out to meet this guy."

Gray felt impatient. "So?"

Kenny huffed as if his own impatience grew. "So, her friend tells me they talked at eight o'clock. There's no way Marilyn's going to meet Stuart."

Gray's insides churned. "You mean she was meeting somebody else?"

Kenny paused. "Yes. That's exactly what I mean."

Gray felt the color drain from his face. He knew what Kenny was implying. "Stuart didn't do it, did he? He didn't kill Marilyn." He looked between Royce and Eve. "It was someone else."

Kenny expelled a deep breath. "I know this sounds crazy, and I may be making a leap here. Maybe Marilyn was just in the wrong place at the wrong time. But if someone else wanted her dead, then there's the possibility that maybe he might want Gillian dead too."

Gray tried to force air into his lungs. His mind went blank. He stared at the floor and tried to comprehend the situation but raised his head when he heard Eve begin to hum.

"I'd feel better if I knew she was safe and sound," said Kenny. "Is she there?"

Gray heard him but was distracted by Eve's apparent attempt to share a song at an unusual time. Max woofed as Eve continued to hum.

"What are you doing?" asked Royce, listening to Eve.

Gray tried to follow the tune, but Kenny interrupted. "Gray?" he asked. "Is someone else with you?"

Gray tried to place the song Eve sang. As he listened, he began to recognize the tune. It was a song from the past. They'd played it at his prom. It was "Under the Boardwalk," by the Drifters.

"Gray?" asked Kenny.

"Yeah, Kenny. I'm here." He stared at Eve. She rose from her seat, and Max walked up to her. She squatted down, petted his head, and held his face in her palms.

"Did you hear what I said, Gray?" asked Kenny.

Gray was transfixed as he watched Eve with his dog. "I heard you, Kenny. I..." He didn't know how much to say. "She's not here. I've been trying to reach her."

"Cell coverage is shit right now with this weather. I'm surprised I've been able to talk to you this long without the signal cutting out."

Gray figured that had something to do with Eve's magical touch. "I'm surprised too." He kept his eyes on Eve.

"You think she's still in town?"

Gray watched Royce watch Eve. The big man looked just as curious as Gray.

"Yes. I think she is." He wanted to tell Kenny his fears but had no idea how he'd explain the situation.

"I'm going to the hotel to see if I can find her. You stay put in case she comes to your place."

"I will, Ken," he said. "You call me if you find her."

"I will."

Eve broke from her stare at Max and stared up at Gray in alarm. By the look in her eyes, he knew she'd discovered something important.

"Kenny?" he asked before Kenny could hang up.

"Yeah?"

"If something happens..." he couldn't finish his sentence. Eve stared back at him in fear.

"What, Gray? Do you know something?"

He didn't answer because Eve had his full attention. Her face was white and her eyes wide. "Who's Franklin?" she asked.

Gray thought of Cooper's assistant. His skin prickled, his mind raced, and he began to put the pieces together. Franklin had the keys to his house. He could have easily accessed Gillian's notebook. He thought back. He remembered Franklin in his kitchen, at Cooper's birthday and dinner party, at the hospital. He thought about Marilyn. Had Franklin been the man she'd gone to meet?

Royce stepped forward. "It's him, isn't it?" he asked Eve. "He's the Red-Line."

"Shit," said Gray over the phone.

"What the hell is going on over there?" asked Kenny.

"What's the significance of the song?" asked Royce.

Eve let go of Max, who trotted up next to her and sat at her feet. "He was humming it."

"Who was?" asked Gray.

"Franklin," said Eve. "He hummed it while he was here, in your house. You and Gilli were still at the hospital. He went through her things. Made a phone call. Wrote in her book. Max watched the whole thing."

"Son of a bitch," said Gray.

"Gray," said Kenny. "What's wrong?'

"Just a second, Ken."

"That bastard," said Royce. "He set her up."

"And I fell for it," said Gray.

"Fell for what?" asked Kenny.

"But why the song?" said Eve, thinking to herself. "It was as if he knew I would hear it."

"It's 'Under the Boardwalk,'" said Gray.

"What's under the boardwalk?" asked Kenny.

Gray's heart thumped at Kenny's question. "Holy hell," he said.

"What?" asked Royce.

"Kenny," he said into the phone. "I've got to go." He paused. "If something happens..."

"Gray, what is the matter?"

"If something happens and you find Gillian before I do, tell her I love her."

"Gray, wait..."

But Gray hung up before Kenny could finish.

CHAPTER TWENTY-EIGHT

GILLIAN TRIED TO PUSH up, but her strength had not returned. She managed to tip her head up and whisper his name. "Franklin."

His stare remained on her. "Feeling better?"

She swallowed but her throat stuck. She wished she had some water. She blinked her eyes again. "How long?"

"How long what?"

The heat in her belly receded further, and she took a deep breath to steady herself. "How long have you been looking for me?"

He looked up. "I don't know. A couple of months?" He flicked something off of his pants. "I knew you existed. I just wasn't sure where to start. But I know my brother. I just focused on him and his energy. After a while, I narrowed it down a bit. The more I tuned in, the closer I got, but I still couldn't pinpoint your location. If you'd stuck together, it would have been much easier. But I'm tenacious. After a couple of weeks, I'd narrowed in on you. I found a few people you'd helped, including Mr. Horn. Once I found him, I knew what to look for. The trick was not to look for you but to look for your next sob story. Didn't take long after that before I zeroed in on Steele. He had the perfect tale of woe. I just sat back and waited for you to show. I managed to find employment with Stone in order to get close. But after waiting a while, I began to get impatient." He sighed and looked out the window at the rain. "It was then that Marilyn showed. It was the perfect opportunity. All you needed was a reason to jump in with both feet. She provided that."

Gillian stared in shock. "You killed her."

He smiled. "Of course I did." His eyes met hers. "And you showed up right on cue."

She pulled herself into an upright position and peered around the room. She appeared to be in a former retail store. Empty racks with naked hangers lined the back walls and wide shelves were covered in dust and random dead bugs. An armless mannequin stared blankly through the store window, looking out at the gray skies and murky rain. Another boom of thunder startled Gillian.

Seeing him clearly now, she asked, "Why not kill me back then?"

He made a pitiful face. "Because, as I explained, I wanted your siblings too." He crossed his arms. "I figured out the plan you concocted with Steele and decided to use it to my advantage. If Stuart were to try and kill you, then brother and sister would surely show." He studied her. "They did a good job though of protecting you, even at a distance."

"You knew Stuart was the killer?"

His tone remained casual. "Of course I did. I knew it the moment I met him. I'm surprised you didn't." He leaned closer. "You're supposed to be the more sensitive one, aren't you?"

She didn't answer him.

"Just lack of practice, I suppose," he said. "That and you were obviously preoccupied with Steele." He chuckled. "I didn't realize it at first, but then it became apparent who he was to you."

Gillian couldn't hide her confusion. "What do you mean?"

He shook his head. "You still don't know, do you?"

"Know what?"

"Steele," he said as he relaxed in his seat. "He's your mate, or at least that's what you made him."

She tried to make sense of what he said. "My mate?"

"Poor Miss Fletcher. He really didn't prepare you, did he?"

"Prepare me for what?"

"You're a female Red-Line, Gillian. You have some powerful...how shall I say it...urges. Especially when you meet the man you wish to Bind with."

She did not understand what he was talking about. "Bind?"

"Yes. Which is exactly what you did with Steele."

"I did?"

He grinned. "I'm assuming you two didn't spend your time playing checkers after you left the hospital."

Her face warmed.

"And since you knew nothing about it that means you took no precautions to prevent it."

"I don't understand."

"No, I know you don't. It's a good thing. It's better you don't know what typically follows once a Binding is complete."

Her eyes conveyed her confusion. "What follows?"

He didn't say anything at first, and her heartbeat picked up in speed. "As I said, it's better you don't know. You won't live long enough for it to matter anyway."

He stood and walked to the window, staring out with empty eyes similar to those of the mannequin. Gillian shifted into an upright sitting position and tried to think. Her fingers shook with fear, and she clenched them into fists. She thought of her siblings and tried to reach out to them, but she felt nothing.

"That won't work," he said.

She heard him but didn't answer.

"I can't let you stop them." He turned back to face her. "Besides, it wouldn't help. They'll still come for you."

Remaining quiet, she watched him walk up to her and she fought the urge to back away.

Standing over her, he asked, "Did he tell you about me?"

Not understanding, she replied, "Who?"

He shook his head as if he considered her slow-witted. "Carson, my brother."

"No. He rarely spoke of his home."

Staring at her for several seconds, he finally looked away. "I'm sure he mentioned something. What did he tell you?"

Gillian considered her answer. "Not much. He only told us who we were after the Shift occurred for us. Even then, the most he offered was to warn us that we were at risk. That's when we separated."

Franklin tensed. "Fool. He should have prepared you. He should have suspected this time would come."

She stared at his profile. "I'm sure that his brother killing his family was the last thing he planned for."

Franklin turned. "His family?" he asked with a wicked smile. "His family is alive and well and living on Eudora."

Gillian felt her stomach drop.

"That's right," said Franklin. "He lied to you. Carson Binded with another Eudoran Red-Line. They have two children." When he saw her shocked look, he smiled. "Did you honestly think he'd remain faithful to a human and her three half-human children?" He chuckled. "You're naïve."

"He has another family?"

"Of course he does."

Gillian didn't know what to say. It made sense she supposed, but still the realization stung.

"So you see," continued Franklin. "He's lied to you just like he lies to everyone else."

The shock eased, and she put on a calm facade. "He's still my father."

"And you're my niece. What's your point?"

Her mind raced for an answer. "Why bother killing us? We're not a threat to you. We will never leave this planet." He straightened as she spoke. "Whatever grudge you hold, why take it out on us?"

His face turned angry. "He slept with a human. He had children with her. Half-human, half Red-Line children. We don't do that, Gillian. Never have and never will. Once it starts, it becomes rampant. Before you know it, our Red-Line genes become diluted and obsolete. It's unthinkable." His face relaxed and his casual mood returned. "It's not personal. It's just necessary."

His argument upset her. "Just what exactly are you threatened by? Our human genes? Our lack of Red-Line perfection? Our budding, but unknown abilities? What can we possibly do to harm you or your precious bloodline?" Her tone turned sharp, and she felt the energy in the room electrify. "From what I do know about your people, you travel extensively throughout space. Do you honestly think that Red-Lines, either male or female, have not propagated with anyone else outside their species? Now who's being naïve?"

He put his hands in his pockets and rocked on his feet. "You should respect me, Gillian. Remember, I'm family."

She stared pointedly back at him. "I guess that's the flawed human in me. Is that what makes me disposable?" Despite the warning tug she felt to stay quiet, she kept going. "And we may be related by blood, but you're not my family. You think I'm horrible because I'm half-human? Well, you may be one hundred percent Red-Line, but you disgust me. If anyone deserves to be destroyed because of who they are, it's you."

The energy ramped up further, and he stepped closer to her. His face turned red and before she could react, his hand came down and he slapped her across the face. Her head rocked back and her cheek stung with the impact. The shock of the hit stunned her, and she rubbed the raw skin of her cheek with her fingers.

"You're just like him," he said, breathing hard.

She said nothing, although she considered continuing to provoke him. If he killed her before Royce and Eve arrived, then perhaps she could spare them. As soon as she had the thought though, she knew it would only make matters worse. Staring down at the floor, she said nothing, but his words penetrated and a theory occurred to her. Facing him, she responded, "This is about him, isn't it?"

His jaw clenched, and she knew she'd hit a chord. "It is, isn't it? You hate him. This is some sort of revenge. It has nothing to do with us being half-human, does it?"

Her words incited him. He reached down and grabbed her arm, pulling her up on her feet. She stifled a moan but found her footing and managed to stay upright. His face close to hers, he sneered at her. "You should keep your mouth shut about matters you know nothing about." Spittle flew from his mouth, and she tried not to flinch at the iron grip he had on her arm. "The only thing you need to know is that you are going to die today. Right along with your brother and sister."

Something inside her snapped and before she could stop herself, she spit in his face. She braced for his reaction. The spit ran down his cheek. He reached with his free hand and wiped at it. Thunder boomed just as she felt a tingle in her body and then she shot backward, hitting a wall behind her with force. Her forehead hit a free-standing empty clothes rack and she felt the warmth of her own blood as it began to stream down the side of her face. She crumpled to the floor and tried to collect herself, but her head buzzed and her body shook. Another wave of pain shot through her midsection and she whimpered, not caring if he heard.

Huddled in a ball, she heard his footsteps as he neared. "It would be so easy," he said, and she felt his hand on the back of her head. She squirmed and tried to pull away. "To kill you now," he finished. Looking up at him, she could see his eyes held a faraway gaze and she trembled. Returning his attention to her, he focused. "But it's not time yet. I have..." He stopped and listened, his head cocked. She wondered what had made him pause. All she could hear was the downpour of rain against the roof. Scooting back from him, she stilled when she felt it too. She understood then what had gained his attention. Royce and Eve were coming.

· · · · ● · ● · · ·

Royce drove Gray's car into the empty parking lot. He stopped at the entrance to a wooden stairway leading to the pier below. The storm had intensified, and the waves crashed hard onto the wooden support beams. Ocean spray shot high into the air and mixed with the rain, creating a heavy mist that blew erratically through the air. The vibration of the waves pounding the boardwalk's support structure shook the vehicle. The stores lining the pier stood empty and dark. They had long since been evacuated and maintained a lifeless stare. The rain pounded the roof of the car, and Max woofed.

Gray stared out at the downpour from the backseat. "You sure we needed to bring Max?"

Eve's concern was evident. She squinted and looked out the passenger-side window as if expecting to see her sister walk out of the rain. "We need him," she said. She faced Gray. "He might come in handy."

Gray reached out to pet Max, who jumped into his lap.

"You're right," said Royce from the driver's seat. "She's here."

Thunder boomed and Gray jumped. "Is Franklin here too?"

Eve paused. "Yes. He's waiting."

"He wants both of us. He's using her."

Gray was anxious but felt his anger build. "How do we get her back?"

Royce and Eve faced each other, and Gray knew they spoke in words he could not hear. "What?" he asked.

Royce popped the driver's side door open and the sound of the rain invaded the car. Max jumped into the front seat. "You stay here. Eve and I have to deal with this. Not you."

Gray voiced his disagreement. "The hell I will. I'm not going to sit here while Gillian's life is at risk. I'm going with you." He popped his own door open.

"Gray," said Eve. "This is dangerous. He plans to kill us. We won't be able to protect you."

"I don't want or need your protection. You think for one second if she winds up dead that I'll want to live either, knowing I didn't do anything to help? No. I finally found someone I love…"

Royce and Eve waited for him to finish. Royce eyed Gray from the rear-view mirror. "You're sure?" he asked.

Gray realized what he wanted to say. "I want to be with her. She made it possible for me to do that." He leaned forward. "Alien or not, she risked her life for me and I'm willing to risk mine for hers." He paused. "I'm going with you. I know this area. I hung out here as a teenager. That might come in handy. And if something happens and you can get her out, then don't worry about me. Just go. All of you. Take Max too if you can."

Royce's stare did not waver. "That goes for you too," he said. "If this goes bad and things turn against us, then get out of here. You're not strong enough to stop him. You try and be a hero and you'll end up dead."

Gray nodded. "Listen, this pier is old. It's needed renovation for years. I don't have to tell you that one nasty wave could bring this thing down. So, whatever it is you're planning, don't linger. We all need to get off this thing or Franklin's job is going to be easy."

Royce and Eve nodded, and Eve opened her own door. "Then let's not dawdle," she said. She stepped out into the hard driving rain, zipped up her jacket, and flipped the hood to cover her head. Royce exited the car as well, and Gray and Max followed. Gray wore a raincoat, but Royce walked without one, seemingly oblivious to the rain.

They walked to the staircase and without hesitating, headed down toward the pier below.

· · · · •· • · · · ·

Inside the store, Franklin yanked at Gillian and pulled her back to her feet. Her body aching, she managed to find her balance and fought the urge to hold onto him for support. Holding her, he pulled her across the floor. The blood dripped down her face, and she wiped it away with the back of her hand. He grabbed the chair he'd been using and dragged it over to the window that looked out over the boardwalk. Looking though the rain, Gillian could see the angry sea beyond the pier. The water churned and rolled as powerful waves hit and splashed up across the walkway that led out over the water. She wished she could quiet her mind and go silent, in hopes of somehow hiding her signal from her family, but her turbulent emotions betrayed her. She was frightened, and she didn't know how to silence her fear. Even if she could, she knew Franklin would still lure them in and there was little she could do to prevent that. She closed her eyes and thought of her father. She thought back to all that he'd told her about protecting herself. She remembered his conversations with all three of them. And the conversation he'd had with her alone. A stillness enveloped her and for a brief moment, she felt peaceful when she accepted what she would have to do. Franklin shoved her hard into the chair and then walked to the window.

He stood there for several minutes and said nothing. Finally, he turned to her.

"Get up," he said, advancing on her. "Let's go."

· · · · •· • · · · ·

The wind and rain lashed at them, soaking them despite their rain gear. They walked down the stairs to the pier. The wood creaked as the waves slammed into it from below. Water sprayed and the wind whipped, and Gray felt the moisture seep into his clothes. Royce was drenched, and Eve gave up on keeping her hood up and pushed her sodden hair off her face. Max raced ahead of them, his fur dripping. At the bottom of the stairs, they paused. Royce and Eve stopped to listen, despite the noise of the storm. After a few seconds, they began to walk. Waves battered the pier and the ground shuddered beneath them. Gray hoped it would continue to hold. The structure had survived eighty years of storms. He hoped it would survive one more.

He followed Royce and Eve. They passed locked businesses with dark store fronts and Gray peered inside each, wondering if Gillian was nearby. As they continued to walk, he looked ahead and saw the familiar large, blue and white tiled fountain. It was original to the site and in the past, when the stores were open, skies were clear and the day was warm, the fountain would run and the water would spray and gurgle. It was large and shallow enough for small children to run barefoot and play within it, water up to their knees, screeching in delight and drenching their pant legs. A bronze dolphin sprang upward from the water's surface, its nose reaching skyward as if jumping to escape from the shallow confines of his enclosure.

Gray stared at it now as the water lashed off the dolphin's back, taking the place of the routine spray that normally spouted from its blowhole, and the fountain water below churned from the rain and wind, its color now dark and murky from debris that had blown into it.

As they approached the fountain, their pace slowed and Max barked, becoming more animated. Royce and Eve stopped and Gray stared ahead, beyond the dolphin. Seeing what had alerted them, he froze where he stood. Another crack of thunder boomed, but he barely heard it. Gillian stood on the opposite side of the fountain, with Franklin gripping her hard at the waist. Despite the rain that lashed at her, blood dripped down her face. Nobody moved.

CHAPTER TWENTY-NINE

GILLIAN SQUINTED AGAINST THE rain. Within seconds of stepping outside, she was soaked to the skin. Her brother and sister were getting closer. Closing herself off as much as she could, she steeled herself for when she would see them. She gasped when Franklin pulled her up close and held her next to him. She cringed at the contact. The weather had worsened, and she could feel the creak of the wood beneath her feet. The spray from the breaking waves combined with the rain made it feel like she was in a washing machine, and as the ground shook, she could only hope that they all didn't end up in one. If the pier failed, they would all succumb within minutes.

Wiping her face, she looked to see a large tiled pool in front of her. A copper-colored dolphin rose from the surface. Franklin halted his movement and pulled her closer. She looked beyond and stilled when she saw Royce and Eve and, shockingly, Grayson too. Above the sound of the thunder and rain, she heard barking and knew it was Max. Her gaze met Gray's. Everything that had happened before this suddenly seemed petty and insignificant, and although her heart leapt at the sight of him, she wished he hadn't come.

Royce yelled through the rain. "Let her go."

Franklin's arm pulled tighter around her, and she fought the urge to push away. Something told her to remain quiet and show no signs of struggle. She needed to keep Franklin convinced that she would not fight back.

Franklin chuckled. "You want her? She's right here. Come and get her."

No one moved.

Eve spoke next. "You okay, Gilli?"

Thunder cracked again. "I'm okay," Gillian answered. "You shouldn't have come."

Eve walked closer to the fountain's edge. "Would you have come for me?"

Gillian didn't answer.

Grayson finally spoke. "What the hell are you doing, Franklin? You let her go and they'll go easier on you."

Franklin didn't hide his amusement. "Unless you're as incompetent as your partner, Steele, you know what you're dealing with. Go easy on me? After I kill all of you, I'm simply going to walk away. By this time tomorrow, I'll be finishing up one last job and then after that, well, let's just say I won't be in the vicinity anymore. Fear of your authorities is one thing I do not have worry about."

"Why do this?" asked Royce. "There's nothing to fear. Just let us be and go home. You'll never have to worry about us."

Franklin scowled. "I didn't travel the mileage I did to have a conversation about our grievances, dear nephew. I came here to kill my brother's children. Regardless of whatever admirable qualities you all may have, your father broke the rules and he'll answer to that. He made the mistake of bringing you into this world, so now he must deal with me taking you out of it. I don't compromise."

The word "nephew" hung in the air, and Gillian could feel Royce's confusion, as well as Eve's. She silenced her mind and tried not to let the emotions of her brother and sister, nor that of Grayson's, impair her ability to think. Another memory of her father popped into her head. At that exact moment, she made eye contact with Royce and Eve. Her mind raced, and she wondered if they'd had the same flashback.

"Dammit, Franklin," Gray said. "Don't do this. You can't kill us all. One of us will get to you. You won't get out of here."

Franklin didn't answer. Standing beside him, Gillian felt chills course through her and she knew it wasn't from the cold. Suddenly, his weight shifted, and within seconds, she felt herself lifted with unseen hands. And then she was in the fountain, struggling, with her head submerged beneath the murky water.

· · · ● · ● · · · ·

Everyone moved at once. Royce and Eve jumped into the fountain and were at Gillian's side in seconds. Grayson followed. Max leapt in with them, his legs just long enough to keep his head above the water. They grabbed at Gillian to pull her up, but she felt heavy as if she'd been chained to the bottom. Royce and Eve pulled at her arms and Gray grabbed at her waist, but it felt like she was encased in concrete.

After several panicked seconds, Royce stopped pulling and grabbed Eve's elbow. She continued to yank frantically on Gillian's arm.

"Eve!" he said, over the noise of the storm. She stopped. "Take my hand!" He grasped Eve's palm. They both reached down with their free hands and held Gillian at the shoulders. Gray didn't understand what they were doing. The siblings went still and closed their eyes.

Her arms now free, Gillian flailed as she tried to push herself up for air but was unable to free herself from the invisible grip that held her down.

"What are you doing?" Gray yelled at them. He continued to pull at Gillian with no success. "We've got to get her out of here!"

A chuckle caught his attention and he looked over at Franklin, who now stood beside the fountain, watching the scene unfold.

"They're trying," Franklin said, blinking against the rain. "But they will fail." He shrugged. "This is just too easy. You really should have stayed home. Nobody should have to watch their intended die."

Gray felt the anger bubble up and fuel him. He didn't understand why Gillian couldn't be freed, but he knew Franklin was somehow responsible for it.

"I'll kill you, Franklin," he shouted into the storm. "There's no where you can hide."

Franklin's grin widened. "Your money can't get you to where I'm going, Steele." He wiped the water off his face. "Not yet at least." He observed Gillian's struggle. "Just another minute..."

As Franklin stared at the scene, Gray saw a gray blur launch upward out of the fountain and contact Franklin at mid-thigh, knocking him backward. Through the driving rain, Gray could see Max, his jaws securely locked at the juncture of Franklin's thigh and groin, biting down hard. Franklin, shocked at the impact, grunted and fell down onto the pier, just as Gillian shot up from the water, sputtering and gasping for air.

Royce and Eve grabbed at her and helped her up. Grayson came up behind her and grabbed her around the waist to support her.

"Get her out of the water," yelled Royce. He ran for the side and jumped out of the fountain. Supporting her, Gray moved her to the edge and handed her to Royce who lifted her out. Eve exited also and helped Royce carry her away from the fountain and lay her on the pier. Gillian continued to cough and gasp but was conscious and breathing.

Gray jumped out of the water and looked over in time to see Franklin recovering as Max maintained his painful hold on Franklin's thigh. Franklin sat up and touched Max's back. Max instantly released his bite and made a strangled high-pitched yelp.

"No!" yelled Gray, but he could only stand helpless as his dog flew through the air. He hit the ground hard about fifteen feet away from Franklin.

"Damn mutt," said Franklin, studying his wound. Despite the rain and his wet clothes, blood seeped up through his trousers. He touched the area, and his fingers came back red.

Seeing his dog lying unmoving on the ground, Gray stood in shock. He turned to confront Franklin but found that the man had returned his attention back on the Fletcher family.

Gillian had managed to sit upright. Satisfied that she was okay, Royce faced Franklin, who approached slowly, limping from his injury. The rain continued its unrelenting descent and both men braced against the wind as a hard gust blew across the pier.

Royce noticed the blood on Franklin's pant leg. "You have some vulnerabilities."

Franklin glanced down at the wound. "A few." He wiped his bloody hand on his pants. "But not many."

"Is this where it ends then?" asked Royce. He glanced at his sisters. "You're going to kill us and dump our bodies into the water?"

A wave slammed hard, water sprayed, and the pier groaned. Franklin looked out over the sea. "I'll admit, I imagined it differently, but now that we're here, it has its advantages."

"What about Steele?" asked Royce. "You going to kill him too?"

Franklin's lips curled up. "If he gets in the way."

"He knows about us...and you."

"What's he going to do? Tell his policeman friend?" He chuckled. "They'll send him to a doctor, prescribe him the appropriate sedative, and send him home."

Royce held his ground. "I know about your plans," he said. Lightning flashed.

Franklin paused. "My plans?"

"I know about the other community, where there are others like us."

Thunder boomed. "Really?" asked Franklin. "Do tell."

"I warned them about you."

Franklin's face dropped. "You did?"

"I did. They'll know you're coming."

"You're lying."

"Am I?"

The two men stared, their faces like stone. Eve leaned down to help Gillian stand.

"Royce," said Gillian, still sputtering.

"I'm going to kill your sisters."

The vigor of the storm suddenly felt dwarfed by the energy generated between Royce and Franklin.

"Not until you kill me first."

Franklin's eyes flared. "And I'll enjoy every short-lived second of it."

"Hey, Frank."

Both men, caught up in their energetic confrontation, turned to see Grayson came up from behind Franklin with a large pipe in his hand.

"Enjoy this," he said. He swung the pipe back and took direct aim at Franklin's head.

A surge of energy flooded the area.

"No!" yelled Gillian.

Before Grayson could bring the weapon down, he felt himself flung backward. He slid across the deck and his side hit hard against a wooden support post. He heard a loud snap as his arm took the brunt. Pain flared through his body.

"Grayson..." Gillian moved to help him but only took two steps before dropping to her knees.

"Gilli," said Eve, who kneeled beside her. "What's wrong?"

Gillian's face turned white.

"What?" asked Eve.

Gillian's hands went to her throat.

"Oh, god," said Eve. "She can't breathe." She reached out for her sister but then froze herself.

"Eve?" asked Royce.

Eve's hands came up to her own throat, she dropped to a crouch, and her eyes flared.

"No," said Royce.

"Looks like you've got a problem," Franklin said. "I'll give you a choice. Which one do you want to save?"

Royce stared in horror as both his sisters struggled for air. They clutched at the ground and dropped low, their faces tight with terror.

Royce bellowed, turned, and launched himself at Franklin. His upper body slammed into Franklin's and they both fell down hard onto the pier. Royce wrapped his hands around Franklin's throat and he squeezed, his face clenched in fury.

Despite the grip on his neck, Franklin reached out his hand and touched Royce's side; the reaction was immediate. Royce groaned and pulled back, his hand clutching at his abdomen. He rolled off of Franklin and curled up, gripping his midsection.

Franklin rose up slowly, holding his neck and watching Royce attempt to uncurl and fight the pain assailing him. "That's called a heat flare. Something your dad should have taught you." He stood, straightened his soaked shirt and jacket, and walked over to Royce's slumped form. "It's painful, but the zap I gave you would be considered mild." He squatted down. "It can be much worse, as you'll soon learn."

Franklin loomed over Royce, who lay huddled on the ground in puddles of water, gripping his side. Both Gillian and Eve, heads dropped and hands at their throats, struggled to breathe. Forcing himself up, Grayson felt intense pain flare through his left arm. He cradled it close and held it against his body. The pipe he'd dropped lay nearby, and he reached for it, gripping it in his right hand. His face dripped water and he wiped it with his uninjured arm. He didn't know if he could stop Franklin or not, but if Franklin was going to kill Gillian and her family in front of him, then he would die right along with them. Bracing himself against the beam he'd fallen against, he held the pipe, steadied himself, and began to walk toward Franklin.

••••••••••

Franklin lifted his hand, ready to zap Royce again but he paused. He turned and saw Grayson, who approached with one arm against his torso and the other still wielding the pipe. Lightning hit close by, and thunder cracked, but Grayson didn't flinch. Neither did Franklin. Another wave hit hard, and water sprayed up. Grayson squinted against it. The pier shuddered and groaned as another crack of thunder shook the air. Despite the weather, both men faced each other, neither backing down.

"Haven't had enough yet?" Franklin asked.

"Not until I splatter your brains into fish food," said Gray. His jacket blew open, but he paid no attention.

"Colorful." Franklin looked him over. "I'll never understand how you and that idiot Stone made yourself into millionaires. Just goes to prove the inadequacies of the human race."

Lightning flashed nearby, and the air sizzled. Grayson stood still, but his heart raced. "We have a few advantages."

"Name one," said Franklin. He nodded at the woman fighting for air. "And maybe I'll take pity and let your girlfriend breathe one last time."

Gray gripped the pipe in his hand. He tried not to think of Gillian struggling for air just feet away from him. "We know that no matter how bad things may seem, we can still come out ahead."

"So, you're over-confident." He shook his head. "Sorry. That answer gains you nothing."

"That's where you're wrong, Frank," said Gray, and he raised his pipe. "Because you're about to find out just exactly who you're dealing with."

Thunder and lightning hit simultaneously, and the boom of thunder sliced through the noise of the pounding rain and crashing waves. A current of newfound energy coursed through Gray just as a sudden wave of nausea hit him and he swayed, but it passed quickly, and he regained his balance. "And I'm not the one who's over-confident," he said waving the weapon. "You are."

Lunging forward, he swung the pipe, noticing that the piece of metal almost looked luminescent in his hand. Something inside him churned and, despite his injuries, he felt ten feet taller and the pipe felt as light as a cardboard tube. He swiped the metal out in an arc, but not toward Franklin. Surprised, Franklin's eyes widened as Grayson slammed the weapon into the wooden pier and the pipe bounced back up from the force of the hit.

"Proving my point, I see," said Franklin.

Gray raised the pipe again and slammed it back down onto the pier. The structure moaned and creaked. The electricity running through Gray's bones and muscles made him wonder if he'd somehow been struck by lightning. He felt no pain. "No," he said. "You're proving mine."

Another powerful wall of water hit the pier just as Grayson slammed the pipe into the deck for the third time. The pier shuddered, split, and cracked opened beneath Franklin's feet. The wood beneath him began to separate.

"You should watch where you stand, Frank, or should I say Galen?" Gray stepped away from the widening crack. His voice didn't sound like his own, but he didn't have time to think about it. "It's not too stable around here."

At the mention of the name "Galen," Franklin's face turned white. "How did you..."

Another strong wave hit, and the crack doubled in size. Franklin jumped back. The distraction gave Gray the opportunity to swing the pipe one last time, only this time it connected with Franklin's shoulder.

Franklin fell back hard against the ground and grabbed his arm. The moment he fell, Eve and Gillian gasped and sucked in deep breaths of air. Royce uncurled and managed to stand. He rushed to his sisters' aide, pulling them away from the widening fissure.

The crack grew, and Gray swayed but stayed rooted to his spot. He cocked his head. "Wondering how I know your true name?" Gray braced himself against the wind. "You know how I know, Galen."

Franklin rolled away before the widening opening could suck him in. He winced and held his shoulder but managed to dodge the growing hole in the wood. He pulled himself up. His face bunched in anger, and he briefly glanced up at the sky, as if staring at more than storm clouds, but then he looked back at Grayson. His lip curled. "You can't save them."

The wind and rain pelted everyone. Franklin swayed, but he reached out and braced himself against an empty iron bench. Grayson held the pipe and used it to support his weight as the pier continued to rock beneath him. "They don't need me."

Franklin narrowed his eyes and returned his attention to Royce, Eve, and Gillian, who stood together. His hand gripped his wounded shoulder. "Don't get too comfortable." He rubbed his injury. "We're not through here."

Nobody said anything, but Gray saw Royce take Gillian's and Eve's hand in each of his. Their fingers turned white from their grip. Electricity tingled through Gray but with less intensity than before, as if some part of him knew that his role in this drama was now complete.

"Ready?" Gray heard Royce ask.

Neither woman responded audibly, but Gray felt sure that some sort of communication had been sent.

Franklin wobbled, but he let go of the bench. "I've wasted enough time. Let's end this." He advanced on the trio. "I should have finished you all the moment I saw you."

The Fletcher's remained where they stood. Gillian, intently focused on Franklin, broke her stare long enough to meet Grayson's eyes. The words

"I love you" popped into his head just before she turned back toward Franklin.

Icy fear ripped through Gray, and he dropped the pipe. The energy previously coursing through him suddenly evaporated; he couldn't summon any more. Everything seemed to move in slow motion. His feet seemed frozen in place, and he watched in shock as Franklin bore down on the siblings. The man raised his hand as if directing an unseen force. But just as suddenly, an unexpected flash of light brighter than any lightning bolt pulsed outward from the siblings and the air popped as if a sonic jet had passed over them. A dry wave of heat hit Gray in the chest, and he flew backward and fell hard onto the wooden deck, just as a wrenching crack sounded. Gray, dazed but hearing screams, raised his head and caught a brief glimpse of Franklin engulfed in flames before the pier lurched violently beneath him. Another wave smashed and the wood buckled, spraying shards of wet splinters into the air. Before he could move, the ground beneath him completely gave way and he was plunged into a wet abyss.

CHAPTER THIRTY

INKY BLACKNESS ENVELOPED HIM, and he fought to push through it. A force held him down, and he couldn't breathe. Panicked, he struggled, desperate to find relief. There was nothing to help him though. It was as if he floated in the void of space but without the stars to guide him. He tumbled and flailed but was at the complete mercy of the sea. He stretched his hands blindly, searching for a lifeline, but they grasped at emptiness. He rose and fell, but the surface eluded him. Lungs bursting, he gasped and water filled his lungs. Strength vanishing, he gave up and let go, allowing the current to carry him. But his survival instinct remained and with one last effort, he lunged for the surface and felt a shockwave of relief when a hand grasped his wrist.

Gray startled and opened his eyes. Everything was hazy. He blinked and awareness began to creep in. He could hear the sound of faint beeping. As his vision cleared, he realized he was in a bed, and more importantly, he was warm and dry. He swallowed, but his throat stuck. The more conscious he became, the more the aches and pains in his body blossomed. Blinking again, he looked around and realized he was in a hospital. He tried to move and groaned. His arm and side flared, and his vision spun.

A chair creaked, and he heard a voice beside him. "Hey, Cochise. You awake?"

His head still muddy, Gray turned toward the sound and saw Cooper sitting next to him. He tried to talk, but nothing came out.

Cooper retrieved a water glass with a straw. "Here. Drink some."

Gray sucked at the liquid and gave silent thanks. The water opened his throat and helped to negate the nagging taste of seawater.

"Thanks," he whispered.

Cooper put the water down. "How are you feeling?"

Grayson swallowed and closed his eyes against a pulsing headache. He managed to speak, although his voice sounded more like a croak. "How do I look?"

"Like shit."

"That's how I feel."

"I'm guessing."

Gray tried to think back, but his head hurt. "What happened?"

Cooper pulled his chair closer. "I'd like to ask you the same question."

Gray cleared his throat. "What do you mean?"

"Kenny found you unconscious on a section of pier down by the boardwalk. It was one of the few sections that hadn't collapsed. He called for help and the ambulance brought you here. You've been unconscious for two days."

"Two days?" he asked, still sluggish.

"Yes. You almost drowned. You had water in your lungs, you've got a broken collarbone and three cracked ribs. You're lucky to be alive."

"I've been here for two days?"

"Yes. Is your brain impaired too?"

Everything was a blur, except for an image of him riding in a car with Max. "Max. Where's Max?"

"Relax. Max is fine."

Gray tried to sit up. "Where is he? Is he okay?" Gray bit back another moan when his side flared and his head throbbed.

"Sit back, will you? I told you he's fine. He's the reason Kenny found you."

Gray lowered himself back down. He sucked in a breath when his ribs pulled. "What are you talking about?"

Cooper pulled the sheets up. "Kenny went looking for you. Said you were talking crazy over the phone and mentioned the boardwalk. It worried him enough to go looking for you. He went to your house, but you weren't there. He headed to the pier and found your car, but not you. He saw that the pier had collapsed and a good portion of ocean front property had gone with it. He was about to call in the cavalry when he heard barking. He followed it and found his way to a section that was still intact and found you."

"Max is okay?"

"Apparently your hearing has also been affected. Yes. He's at your place. I've asked Maria to keep an eye on him. He's up to his eyeballs in home-cooked meals, I'm sure."

Gray finally eased back fully and rested his head into the pillow.

"You gonna tell me what happened?"

Gray closed his eyes, but all he could see was darkness, and then he felt himself tumbling, as if the sea had him again in its grip. He grabbed at the bed sheets. His eyes shot open, and he gritted his teeth.

"Hey, take it easy." Cooper put his hand on Gray's forearm. Sweat popped out on Gray's skin. "You want me to get someone?" He reached for the call button.

"No," Gray managed to say. "Give me a second." He took a deep breath and tried to calm his nerves. "I'm okay."

"You don't look okay." Cooper studied him. "Try to relax."

Gray took another deep breath and the vertigo began to ease. "I'm all right."

"Did you remember something?"

Gray tried to clear the fog from his brain. He remembered the swirling water, but this time the vertigo did not return. "I fell in the ocean."

"Thanks for the tip, but we know that much. The question is how did you get in there? And how did you get out? Why were you at the pier? What does this have to do with Gillian?"

Gillian. He pushed up again and ignored the pain it caused. "Gillian. Where's Gillian?"

Cooper put a hand on his shoulder. "I don't know. Lay back..."

"Did Kenny find her?" Gray shivered, although he was sweating. "Is she alive?"

"Why wouldn't she be? Is she the reason you were out there? What's going on, Gray?"

"Where is she? Is she all right?"

"Grayson..."

Gray turned his tired eyes toward his friend. "Answer me. Have you seen her? Did Kenny find her?"

"Sit back..."

His muscles shook with exhaustion. "Stop telling me to sit back."

"She's fine," said Cooper. "What the hell is the matter with you?"

Gray stilled. "She's fine? How do you know?"

Cooper paused. "Because I saw her."

Gray's hair stood up. "You saw her? When? Where?"

"Here. At the hospital. Yesterday."

"Yesterday?"

"Yes. She came to see you."

"She did?"

"Yes. But she didn't stay long."

"Where is she? Is she here?" Gray noticed Cooper's worried look. "What is it?"

"Gray..."

"What?"

Cooper's discomfort increased. "She left."

Gray's heart thumped. "She left?"

"Listen, buddy. Maybe you should rest..."

"Dammit, Cooper. What the hell happened? Where is she?"

Cooper hesitated. "Gray," he finally spoke. "She's gone. She's not coming back."

"What? You mean to the hospital?"

Cooper hung his head. "No. I mean at all." He sighed. "She left you a note." He bobbed his head toward the small side table next to the bed. Gray saw an envelope with his name written across the front. Next to it sat a can of wet dog food.

"I'm sorry, Gray. I came in and saw her sitting with you. She couldn't have been here long. I tried to talk to her, but she was upset and wouldn't stay. She didn't look too great, either. It was obvious she was in distress."

"She left?" Gray continued to stare at the envelope.

Cooper paused. "Yes."

Gray's body protested its upright position, and he flinched. "How do you know she's not coming back?"

Cooper hesitated again. "She told me to tell you that she was sorry about what happened. That she didn't mean for you to get hurt and..."

Grayson waited. "And?"

"And that she loved you." Cooper's eyes softened. "In my experience, those are not the words of someone who's coming back, especially if she's telling them to me."

Gray deflated. With shaky arms, he eased himself back down on the bed, groaning as he laid back. His head flared and he wished he could return to his numb-like state.

"I'm sorry. I hate being the bearer of bad news."

Gray stared up at the ceiling. "It's not your fault."

"You want to read the letter?"

Gray shook his head. "No. Not right now." His eyelids felt like stones, and he blinked.

"You want to talk about what happened?" Cooper asked. "How you got here? You know Ken's going to have some questions."

His haze clearing, Gray almost chuckled at the thought of what his friend would think if he knew what had occurred. "No," he said. "Not now." His heavy lids drifted down, but he forced them up. "You're sure about what she said?"

Cooper nodded slowly. "I'm sure."

"She wasn't hurt?"

"Not that I could tell. At least not physically."

Gray wished he had the energy to ask more questions, but his eyes would not stay open.

"You need to rest. Get some sleep. We'll talk when you're stronger." He pulled the sheets up again.

Gray let his eyes close. "Yeah. Sure," he said. His mind went blank with fatigue. Gillian's face appeared and he tried to hold onto the image, but it faded as his weariness took over and he slept.

·· · • · • • • · ·

Gillian spoke, her voice distant but clear. "I'm sorry," he heard her say. "I'm sorry." He reached out for her, but she vanished. Another face came into view, and he pulled back when Franklin sneered at him.

"Time to end this." Franklin's voice echoed in his head. The sound of waves slamming against the shore reverberated and Gray shivered. "Time to end this," the voice repeated as everything went dark and Franklin's face receded although his voice did not. And then clearly, he heard a name whispered in his ear. "Galen."

Grayson jolted awake. It was quiet. He was back in the hospital room, the machine beside him now silent. The room was empty; the light was muted. The sound of shuffling feet made him turn, and he saw a nurse at the foot of his bed. She studied a computer tablet in her hand. He cleared his throat, and the nurse looked at him.

"Hello, Mr. Steele."

He swallowed but didn't say anything. She moved beside him. "How are you feeling?"

He spoke groggily. "I've been better."

She smiled. "Well, it's good to see you awake. I'm glad to say you're doing well."

His shoulder ached. "This is well?"

"Better than you were. You'll be on your feet soon."

"How soon?"

She studied her tablet. "Couple of days."

He looked around the room. "Where's Cooper?"

"Your friend?" She tapped at the screen with a stylus.

"Yes."

She put the stylus in her pocket. "I think he went to the cafeteria to get something to eat."

"He's been here the whole time?"

"Most of it." She pointed toward the opposite side of the room. "He's set himself up a little office in the corner."

Gray saw a laptop, papers, and a pen sitting on a makeshift table by a small couch in the room. "He's been working from here?"

"It looks like it." She put down the tablet, reached up and pulled down a nearly empty IV bag hanging on a pole. She detached it and threw it away. She picked up a new bag off the nearby counter and replaced the old one. "I think he's been worried about you."

Gray blinked. He thought of Gillian. "Have I had any other visitors?"

After adjusting the IV bag, she checked another device beside his bed. "Well, from the times I've been on duty, yes. There was a police officer here."

"Kenny."

"And there was a woman."

"A woman?"

"Yes. She was with your friend. I think her name is Fran? She's been here a couple of times."

Gray sighed. "Anyone else?"

The nurse picked up her tablet. "Not that I know of. The night nurse, Donna, will be on duty soon though. You might ask her."

Gray nodded his head.

"You need anything?"

Thinking, he looked over at his side table. "Can you hand me that?"

"What?"

"The envelope."

"This?" she asked. She picked up the letter with his name on it.

"Yes. Thanks." She handed it to him. He slid his thumb over his written name.

"Anything else?"

He stared at the letter. "No. Thanks."

"Okay. Hit the button if you need anything."

"Yeah." He heard her walk away.

Gray slid his finger under the flap and opened it. He pulled the letter out. Finding the bed controls, he raised the bed slightly. Staring at the folded sheet, he unfolded the paper and began to read.

Dear Grayson,

I don't know where to begin. I don't know how we ended up here. When we first met, my only thought was to help you find the answers to your questions and to end the curse and suffering that plagued you. I didn't know where it would lead or what my role would be. I only knew I had to follow my instincts. I didn't know at the time that we would catch a killer, or that I would fall for you. I never expected to tell you who I was or let you into my world. I always thought that because of my origins that I would always be alone. That I would never be able to reveal my secrets or those of my family to anyone. I resigned

myself to that, as I'm sure Eve and Royce have as well. I didn't let it stop
me though from wanting to help those in need, and it didn't stop me from
helping you. Nothing could. It's like a wave headed to shore (maybe not the
best analogy right now, but it fits.). Nothing can stop it.

I told myself I would leave after I helped you. I planned to after we stopped
Stuart. But I couldn't do it. You pulled me in just like that relentless wave,
and I couldn't resist you. It was like you and I were sucked into the center of
a whirlpool. The time we spent together was magical and I held onto it like
a lifeline. I think of it now as I write this and wish you were here.

But what I didn't think about was the future. Because of who I am, I put
you and Royce and Eve at terrible risk. I can't do that again. Franklin is just
the first. There will be others. Seeing you fall into the water terrified me, and
if it wasn't for Royce and Eve's help, you would have died. I can't risk your
life again. Because of that, I must leave.

I know that you will think of the curse. That this is somehow related to you.
But it is not. I am alive and well. My life will continue, although it will be
missing something special—you.

Please understand and do not come looking for me.

I love you and miss you.

G.

Grayson let the letter fall in his lap. He dropped his head back onto
the pillow and stared at the ceiling. Emotions bubbled up and his chest
constricted. Denial, anger, frustration, sadness, despair. He rubbed his eyes
and wondered what he had done wrong. How had he ended up here again?
Even though he knew he couldn't blame a curse, he couldn't help but feel
bitter and angry. He couldn't comprehend not seeing Gillian anymore.
His thoughts drifted to their time together. Their first meeting on the
beach, seeing her at Cooper's party, talking to her in the moonlight, their
interview on his patio, their plot to catch Stuart.

He swallowed, and his breath caught, and the memories continued—kissing her on the deck, watching and wanting her for three days

while she stayed at his house, searching for her in the fire, rescuing her in the hospital and finally having her in his bed... her laugh, her smell, her skin, her touch. He shut his eyes as the pain in his heart grew greater than the pain in his body, and tears sprang into his eyes. He wiped at them, trying to hold them back, but the more he thought of her, the harder they fell.

CHAPTER THIRTY-ONE

THE CALM OCEAN AND its gentle waves kissed the sand, the peaceful sound masking the destructive secrets the water held within it. The sun blazed above, but hints of a chilly breeze lingered in the air.

Gray pulled the blanket over him. He sat in the lounge chair, watching the water. Max sat by his feet, occasionally popping his head up whenever Gray shifted as if hoping Gray might want to play Frisbee. But Gray did not. He dozed on and off. He'd been home for two weeks but had done little since returning. Cooper had asked Maria to check in on him and Max to make sure they were well-fed and alive. She'd done both. Cooper had visited twice, as had Kenny. Fran had brought him lunch one day. He'd said little during their visits. Kenny had asked for details about what had happened that day on the boardwalk, but he'd feigned forgetfulness, saying only that he'd gone to look for Gillian and had ended up at the pier. The storm had worsened, and the structure had failed and he'd fallen in, but he remembered nothing after that. Gray knew Kenny didn't believe him, but he didn't care. It didn't really matter anyway. It wasn't as if they would ever find Franklin, and even if they did Gray couldn't explain Franklin's actions. Gray wasn't sure if even he could understand them. All he knew was that after all he'd been through to end his curse, he'd found himself right back where he'd been. Although this time the woman he loved was not dead, but still gone, and that somehow felt even worse. Because she was out there somewhere, yet he couldn't have her.

He tried to find a comfortable position. His pain pills were in the kitchen, but he had not taken them in a week. He preferred the discomfort. It helped to distract him. His ribs were better and they rarely ached, but his left arm remained in a brace. The shoulder was painful and it hurt to sleep, but he doubted he would have slept anyway. Ten-day old stubble grew on his face because he couldn't summon the motivation to shave.

Footfalls on the back steps drew his attention, and he turned to see Cooper climbing the stairs. Max jumped up and greeted him, excited to have something to do. When Cooper reached the landing, he petted Max and sat down on a patio lounge chair. "Not answering the door?" he asked.

"I didn't hear the bell," said Gray.

"I thought you could hear it out here."

"I've been dozing. Must have missed it."

Cooper studied him across the table. "How long have you been out here?"

Gray settled back against his seat. "About an hour." He could feel Cooper's gaze, but he ignored it.

"You decide to stop shaving?"

"I'll shave eventually."

"Did you shower?"

"This morning."

"About time. Last time I was here there was a distinct odor."

Gray didn't take the bait. "It was probably Max."

"Since when does a dog have B.O.?"

"You've obviously never owned a dog."

"You don't need to own a dog to know what they smell like."

"I disagree."

Cooper chose not to argue. "How's the collarbone?"

"It's better."

"Ribs?"

"Barely notice them now."

"When do you see the doctor again?"

"Tomorrow."

"You need a ride?"

Gray shrugged and winced. "You offering?"

Cooper snorted. "No. I just thought I'd laugh and point at you if you said 'yes.'"

"I'm not cleared to drive yet, so I guess I do."

"What time?"

"Appointment's at two o'clock."

"I'll pick you up at one-fifteen."

"Fine."

They stopped talking and stared at the sand.

"How's work?" asked Gray.

"Work is work. Although I have to admit, it's been hell trying to replace Franklin. I wish to hell I knew where he went and why he just disappeared."

Gray made no reaction but simply said, "Strange."

"Very strange. Guy doesn't answer his phone. His address is a vacant lot. It's like he never existed."

Gray fiddled with his blanket.

"I mean where the hell did he go?"

"I don't know," said Gray. "How's Fran doing?"

The question caught Cooper off guard. "Fran?"

"Yes."

"She's okay. Did she come by?"

"Yes. Couple of days ago."

"Good. She seem okay to you?"

"She seemed fine."

"Good."

Gray squirmed in his seat. "Yeah."

"You talk to Kenny?" asked Cooper.

"About what?"

"About anything."

"He stopped by for a few minutes yesterday. He apologized."

"He did? For what?"

"For not believing me. For saying the things he said."

Cooper grunted. "It's about time."

"He had his reasons."

"He should have known better."

"Maybe." Gray tried to pull himself up in his chair without using his shoulder.

"You taking your meds?" asked Cooper.

"No," Gray said.

"Why not?"

"Don't want to."

Cooper nodded. "That's a good enough reason, I suppose." He eyed his friend. "You sleeping?"

Gray paused. "Not really."

Cooper reached down to scratch Max's ears. "You left the house since you been back?"

"No."

"You're eating?"

Gray shifted his eyes in Cooper's direction. "Yes."

"You've lost weight."

"I'm not that hungry."

Cooper sat back. "The dog's still alive. Obviously you're taking care of him."

"Yes."

The two went quiet again. After a few silent minutes, Cooper spoke. "Well, this has been scintillating conversation."

Gray continued to watch the waves. "Sorry."

"You've been home for two weeks. How much longer are you going to do this?"

"Do what?"

"Feel sorry for yourself?"

Gray frowned at Cooper. "Excuse me?"

Cooper leaned forward. "Listen. Whatever happened to you was bad. You almost drowned. It had something to do with Gillian and she left. I get that."

"You don't get anything."

Cooper raised a palm. "Then tell me what I'm not getting."

"There's nothing to tell."

"Dammit, Gray. Yes, there is. I know you. I know when you're keeping something from me."

Gray held on to his temper. He understood why his friend was frustrated. "I just need some time. I know you want to know, but the fact is, there's nothing I can tell you that will make this situation any easier." Cooper rubbed his face. "All you need to know about that day is that I went looking for her. I found her. What happened afterward is just drama. But because of it, I ended up in the water and she left. She's chosen not to come back. I…" He stopped talking when he realized what he was about to say.

Cooper waited. "You what?"

"Nothing."

"What were you going to say?" asked Cooper. "You what?"

Gray debated not answering. "I wish that I could have talked to her before she left. There were things I should have said. Things I needed to tell her."

Cooper nodded. "She knows."

Gray met Cooper's gaze. "It doesn't matter what she knows. She needed to hear it from me. And she didn't."

"You don't know where she is?"

"I have no idea. Hotel has no record of her address."

"Did you ask Nelson?"

"I called him when I got home. He's had no luck."

"You're kidding. Nelson? He could find Atlantis if we gave him the budget."

"I know. Apparently, she doesn't want to be found."

"Did he try Horn?"

"No luck. Horn hasn't seen her in months and has no address for her."

"Who is this woman?" asked Cooper.

Gray said nothing.

"She can't disappear forever. We'll keep looking."

"There's no point."

"Yes, there is. You want closure, we'll get you closure."

Gray offered a sad smile that quickly disappeared. "I want more than closure, Cooper." He felt the weariness return. It was as if his energy had been sucked from him since his return home and he had no idea how to get it back.

"What else do you want?"

Gray stared with solemn eyes and answered truthfully. "Her," he said. His gaze drifted back to the water. "I want her."

Cooper didn't respond, and they sat in silence. They listened to the surf until the quiet was broken by the sound of the doorbell. Neither moved.

"I thought you said you couldn't hear the doorbell out here."

"Apparently I can."

"So you lied to me?"

"Apparently I did." The doorbell rang again.

"You going to get it?" asked Cooper.

Gray sighed. "Wasn't planning on it."

"Why not?" asked Cooper. "You think it's a repor—" He winced. "Sorry."

Gray threw off his blanket. "Don't be. It probably is a reporter." He swiveled his legs over the side of his patio chair. "You want to get it for me?"

Cooper shook his head. "What? And steal all your thunder when they see me at the door instead of you? No. Besides, you could use an excuse to get your ass up out of that chair."

Gray stood and bit back a moan when his shoulder complained. He adjusted the brace and waited a few seconds to get his bearings.

"You all right, Grizzly Adams? You're not going to faint on me, are you?"

Gray took a deep breath and let it out. "No. I'm not going to faint. Knowing you though, you'd just leave me on the porch."

"Nah, I'd get some water and throw it on you."

Gray didn't doubt it. "Thanks."

Cooper grinned. "You're welcome."

The doorbell rang again. "I'm comin'," said Gray. He reached the back patio door and slid it open.

"It's probably your mother."

"God, I hope not. That's all I need." He stepped into the house. "I'll be right back."

"Take your time," said Cooper. He settled back in his seat and closed his eyes, prepared to take a nap. "If it's the Girl Scouts, get me some Thin Mints."

Gray muttered as he shut the door. "You can get your own damn Thin Mints."

He walked to the front entry and the bell rang again. "Jeez," he said, "What's the hurry?" Peering out the peephole, he froze, not believing his eyes. "Hell," he said. He grabbed the doorknob and yanked it open. He stared at the female standing on his doorstep.

Her gaze found his and she looked nervous. "Hi, Gray," she said.

He felt numb, but he managed to answer. "Hi, Eve."

The two of them stared across the threshold. Grayson couldn't believe it was her. She wore slim cut jeans and high-heeled wedge shoes, and her fitted shirt dipped low to reveal a comfortable view of cleavage. Her hands were in the pockets of her blue-jean jacket and her auburn, curly hair was down around her shoulders and was tousled by the wind. Her flawless face was marred only by her sad eyes. "Can I come in?"

Gray made himself move. "God. I'm sorry." He stepped back. "Yes. Come in."

Eve stepped inside, and he shut the door behind her. She stood there in his foyer and his mind raced with a million questions, but he said nothing.

She looked him up and down. "You look terrible. What's up with the beard?"

Reaching for his jaw, he rubbed at the stubble. "I haven't felt much like shaving." He thought about it. "Guess I haven't felt good in general. I've been keeping to myself lately."

She studied his brace. "How's the collarbone?"

He touched his shoulder. "It's okay." He noted how she shifted on her feet. "How are you?"

Preoccupied, she looked into the den. "You alone?"

"Eve," he said, ignoring her question. "What's this all about? Why are you here? Where's Gillian?"

Taking her hands out of her pockets, she crossed her arms in front of her. She hesitated as if trying to make a decision. "I need to ask you something."

"What?"

She looked down.

"What, Eve? Tell me what's going on."

"How have you been feeling?"

He knitted his brow. "What are you talking about? What does that have to do with anything?"

She became impatient. "Just answer the question, will you?"

Frustrated, he almost argued with her, but then thought better of it. "My shoulder hurts..."

"Not about the shoulder," she interrupted. "I mean in general. Are you sleeping?"

He paused, unsure where this was going. "If I'm lucky."

"Are you eating?"

"Only because Maria won't leave until I do."

"Lethargic?"

He sighed. "Let's just say I almost didn't answer the door because of the energy required to do it."

"Sad? Depressed?"

He opened his mouth to speak, but stopped and changed his answer. "What the hell do you think, Eve? I've fallen in love with a woman that I can't have again. Happy is not an adjective I would use to describe myself right now."

Eve nodded. "Did you get her letter?"

Moaning to himself, he walked into the living room toward the couch. Standing had become difficult at the barrage of questions, and he was tiring fast. Eve followed him, and he slowly sat. He knew he looked pale, and he rubbed his eyes. "Yes. I got her letter."

"You got the dog food?"

Just then, Max popped his head in the dog door and woofed. Running inside, he stopped at Eve's feet and she dropped down to pet him. "Hey, boy," she said, ruffling his fur. "He treating you right?"

Max jumped up on her knee, soaking up the attention. Gray cocked his head. "You left the dog food?"

She smiled. "Yes. I knew he would like it."

"He loves it. I've been putting it in with his dry food."

"Good," she said. "It's good for him too."

She continued to minister to Max when a thought occurred to Gray. "You saved him, didn't you?"

Her hands stopped in mid-pet, but she patted the dog's head and stood. "What do you mean?"

"I saw Max lying on the pier. He was injured. But when they found me, Max was standing over me, barking his head off and in good shape. How is that possible?"

Eve studied a fingernail.

"You did it, didn't you?" asked Gray. "You saved him?"

She finally looked up. "I may have had something to do with it."

"How?"

She shrugged. "It's just something I can do with animals. I haven't had a lot of practice though. I wasn't even sure I could help Max until I tried."

Gray shook his head. "I see." He wasn't sure what he thought about this new revelation. "Thank you."

"You're welcome."

Gray considered something else. "And who saved me?"

She paused. "Royce. We saw you go in. Royce jumped in after you. I got Gilli off the pier before we fell in too."

"But how is that possible? Most of the pier collapsed. And how did Royce not get swept away with me? There was no way out of that water."

Eve sat across from him. "Let's just say we may have had a few more abilities up our sleeve than we were letting on."

"More abilities? What? Are you Moses now?"

Eve made a small chuckle. "No. I'm just saying that we had to act weaker than we were."

"Act?"

"Yes," said Eve. "It's complicated. Our dad told us things about ourselves, but individually. None of us knew how it would play a part later, but he prepared us without us realizing it. When we finally all came together on that pier, that's when it hit us."

"What hit you?"

"Something about the situation triggered a memory. It happened to each of us. On our own, we couldn't defeat him. But if we worked together, then we had a chance. Somehow, in that moment, we knew exactly what we had to do to defeat Franklin."

"You mean your energy combined was stronger than your energy apart? Sort of like," he made a fist and bumped it against the couch, 'wonder twin powers activate?'"

She smiled solemnly. "Yes. Something like that."

"You weren't aware of that ability before? It would have been helpful."

"Maybe, but my theory is if he'd known we were stronger, he would have prepared for that. He would have been that much harder to defeat."

"So it allowed you to play him? Lure him in?"

"Yes."

"Pretty damn risky. Gillian almost died. We all almost died."

"I know. But thankfully, it worked."

He thought back to his encounter with Franklin. "Wish I could have had some of that ability."

Her eyes tightened. "I think you did."

"What do you mean?"

She bit her lip as if gauging what to say. "How much do you remember from the pier?"

His memories were vivid. "It didn't go well. I tried to knock his head off with the pipe and he threw me into a beam. Next thing I know, I'm in the water."

"You don't remember hitting the deck with the pipe?"

He narrowed his eyes. "I what?"

"After he threw you into the beam, you got up. You had the pipe, Gillian and I couldn't breathe, and Royce was down. You swung the pipe and hit the pier. It cracked. You did it two more times and it started to give way."

Gray struggled to remember. "When did I do that?"

"Right before you went into the water. It distracted him long enough for you to knock him down. It's how we managed to get loose from his grip."

"I don't recall any of that," said Gray. "I did that? Are you sure?"

"Gray, you swung that pipe so hard, it cracked the pier. That's not ordinary strength. What you did should have been impossible."

Gray scoffed. "You must have been delusional. I never did that."

She shook her head. "I'm not delusional. We all saw it. And you did something else. You called Franklin 'Galen.'"

"I called him what?"

"Galen."

"Who the hell is Galen?"

"That's just it. I don't know."

"Why would I call him Galen?"

She paused to think. "I think it was Franklin's real name."

"His real name?"

"That's my assumption. Why else would you say it? But there's no way you could have known that."

"Exactly. Which is why it didn't happen."

"But it did. You knew his name, and it shocked him. You swung that pipe and knocked him down, and because of that, you gave us the upper hand. You saved our lives."

Grayson couldn't believe it. He had no memory of injuring Franklin, swinging a pipe, or calling anyone 'Galen.' "What happened out there?" he asked.

"I don't know," said Eve. "But we had more help than we realized, and obviously you were the conduit."

Gray didn't understand. "You mean somebody used me?"

"Sounds like it."

"But how?"

"Anything's possible." She stared off. "I have my suspicions." She swiped at a dog hair on her pant leg. "Maybe one day we'll find out."

Grayson recalled another question. "And what about that other community?"

Eve raised a brow. "What other community?"

"I heard Royce tell Franklin, or Galen, whoever he is, that he knew about another community. What was that about?"

Eve clasped her hands. "Apparently we're not alone."

Gray dropped his jaw. "You mean there are more of you?"

"You might say that. Royce, Gillian, and I are Red-Lines. But there's a group of Gray-Lines that live here as well."

The fact that more aliens existed made Gray's head swim. "What are Gray-Lines?"

"They're like us. They have similar abilities but are less advanced."

"Do they know about you?"

"No, I don't think so."

"And how does Royce know about them? Did he warn them about Frank?"

Eve sat back. "No. He lied about that. He said that to unnerve Franklin. He's never met them, but he knows where they live. Dad told him about their existence, just in case."

Gray shifted on the couch to ease the ache in his shoulder. "In case what?"

"Maybe he wanted us to know we weren't alone." She rubbed her eyes in a gesture of fatigue. "It seems they've lived here a while, but based on what Franklin said, it sounds like they have someone else like us, a Red-Line, among them. Royce didn't know that."

Gray remembered Franklin's words. "If that's all true, they should be told about the possible threat against them. If Frank knew about them and your family, then maybe someone else does too."

Eve nodded. "I agree." She stared out the window.

Gray followed her stare. Cooper was still out on the deck, and had, so far, not interrupted. Gray figured he had probably dozed off. "I still don't know if I buy all this."

She swiveled her head toward him. "After all you've witnessed? How could you not?"

"Maybe in some sort of small part of my brain, I can buy the existence of life elsewhere and maybe even of alien life among us, but being chased and nearly killed by one? Not to mention having someone or something use me to confront Franklin."

Eve lifted a brow. "I can't explain that either. But keep in mind, you're sitting here talking to one very good-looking, animal-talking, water-dodging extraterrestrial, so I think it's time to consider a variety of possibilities."

He couldn't deny that. "No, offense, Eve" he said, feeling the weight of his sadness return, "but the only extraterrestrial I want to talk to right now is Gillian."

"She doesn't talk to animals."

He sighed. "I can live with that."

She reached out and took his hand. "What if I told you I could arrange that?"

CHAPTER THIRTY-TWO

GRAY DIDN'T KNOW WHAT to say. "What do you mean?"

Eve didn't reply.

"Where is she?"

Eve let go of his hand. "Before I say anything, I need to be sure about something."

Gray's heart rate picked up. "What?"

She eyed him intently. "What exactly are your intentions with her?"

"My intentions?"

She leaned forward. "I'm not going to tell you where she is just so you can tell her your problems, blame her, or get angry with her. I need to know that you won't hurt her."

Gray sat up straight. "Hurt her? I would never hurt her."

She studied him. "Royce and I argued over me coming here. He disagreed that you should remain in Gillian's life."

"Why?"

"Because despite whatever courage you may have showed on that pier, he doesn't think that you are what's best for Gillian."

"Isn't that up to her?"

She didn't answer immediately.

"What do you think?" asked Gray.

She paused. "Honestly, I think it's already out of our hands."

"What do you mean?"

Her head dropped. "There's something you need to know."

Grayson's chest constricted. "What? Is she okay?" Eve remained quiet. "What's wrong?"

Eve's head bobbed up. "She's sick."

Something cold moved through Gray. "She's sick?"

"Yes."

"How sick? Is it because of what happened on the pier?"

"No, it's not because of that."

His heart skipped. "Then what? Is it serious?"

"I...we didn't think so at first. But it's gotten worse. Royce thinks she'll get better eventually, but I..."

"You what?"

"I'm not so sure."

"Did she see a doctor? Is she in a hospital?"

"No. It's not like that."

Gray groaned. "Then what is it? What's wrong?" Watching Eve, he could tell she was concerned.

"Listen, there are a few things that you're not aware of about us. In fact, even Gillian wasn't aware of everything."

"God." He rubbed his face. "I'm afraid to ask." He tried to prepare himself.

"It has to do with females of our kind."

He swallowed. "Okay."

"I'll try to keep it simple."

"Please do."

She thought for a second. "As I mentioned before, those of us from our father's planet are either Gray-Lines or Red-Lines. Red-Lines have advanced abilities which Gray-Lines do not."

Gray tried to keep an open mind. "You mean the whole intuitive, tele-pathic, animal-talking, furniture-moving thing?"

"Yes."

Gray nodded his head. "I'm with you so far."

"Red-Line females have their own unique traits as well."

"I can only imagine."

Eve played with her fingers and seemed to gather her courage. "They take mates."

"They take what?" Gray felt a strange heaviness wash over him, as if he was back in the water again and it was difficult to find air.

"Mates," said Eve.

"Mates? You mean like a significant other?"

Eve nodded. "That's one way of putting it."

"Why am I afraid you're about to reveal another way?"

"Because I am."

The air thickened and he tried to relax. "What is it?"

She stared as if measuring his ability to hear what she was about to reveal. "When a female Red-Line falls in love, there is a reaction that occurs. As it was explained to me, precautions can be taken to prevent it, but if that doesn't happen, nature takes its course."

Gray continued to listen.

"What happens next is a very strong physical reaction."

Gray began to understand. "Are you saying...?"

"When you brought her home from the hospital, was she..." She paused. "Did she..."

Gray helped her. "Become rather assertive in a sexual way?" Eve nodded and looked relieved that he'd said it instead of her. "Yes," he said. The memory of her sliding on top of him flashed in his head. "She was, but I sure as hell didn't stop her."

"You felt just as strongly as she did?"

"As you say, that's one way of putting it."

"And how long did it last?"

More memories surfaced and he tried to focus. "Can you rephrase the question, please?"

"Sorry," she said. "Better said, how much time did you two spend together before it abated?"

He didn't understand her question. "Abated?"

"Yes."

"It never abated."

Her eyes narrowed. "It never abated?"

"Well, we spent twenty-four hours together and we would have easily continued, but then..." He hated to think about what happened next.

"Then, what?"

"That's when I learned she was not a reporter. I learned that she'd lied. Then she told me who she was."

"Is that when you threw her out of the house?"

Guilt washed over him, and he sank in his seat. "It wasn't one of my better moments. But you have to admit, it was not something I was prepared for."

She paused. "So she left before the process ended."

Eve's words surprised him. "Process? What process?"

"She instigated a Binding with you."

"A what?"

"A Binding."

"What's a Binding?"

"It's what a female Red-Line does when she takes a mate."

He clenched his hands. "Wait a minute. A mate? She took me as a mate?"

"She did. She didn't know it at the time, but that's exactly what she did."

Grayson took a second to assimilate this new information. "So what, does that mean we're married or something?"

"Again, that's one way of looking at it."

Gray huffed. "I'm beginning to hate that phrase."

Eve pursed her lips. "Gillian didn't know about this. Our dad told me about it, but not her. Probably because I'm a bit more...extroverted."

Grayson got the point. "And Gillian?"

"Much quieter. She kept to herself much of the time. Dad probably thought she had more time, or he expected me to tell her." She studied her toes that peeped out from the tips of her shoes.

"And you didn't?"

She looked up with guilt-ridden eyes. "It was stupid. I should have. I just didn't think she'd fall in love with..." She stopped.

"With who...a millionaire playboy?"

"I was going to say a human."

Gray almost laughed. "Well, who the hell else was she going to meet?"

Eve held her head in her hands. "I know. It makes no sense. I was stupid and I underestimated her." She rubbed her forehead. "I think we just all thought that she'd be the last to fall in love."

Gray offered a surprised look. "I don't know why. She's got the biggest heart out of the three of you." He shrugged. "No offense."

"None taken because you're right."

Grayson sighed. "So what does this mean now? Have we broken the Binding vows before they ever began?"

"That's the tricky part."

"What is?"

"I'm not sure, but I think once a Binding occurs, the connection is permanent. But in your case, the Binding isn't complete."

"You mean this Binding is still going on?"

"Very much so. I think that's why she's sick."

"Because she Binded with me?"

"No, because you didn't finish it. It's supposed to end of its own accord. There's a progression to it. It usually lasts twenty-four to forty-eight hours, sometimes longer."

"Ours was around twenty-four hours."

"Would it have ended if you hadn't kicked her out?"

He remembered clearly. "Uh, no. Not by a long shot."

"Then it wasn't over."

Gray shook his head. "So we need to finish it?"

Eve sighed. "I think it's too late for that."

The wave of heaviness returned. "What are you trying to tell me, Eve?"

She hesitated. "There's something else that results from a Binding..."

"What's that?"

"Grayson..."

Forcing in a breath, he tried to not think the worst. "Just tell me."

She held his look. "Pregnancy."

The color drained from his face. "Oh, my god. She's pregnant?" He thought back. "But..but... that's not possible."

"You used protection?"

"Yes."

"Doesn't matter."

"Why not?"

"It just doesn't. There are some forces that can't be stopped no matter what you put in front of them."

Gray struggled to speak. "She's pregnant?"

Her face dropped. "That's just it, Gray. I think she was, but she's not anymore."

His hope deflated. "What do you mean?"

Eve's face went pale, and he could see the fear in her eyes. "She's lost the baby, Gray. The Binding ended too soon, and she couldn't sustain it. She's been sick since we got her home. She told me she'd been cramping. And then I realized what that probably meant. Royce and I thought she would recuperate, but she's not getting better. If there was a way for her to break her bond with you, then it might help. But she's not going to do that. She's getting weaker, and it scares me."

Gray stared vacantly as Eve's news began to sink in. "Gillian was pregnant." The blossom of excitement that had sprung up disappeared just as quickly. Feeling the sadness of the loss, he thought of Gillian and how she must have felt. He knew immediately what he had to do. "Where is she, Eve?"

Eve met his intense stare, and he could see that she had been as deeply affected as him. "You promise me you won't hurt her? She's been through enough. If you aren't going to..."

"You don't have to worry about that," he interrupted. "Where is she?"

She took a second but finally answered. "She's outside, in the car."

He stood fast and gasped when his shoulder flared. White spots flashed in his vision, and he swayed. He grabbed at the mantel until the dizziness passed.

"Looks like you've been dealing with the after-effects too," she said, watching him. "You all right?"

He stood up taller. "I'll be better when I see her."

He began to walk past Eve when she stood and put her arm on his elbow. He stopped. "What?" he asked.

She hesitated. "I'm sorry."

"For what?"

She searched for words, and he saw the shine of tears in her eyes. "For what's happened. For not handling things differently...the baby."

He'd built his own wall of regret, but he wouldn't let it affect him. He'd done enough of that already. "It's not your fault. It's not anyone's fault."

"We should have intervened sooner."

"And what would that have accomplished?"

Eve sniffed. "Maybe..."

Gray knew what she didn't want to say. "Maybe you would have taken her away. Protected her? Left me to fend for myself with the curse."

She averted his eyes. "Something like that."

"And have Franklin...or Galen, whatever his name is, still hunting you?" Eve remained silent, but he continued. "If there's anything I've learned through all of this, it's that we have to trust what happens. Do I wish I hadn't thrown her out of the house? God yes. If I hadn't, she might be healthy and we might be together right now." He tried not to think about what might have been. "But if I hadn't, and she'd stayed, she could be dead, right along with you and Royce because Franklin would have killed all of you." Eve said nothing. "And why did I have an insane stalker kill four beautiful women in my life? Without me realizing who it was?" He thought about the insanity of it. "I don't know. Maybe in some crazy way it was destined for Gillian to be in my life, and she wouldn't have been otherwise."

"It's a big price to pay," Eve said.

"It is. But we can't understand everything. I showed up for a reason too. Maybe to keep all of you alive." He shook his head. "All I do know is that all of that is in the past, and we don't have time to be sorry anymore. Too much has happened." She wiped at an unshed tear. "If Gillian and I are meant to have children, then we'll have them. If we're not, then we won't. That's the least of my issues right now. All I want right now is to see her and know she's all right."

Eve's eyes shimmered, and Grayson lightly took her hand. "You realize by bringing her here, she's staying with me, right?"

A faint smile grazed Eve's lips. "If that's what she wants, then I figured as much."

"And you can tell big brother to shove it up his ass if he has a problem with that."

Her smile grew bigger. "I'll let you tell him that."

He smiled back and dropped her hand. He began to walk toward the front door when he thought of Cooper on his patio. He stopped and turned. "You want to have some fun?"

Eve shook off her melancholy. "What do you mean?"

Grayson eyed the porch. "Cooper's outside, probably dozing in his chair. Why don't you go say 'hi'?"

"Cooper?" she asked. She looked back toward the patio and her eyebrows arched. "Really?" she asked, as if some unexpected plan had formulated in her mind.

"I'm sure he'd love to see you."

She looked back at him with the eyes of a cat, and Gray almost felt sorry for his friend. "Well," she said, walking toward the back door, "let's not keep him waiting."

CHAPTER THIRTY-THREE

GRAYSON OPENED THE FRONT door and raced down the front steps, taking them two at a time and ignoring the aches and pains in his body. Spotting the car parked on the side of his driveway, he ran over and approached the passenger side. Seeing a reclined figure in the seat, he opened the door. Gillian lay back, her eyes closed. Hearing the door, though, her eyes opened. Grayson dropped low beside her.

"Gillian?" he asked. Looking her over, he saw her pale features, the circles under her eyes and her thinner frame.

Her lashes fluttered. "Gray?" she whispered. "Is that you?"

He leaned in the car. "Yes. It's me, sweetheart." Bringing his hand to her face, he grazed his fingers over her cheek. "How are you?"

Smiling softly, she answered. "I'm fine."

Seeing her weakness, he masked his worry. "Yeah, I can tell." He reached in and snaked his good arm beneath her legs. "Let's you get you out of this car."

"I can walk."

He didn't care. All he wanted to do was hold her. "Put your arms around me," he said. "I've got a bum arm."

Not arguing with him, she brought her arms up and wrapped them around his neck. He pulled her out of the car and kicked the door shut.

"How's your shoulder?" she asked, resting her head in the crook of his neck.

Surprisingly, he felt little pain while carrying her. "It's okay." He took the stairs back up to the house and carried her inside. Kicking the front door closed, he brought her to the couch and sat her down, ensuring she was comfortable. He grabbed a nearby blanket and covered her with it.

She watched him tuck the covering around her. "It's good to see you."

Making sure she was warm, he sat down beside her. "I've been looking for you," he said. "You're not an easy woman to find."

She blinked tired eyes at him. "I didn't want you to find me."

"Why not?"

Her eyes turned sad. "Did you read my letter?"

"Yes. I read it."

"Then you know why. Too much has happened. It's better I stay away."

He scoffed at her. "That's just a load of horseshit."

She blinked. "Gray..."

He didn't let her finish. "Just wait a minute. You had your say. Now let me have mine." When she didn't respond, he continued. "I know a lot of stuff has happened. Stuff I still can't explain and may never be able to." He tucked in her blanket some more. "There are things about you I don't understand, but hell, my past is not exactly boring either. I had a stalker after me who almost killed you. That's not exactly endearing." She shook her head, but he kept going. "I said some things to you I shouldn't have said. Granted, I was in a poor state of mind at the time, but nevertheless, I regret them and I apologize."

"Grayson..."

"Wait," he said, and she quieted. "I know who you are and you know who I am. We like each other, despite all the crap we've been through. Now, I don't know what the future holds. And you don't either. But whatever may or may not happen, I'm not willing to let that stop us from having what could be an incredible love story." He held her gaze. "Are you?"

She didn't answer, but her hand pushed out from the covers, found his and grasped it. The heat of her skin in his palm pleased him, and he could feel his body warm. It was as if being near her again was charging his batteries. He felt an electric spark move through him. Gillian pushed the covers down, and he assumed that she was feeling it too.

Her fingers wrapped around his. "It's a risk," she said. "This incredible love story could end up as one huge tragedy. Royce, Eve, and I are not out of the woods. If someone else comes looking..."

"We could jump at unknown shadows for the rest of our lives. But you're going to do that regardless. So why not do it together?"

"Because if something happened to you because of me, I'll never forgive myself."

"I believe I said the same thing to you not too long ago." She started to argue but stopped. "Exactly," he said. "It didn't stop you, so why should it stop me?"

"This is different."

"No, it isn't."

She played with the blanket with her free hand.

"I love you, Gillian." Her eyes widened. "I should have told you that sooner."

Tears sprang into her eyes, and she pushed the blanket down farther. Reaching up, she cupped a hand to his face and rubbed at the stubble there. "I like the new look," she said.

Staring at her, he could almost see the dark circles beneath her eyes fading. "You do?" His breathing sped up.

Her thumb trailed over his cheek, and she nodded. "I love you too, Grayson. You know that don't you?"

Nodding back, he stared at her lips. The familiar feelings were quickly returning. He remembered her naked and his skin tingled. "I know," he said.

She trailed her hand down to his shoulder with the brace and she rubbed it. "Does it hurt?"

Heat flooded through him at her touch and an almost numb-like feeling drifted through his arm. Whatever lingering pain that remained vanished completely.

"No," he said, flexing his arm with surprise. "It feels great." After moving his arm with no discomfort, he reached up, pulled the brace, and removed it.

"Good," she said. He noted her flushed face.

Dropping the brace to the floor, he lifted his fingers and touched her neck. His thumb trailed over her jaw. "How are you feeling?"

Her paleness now gone, she answered, "Better than I have in weeks."

Gently, he pulled her in closer, but she held back. "What is it?" he asked. The compulsion to kiss her continued to build, and he fought to wait.

"I..." she said.

"What?"

"I..." A tear shimmered in her eye and threatened to fall. "I think I was pregnant."

"Gillian..."

"I think I lost the baby." The tear fell then, and he brushed it away with his thumb.

"It's okay," he said, and he leaned in and kissed her cheek where her tear fell. "Don't cry."

Another tear fell, and he brought his hand up and wiped it away. He gently kissed her face as she wept.

"I'm sorry," she said. She touched her forehead to his.

"I'm sorry too," he answered quietly.

Their eyes met, and the force between them could no longer be contained. He moved his lips to hers and kissed her gently. She answered him and peppered his lips with feathery kisses. Before it could escalate further though, the back door banged and slid open. They broke away to see Cooper pop his head in.

He eyed Gillian. "Well, well, looks like the lovely Miss Fletcher has returned."

Gillian smiled back through watery eyes. "Hi, Cooper."

"Glad to see you back." He eyed Gray. "This is the happiest I've seen him since you left."

"What do you want Coop?" asked Gray, annoyed.

Cooper looked at Gillian. "Is it true?" he asked. "Is sexy Eve really your sister?"

Gillian laughed softly. "Yes. She is."

"Well," he made a contented groan, "the Fletcher family has good genes."

Gray sighed. "I repeat. What do you want, Coop?"

Cooper grinned. "I'm heading out. Me and the other lovely Miss Fletcher are going for a walk on the beach." He wiggled his eyebrows.

"I won't wait up," said Gray.

"Good." His eyes flicked between the both of them. "I'd asked you two to join us, but I'm guessing you've got other plans."

"Get the hell out of here, Cooper."

Cooper winked and closed the door. They watched him and Eve walk past and down the steps.

Gray looked back at Gillian. "Now, where were we?" He slipped his hand to the back of her neck and pulled her close. Pushing the blanket away, she moved into his lap and wrapped her arms around him.

"Right about here," she said. She dropped her lips against his and breathing hard, she opened her mouth and his tongue darted in, tasting her. He couldn't believe how much he wanted her. The energy between them had magnified from the moment he'd picked her up from the car. He pulled her down against him and kissed her hard. She wrapped around him and moved her hands down his back; the two of them clung to each other. His strength returning at a rapid rate and feeling no pain, he pushed up from the couch and stood, carrying her with him.

Pulling away from her lips, he managed a breathless whisper. "God, I've missed you." Capturing her mouth again, he stopped her from replying. He could feel her hands grip at his shirt and her legs wrap tightly around him. He moaned in his throat as he dragged his lips to her neck and kissed her soft skin. He heard her moan.

Somehow, he managed to find his way to the stairs without tripping over anything. As he began to climb them, she spoke into his ear.

"You realize that this means you're stuck with me."

He nibbled on her earlobe but managed to answer. "You mean like a curse?"

Her laughter made his heart race, and he couldn't get her upstairs fast enough.

She pulled back and looked at him. "You worried?"

He kissed her again and felt her hands move through his hair. Navigating his way into his bedroom, he carried her to the bed. "No," he answered, laying her down.

"Why not?" she whispered. He laid down next to her and pulled her up next to him.

His lips barely touching hers, he said, "Because now I've got a secret weapon."

She brushed her lips against his. "What's that?"

Pushing up, he rolled above her. "You," he said in a husky voice. He let his fingers trail over her cheek. "You're my curse breaker."

She stared back with hazy eyes. "And you're mine," she whispered.

Warmth flooded through him, and he covered her lips with his own in another fiery kiss.

What happens next?

If you enjoyed Gillian's story in *Curse Breaker*, then check out Royce's story next in *High Child*. Royce's solitary existence is about to end when a surprise visit from two strangers leads to love and unexpected revelations, but their visit may get him, and his family killed.

Want more from J. T. Bishop?

Sign up for her newsletter at jtbishopauthor.com to get a Daniels and Remalla prequel novella, plus missing scenes, excerpts, and more books for **free**.

How did it all begin with the Red-Lines?

Discover the *Red-Line Trilogy*, which started the Red-Line story. Sarah Randolph holds the key to the survival of a secret community. But first she must survive her "Shift." Her protector, John Ramsey, is assigned to keep her alive, but falling for her was never in his plans. When a powerful adversary reveals himself and his intentions for Sarah, her unique destiny may be their only hope.

It includes *Red-Line: The Shift*, *Red-Line: Mirrors*, and *Red-Line: Trust Destiny*. A boxed set is available, too!

And what's after the Red-Lines?

Get ready for Bishop's paranormal thriller series, the *Family or Foe Saga*, which introduces Detectives Daniels and Remalla. This set of four books will follow the trail of a murderer determined to exact revenge on those he believed wronged him. But there's more to the story when his secrets reveal unexpected connections and shocking revelations. A boxed set is available for this one, too.

Detectives Daniels and Remalla get their own series.

After *The Family or Foe Saga*, the two charismatic and affable detectives battle psychopaths, unexplained evil and unsolved cases. In *Haunted River*, book one in the series, the ghost of a woman haunts a small town where she lived and died. When a second woman's body turns up twenty-five years later, Daniels and Remalla become suspects, and the next targets.

Or pick up the omnibus *Shadows and Secrets*, which contains *Haunted River*, *Of Breath and Blood*, and *Of Body and Bone* (books one through three) of the paranormal thriller series.

A NOTE FROM J.T.

I love to hear from my readers about their experiences with my books, and I'd love to know what you thought about *Curse Breaker*. This book was fun and a challenge to write. If you know my work, then Gillian's secret was probably anticipated, but if you don't, it might have been a bit of a shock. I couldn't reveal too much in the blurb but wanted to give the reader at least a small idea that there was a big change a comin'. I hope you liked it and are ready to read more. Royce's story is just as intriguing if not more so. And if you've read my earlier books, hang in there because some familiar characters are about to turn up.

I've always loved the thrill of the paranormal and the unknown. It allows me plenty of opportunities for compelling story lines, dangerous bad guys, and irresistible good guys. I also love a good mystery thriller, too, so I thought I'd combine the two. I added a little romance too, because how could I not, and that's how this series, plus the original Red-Line series, was born. They are fun to write, and I hope you're enjoying them as much as I am.

Reviews are a huge plus and big help for an author, as well as potential readers. I would love it if you could please take a couple of minutes to leave a review for *Curse Breaker*. And if you'd like, please leave a few comments, too.

As always, thank you for your time and readership. It is deeply valued and appreciated.

Now, on to the next book!

ABOUT THE AUTHOR

Award-winning author, J.T. Bishop, is a writer of mystery thrillers with a paranormal edge. Growing up, she read Stephen King, Mary Higgins Clark, and Dean Koontz, devoured every episode of the X-files and watched plenty of TV shows with great partnerships that leave you wanting more. She loves tangled relationships, unexpected twists and turns, heart-stopping love stories and the complications that come with all the above. Throw in a little supernatural fun and she's hooked. Her evil plan is to hook you, too.

She's the author of The Red-Line Trilogy and its sister series, The Fletcher Family Saga, which features touches of urban fantasy, light sci-fi, and paranormal romance. She's also happily writing mystery thrillers featuring two charismatic detectives who may occasionally encounter a supernatural villain or two, and a crossover series which follows the exploits of a gifted, but troubled, paranormal P.I. and his spunky sister.

All the above keeps her busy, but in her spare time, she loves good movies, tasty food, an unfortunate sugar addiction, and traveling..

BOOKS IN CHRONOLOGICAL ORDER

ALTHOUGH RECOMMENDED, BUT NOT required, in case you like to read in order...

Prelude to The Shift, a short story (subscribers only)
Red-Line: The Shift
Red-Line: Mirrors
Red-Line: Trust Destiny
Curse Breaker
High Child
Spark
Forged Lines
**
The Girl and the Gunshot, a novella (subscribers only)
A Hamburger Christmas, a novella
The Magic of Murder, a novella (subscribers only)
First Cut
Second Slice
Third Blow
Fourth Strike
Murder Unveiled
Haunted River
Of Breath and Blood
Lost Souls

Of Body and Bone

Lost Dreams

Of Mind and Madness

Lost Chances

Of Power and Pain

Lost Hope

Of Love and Loss

Lost Lives

Dominion

Lost Time

Illusions

Lost Love

Vendetta

Black Bird

ACKNOWLEDGEMENTS

NONE OF THIS would be possible without the support of my family and friends.

Thank you to Mom and Dad for always believing in me, to Nick and Cathy for their constant support, and to Suzzie, Jack, Alejandro, Jessica, Paula, Anne, Bob, Taylor, Alex, Sydney, Colson, and Leighton—you make life so much fun, plus you like my books, and I thank you for both.

To my wonderful friends (and I'm blessed to have many), thank you so much for being there for me. You're my biggest fans and you keep me sane.

To my lovely photographer, Mayza Clark, thank you for making me look gorgeous.

And to my amazing editor and cover designer, Amie—thank you for helping me make this book beautiful. I appreciate your help.

I would also like to thank my fans for their support. That's the whole point of this fun adventure and all of this is possible because of you!

An Excerpt from High Child, Book Two in Red-Line: The Fletcher Family Saga

THE QUIET MAN WALKED out of the woods and strode toward the porch. His easy gait and relaxed posture revealed his complete comfort with his surroundings, as if walking out of the dark woods at night were as normal as getting a glass of water before bed. Royce watched him approach. He took in the man's dark complexion and long, black hair. A necklace with a long gray and white feather was hanging from his neck. "What the hell are you doing out here, Chief?" asked Royce.

The man got closer and Royce could make out his visitor's deep set, dark eyes. The man smiled and the lines on his face creased deeper. "I could ask the same of you, Starman." He walked on to the porch and eyed Royce's beer. "You sharing?"

His friend walked across the porch and sat down in one of the patio chairs. Shaking his head, Royce headed into his house, accessed the fridge and grabbed a beer. He returned to the porch, sat, and tossed the bottle. The man caught it and twisted the cap. "How you been, Gus?" asked Royce.

Gus took a swig and set the bottle on the side table. "Good. You?"

Royce rested a foot on the scarred wooden patio table. "Fine."

"I see you have company."

Royce was not surprised Gus knew about RJ. "His dad dropped him off for a few days." He didn't elaborate. "How long were you gone this time?"

Gus picked up his bottle. "About a month."

"That's longer than usual," said Royce.

"This one was different. Took a little time." Gus took another swig of his beer. "How's RJ?"

Royce nodded toward the house. "His dad asked me to keep an eye on him. Rick's working on an apparent murder investigation."

"I heard," said Gus. "Up near Shady Point."

"When did you get back from your walk?"

"This morning," said Gus. He studied Royce who picked at the label on his beer bottle. "One of these days maybe you'll join me."

Royce didn't answer but considered his reply. He'd known Gus Longcreek for three years. He was a descendant of the Iroquois tribe and legendary in the area for being a master tracker and medicine healer. Raised by his grandfather, he knew how to live off the land. Naturally in tune with the animals and familiar with the various plants and vegetation of the forest, he took frequent trips or "walks" as he called them where he disappeared for days and weeks to "spend time with Mother Earth." Royce had met him after he'd bought his land and began to build his cabin. He'd been camping nearby and Gus had walked right up to his fire while Royce was roasting marshmallows. They'd begun talking and struck up an easy friendship. Despite Royce's attempts to reveal as little about himself as possible, Gus had known from the start that Royce was different. Said he'd seen it in one of his visions. Since then, he'd started to call Royce "Starman" and the name had stuck.

"Maybe one day," Royce finally answered. Although the thought of joining Gus on one his walks intrigued him, Royce knew that keeping his secrets only became more difficult the more time he spent with the mystical man. "You see the bear?" asked Royce. He took another swallow of his beer.

"Not this time," said Gus. He held a flat stare. "But I know you did."

Royce choked on his drink and coughed. He had not told Gus of his experiments with the large animal that frequented the land around his property. "What do you mean?" he asked, wiping his mouth.

Gus chuckled. "Come on, Starman. You know what I mean." He raised his bottle. "I saw you in my vision."

Royce shot a glance at his friend. "Really. What kind of vision? Were you maybe smoking something at the time?"

Gus grinned. "Sometimes that's the best way to ensure a vision."

Royce made a half-smile. "I'm sure it is. But how accurate is it?"

"You saw the bear, didn't you?" He winked. "But he didn't see you?" Royce raised a brow. "You forget who you're dealing with Starman."

Royce wasn't sure what to say. "Apparently so."

The two sat quietly before Gus finally spoke. "How'd you do it?"

"Do what?"

Gus put his drink down. "How did you hide from him? Disappear from his sight?"

Royce rubbed his fingers over the stubble on his jaw. He debated how much to say. "It's just something I'm practicing."

Gus's eyes widened. "Practicing? For what? You planning on joining the circus? What would you have done if he'd seen you?"

Royce shrugged. "I don't know." He thought about it. "Run?"

Gus said nothing. Royce decided to change the subject. "How'd you know about Shady Point?"

"What?" asked Gus.

"The murder?"

"Oh, that." He picked up his beer. "Saw Rick on my way in. He asked if I could help."

Royce was curious. "Help how?"

"They're looking for a shoe. They also want to see if I can track any movement through the woods."

"After the police have been through there?"

Gus shook his head. "Probably won't find much, but they think the murderer may have been at the Shady Point campsite earlier in the evening. He hopes I might find something there."

"Well, good luck. Shady Point is a gathering place for teenagers at night. Especially out by the park." said Royce.

"Don't need luck," said Gus. "Mother Earth will guide me."

"Well then good luck to her." He took a final swig of his beer and put the bottle on the table. "She's gonna need it."

Gus laughed. "I won't argue with that." He eyed Royce's empty bottle on the table. "Do your trick."

Royce rolled his eyes. "No."

Gus put his own bottle down. "Come on, Starman. I want to see."

Royce tried to divert Gus's attention. "Why do you insist on calling me Starman?"

Gus eye's narrowed. "You know why."

Royce studied the trees. "I know. Another one of your visions." He sighed. "You should stop calling me that."

"Why?" asked Gus. He settled back in his seat. "Does it make you uncomfortable?"

Royce shrugged. "It's not something I talk about."

Gus's mouth turned up. "Don't worry. It's not something I plan to share."

"I don't even know why you believe it. It was just a vision."

Gus spoke with certainty. "I always trust my visions. And I know what I saw. You come from the stars." He raised a hand to the sky.

Royce sat up but didn't respond. He stared at his fingers. Gus continued. "I suppose that has something to do with how you hide from bears that are standing right in front of you." He watched Royce fidget. "And how you do your trick." Gus raised an ankle and rested it on his knee. "Which I'm still waiting for by the way."

Royce grunted and sat still. He didn't know how to feel about what Gus knew and how he knew it. In some ways it scared him and in others he felt relief. It felt good to share a secret that only his family knew. But he also realized the risks. Gus's foot bounced up and down and Royce realized the man would only continue to pester him. He took a second to gather his thoughts and focused on the beer in front of him. A second passed and then his bottle slid across the table toward Gus without anyone touching it. Then Gus's bottle moved. It slid on its own toward Royce, did a reverse turn, and headed back toward Gus. When it hit the edge of the table, it lifted and traveled into the air where Gus reached up and grabbed it.

Gus hooted and gripped the bottle in his hand, looking at it as if he'd never seen glass before. "Shit. That's awesome." He slapped his knee. "How do you do that, Starman?"

Royce tried not to squirm but failed. "It's just something I learned a while back. Not that big a deal." He thought back on his Shift that had occurred three years earlier. Born to a human mother and Eudoran father, Royce and his sisters had all experienced a transformation, or Shift, as his father called it. It was an important transitional event for all Eudorans, similar to moving from adolescence to adulthood for humans, only at an accelerated pace. And for Royce and his siblings, it was a crucial milestone. And because his father was a Red-Line, a unique species capable of unusual abilities, including energy manipulation and intuition, telepathy, telekinesis and cloaking, Royce and his sisters had inherited a mixture of these powers. But they'd all had a strength, and Royce's was moving objects with his mind. He was also practicing the skill of cloaking by hiding in plain sight of the bear. His abilities had revealed themselves shortly after his Shift and his life had changed dramatically ever since. He wondered what Gus would think if he knew what Royce's sisters could do.

Gus took another swallow of his beer. "Can you turn water into wine?" he asked.

Royce finally cracked a smile. "I'm not that skilled. I'll leave that to a higher power."

Gus put his bottle back on the table. "Smart." He leaned back and stared out at the trees. Royce immediately felt his change in mood.

"What is it, Chief?" he asked. "Something on your mind?"

Gus was quiet and Royce waited. They both listened to the wind stir the leaves. "On this walk...I had another vision," Gus finally said.

"You told me," said Royce. "You saw me with the bear.'

Gus shook his head. "Not that," he said. "Something else."

"What?" Royce tuned in to Gus's energy and felt the concern drift off the man. Since Gus rarely worried about anything, Royce perked up.

Gus shifted and held Royce's gaze. "You, my friend."

"Me, what?"

Gus studied his palms. "I saw death."

That made Royce straighten. "You saw what?"

"And there's a woman."

Royce didn't understand. He thought of his mother and sisters. "A woman? What woman?"

Gus's eyes drooped. "She will break your heart."

Royce didn't understand. He wasn't dating anyone and considering who he was, he wondered if he ever would. "What the hell are you talking about, Chief? Other than my family, there are no women in my life."

Gus held his gaze. "Not yet."

Royce felt his body stiffen. "What are you saying?"

"I'm saying that there's trouble on the horizon. Someone's coming."

Royce thought back on the previous six months and felt his belly curl in fear. He gripped the chair. "Who's coming?"

Gus was unfazed. "Two, maybe more. I can't be sure."

Royce thought of Eve and Gillian, his sisters. Their safety was his primary concern. "What do they want?"

"I don't know."

Royce's mind whirled. "When will they be here?"

Gus barely moved. "They're already here."

Royce sat for a moment, but then stood and stepped to his porch railing. He stared out at the trees and thought back to six months ago. His mind flashed to violent seas, flashing lightning and a collapsing deck. He remembered racing to save Gillian. "My family? Are they safe?"

Gus paused. "I didn't see them. Only you."

Royce gripped the rail. "Should I leave?"

Gus shook his head. "It's too late for that."

"Where? Where are they? Do you know?"

Gus stood and went to stand next to Royce. "I didn't see that in my vision."

Royce didn't know what to think. "Damn it..." It was all he could think to say.

Gus spoke calmly. "But that might be the reason there's a car on the road, watching your house."

Royce whirled. "What? You mean now? Out front?" He didn't wait for an answer and jumped off the porch and ran toward the front of the cabin.

"Wait for me," said Gus and he followed Royce into the woods.

Royce moved fast, but Gus kept up. The front porch light was on which helped to illuminate the entryway, but both men were comfortable in the woods and jogged easily past the side of the house and up onto the pebbled driveway. Royce picked up speed and in a few long strides he reached the side of the road with Gus right behind him. The street was quiet and no cars were visible.

Despite his sprint, Royce's breathing had barely changed. "There's nobody here," he said.

Gus stood beside him. "Good observation."

Royce reached out with his senses to see if he could pick up on anything, but he could only feel the familiar sights and sounds of the quiet woods around him. He looked sharply at Gus. "Why didn't you tell me sooner?"

Gus shook his head in the dim light. "It makes no difference."

Royce attempted to calm himself. "What do you mean? They were here. If you'd said something before..."

Gus's expression remained unchanged. "It doesn't matter. They will return."

Royce's mind rushed. He didn't know what to think. Was he in danger? What about his sisters? Should he contact them? Gillian was living with her fiancé and Eve had returned to the city. "The hell it doesn't matter." He strode off and headed back toward the house.

"Starman…"

Royce stopped. Gus stood unmoving and Royce could feel his friend's unwavering certainty. "You will have a decision to make."

Royce nodded. "I know. I'm making it right now."

"That's not what I mean."

"I have to protect my family."

"Leaving won't help. You must face this," said Gus. "You cannot run from it."

"Run from what?" asked Royce. "What exactly am I running from?" He itched to race back to the house and start packing.

Gus didn't hesitate. "Your destiny, Starman. You have one and you must prepare for it."